THE THIRD BEST THING

MAYA HUGHES

Cover Design: Najla Qamber, Qamber Designs

Cover Image: Rafa Catala

Editors: Tamara Mayata, Lea Schaffer, Sarah Kremen-Hicks, Sarah Kellogg

To Nicole, our walks bring more laughter to my life and stories to my imagination.

CHAPTER 1
JULES

I tugged the drawstrings of my hood tighter around my face and crept across the street. My breath came out in small puffs in front of my face, and I prayed no one would see me. Each step made the note in my pocket crinkle, the sound so loud that I froze in the middle of the street, as though no one would notice me in black, creeping across of the road.

A door opened a few houses down. Fear shot through me. Some people came out onto a porch halfway down the block, laughing, and the bass from their music filled the silent air. Not everyone had gone home for the break. My heart skipped into overdrive.

My gaze darted to the house looming in front of me. The two-story townhouse was the nicest on the street by far. It was a former frat house that had been taken over by the Fulton U Trojans' star players earlier this year when the frat had been kicked off campus.

Do it. Go for it and no one needed to know. Be quick, Jules. In and out. I snuck a glance over my shoulder and scurried to the other side of the street. The cold barely touched me with the liquid courage coursing through my veins.

Someone turned the corner, driving down the block. I dove for the bushes, hoping that with my black hooded sweatshirt and black jeans, they wouldn't spot me. Not that it wasn't suspicious tiptoeing around the neighborhood in my attempt at inconspicuous attire.

After a bottle of wine and way too many chocolate chip cookies, here I was with a dirty note in my pocket and liquid courage that waned with each second, standing at the foot of the steps leading up to the porch. What was I doing? What would I do if I got caught? If one of the football players came out and found me crouched in front of their porch? Would I play dumb? Run for my life? Drop out of school and start riding the rails?

The house had been dark for the past few days. I'd only managed at home through Christmas morning before I'd bolted back to campus. My gift of socks and a low-calorie cook book had been the last straw after a week of needling and snide comments. Mom had said I'm hard to shop for, but she knew what I needed. Thanks, Mom.

My sister had gotten a new Audi. Seemed comparable. I'd fled and immersed myself in the kitchen—baked until I thought the house might burn down from the oven being on for almost two days straight.

I was stalling. The longer I stood out here the greater the chance that someone would catch me. Someone like Berk. Elle would freak when she got back to campus and I told her. Was I going to tell her I'd done this?

Now or never. My hands clasped tighter around the envelope in my pocket.

It had taken me eight drafts to finally write out everything I wanted to say to him. Putting pen to paper and letting every dirty, naughty thing I wanted to do to him and have him do to me loose in all its inky glory. Dr. Schuller had said I should embrace my sexuality and take risks. I don't think he thought getting shitfaced and writing raunchy notes was the best outlet, but, hey, I was improvising.

Darting up the stairs, I looked over my shoulder and slipped the note into the mailbox. Odds were, I'd chicken out and grab the note tomorrow morning once the booze and hangover wore off. A little of my anxiety ebbed away. I'd have my night of bravery and adrenaline, but I could take it back. The gold metal lid banged against the body of the box, making a loud clang. This was totally reversible.

The porch light flicked on and I slapped my hands over my mouth to hold back the yelp. Scurrying down the stairs, I dove for the bushes again, making the acquaintance of the leaves and twigs.

"Hey, no parties tonight." The spine-tingling timbre of his voice cut through the night air. Oh god, it was Berk.

I buried my head in my hands. Why was he here? Not that he shouldn't be in his own house, but why the hell was he there? Had he come back while I was drinking and baking? Why weren't his lights on? I almost jumped up to shout those questions at him.

The creaking of the mailbox sent my stomach plummeting through the earth to its molten core.

Under his breath, he muttered a "What the hell?" Probably trying to figure out who wrote letters nowadays. The answer was drunk college juniors who barely had the balls to talk to you in person. "Who's out there?" He leaned against the railing just over my head.

My heart pounded in my ears. I expected him to transform into Edgar Allen Poe and discover me under his porch. I peered up with my back glued to the brick.

He looked up and down the street with the note out of the envelope in his hand.

Every cell in my body screamed to run, tingling and firing all at once. If he looked down, I was dead. They could just bury me here. My mom and sister would visit—maybe.

"Fuck me." The paper rustled and he turned it over. "I want to feel every inch of you inside me." Oh god, he was reading it.

That meant he'd already read the part where I detailed what I wanted to lick off his body. If I hadn't been petrified into stillness, I'd have slapped my hands over my face, which was glowing red with embarrassment.

"Is this a joke?" He came down two steps. "I've been working on my flexibility; would you like to put it to the test? Who in the hell?"

My fingers clawed at the brick behind me.

More paper rustled and the heavy thud of his footsteps retreated before the front door closed. Minutes stretched out for so long my thighs ached from my crouched position. I stood there until it was nearly sunrise before bolting back across the street and swearing off booze for the rest of my life. But I'd done it. He'd probably have a good laugh, throw away the note, and move onto the parade of women who strutted in front of him like peacocks whenever they had the chance.

But two days later, while in my kitchen scooping out the last of the brown butter and toffee chocolate chip cookies, I spotted movement on the other side of the street.

Berk stood on his porch staring at the mailbox.

I jumped over the kitchen chair and plastered my face against the glass. What was he doing out there? Was he dusting for prints? Oh god, he was going to know it was me, he was going to walk straight across the street and ban me from ever going near his house again. Was this what a panic attack felt like? Like my heart was going to explode?

He waved to someone who walked by. One minute went by and he slipped something into the mailbox. Another minute and he took it out. Tapping it against his leg, he glanced over his shoulder.

I flew back from the window, hiding behind the curtain. Oxygen became something I remembered breathing once.

He dropped the white piece of paper back into the mailbox.

Was that a note for me? Was he responding? Had he written me back? I yelped and did a happy dance for all of ten seconds before freezing with the dough-covered scooper in my hand.

I couldn't wait to read what he had written to me. Was he telling me to leave him alone or was it a reply? Was it his response to everything I'd described?

I had to go get it.

Oh shit.

CHAPTER 2
JULES – THREE MONTHS LATER

I stared at the pole in front of me, daring the shiny brass not to cooperate. Bass from the speakers rumbled the floorboards under my bare toes. It was always better when I couldn't hear anything other than the music, not even my own thoughts. "Let's try not to split my shorts this time."

Gripping the pole, I let out a sharp breath and swung around it, letting my body weight pull me in a complete circle. Momentum wasn't hard to achieve. The heavier something is, the faster it can be whipped around three inches of brass.

You've got this, Jules. Staring down the pole and daring it to let me fall on my ass, I tightened my grip. Maybe attempt number thirty-seven would be the magic number. The muscles in my arm bunched, ready for action. I swayed and dipped to the music, creating a routine I'd gone over in my head. The smaller tricks helped distract me from what I was about to do.

I braced my arms and death-gripped the warmed metal. The blood rushed to my face as I lifted my legs over my head. I probably looked like a splotchy tomato. I wrapped my thighs around the pole, using my non-existent thigh gap to my advantage.

The intensity of the music drove higher, getting closer to the bass drop. I changed my hold and grabbed onto the brass, going high enough to nearly bang my head into the ceiling. It probably wasn't the smartest idea in the world to climb this high when I tried this, but since when had anyone accused me of thinking things through? The stack of handwritten letters tucked under my bed were a testament to that.

I switched my hands, holding on behind my knee and kicking my other leg out straight. My heart hammered against my chest double-time to the driving beat of the music. *Core muscles don't fail me now.* I let go with my hands and swung my upper body out using only my legs to anchor me. I was spinning like a character in a music box—albeit a kind of screwed up one. I stretched out my upper body perpendicular to the pole and struck a fierce pose. At least, I hoped it was fierce. The website had called it the Divine Diva. Apparently, I'm a glutton for punishment.

Sneaking a glance at my mirror, I looked more like a spider monkey clinging to a tree to stop from dropping out of the rainforest canopy into the jaws of predators down below, complete with profuse sweating and shaking. Panting and sweating didn't feel very diva-like. Taking a deep breath, I relaxed into the pose, pointed my toe straight up at the ceiling, and extended my arm like the jiggly bingo wing it was.

A giddy laugh bubbled up from deep down. I snuck a glance at myself in the mirror again. I was a lumpy diva, but, fuck it, I was a badass, too. And I was slowly skidding closer to the ground as the sweat that gathered behind my knee loosened my grip.

Every move I nailed got me a little closer to appreciating how far I'd come. From the first days of slipping off trying to do a basic spin with my feet planted firmly on the floor, to being a diva. This was my freaking body and I loved the shit out of it.

And if I kept telling myself that, maybe one day I'd believe it.

I lowered myself onto my bedroom floor with a flourish, throwing in one more spin for my imaginary audience.

The song ended and I braced my hands on my hips, panting and sweating like I'd run a 5k, with a grin so damn wide I felt it in my toes. Jumping up and down, I gave myself a high five and a few club-worthy *woo*s. It made it harder to figure out if I was doing the tricks one hundred percent correctly, but I sure as hell wasn't going to record myself to watch later or head to a pole dancing studio with full-wall mirrors. I wasn't at that level of okay with me in all my glory—yet.

I flopped onto my bed and stared up at the ceiling. My hip-hugging short shorts and sports bra gave me little coverage, but pole dancing wasn't exactly about modesty. I'd given it a try at the urging of my therapist during freshman year and hell if it hadn't helped—some. It was a way for me to build strength, body confidence, and maybe attempt to feel a little sexy.

The door slammed downstairs and I shot up from the bed.

"Jules!" Berk's unmistakable call sent me from pole dancing heart racing to 'floor it, Louise,' careening toward a cliff. I shot up and fell off my bed, rattling the perfume bottles on my dresser. Scrambling off the floor, I grabbed my sweatpants and tugged them on, hopping from foot to foot and sounding like I'd taken up bowling in my bedroom. I snagged my glasses off my desk and shoved them onto my face.

Berk was probably wondering how I'd trapped a wild animal up in my room. I grabbed my long sleeved T-shirt and hoodie off the back of my chair even though it was August. The fabric clung to my sweaty skin and I probably had a sweat-stashe going on, but that was better than him walking up here and finding me half naked. A panic spiral shot through me and I got dressed even quicker and threw open my door.

My feet barely touched any of the steps as I flew downstairs.

"Berk." I fell into the kitchen, bracing my arm against the doorway. The butterflies in my stomach were replaced by a whole freaking safari. I tightened my lips to what I hoped was a non-serial killer level of smile. My heart was glowing like a spotlight, so I wrapped my arms tighter around myself. Tingles tiptoed up and down my spine at the sight of his floppy hair and jeans that hugged his ass and trim waist better than mine ever fit me.

His head shot up and the half of the cookie sticking out of his mouth broke off and dropped onto the counter. "There you are." His words were muffled behind two manhole cover-sized cookies.

"Did you think I was hiding in my cookie box?"

"Is that what you're calling it these days?" Killer smile and a direct hit. "The old cookie box." The edges of his eyes crinkled and his mop of hair was tousled and still a little damp. Probably from the showers over at the stadium. He'd made it a habit of stopping by after football practice.

Do not giggle like an idiot. Be cool, Jules.

"Among other things."

He tilted his head to the side, his gaze licking its way up and down my body. Okay, maybe that was wishful thinking, but it was equal parts terrifying and exhilarating. "Why are you so sweaty?"

Oh. Of course he wasn't actually checking me out. "From…" My brain stalled and sparks started shooting out at six different angles like an under-oiled engine. *Abandon ship! Abandon ship!* "Running down the stairs." I squeezed my fingers into a fist at my side to keep myself from slamming my hand into my forehead. *Awesome, Jules. Now he thinks you're so out of shape you can't even run down the steps without pouring sweat.*

He nodded like a dude who streaked across a football field without getting winded had the same issue.

"Did you break in just to steal cookies or was there something else?"

There was a sheepish glint in his toffee-colored eyes. He dusted off his crumb-covered hand and held it up to his mouth, clearing his throat. "Do you have some milk?"

I laughed and grabbed some out of the fridge, pouring him a glass. Sliding it across the counter, I kept my fingers on the far side of the water droplet-covered glass and away from his.

Crossing my arms, I leaned against the counter. "Have you ever read that book, *If You Give A Mouse A Cookie*? Although in this case it's like, *If a Mouse Breaks into Your House and Steals a Cookie*." I lifted the corner of my mouth.

"It was unlocked." He downed the glass and set it back down. "Leaving your door unlocked on a street full of degenerates isn't the best idea."

"Exactly. Who knows what crazy person could show up and start raiding my food supply."

"Exactly." He tapped me on my nose with one of the cookies he'd weaseled out of the box when my back had been turned. "This isn't a social visit. It's time for some serious business."

"Are we in the same Philosophy class again this year?" I'd gotten the seat behind Berk last semester in Political Philosophy.

He shrugged. "No, Ethics, but that's not what this is about." His gaze turned razor-serious. "This is about The Letter Girl."

Like a T-Rex had wandered into the kitchen, I stood stock still. *Breathe, Jules. Breathing would be good about now. The Letter Girl.*

The girl I'd volunteered to help him find.

The girl who had been writing him filthy, flirty notes last semester starting with one after a drunken winter break bout of insanity—and had continued for months.

The girl he'd never have a real crush on, if he saw what she looked like.

The girl who was standing in front of him in her too-warm kitchen in some too-warm clothes getting way too warm with each passing second.

"What about her?" I sure hoped he liked my Minnie Mouse impersonation.

"Have you thought up anything else on how we can find her once the semester starts?"

"Maybe she doesn't want to be found."

His eyes went wide and he shook his head with a steely look of determination. "That's not an option. The things we talked about…"

He wanted to find the woman who'd described doing all kinds of confident, sexy things to him. Things I wanted to do to him, but here I was, covered up like I was staving off frostbite. "The sex stuff?"

The corners of his mouth turned down. "Not just that."

The notes had started off as an exercise in expressing my sexuality in a safe environment just like Dr. Schuller recommended. Who am I kidding? They started because I was a drunk coward. There was no way I could walk up to Berk and say the things I had anonymously written, but over the months, things had changed and we had started sharing more of ourselves in the letters beyond what we wanted to do to each other's bodies—not that there wasn't a heaping helping of that as well.

"She was—*is* someone I need to meet in person."

I opened my mouth to throw out nine hundred reasons why that was a terrible idea. Then the front door creaked open as someone knocked.

"Told you you needed to lock it." Berk stepped up like he was ready to throw down in case someone from the street had actually decided to show up and cause trouble. We'd only had one drunk party-goer wander into the house, and that had been fairly anti-climactic. We'd woken up to find them passed out on our living room floor. Okay, it was three times, but who's counting?

"Julia?" The soft and sweet voice drifted in from the entryway.

Yeah, I'd much rather face down some post-apocalyptic motorcycle-riding cannibals right now than answer the door. An attack was incoming, but only my feelings were in danger.

"Stand down." I dropped my hand onto his shoulder. "It's my sister." Giving him a barely-there smile, I walked out of the room. I was hoping that maybe after all these years I'd misremembered her voice and it wasn't her, but there were a handful of people in the world who called me Julia.

I rounded the kitchen doorway and was nearly blinded by her brightness.

The pale pink blazer with sleeves pushed up just below her elbows.

The pristine white t-shirt—that probably cost more than my rent—and perfectly-ripped jeans that hugged her legs made her look like she'd stepped out of the latest influencer campaign.

Throw in some pale pink heels that I couldn't even pole dance in, her Hermes purse, and tastefully simple jewelry accents, and Laura was the picture-perfect replica of our mother, aged down to twenty-eight—although Mom told everyone there were only twenty-one years between them.

"Hi, Laura." I crossed my arms over my chest. My earlier bravado slowly leached out the open door.

"Is that any way to say hello to your sister?" She held out her arms as she stepped into my house, not for a hug, but like she expected roaches to scurry past and carry her away.

I wrapped my arms around her and matched actual contact to her air hug.

"Why are you so sweaty?" The undertone of censure rippled through her words.

I dropped my arms and stepped back. "I was working out."

Her eyes widened, the hint of a smile skittered across her lips. The kind that was at home with a group of mean girls laughing at someone finally finding the courage to go to the gym to jumpstart a healthier lifestyle and maybe shed some pounds. "That's great, Julia."

"Why are you here?" I crossed my arms like they'd shield me from whatever strike she had planned.

"Can't I drop by to visit?" Her gaze swept over my place. It still wasn't much, but at least she hadn't seen it last year, before it had taken the turn from barely habitable to you-probably-won't-catch-a staph-infection-here levels of sketchiness.

"You haven't in the past three years."

"There's a first time for everything. And Mom wanted me to make sure you were coming to the engagement party this weekend. You haven't replied to her messages."

More like chosen to avoid them, hoping that perhaps a meteor would crash into the planet or I'd come down with bubonic plague and have an excuse not to come.

"I have a lot going on, and three full days away is tough at this point in the year. Classes are starting. I've got to start the job search." I dragged my hand through my hair, acutely aware of how my messy bun contrasted with her every-strand-in-its-place mussed perfection.

"But this is my wedding."

"It's your engagement party. Most people don't have three-day engagement parties."

"But this needs to be special. An amazing trip no one will forget to celebrate the love between Chet and me."

It took everything in me not to puke. I pinched my lips together tightly.

She rushed in close and held my hands. Her fingers were freezing cold even though it was ninety degrees outside. "You're my only sister, Julia, and this is my wedding we're talking about."

"No, it's the engagement party."

"What would everyone say if you weren't there?"

"I'm sure they'd get over it."

"Dad would want us to be together during these special times, sharing them."

I fought against my wince. Bulls-fucking-eye. So practiced and routine. After all this time, I should be able to keep myself for falling for these manipulations. Dad would've wanted us all to be together, but when he'd been here it hadn't felt like someone was standing over me with a ream of freshly-printed paper and a gallon of lemon juice ready to slice me to ribbons.

"Mom wants you there. I want you there." Laura touched the back of my hand like she was trying to reassure me. "And Chet wants you there." Her brightest smile was turned up to eleven.

Chet. I should've known from the moment we met that he was trouble—just from the name alone. My sort-of ex and now my sister's fiancé. I'd met the insistent requests from my mom and Laura to bring around the boy I'd been seeing with every kind of dodge I could think of, until he finally did meet them and the inevitable happened.

In the ninth grade, I'd gotten one candygram for Valentine's Day. Laura had gotten over twenty, and she made sure to carry them in her arms so everyone could see. She was the homecoming queen as a sophomore, something unheard of at our school, and prom queen after getting invited by a senior. The family measuring stick had always been just a few inches too tall for me. Once she'd graduated, I'd breathed a little freer, thinking I wouldn't be compared to her anymore. And then Chet came to town without the baggage of twelve years of school with the same people. For a sliver of a school year, I'd had a glimpse of what it was like not living in her shadow —and then the lifelong eclipse circled right back around.

Jules was put out to pasture like an old, crusty cow, and Laura became the sun to his piece-of-crap-no-good-son-of-a— stars. And now they were getting married, having conveniently forgotten where their happily-ever-after started.

We met through a mutual friend.

It sounded less scandalous the way they told it.

So I wasn't exactly jumping for joy about being stranded on the country estate where the social-climbing members of the Kelland family would host their non-ironic Great Gatsby-themed engagement party. As though stealing my boyfriend wasn't enough, Laura was moving the scene of the crime to the place *I'd* always wanted to exchange vows with a man who looked at me like no other man ever did. She'd always been too busy to go there with Dad during the summers.

Pardon me for not RSVPing.

"Jules, do you mind if I take a few with me?" Berk popped out of the kitchen with his winning, knee-weakening smile, and a huge tub of cookies in his hand.

"Why, hello there." Laura nearly knocked me over as she executed a model glide past me, heading straight for Berk.

"Hey." He looked around like a deer caught in headlights.

"I'm Laura Kelland." She looked over her shoulder at me. "A friend of *yours?*"

Berk's gaze bounced between me and Laura. My shoulders hunched and I tightened my arms across my chest. The pit in my stomach sprouted a trunk and a few branches as I braced myself for the questions I'd been asked so many times.

Standing beside my mom and sister, I always looked like the weird cousin they introduced for comedic relief in every sitcom when things got stale. When Dad was alive, it had all made sense. Laura looked like Mom's mini-me, I took after him, and our picture was complete. When he was gone, I was the odd one out—always.

"Laura, this is Berk. Berk, my sister Laura."

Here come the wide-eyed glances between me and her. I was tallish, taking after Dad at five-eight, whereas she was a petite but willowy five-four. Next to me she almost felt pocket-sized.

She had bright blue eyes, but mine were a muddy-mossy mishmash hidden behind my glasses.

And then there was the extra fifty pounds I had on her. Standing next to my sister, I always felt like I should be named Helga and have a place on the Soviet female shotput team.

But Berk's eyes didn't have the same questions or comparative judgments most people's did. He shook her hand like we made sense as siblings, even though *I* didn't get it sometimes.

"I didn't know Jules was seeing someone. You've got to come to the engagement party. It would be so wonderful to have you come."

I clenched my fists at my side and my heart did a skitter-patter. She was doing it on purpose: inviting someone she knew could never be my boyfriend, so she could laugh at her silly mistake and rest her hand on his chest, flirting to within an inch of her life with the added bonus of pointing out how silly she'd been for even assuming.

"Berk's not—"

"Sure, I'm always up for a party." He shrugged and nodded.

Laura threw her head back, but only half the laugh came out. Her head snapped back down and she stared at him. "What?"

"Jules mentioned it before. The wedding's in spring, right? Sure, I'll go."

"But—" Her gaze swung to the side, meeting mine. "You're actually—"

I plastered on a smile. "You heard him. He'd love to go. You still have room for him, right?" I took her by the shoulders. "We'll see you this weekend."

Shell-shocked and still looking like she couldn't believe what had just gone down, Laura nodded.

"Perfect." I pushed her toward the door. "We'll be there at five, see you then, so happy for you both, love you, bye."

She turned around on the porch.

I slammed the door closed and rested my head against the solid wood, closing my eyes.

"Should I be ready at five on Friday or Saturday?" Berk waved around the salted caramel chocolate chunk cookies with the espresso chips I always kept on hand for him.

Oh god, did he think I'd told her we were dating? "I only said that to get rid of her. You don't have to go." I'd delayed humiliation right now for the humiliation in three days when I showed up with no Berk. "I only let her believe we're dating to get rid of her."

"You don't want me to go?" A sliver of hurt fluttered across his face.

Did he really want to come with me? As if—he was just being polite. "Of course I do, but I can't ask you to do that. You've got practice. The semester starts as soon as we get back." There, I'd given him an out so he could back out gracefully.

"I wouldn't mind getting out of here for a few days. You mentioned this thing before, right?"

"As a joke. I don't want you to think you have to come."

"I wouldn't have offered if I wasn't cool with it. The season will be intense. A party with good food and top-shelf booze that I don't have to clean up from sounds good to me. If you're good with it."

My mouth opened and closed. "Sure, I'd love it if you

came." I needed a gold star for not digging a hole into the ground to disappear into after saying that.

"We'll have fun. I won't embarrass you, don't worry." He ducked back into the kitchen.

"I'd never think you could."

After the roots holding me to the floor dissolved, I followed him.

He downed another shot of milk. "Now that we've gotten that out of the way, let's figure out how we're going to track down TLG."

"TLG?"

He stared back at me with determination glinting in his eyes. "I'm not stopping until I find The Letter Girl."

CHAPTER 3
BERK

The brown sugar, cinnamon, chocolate, and vanilla smells made walking into Jules' kitchen one of my new favorite things. My mouth watered every time I stepped through her door. It made me want to take a bite out of the countertops. It was like being in a movie set version of a perfect house. Not that her house was perfect. The landlord had fixed it up some from last year after Jules' old roommate reamed him in court for not keeping the house up to code and making repairs as needed, but it had nothing to do with the way the place looked.

Walking into Jules' house was like walking into a home, complete with a cute apron hanging beside the doorway, stacks of neatly wrapped treats and Tupperware full of even more. I could sit there for hours soaking it all up. And eating mountains of treats that were always on hand.

"I could put flyers up all over campus with a picture of one of the letters." A highly censored version of the letters. Maybe a small excerpt.

"But who sees anyone's handwriting? Most people use their computers or phones for everything." Jules rubbed her thumb along her bottom lip. Did it taste like sugar? I dropped my gaze from her lips. Don't go there, man. Jules was awesome, but I wasn't going to be distracted from my search.

"You're right."

How can you lose someone you've never met? The Letter Girl had careened into my life like a damn smash and grab pro and wormed her way into my heart before I knew what happened.

She was everything I'd ever wanted in a girl. Hot as hell. Smart and caring. The slow slide of the notes from X-rated to something more caught me off guard, but she became someone I could talk to. Someone I could share parts of myself that I didn't share with other people. Even if she didn't know everything about my past, she knew more than most.

No one wanted to be sexy pen pals with a former foster kid who had almost no one in the whole world. Nah, that was for the college senior, soon to be pro athlete.

Don't ever let anyone see things bother you; I learned that in foster home number four. If everything's a joke, there's nothing they can do to hurt you, but losing TLG when I thought I'd finally found someone who knew me for me and actually gave a shit? That hurt. It was an unexpected squeeze on my heart every so often that made it hard to breathe.

Jules slid her hand closer, herky-jerky like she was in a stop motion animation movie before it finally landed on top of mine with a gentle pat. "Is it really that important for you to find her?"

I shrugged. "Maybe not. She probably got tired of trying to figure out my fucking chicken scratch." I forced out a laugh through the tightness in my chest.

"Once the season starts things will be crazy for you, right?"

"You're right. I guess I'm fixating because not much else is going on." No, this would always be a question I needed answered. Who is TLG and did all the things we'd written about mean as much to her as they meant to me?

I slid the plastic container closer to the edge of the counter. "You're good if I take these?"

She smiled and it shone through her eyes. "Who do you think I made them for?" Turning, she put the now empty plate into the sink.

A wave of heat spread in my chest and stopped me in my tracks. "You baked these especially for me?"

"It's the only way I can save the rest of my cookies from your stomach. Sometimes I think a bear has been foraging in here."

"You could always lock the door."

She peered at me sideways with the side of her mouth quirked up. "I could."

I stepped back, wanting to step forward. *Slow your roll, Berk. This is Jules. Don't toy with her when you're dead set on finding TLG.* "Thanks for these. I'll get out of your hair. And I'll be here on Friday for the thing."

She nodded and dried off the plate in her hand.

Outside, I jogged across the street and went straight for the mailbox, flipping up the brass lid on the rectangular box next to the front door. A crater of disappointment thudded in my chest.

We'd upgraded the place a little bit now that we'd managed to keep the roving party monsters out of our house. For two years we'd had parties appear in our house like something out of Harry Potter. Blink and there's five kegs, a DJ, and red plastic cups everywhere.

In the kitchen, I looked over my shoulder making sure no one was around and opened one of the upper cabinets beside the back door. I slid the box of kale chips aside and put the Tupperware up there, putting the chips back where they'd been. I'd learned my lesson about hoarding food in my room after the mouse fiasco of sophomore year, but that didn't mean it was free rein on Jules' cookies. Especially, since she'd made them for me.

The front door opened and I slammed the door shut and spun around, crossing my arms over my chest.

Keyton came in the front door with a backpack and a guitar case in his hand. He froze when he spotted me.

"I didn't know you played."

A muscle in his neck tightened. "I don't."

LJ and Marisa barreled down the steps arguing about something. Anything. Probably whether or not an ant could lift an ant-sized car or who could hold their breath the longest. They'd never learned the fine art of not sounding like they were in a wrestling match whenever they went anywhere together.

"Oh, a guitar. I didn't know you played." Marisa hopped down from the last step.

Keyton ducked his head. "I don't."

"What's up with the guitar if you don't play?" LJ jumped in with the question before Marisa could get it in.

Keyton shifted the case and held onto it with both hands. "I—I'm hanging onto it for a friend."

Marisa laughed. "That's so sweet of you. Nice and caring to do something for a friend. Storing something like that in your room when it takes up a lot of space. That's a big deal, not something small like showing someone how to make ramen noodles or French toast."

And just like that the conversation had nothing to do with Keyton. He took the opening to dart upstairs.

"Ris, we had to throw out that pot the last time you attempted to make pasta."

I shuddered. The burnt smell had lingered in the house for a week.

"That's why I need you to show me. We can make up a battle plan."

"I'd need some armor, that's for sure," LJ grumbled.

I grabbed a twizzler from my stash on the counter. Food always comforted me. If I could fill my stomach, then everything would be okay. That's what happened when you didn't grow up with much of it.

But I had my chance. This would be my year, but there was still that faint nails-on-a-chalkboard fear that things wouldn't pan out the way I dared to hope they would.

TLG, my senior year season as a Fulton U Trojan, the draft, and a plan I'd set in motion that could bring it all crashing down with one blown out knee. One bad grade. One fuck up.

There was a lot on the line this year. I took a bite out of the licorice and followed LJ and Marisa into the living room.

Keyton came back down, sans guitar, looking a lot less like he wanted to bolt at any second. "Anyone want a drink? I'll get drinks."

"We should upgrade the TV for this season. Reece's first game is in a week."

"I'm always up for a bigger TV." LJ sat on the couch beside Marisa.

"Do you have 'upgrade the TV' money?" Marisa crossed her arms over her chest.

"Gee, thanks for asking, Mom."

"Can you two cut down on the foreplay for five minutes?" I took another bite of my strawberry-flavored snack and wedged myself between them like a parent separating their two bickering kids. Only these two weren't siblings or children and they wanted to bang. They hadn't come to terms with that yet, but it was only a matter of time.

Both their heads turned and their double glare made me grin even harder and pick up the game controller off the coffee table. "I'll take a beer and two glasses of shut the hell up for these two."

Keyton disappeared into the kitchen with our requests and came back with three beers, and a Shirley Temple complete with maraschino cherries for Marisa.

"What college student has a coffee table? Shouldn't this be a couple milk crates with some plywood balanced on top?" Marisa took the drink from his hand. "I'd have sworn you were a senior last year. You're the only adult in the house."

"I had an off-campus apartment before. I've been lugging things around for a while." He slid coasters across the table for us to set our beers on.

"If everyone pitched in, it wouldn't be so bad." I hadn't done my textbook buy back from last year. It would come to a whole forty bucks if I was lucky.

"Not all of us will be bringing in pro football paychecks in less than a year, people." Marisa waved her hands like none of us had noticed she was there.

"Not all of us is right," LJ mumbled beside me, picking at the label of his beer.

Marisa sighed. "I can put in thirty-five cents and a hand-written back massage coupon."

"No need to break the bank, Ris. I'm sure Reece will be touched you're digging deep for him. And if Marisa wants to kill our joy and support for the former Brothel resident by denying the TV purchase, Nix said we can watch any of the games at his place with a free food bonus."

My already full stomach rumbled thinking about the saucy pasta dishes he used to make when he lived here. "Do you think he regrets not going pro?" He'd been better than all of us—hell, probably all of us combined—and had walked away from the game just before the draft last year.

"Nah, he's got Elle and the restaurant. He's thinking about getting surgery on his shoulder to help with the pain now that he knows he's not going to be getting knocked around on the field again." LJ took a long drink from his beer.

Going pro was my future. I'd do whatever I needed to

make that happen. It was a short career at best, but I'd invest my money wisely and never have to worry about ending up on the streets again. That looming fear lingered in the back of my mind. Gnawing hunger that made it hard to think and clothes with non-manufactured holes in them. That I'd end up back in some shelter or wake up and find this was all the dream of a thirteen-year-old kid living in a group home, sleeping on top of his meager possessions to keep the other kids from stealing them.

I didn't need sneaker deals or a car dealership. I'd take that money and finally have a home. Find someone to share it with. Make a family. A huge one with kids who never had to worry about being kicked out. I'd do it right, at least as right as I could figure out with no clue how a real family worked.

My phone buzzed in my pocket. I tugged it out and the screen lit up.

ALEXIS: Berk, I need you.

My muscles tensed in that old fight or flight response programmed in me from years of being in the system. I needed to find her and save her from whatever situation had her sending me a message. It was almost always, 'there's a raging inferno of madness around me, please help me put it out.'

LJ tilted his head when he spotted the name blazed across the screen, and made a sharp sound of disapproval. "Don't."

"Alexis needs me." I pressed my lips together, shaking my head, and jumped up from the couch. Taking the stairs two at a time, I ducked into my room and grabbed my keys.

"What's the deal with Alexis?" Keyton asked as I hit the top of the stairs.

I could feel LJ's eye roll from downstairs practically shift the foundation of the house. "Long story."

Hustling down the steps, I didn't look at them. At least Nix and Reece weren't here to add to the pain in the ass levels. "See you guys later."

"Do not bring her back here." LJ stood behind me like he was standing sentry over the house.

I slammed the door behind me. They didn't understand. Couldn't even begin to understand what it was like to be the only person someone could count on.

CHAPTER 4
JULES

"**H**e was there when Laura showed up. And he was like, 'yeah, sure I'll go.'" I put on my best superhero swooping in and saving the day voice.

"I'd have loved to have seen her face." Elle laughed and scribbled something down on her tablet, wiggling her painted pink toenails.

Elle had moved into an apartment over the summer, leaving me back at the house all on my own. It was so quiet without her and our ghost roommate, Zoe. Any time she'd popped into our place it was from a changing of the boyfriend guard. It only lasted a few days at most before the next guy on deck swooped in. He'd show up on our porch and she'd bounce out of the house again with her bags packed.

Most people would be happy to have a house all to themselves. A three bedroom by myself didn't exactly scream wild and crazy senior year, but if felt weird looking for a new roommate, and Zoe's checks still cleared, even after I emailed her about the rent hike since we'd only be splitting it two ways. My email asking if she was moving out after graduation was met with silence.

Pictures were hung up all over the walls of Elle and Nix's apartment, which had been freshly painted a light gray. Great shots of me and Elle and Nix with the rest of the guys from The Brothel, including Berk. Nix's grandfather owned the restaurant downstairs and had been using the apartment for storage until the guys had fixed it up.

It was cozy and I'd never seen Elle happier. It probably helped living in a place where you weren't afraid part of the ceiling might cave in on you at any minute and there was a hunky boyfriend to snuggle up to and cook delicious food all the time.

I snorted. "I wish I'd had a camera, but I'm sure my face was just as shocked."

"It shouldn't have been. Who wouldn't want to be tucked away in some country estate with you all weekend?" She waggled her eyebrows.

"This weekend is not even a little bit like that."

"Maybe it'll be the perfect time to tell him about how well you two actually know each other." She kept her gaze trained on her screen.

"No, absolutely not."

She set the tablet down beside her. "He deserves to know you're The Letter Girl. And you two are friends now. Tell him. He'll be so happy."

"More like crushingly disappointed."

She grabbed onto both of my shoulders and stared into my eyes. "Jules, you've got to stop. No one would ever be disappointed in having a sexpot, pole-dancing baker as their secret sex pen pal."

"Have you seen the girls at the parties at The Brothel and the ones at the FU games?"

"Do you remember me dating the all-star quarterback who was a sure lock for the first round draft pick and had just won the national championship?"

I tapped my finger against my chin. "Doesn't ring any bells, sorry."

A pastel blue pillow whacked into the side of my face. "Pain in the butt."

"Maybe you knocked something loose, it's coming back to me now. Regardless, it's different... You're objectively gorgeous."

"He was so over that scene by the time I arrived. It's not about looks. Do you think I'm with him for his glorious ass, sinewy arms with veins that pop out a little while he's cooking, and abs made for washing laundry?" She got a faraway look in her eyes and bit her bottom lip.

"You're not helping." I returned the pillow straight to her head.

The door to Elle's apartment opened, keys jingled.

"Honey, I'm home." Nix walked in with a huge smile on his face and his arms loaded with containers. Garlic, butter, and cheese smells combined and my stomach made an attempt to climb out of my mouth to wolf down the contents.

Leaping from the couch, Elle clapped her hands together. "You're a saint. I'm so hungry."

He kissed her, trapping her between him and the counter and setting the food he had in each hand down without even looking. "I told you to come down an hour ago." His fingers trailed over her cheek.

"I lost track of time. Jules was here and we're working with August Niles for five events in the next four months. I'm three seconds away from throat-punching him. He's been through eight assistants in nine months. I'm working with his new one now and she's sweet. I hope he doesn't chew her up and spit her out. Everything has to be perfect or he'll probably incinerate me with his dragon fire."

"If someone's giving you trouble, tell me and I'll deal with it." His face was a mask of seriousness. And he'd kick whoever's ass he needed to when it came to Elle.

After everything that had kept them apart—mainly Elle's stubbornness—they were living their fairy tale in a two bedroom apartment above Nix's grandfather's restaurant, Tavola. My happiness for her was absolute, but tinged with the sadness that I'd probably never experience it. The closest I'd come was thirty dirty notes to a guy who'd pushed me so far into the friend zone I could smell the freshly mown grass.

"Oh no." She ducked out from under his arm. "You're not getting involved."

"Help me out here, Jules." Nix looked to me with his *talk some sense into her* look.

I jumped a little. His focus had been so completely on Elle, I hadn't realized he knew I was there.

"I'm siding with Elle here on the argument of whether or not to beat up some guy she works with. Sorry, Nix."

He shook his head and unboxed our food. "Did Elle tell you she gave your cookies and brownies to Avery Cunning from Bread & Butter?"

I nearly tripped over the coffee table and braced my hands on the smooth table top. "You what?" It was a screech to end all screeches. Some of the newly dried paint peeled off the walls.

Nix winced and stuck his finger in his ear.

"I can't believe I forgot." Elle smacked her hand to her forehead. "I was so distracted by your other news. It slipped my mind."

"What news?" Nix looked between us.

She waved him off. "Nix has been looking at new dessert providers since the pastry chef left and they're focusing more on the savory dishes. And Avery's name shot to the top of the list, since you've turned down my offers to run your own little dessert factory out of our old place. They've been looking to branch out with collaborations and trying new things. And everything that comes out of there makes me want to die so it's the last thing I've ever tasted."

I sputtered. "I freaking know." Covering my face with my hands, I sank onto the couch. "Did you actually give her something I made?" It was like showing up to a master art class with your paint by numbers coloring book.

"It was the salted caramel you've been making a lot of lately, the peanut butter chunk brownies, and the toffee espresso cookies. I gave her the container you brought over two weeks ago. Letting them go was probably the third hardest thing I've ever done."

Throwing my arm over the back of the couch, I stared at her as she described the interaction like it was no big deal that Avery Freaking Cunning, owner of one of the best bakeries in the city, had my cookies in her possession.

"Well, not all of the cookies." Nix bumped her shoulder.

"I only stole a few out of there. I didn't hear any complaints when you wolfed down all but a half of one I rescued from that non-stop chewing machine you call a mouth."

He ducked his head and pretended he hadn't heard that last little bit.

"She probably threw them out the second she had the chance." I dropped my head against the back of the couch and squeezed my eyes shut, trying to breathe through the teacup terrier racing around my stomach.

"Not even close." Elle leaned against the couch beside my head. "She took a bite and her eyes fluttered closed and she even moaned a little."

My head popped up. "Shut up!" I shoved at her shoulder and she nearly fell back over the couch.

"Yes, really. Do I ever joke when it comes to your food? Would you stop it! Everyone loves everything you make." She locked onto my gaze. "Everyone. But I didn't want to tell you anything until I knew for sure."

"Knew for sure what?"

"I mentioned them branching out and toying with the idea

of collaborations, well, she was talking about this new thing she's thinking about. And she asked you to come in for an interview."

I shot straight up. "Interview?"

"Sort of. She knows you're still in school and have classes and stuff, so it's not like working there full time or anything, but she was thinking you might be interested in an internship of sorts."

Containing the giddiness at working alongside Avery Cunning in the kitchen wasn't happening in the slightest. I bounced on the couch, rocking the whole thing, but I didn't care. "I'll clean the ovens if that's what she wants." Bread & Butter had been featured in every city magazine over the past couple years. If I worked with her, learned from her, I'd have an in with most bakeries and restaurants in the city. I didn't have a formal culinary education, so I'd been trying to figure out how to break into the business with my Philosophy degree.

"Perfect. Here's her number." Elle scrounged around in her purse and pulled out a business card.

"You've had her number all this time and you've been holding out on me?" I snatched the paper from her hand, clutching it to my chest like a goblin with some newly-discovered gold coins. I kept myself from whispering 'precious,' but only just.

"Not like you'd have done anything other than stare at it, which is why I gave her yours, so if she calls, please pick up." She took a plate from Nix and handed it over to me.

I waved it off. Eating wasn't happening until Avery Cunning spoke those magic words to me. I clutched the pale pink rectangle of paper against my chest even harder. Avery's personal number was scribbled across the back.

I left Nix and Elle to do the thing couples do when they're completely in love—make out. The third not-so-stealthy kiss between those two was my cue to go.

Once off the bus, triple-checking that my ringer was on and at full volume, I held on to my phone, afraid it would get lost in my bag and I'd miss the call. The call.

Avery was calling tomorrow. I did a little dance and my steps quickened.

I stopped at the bottom of the porch steps. The lights were on across the street in Berk's room. I looked up at his window and had to wrestle the nearly overpowering urge to run up there and tell him my good news. Or head back inside and write him a note the way I used to.

There was a hole in my life where our letters used to live, but after baking a cake for the mysterious Alexis last year, I'd had to cut myself off. And I didn't have the balls to ask him who she was, but who, especially a college football player, ordered a cake for someone they didn't care about. Not like I'd have had a right to pry. The Letter Girl would've deserved an explanation, but I was just his neighbor across the street. That would've made me come off like the weirdo girl who was way too into him.

Obviously he cared about Alexis, even the other guys knew about her, although they didn't really seem to have high opinions of her, and I hadn't been able to glean any specifics.

The thrown hands and glares when he'd mentioned her one day told me whoever she was, she was bad news—and she was here to stay. And I didn't need to put my heart on the line up against another girl. I wasn't exactly the girl guys fought over. I was the one they settled on dancing with when my much prettier sister or friend was taken. The consolation prize. But I couldn't be that with him. I'd rather stand on the sidelines than jump into the game and get pulverized.

Protect my heart. Figure out what the hell I wanted to do with my life. And not get any crazy ideas during this weekend with Berk, especially while in a vulnerable place. Actually, I should just cancel. It was better to cancel on him than endure whatever my mom and sister had in store for me this weekend.

Berk may not see me as an option, but I didn't want him to see my mother and sister turn me into a victim, and they had a nasty habit of turning me into their whipping post whenever we got together.

Hence me avoiding that as much as possible.

What the hell had come over me, allowing Berk to come?

I spun on my heel to walk across the street. I'd rather Berk not witness the impending emotional blood bath. I'd hidden from my mom and Laura for nearly six months—other than that drive-by invite. The pent up shitty-things-to-say-to-Jules dam had to be overflowing. Halfway across the street, my phone buzzed. I whipped it out and answered it immediately, primed for Avery's call.

But that wasn't until tomorrow.

"Julia."

Mom's voice was like a full glass of ice water to my face.

"Yes, Mom."

"I'm double-checking on everything for tomorrow. I'll be meeting everyone at Kelland, but I wanted you to know that even with your late rsvp we've got a room big enough for you and your friend. Laura mentioned it in passing, but I wanted to double-check that you're actually bringing a guest." She said the word like it was something made up that most likely didn't exist.

"Absolutely, Mom."

"A friend, of course."

What would be so outlandish about someone wanting to date me? My blood pressure soared as my pride screamed. "No. He's my date. I have a date." The words came out and were met with a thunderous silence I felt the need to fill. "Laura was one hundred percent correct. Berk's my date. We've been seeing each other for a while now."

Ha! For once I'd stood up to her judgy misconception, her

baiting of me. I wasn't a loser, I had a date! I'd locked in Berk's presence to the party and… Oh god, I'd *said the words* 'we've been dating!'

I resisted the urge to scream into the phone. My heart thudded in my chest and I scrambled to figure out a way to backpedal, take the lies back. It was like I'd had an out of body experience and started spewing all that stuff to save face.

"It took quite a bit of arranging and rearranging, so I do hope he'll be there."

I stared up at Berk's window and my shoulders sank. Backing out now would bring on even more of a shitstorm with my mom, especially if her plans were thrown out of whack.

"Yes, of course we'll be there. Berk is so excited to finally meet my family." *What are you saying?! Shut up!* "He wouldn't miss it for the world."

"Good."

"I wanted to ask you about the *Peter Rabbit* books." The ones I kept asking about and never got a response to. Dad had drawn little doodles in the corner of some of the pages of the books we'd read together. They were an irreplaceable part of my childhood and memories of him.

Dead silence on her end.

"It would mean a lot to me."

"Now is not the time. I'm not going to search through those old boxes now, Julia. We're focusing on Laura at the moment. I can't believe how selfish you are. I'll see you tomorrow."

End of call. My heart gave three thumps of sadness over the books before horror of my embellishments with Berk came rushing back in.

Oh my god. What the hell did I do now? I dragged my fingers through my hair.

Well, shit. I stood in the middle of the road until a set of headlights rolled over me. Canceling now wasn't an option. I could just hear her digs all weekend at how sad it was that I was there alone after making such a big deal about 'making room' for Berk. I couldn't take that on top of the whole Chet situation. Now was not the time to hyperventilate.

I shuffled off the street, closed myself up in my house and made a beeline straight to the kitchen. I flipped through my recipe cards, triple-checked my ingredients. It was going to be a long night ahead.

And in two days, I'd be driven an hour outside the city to a place with no wifi and sharing a room with Berk for two nights. I hefted the ten-pound bag of sugar from my emergency stash. Brown sugar, eggs, and enough flour to feed half the campus. Sugar rush, here I come! I'd need all the help I could get to survive this coming weekend.

CHAPTER 5
JULES

I sat in the pastel blue metal chair in the office crowded with baking trays, recipe cards, and bakery boxes. My leg bounced up and down. An employee had led me to the back office and said Avery would be here at any moment. I looked around the room. There were articles framed and hung up on the walls. A picture of Avery with a big guy who had to be her husband sat on her desk. She was in a beautiful and simple white dress and he was in a summer suit and tie.

The place smelled incredible, like my kitchen times ten—minus the lingering mildew smell I hadn't gotten out after hours of deep cleaning.

I'd walked by all the displays. Donuts, croissants, cupcakes, and a few cookies on trays in the back.

The office door flew open. "So sorry I'm late. I'm—"

"Avery Cunning, I know." I jumped up and shook her outstretched hand with way too much force.

She was jerked forward and braced her hand on her desk.

I cringed and let go, sitting back in the chair, balancing the folder with my resume on my lap. Her hair was up on top of her head and she slipped the well-loved apron off her neck and sat it down on the desk in front of her. She had on jeans and t-shirt. Simple and down to earth. I felt a little overdressed in my pants and button-down top.

"And you're Elle's friend with the killer skills."

My cheeks flushed and I tried to keep my breathing under control. "I wouldn't say that."

"I would." She smiled.

"Nothing like yours. The cakes you make are amazing. The donuts too."

"I learned from a great teacher. How did you start baking?" She leaned forward, intently focused.

The flames in my cheeks could keep her oven going for days. "My dad loved to bake. He had a big sweet tooth and he was always experimenting, so we spent a lot of time in the kitchen. And I was an annoying little kid, so I wanted to help and he taught me."

She smiled and it made her eyes sparkle. "Does he still bake? What does he think of what you're doing?"

I pushed through the lump in my throat. "He died when I was nine."

"I'm sorry to hear that. My mom passed away when I was eight. We used to bake together too." A small, sad smile that probably mirrored my own curved her lips. "I can see where the passion comes from."

"It's a connection."

She nodded. "Absolutely, and the joy on other people's faces when they eat what we make…"

"It's like getting a little piece of them back."

"I knew I'd like you, Jules. No one who bakes like you do could be an asshole. I'll lay it all out for you."

I scooted my chair forward, the legs scraping against the polished concrete floor.

"I'm a little short staffed with some of the projects I have coming up. And I'm also hesitant about bringing in new people because of stuff with my husband."

Oh no, was he a total creeper or something? "What stuff with your husband?"

"Emmett Cunning."

I hope my blank stare wasn't taken as a bad thing.

"And if I didn't think I could like you more, I just did. He's an athlete."

"That makes sense. I've seen a few pictures and he definitely looks like he works out."

She chuckled. "Understatement. Being the wife of an athlete comes with some extra spotlight time and crazies, so I've had to be careful with who I bring into the business."

The office door banged open and a woman with ripped jeans who looked like she belonged in an Abercrombie biker gang ad waltzed in. Her rainbow-colored hair was tugged up on top of her head in an I-don't-give-a-shit bun.

"Is she one of the crazies?" I stage-whispered to Avery.

Avery's chuckle turned into a full blown laugh. "Absolutely."

"Did you tell her you want her to be your new intern because you're knocked up with your giant hockey player hubby's baby?"

"Max!" Avery shouted, throwing a stack of cupcake wrappers at her head.

"What? I knew you'd be tiptoeing around the whole situation."

Max pulled up a chair, spun it around on one leg, and sat on it backward. A total cool chick move. If she didn't have a leather jacket tucked away somewhere, I'd eat my hat. Not that I owned one, but I'd go out and buy one and eat it—tag and all. Beautiful tattoos wound their way up one arm from her wrist to her shoulder. She definitely didn't have a problem wearing her arms out in public.

Avery sighed. "I never should've had them put in that door connecting your shop to mine."

"Nope, but you like to tempt my custom cake clients with

your little treats, so it's a win-win for you." Max grinned and turned her gaze to me. "I'm Max. I work next door doing custom cakes. But Avery's got better coffee and I love screwing with her." Her smile was annoying-best-friend levels of hilarious. "Ah, you're the girl she's trying to rope into her little 'taking a break' experiment."

"I—I think so."

Avery shook her head and sat down behind her desk. "As Max so delicately put it, I'm pregnant and being on my feet and baking is going to be hard enough, so we'd like to branch out a little and possibly do some work that doesn't require me to wake up at four AM and be in the shop for twelve hours straight. That's where you'd come in."

"What do you want me to do?"

"Come in and learn the ropes. Help in the front of the shop during the day—around your class schedule, of course. I'd also love to show you some of my recipes, and you can help prepare orders for our bigger events. I have some full time people and they're great, but I'm looking for someone with your kind of talent."

Max reached over and pushed her fingers against my chin, closing my gaping mouth.

"Seems like she's in. Are you in, Jules?" She lifted an eyebrow.

My words came out in a sputter. "Sure, I'll be here for as long as you like. I can be here at 4AM if you need me to be."

"I don't need a morning person, but send me the times you're available and we can figure out a schedule that works for all of us."

————

AN HOUR LATER I'D HAD A TOUR OF THE BAKERY AND STILL couldn't get over the fact that I was here. I'd started the mental catalog of what I needed to look up when I got home.

I wanted this engagement party weekend over, so I could start already.

"These are killer. Avery's still testing them out to add to the menu." Max handed me a mini lemon blueberry cupcake.

"After the long weekend, I'll be here whenever you need me." The bright citrus flavor complemented the vanilla cake so well. It was only one bite, but damn, I wanted more. Like, that whole damn tray of them. And that, ladies and gentlemen, was how I'd ended up with the name Gigantic Jules back in middle school.

"Partying it up before school starts?" Avery pushed the big baking trays out of the way.

"I wish. It's my sister's engagement party."

"That's not a happy face." Avery rested her elbows on the butcher's block counter.

"Understatement of the month. She looked like she said she'd be putting her hand in the garbage disposal."

Was I that transparent? Shit, I've lost my touch. I'd have to work on getting my game face back for this weekend.

"Nothing wrong. There's a lot to get done before the semester starts, and my mother can be...demanding."

"I.e., a total bitch. We hear you loud and clear, Jules. Don't worry, we're not prima donnas here. Other than Preggo My Eggo over here when she's pushing herself too hard." Max licked the icing off her fingers.

Avery whipped a towel at Max's head, which she ducked like she had spider sense.

"As you can tell, I could use some non-smart ass company around here, and I'd love you to bring in some of your own recipes, if you're up for it. We can call them Jules' Specials."

"Yes, absolutely, I can do that." Or I'd kill myself trying. Having something I made showcased at Bread & Butter was insane.

"Yeah, don't screw this up, Jules," Max said through her mouthful of even more cupcakes. And I officially hated her a little bit. She was chowing down on mini cupcakes like they were cucumbers and could rock the skinny chick, 'I can walk into any store and buy off the rack' look, while I'd be on the pole for an hour tonight to make sure that mini cupcake didn't go straight to my already gigantic ass.

I mean, to my well-rounded and strong ass. There, are you happy Dr. Schuller?

"Thanks for the vote of confidence, Max."

Max turned, her face completely serious. "We've got all the confidence in you. If I didn't think you could do it, I'd have run you out of Avery's office in five minutes flat. You've got this."

A compliment from Max was something I didn't think happened too often. In the short amount of time since I'd met her, that comment meant the world to me.

"I won't let you down. Either of you." I looked at both Avery and Max.

They gave me reassuring smiles and sent me home with a bag piled high with donuts, cupcakes, and croissants. I was still in shock in the taxi on the way back to campus.

As I grabbed my phone to text Elle, it vibrated in my hand.

BERK: *When can I taste your frosting again?*

I tried not to blush and failed hard. For some reason writing all the things I'd written him in letters was fine, but by text, real live text where he knew who I was, that was a hell no. He was a flirt. I don't even know if he knew he was doing it.

ME: *On my way home now. And I have extra treats.*
BERK: *Eagerly awaiting your arrival.*

The taxi pulled up and my door opened before I could gather up all the boxes on the seat beside me. I yelped.

Berk shoved his head into the back of the taxi. "You said extra treats? I'm starving." He had a twizzler dangling out of the side of his mouth.

"How can you be starving? You're actively chewing." I nudged him out of the way with my feet.

"This was just so I didn't start gnawing on the planks of your porch. Let me take those." He plucked the boxes out of my hands and nudged at the half-open lid.

I smacked my hand down over it. "Do not pilfer the goods. They're not all for you."

An offended gasp shot from his mouth. "Who else have you been giving away your treats to?"

A deeper level-five blush set into my cheeks. We climbed the steps. "Wouldn't you like to know?" I called over my shoulder as I opened the door.

"I sure as hell would. The only reason I'm looking forward to study sessions this semester is because you always baked for them." He slid the boxes onto the kitchen table.

My head shot up. "I didn't know we had classes together this semester."

"Ethics, remember? A late switch for me into Buchanan's class."

"You willingly switched into his class? I only took it because I needed one last ethics class and his was the only one that fit into my schedule." I grabbed a couple plates from the dish rack.

"Same." He brushed sprinkles off the side of his mouth.

"Berk!"

"What?" His big-eyed innocent look did nothing to remove the splotch of chocolate on the side of his mouth.

I grabbed a napkin and wiped at the spot. "Next time, be better at hiding the evidence." I laughed and opened the boxes.

"What's all this from? It's not your usual baking."

"My new internship."

"It's at Bread & Butter?"

I nodded. "I need to step up my game. Are you willing to be a taste tester? I've got some dough chilling in the fridge."

"I'd taste your dough any day of the week, Jules."

His words rolled down my skin like chocolate syrup. He was way too good at the flirting. Way too good. It almost made me feel like I was special. I cringed, wanting to bury my head in the sand or maybe break my leg to have an excuse not to go to the engagement party. And after this weekend, I could only hope the way he saw me didn't change.

CHAPTER 6
BERK

The driving bass of the club killed the cookie buzz I'd had on the way over. My after practice ritual of grabbing something sweet from Jules' place had been interrupted by yet another text from Alexis.

After the edict from LJ not to bring her back to the house, I'd sleep at her place. I hadn't even realized it was almost eleven when I got Alexis' call at Jules' until I saw the time. Hours melted away when I was watching Jules do her thing. And she did it so well. Every time I walked in the door there was always a huge smile and that warm glowing feeling in my chest.

But vanilla, sugar, and chocolate had been replaced with sweat, beer, and too-sweet mixers.

A head above most people in the club, at least I had an easier time spotting Alexis. Dancing on a table in the roped off VIP area—typical. And slipping off it and falling into one of the couches lined up against the back wall.

I charged through the crowd, not afraid to throw in a few shoulder hits to the people sloshing their drinks all over me. A wet stickiness seeped into my shoes. Reece would probably hold a Viking funeral for them if he found out.

At the velvet rope, the bouncer's gaze lit up with recognition and went from guard dog to a flicker of confusion to a bro handshake and a pat on the back in the space of five seconds.

"I won three hundred bucks on that interception play you ran last season." He let go of my hand, sporting a wide grin.

"Glad it worked out," I shouted back and shoved my hands in my pockets. Getting recognized always felt awkward. Nix handled it like an old pro—he probably got tips from his dad. But I had bigger things to deal with tonight. Namely, the drunk-off-her-ass redhead taking another sip of her drink.

"Can you help me? I'm here for her." I lifted my chin toward the beyond tipsy, stumbling version of Alexis.

"Girlfriend?"

I shook my head. "Nah."

He eyed me up and down and lifted the velvet rope.

Standing in front of Alexis, I stared at her picking herself up off the floor and reaching for another drink.

"Oh no, you don't." I lifted it out of her reach.

Her gaze narrowed and then brightened when her drink-hazed brain registered my face. "Berkie, you came." She flung her arms around me and looped them around my neck.

I wrapped my arms around her and turned my face away from the alcohol-soaked smell permeating a three foot radius around her. "Jesus, Alexis, what the hell are you wearing?" I averted my gaze and was three seconds away from pulling off my own shirt and putting it on her. My backpack was in the car or I'd have had a thermal and some sweatpants to put her into. "Let's get you out of here."

"But I want to stay. Let's have some fun, let's dance." She tried to lift my arm over her head.

"No, Alexis. We're leaving. You're beyond drunk and you're not even twenty-one yet."

"Don't ruin my night. I invited you here so we could have

fun." Only a practiced translator of Drunk-Alexis would even understand what she was saying.

"You didn't invite. You said you needed help."

"I did, but then I found some guys to buy me drinks. Problem solved!" She smiled like she was a genius for hatching that complex plan.

"We're going. You can walk out or I can carry you." I wrapped my fingers around her arm.

"Carry me." She flung her arms out in front of her and pouted just like she had when she was eight and she'd been told she couldn't leave the table until she ate her broccoli. She'd sat there until it was time for school in the morning, bleary-eyed and broccoli-free.

"What the fuck, dude? No poaching." A dude half a foot shorter than me and probably one hundred and fifty pounds soaking wet stepped to me. "We've been buying rounds for her. You can't just swoop in and cock block like that."

Alexis's eyes got wide and she bit her lips like this was hilarious.

I didn't feel like fighting tonight, but I would. The pounding of the bass matched the throbbing in my neck.

"Consider your cock officially blocked. She's my sister and I'm taking her home."

The guy's head whipped back and forth between me and Alexis in the way I hated, comparing the way we looked. That made my skin crawl and want to punch something hard—like his smug face.

"You're not my brother," Alexis slurred, falling into me.

Every time she said those words, it hurt. Even all these years since the first time. "We're not having this conversation here." I turned to the guy, who had been joined by two more of his friends. "She's leaving. Step aside or I go through you." *Don't move, dude.* I didn't want to fight, but I could knock him on his ass in half a second flat.

"He runs through guys three times your size every day of

the week. I'd listen to him," the bouncer called out from his sentry post.

The guy squinted at me and then glared at Alexis. "You would've been a sloppy lay, anyway. Have her."

I balled my fists at my side, grinding my teeth so hard my jaw ached.

I shifted from the balls of my feet, ready to lay into this guy, but then Alexis slipped her hand into mine. "Berk, I don't feel so well. Can you take me home?"

Grabbing her hand, I hustled her out of there and into my car. Street lights whipped by as we drove in silence to her apartment.

My former foster parents had moved her into a studio apartment in the University City area, probably hoping she'd finally make a decision about college by being around so many students. All it had done was open up even more free places for her to get booze until she was twenty-one. Sometimes, late at night, I'd stare up at my bedroom ceiling and try to picture what my life would've been like if I hadn't been kicked out of their house. Would I have had a place to go back to for Thanksgivings? Christmases with presents under the tree with my name on them? Parents who texted and called to check up on me, see how school was going? If I was dating anyone?

Alexis never seemed to care. Never got comfortable there. Never believed it was real. It wasn't like I hadn't been there too. But they actually gave a shit and I'd sacrificed something real for her. Something she still didn't feel she could trust. It broke my heart for us both.

I used my spare key and helped her inside with my backpack slung over my shoulder. It had never failed me yet. Everything I needed and everything I cared about was in the bag.

The light gray walls and coordinated teal accents pulled the space together and made it look like something out of a catalog. Other than the empty pizza boxes, take out containers and half-empty cups on most flat surfaces.

With my lips slammed together tight, I flung open the cabinet under the sink and shoved paper plates and other trash into the garbage can. This place looked worse than The Brothel, and there were four guys living there.

When the garbage bag was filled to the brim, I tied it off and dropped it beside the door, grumbling the entire time. I rummaged through my backpack, gently pushing aside the gift-wrapped box and found the overly large bottle of ibuprofen. After filling a glass of water, I checked the time. *Fuck*, I had practice in less than four hours.

"Are you mad at me?" She stared up at me as I handed her the pills and shoved the water into her hand.

I pinched the bridge of my nose. "No."

She downed half the glass. "You look mad." Her small voice reminded me of the scared little girl on her first night in a new placement. The first time she'd ended up in the system with a paper thin dress in the dead of winter, clutching a stuffed bunny rabbit missing one eye. The grayed ear of that same rabbit peeked out from under her blankets.

And the simmering anger at her irresponsibility evaporated. She was still just my kid sister. "I worry about you. This is the second time you've texted me this week to come get you. You disappear all summer and then football season's right around the corner and you keep having meltdowns."

"Good to know football's more important than me." She crossed her arms over her chest and the SpongeBob T-shirt that might as well have been a tent.

"You're my sister. Nothing's more important than that."

"Except for football."

I threw my arms up. "You're drunk. You need to get some rest and I need to get back to my place. I have practice in the morning."

She grabbed my hand. "Can't you stay?" The puppy dog

eyes. Always with the freaking puppy dog eyes, and she used them because they worked.

"Fine." I grabbed my stack of blankets from the closet.

"You don't have to sleep on the couch."

"Like I want to get punched in the face by your flailing all night. No thanks. Plus, who knows when you last washed your sheets."

"Mom came over last week, so a week ago." Mom and Dad. The same Mom and Dad bankrolling her tiptoes into adulthood that bordered on aimless—outside of partying.

"Still have her doing your laundry." I took a couple pillows out.

She shrugged. "She offers."

"Maybe they don't want you to attract bedbugs."

"That happened one time. They still bring it up every Sunday dinner."

"You mean the ones you don't even go to anymore?"

"I have food here." The eye roll was practically audible.

"When's the last time you went for one?"

She shrugged.

I unfolded everything. Kicked off my shoes and snatched my backpack up off the floor.

"Maybe she's just looking for an excuse to check up on me."

"Like any concerned parent. You're not exactly known for making the best choices."

She flopped back on the bed and flung her arm across her eyes. "Not with this again."

"With what? Me telling you that maybe you need to make some decisions and stop waiting for everyone else to clean up your messes?"

"I don't ask anyone to do anything they don't want to do." She glared at me.

No, she didn't. She never did. It was always a request, but

the vivid images of what kind of trouble she could get herself into always drove me to action, even when I should let her learn from her own mistakes. That was the bitch about caring about someone who didn't seem to have any form of self-preservation—you always wanted to protect them from the fall.

I took my stuff into the bathroom. My toothbrush sat on the sink beside Alexis's. In the studio apartment her parents rented for her. The same ones who had been my parents for a short while. They'd opened their arms to me—to us.

It had taken me a week to finally go to sleep without my shoes on, but then I did and we had movie nights with popcorn and soda. Homework time after school every day. Some of the kids griped about it, but the fact that Barry and Patricia—although she said we could call her Patty—gave a shit about us at all was another way they showed they cared. Like before I'd gone into the system and my biological mom would come home from her second job before her third shift and make sure I'd done mine. It was simple worksheets and stuff, but that didn't matter.

But even after all these years, I'd never been invited back to Barry and Patty's house. Not for a single holiday. Not after what they thought I'd done. Maybe it wasn't worth their time for the kid they saw as throwing their generosity back in their faces. I wasn't bitter about it anymore—at least I tried not to be.

I pushed those thoughts aside. No use dwelling on that shit. Ha, said the guy who'd put his whole damn pro career and this entire football season on something that should've been left in the past. I changed into my sweatpants and T-shirt from my backpack. This tattered navy-and-black Jansport always had my back.

Alexis had turned out the lights while I was in the bathroom. Punching my pillow a few times, I laid down on the pillow- and blanket-laden couch. Alexis had been getting more and more out of control, but it was up to me to be there for her no matter what.

We were family.

"Can you not call me your sister all the time?"

Why didn't she just boot me straight through the heart?

"Everyone always does that mental math when they're looking at me and you and it doesn't add up and that brings on the questions and… I just hate that, okay?"

It didn't make it hurt any less. I hated those looks too. The ones that called you a liar without ever saying a word. It hurt and I hated it, but I understood.

"Please don't be mad. I love you, Berk." Her small voice cut through the apartment.

And that melted all my anger. Wasn't this what little sisters were supposed to do? Push buttons. Make you want to strangle them? And then tell you at the end of the day they still loved you?

"Love you too, Alexis. Night." It was nearly three am. Practice tomorrow would be a bitch. But at least after that I'd get two whole days with Jules, not that I was counting and not that anything was going to happen. Just two friends, hanging out for the weekend.

CHAPTER 7
BERK

An ear-splitting whistle ricocheted inside my helmet. Sweat poured down my face and everything in my body ached. The paint from the lines on the field criss-crossed my back after the drills I'd had for twenty minutes before our scrimmage. The pre-season always stretched on for way too long. Without the adrenaline from running out onto the field in front of thousands of people losing their collective minds, and an opposing team to face down, the grind of two-a-day practices took its toll.

Coach hadn't been happy about my right-on-time arrival, so I'd had to run laps. My own personal hell. Hey, let's get this lineman who's never had to run more than twenty yards at a sprint to do laps. Not that I couldn't use the extra cardio. There was no holding back this year. It was about laying everything on the line and pushing harder than I ever had. I wasn't getting straight As or anything, but I didn't have the luxury of a family business or support to fall back on like Nix. Even with a degree, it would be hard to find work without a safety net. But a few years in the pros and I'd be set for life.

Right now, however, I was eight seconds from puking. I braced my hands on my knees. Sprinting in full pads and going straight to the lineup was what I got for rescuing Alexis last night. The second time this week. This time she'd found herself stranded an hour outside the city at some house party in Jersey.

Two-a-day practices leading up to the season opener were brutal, but no one could question Coach's methods. We'd won the national championship last year, and we all knew that with Nix and Reece gone, there was a lot of ground to cover to get our asses to the dance two years in a row.

Our new QB, Austin, was doing everything in his power to make it happen, and I'd be the guy getting in the way of the other guys trying to take his head off. We huddled up and our QB went over the play.

Breaking the circle, we jogged to our positions. I crouched down, fingertips sinking into the freshly-mown and meticulously-maintained grass. This grass probably got more care and attention than eighty-five percent of people in this world.

Energy crackled along the line as everyone waited for the snap. My legs tingled waiting for the telltale sound of the ball hitting the QB's palm. There was the call and smack. Using muscle memory ingrained from the first time I'd run these drills back in high school, I charged forward, holding off the defense who wanted nothing more than to come out of this practice with the nod from Coach. Not happening.

The ball sailed over my head and my job was done. A touchdown pass and the rookie hunched over, resting his hands on his knees.

"You did good, kid."

He stared up at me with a huge grin. "Kid? I'm barely a year younger than you, fuckface."

"But much wiser, I am." I pressed my palms together and went for the best Yoda impersonation that I could manage while being nearly six-three and hefting at least twenty pounds of gear across the field.

"More like more annoying."

"One man's wise is another man's foolish."

He shook his head and punched my shoulder pads. "Either way, thanks for having my back out there. I won't let you down. I know with Nix gone things are different."

"Things always change." Better than anyone, I knew how quickly life could become quicksand under your feet. Suck it up and adapt or end up in a spiral that shot you out on death's door or somewhere worse.

"You're killing it so far. Don't psych yourself out. Keep running plays like you have been and I'll keep the defensive line off your ass for as long as I can." That was one thing I kicked ass at—protecting the QB at all costs. Better I get my bell rung, the bruised ribs, or a cleat straight to the face than the guy calling the plays. If the ball made it to where it was supposed to, we were good.

"But you throw a few interceptions and I'm going to let them knock you around a bit."

"Thanks." He rolled his eyes. "No pressure there."

I shook his shoulder pads and they clacked against his helmet. "Just giving you a heads up."

"Why'd Coach have LJ riding the bench all pre-season?" Austin shielded his eyes from the late August sun, staring at our should-be cornerback hanging on the sidelines looking like he could bite through steel bars.

"It's complicated." I clapped him on the shoulder.

LJ had made the unfortunate mistake of pissing off our Coach in more ways than one. You'd think being best friends with his daughter would come as an advantage. That was so far from the case it was hovering in the outer atmosphere only visible with a telescope. And it had only gotten worse when Marisa had moved into The Brothel. The name probably wasn't helping things.

Coach had us all huddle up. "You've all hustled hard this pre-season. We're going into the next season and I want you to get it out of your heads that with last year's seniors gone we don't have it in us. Every single one of you—" His gaze froze on LJ and his lips tightened. "Almost all of you have what it takes to make this another winning season. You have Labor Day weekend off."

Guys banged their helmets together and cheered.

"You have these three days off, and I'm trusting you all to rest up and not make me regret giving you some time before the semester starts. Get ready for your classes. Get some sleep. Do not make me have to attend any honor council meetings once you're all back. Dismissed."

The whole team charged toward the tunnel, ready for three solid days off. The energy that flagged during practice roared back. The unmistakable smell of IcyHot, sweat, and soap filled the locker room.

I headed straight for the showers, not wanting to be late to meet Jules. Since I had practice so late, I told her I'd meet at the pickup spot for the shuttle to wherever it was we were going.

She'd had to go earlier to help her sister. I'd leave my car at the house and get a taxi there, so I wouldn't be late. I'd make sure to eat and drink my fill to make up for the ding to my wallet.

Some guys were already slamming their lockers shut and heading outside, clothes clinging to their barely-dried bodies. Classes started in three days and there was no slacking off once the semester began. Sometimes it was hard enough keeping my eyes open after practice, but throw in classes and I'd be 90% powered by caffeine and sugar.

"Looks like someone's ready to party." LJ stood beside me, not a bead of sweat on him.

"I'm sure you and Marisa have some pre-class ritual including face paint, stuffed animals, and tricycles you'll wander off into the woods to complete." I grabbed a towel from the stack and dried off my hair.

"Not the woods. In the backyard," he said absently, tugging his jersey off. He hadn't even been wearing pads.

"Did you talk to Coach?"

LJ slammed his elbow against the open door to his locker and bit out a curse. "He's going to keep me from getting drafted."

"Why don't you play his game? Just enough so you get some time out on the field." I wrapped a towel around my waist, water dripping down my chest.

"And abandon Marisa?" He looked at me like I'd suggested feeding her in little pieces to a swarming sea of crocodiles.

"Asking if she'd go to her dad's weekly dinners by herself is hardly abandonment. She can sit in silence with him all by herself; she doesn't need you there as her white knight. Not at the expense of your career. You'd think she'd care about that."

LJ's lips slammed together. "Oh really? What about Alexis?" His glare intensified.

I grabbed my shirt off of my locker. "That's different and you know it."

"No, it's not different—at all. Remember your words the next time she calls or texts with some bullshit she needs rescuing from."

"Who needs rescuing?" Keyton tucked his towel around his waist.

"No one." I shoved my head into my shirt, trying to get dressed as quickly as possible.

"Alexis," LJ said at the same time.

Keyton's eyebrows dipped. "Is that the redhead? The short one who tried to steal LJ's wallet?"

"Exactly her." LJ chucked his towel into the giant overflowing bin at the center of the locker room.

"She thought it was mine." I pulled my brand-new green with white striped Adidas, courtesy of Reece, out of my locker.

Apparently, my five-year-old, no-longer-white, bordering-on-holey shoes were too much for him to take, so I finally let him buy some for me. After Seph, his soon-to-be fiancée, and football, shoes were the third most important things to him.

They were nice shoes, but even now, I looked over my shoulder as I grabbed them out of my locker and slipped them on. Even four years after leaving the group home, having brand-new stuff made me paranoid. Most people didn't want to steal someone else's shitty stuff. They'd leave it alone and go for flashier, newer things. I needed to break away from that.

"Oh, I get it. She didn't know she was trying to steal from me. She thought she was stealing from you, and that makes it okay."

"It's not stealing if she knows she can take whatever she wants whenever."

LJ's frown deepened like there were weights attached to the corners of his lips, dragging them down to the floor. "Good to know she's got a thievery free pass. Next time she comes by, I'll padlock my door."

Water from my hair soaked my t-shirt as I left the stadium, needing to get out of there. Whenever LJ started up on an Alexis rant, it was easier to bail. At least Reece and Nix were out of the house, so they couldn't gang up on me about her. They didn't get it and they didn't want to. Growing up the way I had, there were some people you counted on and some people you didn't. And she counted on me. Needed me and trusted me. I wouldn't ditch her because sometimes she had a full-blown case of the sticky fingers. Not like I hadn't been there when I was younger. Sometimes the hunger pangs were too strong to ignore and the static in my head would get so loud I could barely think straight, but straight enough to slip an apple or a candy bar into my pockets to tide me over on the weekends until I could get lunch again at school.

Stealing wasn't always about wanting someone else's

stuff, but I wasn't going to correct them. And it was a reminder that my reality wasn't one most people had faced. There were people out there with loving families who'd never known what it was like to chug a liter of water to have *something* in your belly, just so you could fall sleep.

I sat in my car and drummed my fingers against the steering wheel, staring up at the house. Run in, grab my backpack, dump my practice gear, and then meet Jules. I ordered the taxi on my phone. Three minutes.

The street was quiet, not too many people around. The perfect time for someone to be able to slip in unnoticed and leave something sexy behind in the mailbox. I'd just done two hours of hardcore physical activity, and my heart was pumping like I'd just finished a marathon.

Climbing out of my car, I took the steps three at a time and stood on the porch in front of the mailbox. I let out a breath and lifted the lid. The same heart-under-heel disappointment squeezed my chest. It was still there. My note. The one I'd rewritten ten times and it hadn't made a difference. The crushing waves of disappointment only got higher. It would only be a matter of time before I drowned.

Every day with no word from her made the words in her final letter sting that much deeper. It was like losing a connection to someone out there in the world who knew more about me than most people. I'd let her in and now she was shutting me out.

At least heading to this weekend party thing with Jules meant my mailbox wouldn't be ten feet away, taunting me every time I walked in the door. A few days away would help me clear my head and break the spell TLG had on me —maybe.

CHAPTER 8
JULES

I t was almost six. I hadn't wanted to go inside without Berk, mainly so I didn't chicken out and cancel on him at the last minute. Plus, at least if he were here then I'd have a friendly face in the crowd. Hanging with my mom's country club cohorts and Laura's friends wasn't exactly my comfort zone. Laura had already taken my carry-on suitcase and they'd stashed it somewhere.

The building's granite and marble historical structure cast a wide shadow over the city street.

"Sorry, I'm late." Berk walked around from the side of the building. He had a duffle over one arm and a backpack over the other.

The door to the building swung open again and Laura strolled out. Her step faltered for a second when her gaze landed on Berk. "You're here." Her smile was tooth-achingly sweet.

A nightmare scenario ran through my head. One where she spent her entire engagement weekend pretending to be the perfect, beautiful sister, and I caught her and Berk making out in an alcove somewhere.

Or worse, in intense conversation filled with laughter and

any excuse to touch one another like the thought of being physically separated hurt. And they'd pull me aside and tell me that she was calling off her engagement because she and Berk just clicked. He'd say neither of them expected this to happen, but sometimes these things come from the most unexpected places. And then she'd throw in that it wasn't like Berk and I would've lasted, and I should be happy that she'd finally found the one—again. I should be happy she wasn't with Chet anymore—and she'd give me her full blessing to have him back.

Now it felt like my shield might've had a secret self-destruct button I hadn't known about.

"Sorry, practice ran over and I didn't want to show up here all sweaty."

A large black bus with tinted windows pulled up to the curb.

Laura made a sound like she'd have licked him if he had shown up all hot and sweaty—hell, she might do it right now. "What do you play?"

"Football."

"A football player at Fulton? Not exactly your speed, is it, Julia?"

My smile tightened. *My speed is none of your damn business.* "He's amazing. Berk's joining the draft at the end of the season."

The doors behind her opened and everyone who'd been downing glasses of champagne and cocktails like we were in the end of days flowed out like it was an uncorked bottle.

"Everyone onto the bus. And can someone take Berk's bag?" Laura called out to no one in particular, but a guy in a uniform showed up beside her to take Berk's bags.

The duffle he let go with no issue, but when the uniformed guy tried to take his backpack, he held it tight.

"Not that." He jerked the bag back.

The uniformed guy looked to Laura.

"I've got all my books in here to get in some studying over the weekend before classes start. I'll do it on the bus."

Laura pressed one of her freshly manicured hands to her chest. "That's so academically conscientious. How wonderful to find an athlete who also cares so much about his degree." Laura took his arm and led him toward the bus.

Berk checked over his shoulder for me.

I followed along, joining the line of partygoers entering the bus. Everyone moved out of Laura's way like she was on her way to her coronation, because of course they did, and everything would revolve around her this weekend.

Making it to the top of the steps, I expected to see Laura huddled up with Berk under the guise of making him feel more at home before the weekend began. Instead, she was sitting with Chet, who popped open another bottle of champagne, bubbles overflowing all over the floor.

I slipped into the empty seat beside Berk, just as the bus pulled away from the curb and knocked me into him, nearly throwing me into his lap.

Berk braced his hands on my shoulders, so I didn't crush him.

"Sorry," I mumbled and sat, buckling myself in. After a couple minutes of silence—well, not silence from the rest of the bus, they were all standing in the aisles and ignoring even more appetizers that were being passed around in favor of the booze served up in plastic flutes—he leaned over to me.

"Your sister is—"

"Beautiful. Stunning. So amazing. And yes, we really are related."

His eyebrows dipped and he shook his head. "I was going to say kind of pushy."

Relief crashed over me like a wave.

"I know she's your sister and I probably shouldn't say anything, but—" He leaned in closer and I tried not to think about how close he was and how good he smelled after his post-practice shower. He whispered, "I had to tell her maybe it would be a good idea to go sit with her own fiancé. She doesn't seem to like him very much."

"I think the whole stealing him away from me thing probably got her in over her head." My back snapped straight and I cringed. That hadn't come out nearly as jokingly as I meant it. The last thing I wanted was Berk thinking I still had a thing for Chet, who was cheering on his friend chugging a bottle of champagne.

"You dated that guy." Berk nodded toward the crisp and impeccably put-together Chet.

"Hard to believe, I know."

"Inconceivable." Berk's Princess Bride impersonation should've rolled off my back, but it hurt. Like another hit to an already stubbed toe.

He sank back in his seat probably wondering why the hell that guy had even given me a second look. *Don't worry, it wasn't for long, Berk.*

"He seems about as interesting as cardboard. And he's checked out the asses of at least five other women since we got on the bus."

I peered around the side of the seat. Chet's eyes were trained right on the butt of one of Laura's bridesmaids. Maybe I'd dodged a bullet after all. Part of the appeal of Chet had been that I'd held the interest of someone who'd normally never have given me a second look. Those feelings of finally being seen, cared about, desired. I'd mattered until I hadn't, and that made it even harder, made it hurt even more getting a taste and having it turn into sawdust in my mouth. Worse, because he'd betrayed me with my sister, he'd never gone away so I could forget about him.

There was no clean break—never would be.

Berk tried to squeeze his backpack under the seat in front of us, but it wasn't exactly a clutch purse.

"What do you have in there?" I reached for it, trying to help him push it down between us.

Snatching it back, he set it on his lap. "It's nothing. Just some of my dirty clothes I didn't dump at my place before I left."

Touchy, touchy about dirty underwear. Noted. Also, kind of gross.

"And now that the bus is moving and you have no escape, I thought I'd let you know that some people on this trip…" I craned my neck looking out over the seats around us. "Might be under the impression that we're together, like *together* together."

He shrugged. "Boyfriend from the wrong side of the tracks to piss off the parents. Got it."

I waved my hand dismissively. "Nothing like that. Just be yourself. I didn't want to blindside you in case anyone asked."

"Which is why you waited for wheels up on this trip before you spilled the beans?"

My cheeks burned.

"It was a joke. Don't worry about it. I can keep it together."

Berk struggled to keep his eyes open, widening them and running his hands over his face.

"We've got an hour ride. Don't feel like you need to keep me company."

"It's cool. I'm good." His eyelids drooped.

"Berk, sleep."

His sleepy smile made my heart flutter. "Just for a little bit? I had a late night." He rested his head against the seat back and closed his eyes. The steady rhythm of his breathing started in less than a minute. He wasn't kidding.

My head snapped up off Berk's shoulder as I jolted awake. Wiping the side of my mouth, my eyes widened and the dancing flames of embarrassment threatened to consume me. I spotted the dark splotch on his shoulder and squeezed my eyes shut like that would magically make my drool disappear. Staring straight ahead at the geometric pattern on the seat back in front of me, I debated between jumping from the moving bus and checking for an ejector seat.

"You're up, sleepyhead."

A wheezy giggle burst free from my lips.

Berk craned his neck and looked down at the spot on his shirt. "Looks like you got real comfortable."

Was I too old to run away and join the circus?

"Jules, chill out." He rested his hand on my shoulder and pushed me back against the seat. "I'm on buses almost half the season. You don't think I've ever drooled on someone before? It happens." He glanced out the window. "Where are we?"

"Almost at my grandparents' house."

"They're having the party at your grandparents' house? I never knew mine, but I didn't realize that was a thing. Is it a tradition or something?" We rolled down the unpaved drive, kept that way to preserve the out-of-time feeling of the scaled-down regency manor house replica.

"It's not their house anymore. They hold events there. Weddings, corporate retreats. A place out in the middle of nowhere where no one can hear you scream."

His eyes bulged.

I laughed, resting my hand on his arm. I wished I'd told him all this in my letters, that I'd been so open that he could put the pieces together and figure out it was me.

Instead, I'd been guarded, even when trying to express a part of me I'd been afraid to embrace in real life. I missed reading his words and hearing a side of him I didn't think many people got to see. Although, I saw more of it the longer we spent together.

"I'm joking. It's so far away from the main road and other

cell towers, they don't get service out here. So, people use it to get away from it all."

He peered around like he expected someone to jump up behind him and throw a burlap bag over his head. "That's what all the rich people planning to play the most dangerous game say."

I laughed even louder. "If I had to put money down on anyone surviving a game of human hunting like that, it would be you by a long shot."

He sat up straighter and looked over the seats in front of us. There was a mix of people still drinking after the hour-long drive and those who'd probably wake up on the bus tomorrow morning.

The carriage rocked as we came to a stop in the circular drive. The event planner stood up at the front of the bus.

"Welcome to Kelland Estates. We're here to celebrate this amazingly special day for Laura Kelland and Chet. Your bags will be sent to your rooms. There will be photographers covering every aspect of the event—some you might not even see. Be forewarned, the cell reception and wifi is almost as bad as dial up."

"What's dial up?" someone called out from the back.

"Trust me, you don't want to know."

Laura stood up to quell the little ripples of discontent at the unplugged weekend. It seemed she didn't trust her engagement party would've been enough of a draw to keep people from being constantly connected to the rest of the world. "Let's go, everyone. We'll have a technology-free weekend, everyone will wonder where the hell we've gone, and when we come back, they'll freak. Just wait until you see your costumes."

The word came out in a slow motion deep baritone.

Costumes.

We were supposed to get dressed up in costumes? Great Gatsby inspired costumes? Flashes of short silver flapper dresses flashed through my mind. *Sleeveless* dresses that showed my arms.

No. No. Absolutely freaking not.

Jumping up from my seat, I shoved people aside, panic rising, and chased after Laura. She disappeared into the front door being held open by one of the event staff. I thanked them and scrambled after her.

Grabbing her shoulder, I turned her around. "You didn't say anything about costumes."

She tilted her head to the side like she was wracking her brain to figure out how she might've forgotten such an important detail. "Hmm, did I not? I swore I did. It was printed on the invitation." A face of mock surprise. "Oh yeah, the one you never picked up from the house." She shook her head disapprovingly. "It doesn't matter. Here's your costume." She held out her hand and one of the event staff handed her a hanger. She shoved the hanger with a black linen cover at me.

"But I didn't tell you my size."

"Mom picked it out." And then she was gone, enveloped by her party planners and party goers.

I stared at the hanger like she'd offered me a viper covered in razor blades. I hated new clothes. I hated everything about clothes in general other than them covering ninety percent of my body.

New clothes hadn't been tested from every angle in the privacy of a fitting room where they could be abandoned, not walked back out in front of everyone to tell them it doesn't fit.

New clothes hadn't been broken in.

New clothes might not cover every part of me I wanted, and new clothes from Laura or Mom were never a gift. They were just another way for them to show me I was absolutely nothing like them with their tiny bodies.

Flashes of back to school shopping when I'd been growing up sent shivers of panic racing down my spine. Walking back toward Berk like I was on the way to an executioner, I blocked out all the laughter and clinking glasses around me.

Maybe it would actually fit.

Maybe it wouldn't look terrible.

Mom wouldn't want me to look terrible in front of everyone.

No, maintaining the picture of perfection was what she lived for.

Breathing a little easier, I slung the garment bag over my shoulder, nearly falling over as the weight inside shifted.

"I got you." Berk's hand slid along my back.

Looking up at him, I totally believed it. His hold on me was solid without a hint of strain, like I was one of the lighter girls who got tossed over a guy's shoulder on a whim at a pool party.

"Do we change now?" He looked at the black garment bag like it may have been a pack of gremlins masquerading as a suit ready to tear him apart.

"We've got some time. Dinner isn't until nine. And knowing my sister, she won't arrive until ten."

"Did you want a drink? I could murder a beer right now."

"Knowing my sister, you'd have to go into town for that."

"It's their bar bill if there's only booze on tap."

I snorted and jiggled the arm of my glasses. "Don't hold back."

He laughed and walked to the bar.

Every head turned as he walked by. Guys in my sister's crowd weren't exactly built like brick shit houses. I probably shouldn't feel so bad about how my dress would fit. After a three second interaction with Berk, I could only imagine what Laura had picked out for him to wear. If I was lucky he might have to go shirtless with the legs of his pants cut off à la the Hulk.

"Julia." The way he drew out my name made me want to barf. It made it sound like my name was Muffy or Barbie and we were in a John Hughes movie with the rich kids who were total assholes. Only here in real life, these ones were also assholes. But he was an asshole I'd liked, which made it even worse. I'd held off sleeping with him for three months of making sure he liked me, someone special for my first time. It was a whole three days before he decided there was a better Kelland sister for him. I'd been blinded to his douche status just because he'd thrown me a bone.

"Hi, Chet." My best smile was plastered on my face.

"I'm so glad you're here. Laura was afraid you'd back out at the last minute and everyone would be gossiping about you behind your back." He hugged me, smelling like a toxic mixture of his and hers Chanel scents and way-too-expensive champagne. His hold continued even after my ghost of a pat on the back.

"Instead, they can do it to my face."

He laughed, finally letting go and squeezed my shoulders. "You've always had such a wonderful sense of humor."

I looked down at his hands and back up to him. What was his deal?

"Hey, Jules. I've got your drink." Berk broke the uncomfortable staring match I'd been roped into.

He expertly handled the two champagne glasses even with one hand taken by the garment bag, and handed me my drink.

"I'm Berk." He shoved his hand right in front of Chet's face.

Chet turned to my rescuer and his eyes widened. "Can I help you?"

"Sure, you can let go of Jules. My date."

"Jules?! Her name is Julia," Chet snapped.

"My mistake, I just go with what I call her in bed at night."

The bubbles from my glass of bubbly shot straight out my

nose. I'm talking full on spray tan coverage of Chet. All heads swung in our direction.

Berk didn't even try to hide his laughter behind his hand like I did. Between the alcohol burning my sinuses and my laughter there were tears in my eyes.

Chet grabbed a stack of napkins from a passing server before glaring at Berk and rushing off.

"I can already tell this weekend is going to be fun." Berk winked at me.

I locked my knees lest I melt into a puddle beside him.

He stood shoulder to shoulder with me like he was ready to take on every ex-boyfriend that came to give me shit this weekend. Fortunately, or unfortunately, Chet was the only one, but I sure as hell wasn't going to tell Berk that.

Beside him, I did feel like he was ready to take on the world on my behalf. My very own knight in shining armor even if it was only for two days and even if he was just pretending to be with me. I could pretend with the best of them.

CHAPTER 9
BERK

Damn that dude was an asshole. Telling me what to call Jules. And then that stuck in my head. Did she hate when people called her Jules? She was the type to let something like that slide to avoid making someone feel bad.

"You are cool with me calling you Jules, right? That's what Elle calls you," I leaned down and whispered in her ear.

She shivered and I looked up to see if there was a vent over her, blowing the AC, but nothing was there. "You can call me anything you want—except Julia. The only people who call me that are in this room and no matter how many times I tell them differently, they still do it."

"Anything I want, huh?" I ran my fingers over my chin and looked off into the distance. "How about Snowglobes?" I bent down and whispered the word in her ear.

Her cheeks turned beet red and she shoved at my shoulder. "Anything but that!"

"Are you sure? Anything? I'm sure I can come up with something in that same vein. How about Lana?"

Her eyebrow shot up.

"Some things are better backward." I stood there taking a

sip of my drink, waiting for her Wheel of Fortune reveal as she ran through the letters.

"Berk!" She laugh-hissed and shoved at my shoulder. "Anything that you could say in front of a classroom full of second graders."

"What part of the city are these second graders from?"

She laughed and some of her champagne dribbled down her chin.

"Such a messy drinker. And you've only had one glass. Or did you get started before our party bus ride happened?"

"I'm messy because someone keeps making me laugh." Her playful glare shot out from behind her horn-rimmed glasses.

"I'm only clarifying the nickname rules. So far we have 'not Snowglobes' and something that can be said in front of a classroom of second graders and their nannies from the Mainline. Any other requirements?"

"Something you could say in front of your mom." She took another drink from her glass.

I dropped my gaze to my hands and squeezed the stem of the glass. With Jules, I never felt like I had to hide who I was, but I didn't want to be a pity case, a sob story where she'd look at me and squeeze my hand and smile at me because she was that kind of person. But she didn't know everything about me. What would she think if she knew?

My throat tightened and I closed my eyes for a second. Enough time to breathe through that dart to my heart and keep those walls I'd built so high and wide around my heart intact. With a gentle shake of my head, I was back to being Berk. Not Orphan Berkley Vaughn.

"You're taking all the fun out of this, but how about Julienne Fries?"

Her eyes lit up and the corner of her mouth quirked up. If she pushed her glasses up her nose in that certain, adorable way I'd maul her on this dance floor. "That, I can handle."

We found a spot along the wall and Jules gave me the rundown on the ins and outs of our weekend companions.

"He's here with two of his ex-wives and his new fiancée?" I pointed at the guy with a way too perfect, nearly-touching-his-eyebrows hairline, who didn't look much older than us. He had a stick thin strawberry blonde on his arm who managed to drape herself all over him to mark her territory without actually touching him. To other people it might look handsy, but ninety percent of the time she never made contact.

"Technically, only one ex-wife. The first marriage was annulled when she found out he'd regularly snort his monthly trust fund allowance right up his nose before the first week of the month was over."

"He stopped using coke then?"

She shook her head and didn't even try to cover her laugh. "Nope, his monthly allowance just got a whole lot bigger when he turned twenty-five. They paid off his debts and now if he tried to snort all the money every month, he'd be half a step from a coronary, which is why everyone thinks his new fiancée is trying to speed the wedding up to this winter."

"And I thought the football team had drama." I downed the last of my drink.

"They've got nothing on families that have been frenemies for generations with more money than sense."

"What about you? You're one of them, right?" I lifted my empty glass to the walking fashion magazine photoshoot happening in front of us.

"Do I seem like one of them?" Her eyebrow quirked up.

I looked her up and down. Low sensible heels. Plain pants and a top that did its best to hide all the assets I knew she rocked under the nineteen layers she usually wore. "Nah, I guess not. So how'd you end up not getting turned into one of the pod people?"

She looked out over the crowd. "My dad."

"I haven't seen him yet. Where is he?"

"He died when I was nine. My mom was flat out against having kids after me, so I guess I became his boy child. We'd come out here on the weekends and go camping, ride horses and have water gun fights. Laura always preferred to go shopping with Mom even when I came back telling her how much fun it was. I don't think my mud-soaked clothes were the kind of convincing she was looking for."

"It was a lot of rough and tumble stuff?"

"Not all. He used to read me these books when I was growing up, even way after I'd outgrown them, but the way he read the story always kept me riveted." She took a sip of her drink with a smile that only came from those happy child-hood memories.

"Which books?"

"Peter Rabbit."

"Do you still read them?"

Her smile faltered. "They're at my mom's. She's... having some trouble finding them." Each word was a tiptoe like she was walking in a minefield.

"I hope she does. Sounds like you and your dad had a lot of fun."

"We had the best time. He's the one who got me into baking."

"He baked?"

"A guy can't bake?"

"It's not that, I just figured people with money had other people do that for them."

"He wasn't like that at all. My grandparents didn't even tell him they had money until he was in college. They lived in a normal house in the suburbs. But on the weekends they'd come out here too. My grandfather told my dad it was his boss's house and they were allowed to use it. But he didn't drop the fact that my grandfather was the boss. So my dad had a pretty normal childhood until he showed up at college and saw his grandfather's name plastered on one of the academic buildings."

"Had to be a shock." Even rich families had their secrets.

"It was. He didn't do the same to us, plus my mom never would've settled for a middle class existence. She wanted the big house and the even bigger parties. But anytime my dad came out here I'd come with him. The cattiness of all this"— she waved her hand at the couples and groups smiling and laughing all while casting judgmental glances, or checking over their shoulders every couple of minutes to make sure they were being paid attention to—"was something I was more than happy to escape."

"With the food you make, you should've been the queen bee of your own little domain."

A sharp exhale shot through her lips. "Showing up with chocolate and carbs in this crew is right up there with drowning puppies in a shallow creek. Baking did not make me popular. I gave my treats to teachers and the staff at school. My mom forbade having them in the house for more than twenty-four hours, so it kind of became a habit for me to give my baking away. And once my dad was gone…" She got a far-off look and I hurt for that little girl who had wanted to do something that made her feel closer to her dad and had had it taken away by the one person who should've done anything to help her during that time. But having a kid didn't make someone a good parent.

"After my dad was gone, I didn't do it as much as I would've liked, which is why even with how terrible my house is, the kitchen made it worth it. Plus, I snuck in a new oven and fridge. I told Elle the landlord had paid for it."

"Why didn't you tell her?"

"She'd have insisted on splitting the cost and she was strapped for cash. I didn't want her to feel bad about it, so I did it."

"Look at you keeping secrets. I had no idea, Julienne Fries."

She let out a stuttering laugh and finished the rest of her drink. "Just so you know, we have a room together. I hope that's okay." Her hand tightened on the glass like she was bracing herself.

"No problem. I'm cool crashing on the floor. I'm sure even that will be nicer than some of the places I've slept."

Her eyes widened and she waved her hands. "No, I can sleep on the floor or on the couch. I invited you."

"Come on, Frenchie. I might be a jock, but I'm not an asshole. I'm not going to have you sleeping on the floor or the couch, especially when you're supplying me with all this top shelf booze." I snagged two more glasses from the passing server's tray.

"We'll figure it out when we get back to the room. I'll head to the bathroom and then we can find it." She chugged the glass I handed her and handed it right back, laughing at my slack jawed face.

"It's not like it's straight vodka." With her costume bag, she headed toward the bathrooms.

I finished my drink and eyed a table of mini versions of foods I'd inhale if I wasn't trying to keep myself from embarrassing Jules. Slowly, like I used to when I came into a new house, I ate one and counted for a full minute before I ate another.

Showing up to a new house as a foster kid was a surefire way to find yourself locked out of the fridge. Some families were awesome and they'd put a small stash of fruit and snacks in our rooms for the new kids, knowing we'd feel awkward in a new place. Others had locks on the fridges or on the kitchen. It was better to figure out the lay of the land and the rules first.

But I learned early to always eat whenever food was offered. I never knew if a social worker would show up to pick me up and cart me away to somewhere new. Hours sitting in the back of her car or hanging in an office just waiting. I hated that jittery feeling I got whenever I was left waiting for long stretches. It was like sitting in the doctor's office for an appointment cranked up to eleven.

After I ate as many as I figured I could without lifting one of the trays and just pouring the food into my open mouth, I picked up my backpack and the costume bag I'd slid under the table. I hoped this thing didn't include tights or some goofy Shakespeare pants.

I'd never worn a costume like this before. The Halloween parties we threw at the Brothel were usually togas or some other costume that could be thrown together in an afternoon scramble once we'd secured a few kegs. When I was younger, if I was ever in a place that had trick-or-treating, I'd used my football uniform, my pillow case, and whatever face paint I could score off other kids, and go door to door as a zombie football player. With how everyone here dressed, I'd probably be in an outfit three sizes too small.

Finishing my drink, I checked the room for Jules. Had she said meet her somewhere else after the bathroom to find our room, or to just meet at the room? The last thing I wanted to do was screw something up and embarrass her. It was strange how different she was from the pod people all around us. I couldn't blame her for inviting me. She needed someone else to watch her back and make sure they didn't drop in whatever alien parasite or microchip these people had in their brains.

These women looked at me like people who'd never been told no in their whole lives. And I knew firsthand what kind of fuckery that brought about. It made it hard to see Jules rubbing elbows with people like this. She didn't exactly scream 'look at how much money I have' like every other person in this place.

From the watches to the shoes, I'd seen these same looks

on many donors at the fundraiser the Coach and university 'requested' we attend.

I checked the room for Jules and didn't see her. After asking one of the servers to check the bathroom for me, I went in search of my date and the room we'd be sharing. All weekend. I threw up the mental vault to keep any thoughts that weren't strictly friendly from invading my mind. I definitely didn't need to be thinking about Jules under the covers and what exactly she might be wearing or not.

CHAPTER 10
JULES

My low heels clicked on the marble floor on the way out of the bathroom after drying my hands. Turning up my winning smile, one that had hurt my cheeks for days when I was younger—who knew cheek muscles could be conditioned?—I opened the bathroom door.

"Of course she'd end up with a guy that huge. It's the only way she'd find someone she wouldn't crush in bed."

Chet and his friends laughed at the end of the short hallway outside of the bathrooms, right by the bar.

"Those kinds of girls always put in the extra effort. She'd probably have been a good lay."

"With the lights off." Someone else chimed in with that charming little comment.

Ducking back inside the bathroom, I pushed my palm against the door, so it closed slowly, without a sound. That's the last thing I needed—them knowing I'd heard them. It would only make it worse, and I didn't need to hear the fake words of apology or how I'd misheard the comments. *Stop being so sensitive. You're overreacting. Don't make a scene.*

I stood in the bathroom with my garment bag surprise from hell and stared at myself in the mirror until I slammed my eyes shut, unwilling to spill any tears in front of them. Splashing water on my face, I stared at my reflection in the mirror. Flushed, a little blotchy, and apparently only a good enough lay in the dark.

I squeezed my eyes shut and tightened my grip on the edge of the sink. *Breathe through it. Don't let their words chip away at you.* Why was I even surprised? Why had I thought things would be different? And to have Berk have to witness it. Kill me now.

Checking outside to make sure they were gone, I bolted straight for the room and didn't look back. Nothing mattered but getting out of there and trying to hold myself together. Sixty hours. Make it through the next two days and everything would be okay.

I nearly tackled one of the staff and asked about getting the key to my room. Shifting from foot to foot and checking over my shoulder like I was being inducted into the witness protection program, I rushed out of the lobby with my key in hand and an apology that my bags had been misplaced ringing in my ears. This wasn't the airport. How were my bags 'lost' from the bottom of the bus to here? Probably something to do with my mom and sister not wanting me to find alternate clothing options for tonight. I could scream, if I weren't already on the verge of crying.

The garden and greenhouse were where I usually went when I needed to think out here, but the hot mugginess outside was enough to deter me. The last thing I needed was a knockdown, drag out fight with the frizz if I wandered around outside, let alone in the greenhouse. Plus, my room was safer.

Creeping down the hall, I spotted my room number, or, should I say *our* room number. Eventually I'd emerge and find Berk, apologize profusely, but at least I'd maintain a little of my dignity. I hung up the garment bag on the bathroom door and flopped down on the bed. Damn, it was comfy. The people who my mom had gotten to take over the place had nothing if not impeccable taste. I tilted my head to the side.

There was a bottle of champagne chilling in a bucket beside the mini bar. Freshly cut flowers in an arrangement sat on the low table in the seating area by the door.

I stared up at the ceiling. "Dad, I don't know what to do. They're all I have left—but I don't know how much longer I can take it." I talked to him like I had for so many years since he'd been gone. Wishing and praying it had all been a mistake and he was sitting in some hospital somewhere, maybe with amnesia, and one day he'd come back and whisk me away from all this. Somehow it hurt more that they were my own mom and sister, not some evil steps who wanted me out of the way.

It made that pain even worse. I was part of my mom and all she wanted to do was cut that part of herself out and throw the rest of me away. Throw my dad away. But I wanted the books first. I wanted the *Peter Rabbit* books she'd promised me. I needed them to remember those rainy days with my dad, curled up in his favorite window seat while he read them and did all the voices. I could go buy other copies from a store for the stories themselves, but these books were the ones he'd touched and drawn in. That mattered.

Pushing my glasses up, I wiped at my eyes with the back of my hand. So many tears spilled over their words and digs at me.

I longed for those books. Those were happy family memories I couldn't let go.

The door opened and I sat up and stared out the window.

"There you are. I came here first when you disappeared, but you weren't here." Berk closed the door behind him.

"I got a little side tracked."

"Okay, should I check out this costume? I've been dying to see what's inside."

"You don't have to stay if you don't want to," I blurted out.

"You bring me all the way out here and you want me to go." The hint of hurt in his voice pressed the knife in deeper.

What the hell was I doing? Why had I let him come? I wanted to spend time with him, that's why. My pathetic attempt to maybe force some bonding and have one person I knew who would be on my side this weekend.

Tilting my head to the side, I looked at him with what had to be red-ringed eyes. "Do you want to stay?"

"If you want me to. I promise I won't embarrass you— much." He smiled and ducked his head trying to catch my gaze.

"It'll probably be the other way around."

"You've never been to one of our parties. I've been known to bust out The Worm and The Robot on occasion." He swung his garment bag down off his shoulder.

I chuckled. "Doesn't sound too embarrassing."

"I didn't say I was good at them." He crossed the room and threw his bag over the edge of a high-backed chair in the seating area.

If Laura or my mom saw that, they'd have a freaking cow. I stared at my own garment bag hung neatly off the bathroom door and I wanted to run up, grab it, and throw it on the floor. I hadn't looked inside yet. The strength for that would take a few more minutes or hours to gather.

"What's up, Julienne Fries?" The bed dipped as he sat beside me.

"It's been a while since I've been around this group."

"And it feels weird?"

"It's weird hanging out with people I grew up around now that I'm in college. I've... changed." More like gotten used to living my life on my own without the voices in the background constantly reminding me how I'd never stack up. "Is it weird for you, going home?"

In his letters he'd always kept our conversations to the present. The here and now, and never ventured too far into the past. I was okay with that. I didn't want to be the same girl with the even sadder story.

"I don't."

"You don't? As in you don't go home?"

"No, I don't have a home to go back to." He tilted his head and corner of his mouth lifted, but it was a thin ghost of a half-smile.

"No family?"

A flicker of sadness rushed across his face. "I have a sister, but... that's complicated. So, to come here and see a place your grandparents owned, that's pretty cool."

Here I was bitching about my shitty family when Berk barely had any family at all.

He hadn't mentioned it much in our letters. I'd kept things to my sexy thoughts I was too scared to live out in the real world, and things like movies I liked because I didn't exactly feel like delving into my past. It seemed he'd felt the same way. All the time I was worried about him knowing too much, but he hadn't been delving into his past either. As much as our letters had changed over time, we'd both been keeping things from one another. "I didn't know about your family."

"How could you?" He lifted one shoulder. "And I didn't say that to make you feel bad for me or anything." His gaze danced around the room, finding every fresh flower and wallpaper design fascinating and ignoring my own.

"I don't." My small smile caught in the corner of his eye and the tension leaked out of his body second by second.

"Are we doing this thing?" He rubbed his hands together. "Going out there and showing your sister's friends how the FU crew does it?" His tough guy voice made me laugh.

"Yeah, let's do this." I stared at the garment bag like I'd

somehow be able to transform it into a pair of comfy sweat-pants and a long sleeved t-shirt with my mind.

"Did you want to change first?" He lifted his chin toward the open bathroom door.

"Sure, might as well get it over with." The laughter leaked out of my body with each step toward the garment bag. I threw a weak smile to Berk over my shoulder and unhooked it from the door, disappearing inside the bathroom.

Taking a deep breath, I unzipped the bag. A moment of relief that it wasn't a mini skirt was quickly replaced by horror. My eyes bulged at the neckline. Weren't people back in the 20s prudes? What fresh hell was this?

Doing a few 'you've got this' mantras in my head, I took off my glasses and set them down on the counter. I hefted the dress off the hanger. The silky champagne underlay was covered by long strands of shiny material that added about ten pounds to the thing. I slipped the dress on. It was long sleeved, at least, only slightly pinching. It seemed Mom didn't want me to totally embarrass her.

But the front. The neckline plunged way down, showing off the girls like I should be on stage in Vegas. With my arms raised over my head and fingers grazing the top of the back, I spun in circles for at least eight minutes trying to snag the zipper to pull it up. Turning toward the mirror, I stared at my reflection. Finally, using a bit of ingenuity and the shower stall handle, I contorted myself and grabbed the zipper, tugging it up.

Holy hell. My girls, the ones I usually kept well under wraps, were singing to the heavens. So much cleavage. The lacy fringe on the cups of my bra peeked out from the neck-line. I looked like I should've been staked out on a stool at the fanciest hotel in Philly trying to drum up business from unsuspecting businessmen.

Shoving my glasses back onto my face, I stared at myself,

every bit of me, in excruciating detail. The glasses weren't time period appropriate, but Laura would have to deal.

Berk knocked on the door. "Do you need some help?"

"No," I shouted way too loud. They'd probably heard me out by the stables. Collecting my clothes, I clutched them against my chest. My fingers shook as I undid the latch to the bathroom. He was going to laugh at how ridiculous I looked. I could picture it now, Berk rolling on the floor with tears of laughter in his eyes.

The door opened and I stepped back into the room with my clothes cradled in my arms.

I looked up at him and my eyes widened. Had they taken his measurements before we got here? His outfit looked fantastic.

He struggled with the buttons of the white vest. The material of his dress shirt bunched as he pushed at the buttons. The pants hugged his trim hips and stellar ass.

"I can get into my uniform in six minutes flat. These buttons are bullshit."

Pinning my clothes to my chest with my chin, I knocked his hands away and slid them through the navy silk-lined arm holes. "So hard," I teased.

"It's not my fault." He pulled the bottom of his vest down, straightening it.

I spun away, keeping my clothes tight against my chest, aware of how close he'd come to getting an eyeful of me, not that I'd have a choice unless I walked around with my clothes against my chest for the rest of the night.

"I'm going to make us a drink. Top shelf booze doesn't deserve to be all alone at times like these." He cradled the bottles, swaying them back and forth like a doting parent slash total lunatic. Bottles and glasses clinked together.

I crouched to pick up one of my dropped socks. Gathering everything, I turned to dump it onto the bed. Maybe things would be okay. He wasn't freaking out and I wasn't freaking out, so far so good. I could wear this outside of the room.

"Might as well start now." I turned to him and our gazes collided.

He coughed into the glass he had up to his mouth. Wheezing and spraying his drink all over the place, his eyes got anime character wide before he barked out a, "Holy shit."

CHAPTER 11
BERK

Holy shit! The soda water burned my lungs and I coughed, bent over at the waist. There was no saving this and playing it off cool. Water dribbled down onto my pristine white and insanely expensive shirt. At least I hadn't opened one of the bottles of wine sitting on the mini-bar.

Jules stared at me, frozen in her crouch with some of her clothes bunched up in her hands like a deer in the middle of the road with a Mack truck barreling toward her.

I liked Jules. I'd always liked Jules. She's funny and sometimes she lets a little bit of her potty mouth slip out between her unique personality of the next Martha Stewart and a cute anime character. She's not flashy, except when it comes to everything that comes out of her oven.

I'd looked at her so many times and liked exactly what I saw. But I didn't let my thoughts stray to her in any way other than as a friend too often, mainly because she's Elle's best friend and if I went near her with anything other than my friendzone lanyard hanging around my neck, Nix would've mailed my balls back to me and made me pay for the shipping.

She was wiped off the radar before I met her with a glare from Nix and a promise of retribution if I screwed up what he had with Elle in any way, shape, or form, but that's not to say I didn't appreciate Jules' quiet beauty. The kind you found yourself sneaking a glance of when she smiled because it was so completely pure and unworried about being anything other than real.

Or the times I'd sit at her kitchen table and talk for hours about our favorite comic book movie. I'd chalked it up to the fact that I hadn't spent much time around many women who didn't want anything from me. Not status, or a false idea that I had cash to splash around, or any number of reasons. With Jules, I could just be and so could she. It gave me that warm feeling that drew me to her time and time again, but I knew going in it couldn't go further.

I'd never really been just friends with a girl before, and I liked it.

She was kind and I'd never heard her talk shit about anyone or be anything other than awesome, which is why the fucking rack on her showcased with a plummeting, glittering 'look at me sign' that was that dress made me want to bite my knuckle and run around the room like a damn animal.

Who in the hell knew she was hiding all that under those clothes? I was five seconds away from going full wolf-whistle-in-a-nightclub cartoon parody over here. There were those movies where the girl with the glasses gets the makeover and all the sudden everyone looks at her differently. It was like that, except she was still wearing the glasses and was way hotter than any movie star because she was real and two strides away from me.

"Jesus, Jules." I leaned in, trying to keep the need to lick her out of my voice. This was straight up not fair. She was sweet as hell and now I wanted a taste.

Her face paled. "I know," she whispered and tried to tug the edges of her dress's neckline together. She might as well have been trying to fill the Grand Canyon with a bucket. "It's too small. I need to find Laura and tell her it's not going to work." Ducking her head, she tried to run away. "It looks terrible."

I rushed after her and caught her elbow. My fingers wrapping around the soft fabric protecting her smooth skin from my touch, an electric spark licking its way up my arm.

"You don't need to change." I squeezed my lips together, so I didn't bite my bottom one. "You caught me off guard. The dress looks great on you. I just never realized you were hiding those." I nodded toward the cleavage Valhalla peeking out from under her hands.

She punched my arm. "You're not exactly helping on the keep-Jules-from-feeling-self-conscious-and-wanting-to-run-away front."

"If there's anyone who should feel self-conscious, it's all those other chicks who've got absolutely nothing on you in the breast department. KFC is going to burst in here and haul you away."

She snort-laughed and shook her head in disapproval, but her eyes were no longer deer-in-headlights scared. "I just... I can't wear this in public. Maybe at the venue for a bit, but..."

"If you're still feeling weird about it, I've got something you can put on." I crouched down and rummaged through my bag. It was never too far from me and always ready to go at a moment's notice. Old habits, die hard, right? I pushed a few things aside and spotted the light grey material. Tugging it out, I stood and handed it over to Jules.

"You carry a sweater in your bag?" Half statement, half question.

"You never know when you might need one."

She took it from my hands with a grateful nod and slipped it on. A little warmth glowed in my chest. I liked having that for her and I sure as hell liked seeing her in it, even though she was hiding the best rack in three counties under it right now. I'd have to commit it to memory.

"You're saving me from wearing a bathrobe over this getup." Her smile flicked a different switch inside me. One that sent the blood rushing to another part of my anatomy it had no business rushing to as I imagined her in nothing but a robe. The fluffy fabric against her skin. A switch had been flicked and I didn't know how to unflick it.

Then came the guilt. I hadn't really checked anyone out since TLG and I started writing. Once the letters kept coming and I let her in on some of the fears and insecurities I was dealing with when it came to going pro, it had kind of felt like cheating, just like it did when I couldn't keep my eyes off Jules.

What was I thinking? TLG didn't want to talk to me anymore. She was done with me, whatever it was I'd thought we were building was an illusion. After all this time, I should be better prepared for people dipping out of my life like it's nothing.

Mom. Gone. Dad. Locked up for a long time. Foster families who'd pushed me aside. At this point there was only one person in my life who'd always been there and she was flaky at best. No, I didn't need to add anyone new to the Berk Sucks, Let's Stay Far, Far Away Club. But that didn't mean I couldn't admire the view.

———

JULES LED ME THROUGH SOME OF THE DANCES AND I TRIED MY best not to crush her feet.

"You're getting better." She winced as I caught the tip of her toes.

"I'll get you a drink to numb the pain." Leaving Jules, I walked to the bar, passing by guys who eyed me when they saw their girlfriends' and wives' heads turn. It's not my fault

I'm half a head bigger and fifty pounds heavier than most guys here.

"Welcome to Kelland Estate. We're all so happy to have you here for the wonderful occasion of Laura and Chet's engagement." A blonde woman who didn't look much older than most of the attendees stood in front of the band at the old timey microphone. Her warm smile left crinkles at the edges of her eyes and that was the only telltale sign that her smooth skin wasn't one hundred percent genetic.

She held out her arms on the stage like she was prepared to hug everyone. I got the drinks for me and Jules, headed back to her, and slipped one flute into her hand.

"Your mom definitely knows how to work a room," I leaned down and whispered out of the side of my mouth into Jules' ear. Everyone hung on her mom's every word with beaming smiles.

"Yes, she does." Jules kept a smile on her face like if her mother saw it drop she might get into trouble.

The women in the room glittered with different colored dresses. The guys were all in tuxes, looking way more comfortable than anyone I'd seen in one. Like they'd been wearing them since they were little and it was just another set of clothes, not five layers of fabric too many.

I hadn't had to read the Great Gatsby back in high school. Kids on my track had been expected to read The Giver and other way-below-reading-level stories. But I'd seen the movie. Even up on screen, it was a whole lot of over-the-top exaggerations and people with egos way too big for the mansions they lived in. That had nothing on Jules' sister's party.

There was a full band decked out in tuxes matching mine. It was a trial run for all the stuff I'd hopefully be doing next year. Reece already talked about the invites he got to events, parties, and charities. Nothing I'd ever experienced dripped with money like this, and Nix's dad was a former NFL player who definitely knew how to party.

"Looking to enter the draft this season?"

I turned to the older man next to me. "Yes, sir. With the season we had last year, there's been a lot of interest."

"I'm sure there has been. And cut the sir stuff. Call me Felix." The older man with graying temples slipped me his business card. "We've had our eye on you for a while, Mr. Vaughn."

I schooled my expression, trying to play it cool. Fans on campus were one thing, even people screaming out my name on the streets around the stadium, but this was the first time I'd been spotted out in the wild like this. To have a guy like him come up to me and talk to me like an equal. Like I was doing him a favor for even talking sports for a few minutes.

He chuckled. "I can spot a football player from a hundred yards. Comes with the territory."

I checked out his card. Sports Agent.

"I know how hard things can get for you players with all the NCAA rules, but I happen to know more than one team who's been able to help players just like you out. Maybe you've got an eye on some blow-out spring break or summer vacation before the season starts." He leaned in conspiratorially.

Putting my team's season on the line for a party wasn't anything I'd go anywhere near. "I'm okay for now."

"Well, if you need some help, give me a call and I can make it happen." He patted me on the shoulder and walked away.

A passing waiter rammed straight into my shoulder. It was a hit like I was back on the field. My drink flew out of my hand, showering Jules as she approached.

"Sonofabitch." I whirled around to grab the guy, but he was already gone, disappearing into the doorway all the servers flowed in and out of. That hit felt all too familiar, but I had bigger things to worry about. Like the frozen, semi-drenched Jules staring at me with wide eyes.

I grabbed a few handfuls of napkins and proceeded to dry her off. A trail of champagne dripped down the valley of her breasts. One of the party planners had pried the sweater from her grip when we'd walked into the room (for not being time-line appropriate) and I'd never been happier for bizarre, rich people party rules in my life.

She smacked at my hands. "Would you quit it!" she hissed and turned her back to the room, taking the napkins from me and running them over her dress.

"Sorry."

"Not your fault. I saw that guy bang into you like he was headed for the end zone."

"Right?"

"He's lucky my mom didn't see that. She'd have freaked. They had to bring in a whole catering crew from Philly just for this."

"As if the party couldn't have gotten any swankier."

"Har har har."

Another server passed by holding a tray with tiny puffed pastries on it. I could down the entire thing in five seconds doing a two hander.

"I don't think everyone else has stopped drinking since we got here," I leaned in and whispered into Jules' ear, not letting my gaze drift down the soft and ample slope of her breasts and into the forbidden valley that glittered with sequins like a freaking Times Square Billboard. Definitely not doing that at all.

"There are some people who're permanently like that. Hidden flasks, rehab stints, the eventual relapse everyone pretends not to notice, or swears them having a few drinks is no big deal."

"No wonder you invited me."

"It was a tough choice after you volunteered yourself. I thought about backing out and canceling on you, but then I'd be here on my own."

I did another sweep of the crowd. "I can see why it was a tough choice." I stared into her eyes. "And I'm glad you didn't try to cancel on me. I'm glad I could be here with you."

"Julia, are you going to introduce me to your guest?"

It was like a cold front had blown in over the party. Jules stared back at her mom like a boxer headed into the ring. Jules' body went rigid, but she was light on her heels and almost imperceptibly swaying like she was ready for a punch.

Her mom's dress probably cost more than a season ticket to the Trojans' Sky Box. Her gaze bounced between me and Jules with the same smile she'd worn before, the lines at the edge of her eyes crinkling even more.

She held her hand out and her gaze raked up and down my body. "And you must be Berkley. Laura was telling me all about you."

Pretty hard to do when Laura had molested me with her eyes for all of twenty seconds and barely spoken to me during the process. Maybe she'd just been sizing me up trying to figure out if I was an okay dude to be dating her sister, even if it was all pretend.

"It's nice to meet you." I wiped my hand on my pants, not wanting to shove my sweaty palm into her delicate hand. Damn, I felt like I was going to snap every bone in her fingers. I was also slightly concerned about Jules' statue impersonation.

"Evelyn," she offered her name. "Laura wasn't exaggerating when she said you were handsome." Her mom propped one of her hands under her chin. "And how long have you two been together?"

Jules opened her mouth to set her mom straight, but I butted in.

"It's new." I slipped my arm around Jules' shoulder. "But if she keeps baking for me the way she has been, I'll never let her go." I looked at Jules with a distinct roll-with-this-look.

She patted her hand on mine. "Yes, very new."

"Of course you'd know your way into a man's stomach." Her mom's wavy blonde hair bounced as she laughed.

Jules shrank under my hold.

"She's a fantastic baker. One of the best bakeries in the city is bringing her on for a special project."

"Julia has always loved the kitchen. And food. Good thing he looks strong." Her mom spoke to Jules while patting me on the chest.

Jules sucked in a sharp breath.

"She keeps me well fed."

"I'm sure she does. I'm glad she's making enough for you both. Have a lovely time this weekend."

That was one of the weirdest conversations I'd had in a long time, but rich people do what rich people do. It was like she was speaking in code and I didn't have the translation key.

Someone interrupted, pulling her away, and she went on hugging and kissing other attendees.

Jules spun around out from under my arm and rushed out to the patio, disappearing into the inky night beyond the doors.

CHAPTER 12
JULES

Skirting around the people dancing in perfect waltzes, I shoved open the French doors. The gauze curtains billowed out over the stone patio. Outside, the tightness in my chest squeezed so much it was hard to catch my breath.

I braced my hands on the stone railing and stared upwards. Clouds blotted out the night sky. At least the stars weren't here to witness to my humiliation, although everyone else had been, including Berk.

Humidity licked at my skin, making the dress even more uncomfortable, clinging and scratching every inch of me it covered. Dots of water splattered against my arms. At least if it poured I could blame that for why my face was wet. I wiped at my eyes, so sick of letting my family do this to me. The heavy footfalls that could only be Berk's followed after me. No one else had probably even noticed I was gone.

"Jules."

I wiped at my eyes. Not a-freaking-gain. This weekend wasn't going to be the Comforting Jules Weekend Extravaganza. I scurried down the steps leading to the garden.

"Jules."

I kept my head down and kept walking. My heels slid and wobbled on the gravel path.

"If you're trying to hide, the glittering, sparkly dress isn't exactly stealthy. I think that's why the military went with camo over sequins."

Stopping, I sighed and waited.

His crunchy footsteps closed in. His suit jacket brushed against my arm. "At least let me come with you on your walk. Show me around. Maybe one of your old favorite spots."

There were no questions, only comfort. The comfort of his presence and the peace of mind that, for now, he wasn't going to ask me to say anything more than what I was able. "Sure."

I kicked off my shoes, abandoning the pinch of the heels when we made it to the grass. "There's one place I haven't been in a while. I hope it's not locked for the night."

"If it is, don't worry. I'll handle it." Even in the darkness, I could hear the smile in his voice.

"Practiced at forcible entry, are we?"

"Only when I need to be."

Out in the dark with only the stars lighting the way, I felt safe with him at my side. The way you got when you felt like someone could haul you into their arms and run away with you. I didn't get that feeling around many guys, but with Berk, I thought maybe, just maybe.

Then I pushed those thoughts aside. *He's being a friend. Just like he's been a friend for nearly a year now.* Stopping into the house to make sure I'm okay and steal treats. But there's never been more than a hint of interest—other than the way his gaze kept dipping to my chest, but that was probably his overprotective streak—I'd seen it come out more than once. Not that I minded, but I needed to keep things straight in my head.

Don't slip up and don't get any ideas about what this might be.

"I've never seen stars like this before." Berk stopped beside me and stared straight up.

"Less light pollution out here."

"Sometimes I forget to look up."

"You don't see them much in the city. Even on the best days only the brightest stars can shine, but out here even the little pipsqueaks get a chance. We can stay out here, if you want." I flicked my thumb nails together and kept my head down. It was like my chin had a magnet attached straight to my chest. "I'm sorry you had to see that." I couldn't breathe. Her words still rang in my ear, erasing so much of the progress I'd made. I wrapped my arms tightly around my waist, wanting to sink into the floor.

"What happened? One second you were there and the next you were gone."

And now he thought I was crazy.

"It's nothing." Was I overreacting? He'd been less than a foot from me and he couldn't see anything wrong with what she'd said.

"You're upset. Like before. Tell me what happened." The earnest concern in his eyes made me feel even worse. We'd been having a great time and then I went and lost it again because of my mom. You'd think after so many years I'd have a healthy callous built up to her words, but every time she spoke to me it was like someone poking at a throbbing wound only barely starting its healing journey.

I held his gaze.

His eyebrows were furrowed, and he looked ready to take on whatever had upset me. If I hadn't already been falling for him, I was a half-step away. No one had ever looked at me like that before.

"It's nothing you can help with."

"Maybe I can."

His thumb made tiny brushes against the side of my face and I tried to breathe. *Keep breathing, Jules.*

He leaned in closer and the hairs on the back of my neck stood up. His bow tie and tux fit him like they'd gotten his measurements ahead of time. That was what happened when you worked out so much tailors made their clothes to fit someone like you. Someone with a perfect body.

The tendrils of desire fought against the drum of fear trying to overtake my stomach. He was here with me. Not that he had much of a choice since he was pretty much stranded out here, and if it came down to hanging with me outside versus staying inside with my family and their friends, I got it.

But his face did seem to be getting closer to mine… or was I the one leaning in? Were we both leaning in?

"Jules…" He lifted his hand and placed it right at the side of my neck. The rough pads of his fingers caressed the hairs at the nape.

"Yeah, Berk." I wanted to shoot up on my tippy toes and finally know what his lips felt like on mine. The same ones I'd dreamed about and he'd written about using to taste every inch of me.

He ducked his head, totally Berk incoming in three.

Two.

One.

A ground shaking thunder *crack* made us both jump, and it was as if someone had dumped a football celebration-sized cooler over our heads. Water came down so hard and fast it stung my skin. Tiny pelting drops alternated with fat ones that had me soaked in seconds.

Mascara ran into my eyes and I was blinded. Berk's strong hand gripped mine and he pulled me along. With his other arm, he used his suit jacket as a shield. Where were we going? I had no idea because I couldn't see anything. A mix of gritty sand and pebbles dug into my bare feet and I hobbled after Berk trying to shield my eyes.

He pushed open a door and we rushed inside the darkened space. Standing there, panting, we both looked out at the torrential downpour that blotted out everything else beyond the door and hammered against the windows like it was trying to get inside.

"It's a greenhouse." He looked around the space.

The mixture of earthy and floral scents filled the glass structure.

"I got in so much trouble one summer for deciding I wanted to make flower crowns for everyone. And of course I knew the greenhouse had the best flowers, not the ones out in the fields nearby."

"Big trouble?"

"The biggest." I ran my fingers across the brightly colored petals of the flowers. "They made me replant a new pot for every one I'd decimated. It took me an entire day."

"Not the worst punishment in the world."

I laughed. "No, it wasn't."

"Why'd they care so much?"

"They use the flowers for a lot of the events they have. Cheaper than calling in a florist each time, but sometimes, specialty flowers are needed."

"Like for tonight?"

"Oh yeah. I wouldn't be surprised if she'd had them flown in from New York or Fiji or something. If there's ever a chance to one-up someone, my mom will grab onto that chance with both hands and never let go."

"Must have been hard growing up like that."

Here I was complaining about my sister and Berk's situation was way more complicated. I shrugged. "It wasn't that bad." The hours I'd stayed locked alone in my bathroom crying on the floor were trivial in comparison to what other people had been through.

"Don't do that."

"Do what?"

"Minimize what you went through because of what I told

you about me."

My cheeks burned. "I'm not—"

He tilted his head and lifted an eyebrow.

I pinched my lips together. "Are you inside my head or something?"

"No, but I see the way you always want to take care of the people around you, even if it's at your expense."

"I don—"

He cut me off again at the pass. "Don't ever let anyone else make you feel like you're not awesome." He swung his jacket and settled it around me. The weight of the damp fabric settled around my shoulders. I tugged the front of it closed. Even for me it was roomy and dwarfed me. It wasn't like I didn't know Berk was a huge guy. He handled other football players out on the field with no problem, but standing beside him in his jacket, staring up into his eyes lit only by the streaking lightning across the sky, I felt small.

The buttons from his wet shirt brushed against my fingers holding the jacket closed. I curled my toes against the warm tile floor.

Rain hammered on the glass panes all around us like our own soundtrack to go along with my heartbeat, racing not only from the sprint but from the proximity to him.

"Thank you for inviting me." His words were a low rumble accompanied by the thunder.

My throat tightened and I licked my lips. It was like we were under the laziest strobe light known to man. But with each second of full light his lips seemed to be getting closer.

I'd been working on that. Accepting a thank you without the need to minimize whatever it was. Just say 'you're welcome', Jules. "You're welcome."

"I'm kicking myself for giving you my jacket now." His gaze darted down the dark gap between my body and his jacket. "In case I didn't tell you already. That dress looks killer on you."

"Thank you." Our lips were a hairsbreadth away. My body tingled in anticipation of everything he was ready to serve up.

All those nights I read and reread his words. The way my fingers tingled when I slipped another note into his mailbox and grabbed one of his. But this wasn't pen and paper anymore. This was everything we'd written about in our letters. All the promises he made and the months of fantasy-making. I'd figured that was where they'd always live, but miracle of miracles, he was here with me now—leaning in closer for a kiss. He was here with me. He wanted me.

He smiled with a glitter in his eyes and then they closed. With one swift motion the distance between our lips evaporated.

There was the slightest brush of his against mine. Needing more, I rocked onto my tiptoes.

The entire room exploded in bright, brilliant light. A lightning strike shook the windows and thunderclap roared so loudly my ears rang. We shot apart. He stared back at me with wide eyes and a face painted with shock.

We turned and looked outside at the smoking, charred remains of a stone bench on the other side of the glass, only illuminated by the intense lightning streaking across the sky, throwing the landscape around us from night to day in split second chunks.

With wide eyes, we both looked up at the glass and metal structure currently protecting us, and I don't think either of us wanted to test whether the floor would insulate us from a direct hit or the adage about lightning never striking twice.

Bolting toward the main house, we ran all the way back to the room. Our room. As in the room I'd be sharing with him for the next two nights. Sleeping feet away from him with that almost-kiss lingering and leaving me rattled like a ghost with his chains.

"I'm going to change." Not waiting for his reply, I grabbed

my bag, which had thankfully been set on the luggage rack outside the closet door, and ducked into the bathroom. Inside, I shimmied out of my dress. It sank to the floor with a drenched, tinkling thud. My face was a mess of washed away mascara and hints of long gone eyeshadow. Good thing he hadn't seen me in full light, or he'd have probably run right over those lightning struck hills.

I scrubbed my face and slipped on my comfy pajamas. They were slouchy and worn in, just how I liked them. I threw my hair up into a ponytail and brushed my teeth. I even flossed. Yes, I was hiding. Trying to keep my dignity for a few more minutes.

Taking a deep breath, I opened the bathroom door. My stomach was an absolute mess like I'd been doing keg stands since dawn. My one and only keg stand had ended with beer soaked hair and me praying to the porcelain gods to smite me for my transgression.

The room was so quiet, I thought maybe he'd left. My gaze swept over the room. But his large form was folded into one of the wingback chairs in the corner. His head rested against the top of the smooth leather back.

Walking over, I nudged his shoulder. "Berk, the bathroom's free."

He mumbled.

I reached out and shook both shoulders. "You're going to hate me in the morning, if I let you sleep like this." I brought my hands up to his neck and rotated them.

His head shot up and his arms whipped out around me, tugging me onto his lap. His fingers tightened painfully on my hips and I braced my hands on his chest.

I yelped and his gaze focused on me.

The alarm in his eyes melted away as he took in our surroundings and embarrassment took its place, turning his cheeks ruddy under his five o'clock shadow. His grip loosened immediately.

I had no idea what the hell had just happened, but he'd looked so scared for a second, like someone shaking him awake was a nightmare come to life.

"Sorry, Jules. I forgot where I was." He shook his head and released me completely, which still left me on his lap.

"You passed out while I was in the bathroom."

He yawned into his shoulder. "Someone was taking an incredibly long time to just duck in and change."

"Sorry."

He smiled. "No need to be sorry. Thanks for waking me up."

My cheeks burned and I was lucky the only light in the room was the one behind me from the bathroom. "No problem." And then it sunk in that I was still sitting on his lap. All of me, without any bracing or keeping my feet on the ground and I shot up.

He headed into the bathroom and I sank under the covers. The day that felt like it had dragged on for months was finally ending. And my blood thrummed in my veins.

Berk opened the bathroom door and the light from inside cast him in shadow. Outlining every ripple and bulge of his muscles framed in the doorway.

"There are some extra blankets in the closet."

"You don't have to sleep on the couch. It's a big bed. After the day you've had, I can take the couch if you don't want to share. You came right from practice." I pushed the covers down and swung my legs off the edge.

"Don't. That would make me feel like shit if you did. You sure you're okay with sharing a bed with me?" There was an uneasiness to his stance. Like the confident goofball had given way to someone less self-assured. Someone like me.

"I'm good." I got back under the blankets and locked my arms in at my sides.

He went around the bed and sat on the edge. "About the greenhouse…"

I jumped in front of whatever he was going to say, throwing myself in front of the Mack truck of him letting me down gently. "Don't worry about that. I don't want you to feel awkward or anything. You were trying to make me feel better. We were caught up in the moment, no big deal." It came out in a rush, all in one breath.

I turned my head to the side.

He swung his legs up onto the bed and settled on his back, staring straight up at the ceiling.

And now I'd officially decided that inviting Berk wasn't a bad idea at all. It was the *worst* idea.

Because I couldn't stop thinking about that almost-kiss. We'd almost kissed. The way his strong hands had cupped my face so gently as he was a hairsbreadth away from my lips. It was like the lead up to one of the kisses he'd promised me. Like one that had been scrawled across every single one of his letters. The kind that made me touch myself under the covers until I moaned his name just like he promised me I would.

Damn you, lightning!

He was the perfect gentleman, taking me for walks and sharing his contraband ear buds with me that night as we lay side by side in the bed. Then, once the song he'd wanted to share with me was finished, he'd rolled onto the floor, even though I'd told him the bed was big enough for the two of us. Maybe the almost-kiss had only been to lift my spirits. Snap me out of my teary state he'd already seen once today.

With lips like those, I was sure he'd found they were the perfect distraction to nearly any woman. A small streak of jealousy shot through me at all the women he'd probably kissed because he wanted to, not because he'd felt like it was the nice thing to do. My fingers itched to write him a new note, but I couldn't. I'd closed the door on The Letter Girl. But those letters were the closest I was going to get to having him. Berkley Vaughn wasn't interested.

CHAPTER 13
BERK

'd rolled off the bed onto the floor, taking a pillow with me. I grunted as my not-so-friendly erection jammed into the floor. I certainly wasn't sporting boners around LJ, Keyton, or Marisa. But listening to Ed Sheeran with Jules, memorizing every freckle on her face and the way her full lips mouthed the words to the chorus by the end of it had my dick throbbing.

As she peered down at me over the edge of the bed, a curtain of her hair swung down. She tucked it behind her ears. "Crap, are you okay?"

"Yup, I'm fine." I grimaced, clutching the pillow to my slowly, but not slowly enough deflating cock. "The bed's too soft, so I think I'll hang out down here for the night."

Jules' eyes widened and she let the hair fall back over her face. "Oh." She snapped back from the edge of the bed and I flatted onto the floor in relief.

"Are you sure? I can take the floor. I don't mind."

She was too much of a temptation. And I wanted to taste her lips so badly I'd almost rolled on top of her and taken that kiss Mother Nature had stolen from us by trying to murder us in the greenhouse.

"At least take a couple more pillows and the blanket." She shoved a wall of white, insanely high thread count linens onto me.

Her eyes reminded me of the milk chocolate chip cookies she'd made a couple months ago. They had wafers of chocolate in them instead of regular chocolate chips. And they were soft and delicious and I knew she'd taste the exact same way. So I'd banished myself to the floor before I lost my cool and did something I couldn't take back. Namely, wrap her bed head curls around my fist, hold her chin between my thumb and forefinger, and see if those lips were everything I'd been thinking about for the past few days.

The night on the floor wasn't all that bad. I'd slept in far worse places and the pillows and blankets made it easy to sleep through until morning, which didn't happen often. I still couldn't believe I'd fallen asleep in that chair the night before, but I could believe I'd woken up like someone was going to rob me. The look of fear on Jules' face had soured my gut and I'd immediately let her go. A hazard I'd come to expect. If I fell asleep somewhere quiet, I was almost always on edge when someone woke me up.

But even on the floor in this new room, I wasn't on edge anymore. Jules was here. The bathroom door creaked open slowly and her not so quiet rustling let me know she was trying to make sure she didn't wake me up.

I cracked open an eye. She was crouched down by the edge of the bed, tying her shoes.

"Where you going?"

She jumped and fell back onto her ass, clutching her chest.

"You scared the shit out of me." Her whisper-yell made me smile.

"Where are you going?"

Her lips pinched, and she pushed herself off the floor and finished tying her shoes. The mumbled words barely made it out of her mouth.

"Where?" I cupped my hand around my ear.

She let out an exasperated sigh. "For a run. I'm going to go for a run, okay." There was a challenge in her eyes like she'd told me she was going to go up onto the roof to flap her wings.

"Cool, give me three minutes and I'll come with you."

Her deer-in-headlights look was back. "No, you don't have to do that. You don't have to come with me."

I pushed up from the floor and grabbed some sweats and a t-shirt out of my backpack. "Of course I don't have to, but I want to. The season's right around the corner and with the workout from yesterday, I'll be stiff if I don't get my ass up and do some physical activity." I closed the bathroom door behind me, not one hundred percent sure she'd be there when I opened the door.

Brushing my teeth to banish the gremlins that had had a party in my mouth last night, I went out at least smelling like I hadn't been eating bulbs of garlic.

"You really don't need to join me."

I held up my hand. "Julienne Fries, when will you learn? I don't do anything I don't want to, especially not going for a run at—" I picked up my phone and my eyes bulged at the time. "It's not even seven am."

"See!" She took my moan as confirmation that I hadn't actually wanted to go.

"Doesn't matter, we're going." I grabbed her elbow and ushered her out of the room.

There were people bustling around, setting up for what-ever festivities were planned for the day. I didn't give a crap as long as I wouldn't have to wear that tux again. I didn't think rain water and expensive clothes went together.

"There's a gravel path leading down toward the stables. And a loop back up to the house."

"Sounds good to me." I looked over at Jules; she was in a long sleeve t-shirt and sweatpants.

"Aren't you hot as balls in that?"

She shrugged. "No."

"Lead the way." I pushed open the front door and held out my arm. The early morning haziness wasn't at its full last-vestiges-of-summer peak. The downpour from yesterday had taken most of the humidity out of the air.

She walked through the doorway, banging her shoulder on the doorjamb opposite me, like she was trying to stay as far away as possible, but stopped halfway out. "You really don't—"

"Zip it, Julienne Fries. I'm running with you, even if I have to toss you over my shoulders and do the run that way. So let's run this thing." I lifted my hand and froze inches from her ass.

No, don't go anywhere near that. I'd only seen it silhouetted in clothes, but I knew with one touch I wouldn't be able to stop myself from dragging her off somewhere and claiming that kiss that had been stolen from us last night.

Her glare was adorable as she stepped outside. "Fine."

We set out on our run—more of a jog, but I wasn't complaining. I hated running. My number one punishment after a fuck up during practice was laps. My job was to keep my QB from getting demolished. Not sprinting down the field for fifty-yard passes. My position lived in a twenty-yard zone of comfort, and running sucked. But if I got to spend a little time with a certain baker, I'd suck it up and do some of the conditioning work I'd been avoiding.

Jules pointed out more places she loved about this place and had hung out growing up. But then the pace picked up and I kept up with her pace. Our talking got bumped down from a few words every so often to nothing but a steady exhale and the crunch of our feet on the ground.

After we made it to another small rolling hill with Jules' gaze fixed on the horizon, I was ready to crawl back to the house. My legs were on fire, screaming for me to stop. How long had we been running? Thirty minutes? An hour?

Jules was charging along like a cross-country runner just hitting her stride.

"Mercy. I'm calling it." I braced my hands on my knees, stopping in the center of the path. "You're worse than Coach."

She skidded to a stop a few paces in front of me. "Oh thank god." She flung herself on the grassy slope beside us. "I was trying to keep up with you." Her arms were draped over her face, smooshing her fogged up glasses.

"I'm about twenty seconds from my heart bursting out of my chest. Jesus, I felt like you could've gone on forever."

She glanced at me, glistening with strands of hair and bits of grass stuck to her face, and laughed. It was a delirious kind of laugh that infected the air around her. And I was right beside her in the soggy hillside, trying to catch my breath. The rise and fall of her chest made me think of other ways we could be exerting ourselves. Much more enjoyable ways than our torture run, and I was sure I could get her extra sweaty.

"I was already leading us back to the house. They'll be starting the festivities of the day soon. We'll have to get ready."

I groaned. "Only if you protect me and promise not to abandon me this time."

She wrapped her arms around her legs. "I promise."

Those words reached deep down inside, like my joking had revealed something about myself that only she could see. And her promise to do something that other people would laugh off was as strong as any.

We walked back to the house, both a little soggy, muddy, and sweaty, but with something new between us that even the almost-kiss hadn't created.

I snagged a muffin from the breakfast food they were bringing out and chugged a gallon of water.

"Where's the real food?" I had my emergency stash in my backpack like always, but I was sure I could sweet talk someone into bringing me some scrambled eggs with cheese and bacon.

Jules grabbed a plate and filled it with pineapple, kiwi, and a croissant. "They'll do a sit-down breakfast at nine. Don't worry. They have your cheesy scrambled eggs and bacon."

I stopped midway through a bite of my blueberry muffin with real blueberries. "How'd you know that's what I wanted?"

She shoved half a cornucopia of food into her mouth and covered it with her hand, shrugging her shoulders. "Seemed like something a hungry football player would eat."

"Julia."

Jules once again went stock-straight.

Her mom walked across the room with a big smile and an outfit that I'd be afraid would stain if I breathed on it.

"Getting in a little early morning exercise?" Her mom looked from me to Jules.

"Jules was up early and I decided to tag along."

"That's so wonderful that you joined her, Berkley. I hope she didn't slow you down too much."

Jules had her head down, staring at her cantaloupe like she could levitate it into her mouth.

"Nah, she was kicking my butt out there."

Ms. Kelland let out a trilling laugh like I'd said something hilarious. "Such a gentleman."

"Not sure how admitting Jules nearly left me in the dust back there was gentlemanly, but I'll take it."

She tilted her head and patted me on the shoulder. "You two should go get cleaned up before breakfast. Julia, a moment."

"Go ahead, Berk. I'll meet you in the room." Jules sounded like she was getting her last rites.

"I'll hurry up and shower, so you can have the whole bathroom to yourself."

"So kind of you." Her mom beamed. She wasn't the warm and fuzzy type of mom. The pale pink pants and off white top screamed 'children go wash your hands before you touch anything,' but she damn well knew how to throw a party. And she hadn't taken one look at me with Jules and called security to boot me out.

It didn't make sense why Jules hadn't wanted to come this weekend. Her sister's friends were asshole-ish. Her sister and mom were... interesting, but nothing I couldn't handle. Maybe Jules was one of those people who didn't know how lucky they were to have a parent around. But Jules had never been a diva or ever talked badly about anyone, not even her asshole landlord who'd nearly turned her house into a deathtrap.

If I was missing something, I couldn't see it.

CHAPTER 14
JULES

We made it out the other side of the weekend unscathed. Well, Berk did. Every time my mom 'needed a word' I braced myself to feel a few inches smaller.

"Your sister wanted you as a bridesmaid, but we may have to take you out of the pictures if you don't lose some weight before then."

"You're lucky he's even here with you. Why would you try to outrun him? Don't you know men like to feel powerful. Not have a woman try to show them up."

"Please go take a shower before everyone assumes you're sweating because of the heat."

"Where did you get those clothes, Julia? It's a wonder he saw anything in you at all."

I'd been seconds from screaming the truth right in her face, but that would've been worse. That I'd lied about being with Berk—oh, sorry, Berkley—would only be another example of how I suck and no one like him would ever want to be with someone like me. At least once we left, I'd have no trouble floating the lie that he'd broken up with me.

I zipped up my bag in our room, but Berk wouldn't let me

haul it out to the bus. He grabbed it, picking it up like it was nothing.

The ride back to the city would be quieter than the one up. Early mornings were not the thing for this set, so out of the three shuttles they'd run from Kelland Estate, I made sure Berk and I were on the first.

I took the inside seat this time, needing Berk's buffer between me and anyone else who'd decided on an early morning departure. As we pulled down the gravel driveway the shuttle's leather seats weren't even halfway full, but Berk didn't move rows.

The storm clouds were back, rain drumming on the window I rested my head on. The hoodie Berk had let me borrow smelled like him and swam on me, which made it perfect for sinking into.

"What do you have planned before classes start?"

"Stress baking as I try to get everything ready."

"Let me get in on some of that." He unravelled his head-phones from around his phone and stuck a twizzler into his mouth. He had a Mary Poppins-sized portion stashed somewhere.

I shoved at his shoulder and he barely moved; it was like jamming my hand into a brick wall. "You're not supposed to bask in my stress."

"How can I not when your delicious treats are what I get because of it? I'm tempted to stand outside your bedroom banging pots and pans to keep you bleary-eyed and baking."

"Then I'll sick Elle on you and you know Nix'll back her up."

"Playing hardball, I see. He invited us all over to watch Reece's game this week. I think he's just happy he's not doing two-a-day practices and about to head out on the road for the season. Can't believe he passed on the paycheck, though."

"Some things are more important than money."

"Says the person who always had it." He looked at me

with a small grin. The butterflies in my stomach were like a herd. A flock? Whatever the hell a group of butterflies was called, and that was bad, bad news. Berk was so many things, but my new boyfriend wasn't at the top of that list. He had my new heartbreak written all over him, and I'd been there already. Standing inside my front door as he ordered a cake for Alexis. I still didn't know the deal with her and I wasn't going to put my heart on the line to find out.

"Touché."

He held out an earbud to me. "Have you heard the latest James Arthur album?"

"You've got a killer ear. Lay it on me."

"I like listening to new stuff, so I'm always rediscovering things I've forgotten about." He held out the bud to me.

My fingers itched to grab it and let my skin brush against his, accidentally-on-purpose, but this was the time to put that friend barrier firmly back in place. *He's not thinking about you like that. Don't mistake his kindness, or even a semi-drunk almost-kiss, for anything more than it is.*

"I'm not feeling too hot. I'm going to sleep." I stared down at the floor between our feet.

"Was it the eggs? I don't know how you eat them so runny."

"No, it's probably just nerves. I'll sleep it off."

Concern wrinkled his brow and he ran his hand quickly over my thigh.

It was like a Pavlovian response. I'd need to change my underwear as soon as we got back to the house.

"Don't worry about me. Sleep, Frenchie." He pulled the hood up higher on my head.

A weak smile was all I could muster before I leaned back against my seat, wedging my head against the window. All the touches and quiet moments almost made it feel like we were a couple, but I'd learned never to read too far into things.

Guys don't see me that way. The one time I thought a guy did, I'd wound up wanting to bury myself under my high school until graduation. As a member of the stage crew, I was allowed to go on the theater club's weekend visit to a Broadway show back in high school.

Dexter, the cutest guy in drama club, had ended up sitting next to me. We roamed NYC together before the show and grabbed food together. I was so giddy, I was seconds away from floating off like one of the Thanksgiving Day parade balloons. And when he said he needed to talk and told me all about the girl he really liked but was afraid to talk to, I was probably beaming like a spotlight as I inched closer to him.

Maybe he saw the crazy look in my eye or the way my smile changed, but his smile dropped, plummeted straight off his face. "Oh, you don't think I'm talking about you, do you? I meant your sister."

After the way I'd held it together in front of him, I'd deserved to be the lead in the school play. "Of course, who else would you be talking about?" Not a strain in my voice, not a quaver, although inside, I was crawling into a pit of despair.

Nope, not making the mistake of confusing flirting and niceness with him wanting something more from me again. We'd roll back onto campus and things would be back as they should be. No more laying in bed beside Berk. And no more almost-kisses. No more pretending.

————

WE GOT OFF THE BUS AND BERK AND I SHARED A TAXI BACK TO our street. I fidgeted with the strap of my bag at the bottom of my steps and nudged my glasses up. In another world, this would be the big moment before our kiss, but this wasn't that kind of world.

"That was probably the craziest weekend I've had in a

while, and I'm totally including the one where the other team was hazing their freshman with cherries and duct tape."

I held up my hand. "I don't even want to know. Thank you for coming. You were a life saver."

It made it worse that my mom would never say the things she said in private in front of Berk. Way worse because she knew it was wrong. She knew that the words that launched from her mouth like poisoned darts were screwed up, but she did it anyway.

"You've been quiet since we got on the bus."

"I'm tired." Plastering that smile on my face had made my cheeks all achy.

"I get that." He took a breath. "We never really talked about it. But about that—"

I cut him off before he could get the words out.

"And I know we were just pretending about the whole dating thing. And the greenhouse. Don't worry about it. It was nothing. I've completely forgotten about it, so…"

Deflect, hide, run. That was how I handled uncomfortable situations. Run for cover if at all possible.

"Let's just go back to how things were before and leave all that back at Kelland."

"We don't—"

And when all else failed, run away.

"Really. It's okay. I'll talk to you later. Bye." I bolted up the steps.

"See you in class."

Shit. Double shit. We were in class together and we were neighbors. Hiding from him wasn't a solid long-term strategy, but that didn't mean it wouldn't work for right now. I rested my head against the door, closed my eyes, and dropped my bag on the floor.

"What's up?"

I yelped and kicked out with my best Karate Kid impersonation with my heart thundering against my ribs. "What the fuck?"

Zoe stood at the bottom of the stairs with a spoon in her mouth and a jar of peanut butter in her hand. She had her hair up in a ponytail, and pajama boxers and a bright pink tank top on.

It made me miss Elle. Times like these, she'd always been there to pick me up after my mom and sister drained me of happiness like emotional vampires.

There wasn't a stretch mark in sight and Zoe's healthy, glowing skin was on full display. Probably a nice bikini tan line from her summer vacation to wherever the hell she pleased.

"Is that my extra chunky peanut butter?"

"Maybe." She looked from me to the jar. "Whoops." Her mild look of contrition didn't stop her from sticking another spoonful in her mouth—straight from the jar. "Sorry. It was the only thing I didn't feel like a dick for eating."

"What are you doing here?" I grabbed the strap of my bag.

"I live here, remember?"

"Do you remember, would be the better question."

"You got me there. Why the sadness? You're about to make me cry."

"No sadness, I'm fine. It's been a long weekend and I need to crash before tomorrow."

She hooked her arm through mine and stopped me from walking upstairs. "Just pretend that I'm..." Elle's name had escaped her. I could practically hear the gears churning and sparks starting as she dredged her memory for our former roommate whom she'd met twice.

"Elle."

"Yes!" She patted me on the arm and tugged me down to sit on the bottom step.

"You're really weird, you know that, right?"

"Mhmm." She hummed through another spoonful of peanut butter.

"And you owe me a jar of peanut butter." If only I could be that assertive with my mom, or hell, even Laura. Every time Mom said something, a reply shot to the front of my mouth, crushing my dreams of the loving family I'd always wanted and hoped I might reclaim a sliver of someday if I did everything exactly how she wanted.

"And you're sad again."

"Family stuff."

"I hear you. Mom? Dad? Siblings?"

"Mom and sister."

"Mean girls." It was a statement, not even a question.

"Kind of." I tilted my head and looked over at her.

"Here's what I know about them. If you stand up to them and show them you're not going to let them walk all over you? They usually back down."

"I don't think it works like that with parents."

"Can't hurt."

A thud from upstairs shook the floor. "Babe, there's only pomegranate-scented body wash," a distinctly male voice called out from upstairs and a guy strolled to the top of the steps with my blue, extra wide towel wrapped around his waist.

I looked from him to her.

"And I owe you some body wash and a new towel." She tapped the spoon against her bottom lip. "We kind of got booted out of Jaxon's place, so we figured we'd crash here. I hope that's okay with you."

"It's not like you don't pay rent." I shrugged and got up from the step.

"You won't even know we're here."

"Babe, there's a stripper pole in this other room! Can we swap?"

"No!" we shouted at the same time.

Dragging my bag into my room, I skirted around the half-naked man standing at the top of the steps. He definitely fit the Zoe-boyfriend-of-the-month-or-possibly-semester mold.

Rippling muscles crafted over hours at the gym making sure he didn't miss leg day, a legacy admission to the college with grades that would make any regular student lose their shit, and a cocky swagger that would go along with his Fortune 500 job weeks after graduation.

He threw me a chin tilt 'sup' before I disappeared into my room.

I unpacked and printed out my syllabi for all my classes, including a wonderfully aggressive one for Buchanan's class. The one I'd be sharing with Berk.

I stared at my closed blinds like I might suddenly gain X-ray vision and be able to look straight into Berk's room. The room that was the reason my blinds had been closed for the past three years. Because I shouldn't be staring into his bedroom dreaming about him. In big bold letters hanging right over my head like a comic book caption, that was how you spelled heartbreak.

CHAPTER 15
BERK

t was nothing. I've completely forgotten about it. Jules' words were ringing in my ears days after I'd stood at the bottom of the steps to her place, seconds away from making that almost-kiss a distant memory wiped away by my growing hunger for her.

But then she'd put me in my place. She was a rich girl who could do whatever the hell she wanted. Just because I was a starting Trojan at Fulton U didn't mean she gave a crap about all that. And while almost everyone over the weekend had been assholes, there were probably guys on her level who weren't like her sister's friends wanting to take Jules out on fancy dates.

Places I wouldn't be allowed without showing them my bank account—well, maybe in a year. Walking backward across the street, I looked at her house. Why did she live in such a craptastic house? With the money her family had, she could've stayed in one of the swanky houses right across the street from campus.

Tomorrow, we had class together. Excitement coursed through my veins. The same kind I got before one of my games. Tomorrow, I wouldn't be the dude who "happened" to be outside at the exact same time she was coming home, or used cookies as an excuse to hang out. Who does that? Me, apparently, I can't help myself.

In a matter of days, Jules had gone from someone I looked forward to seeing every day, to someone I needed to see. I needed to make her laugh and make sure she was okay. And I wanted her to want that of me too.

There was an awkwardness between us now and I hated every second of it. But I was in this for the long haul, until she told me that under no circumstances was she going to even consider dating me.

My first football game was in two days. I needed to focus. I slung my duffle over my shoulder and opened the front door. Halfway up the stairs, I froze mid-step. Flinging my bag down, I rushed back down the steps and out the front door.

Lifting the mailbox flap, I peered inside. The same blue envelope stared back at me. The crater in my chest formed again, but it was nowhere near as deep as it had been before. I looked across the street and back into the box. There was a new, white, official-looking envelope beside it with my name on it.

I didn't even check the return address, just ripped it open. Flipping through the printed pages, I went back inside, scanning each one.

Records inquiry complete.

No known address.

No known addressee.

No forwarding address provided.

Every entry for Elizabeth Vaughn came up as another dead end.

I sat on the edge of my bed and stared at the folded sheets of paper on the floor. There was no way I could track her down on my own. I'd tried. Researching each state's records processes, paying for them. I'd need help, but I didn't have the money to hire someone to get it done.

That little kid who had stared at the retreating figure of his mom couldn't let this lie. The same kid who had stared up at the ceiling every night hoping she'd show up at the door telling everyone it had been a terrible mistake—he rattled around in my head, unable to let it go. Moving on was impossible when that scared seven-year-old version of me needed his mom.

My phone sat on the bed beside me. The present my mom had carefully wrapped and tucked into my backpack when she'd left me on the screened-in porch of my dad's house sat in the middle of my bedroom floor. The white paper with blue and red balloons had faded over the years and there were a few rips, including an especially long one where one of the kids in the group home had found it and tried to open it. I'd carefully taped it back together with his blood still covering my knuckles.

If I opened the box, it would be the last gift I ever got from my mom. She never even got to see me open it. Every birthday, she'd worked hard to buy me one gift and wrap it. Sometimes it was only in newspaper, but the look on her face when I peeled back the paper always made whatever was inside extra special. It was stupid not to open it. For all I know it was a box of decade old Tastykakes, but I couldn't bring myself to rip through that paper.

I flicked the business card from the sports agent back and forth in my hand. Jerseys were tacked to the walls from charity events the team had run. My lucky number eleven on a few. I'd have a jersey like one of those in a year from now, if I didn't fuck up.

The card stock *thwipped* against my palm. Before my rational brain took over, I snatched my phone up off the bed and made the call.

In less than an hour, I had an agent. A business meeting. Five figures sitting in my bank account.

And a private investigator on the case with the full run

down of everything I could remember about Elizabeth Vaughn.

I'd accepted money from an agent and if anyone found out I was toast and so was the FU season. Everything I'd worked for to set myself up and make sure Alexis never had to worry about a thing could be destroyed in the blink of an eye to track down someone who might not even want to see me. Maybe she'd never bothered looking, or maybe she couldn't find me, but Mom hadn't tracked me down so far, and I needed to know this. I needed to find out why she'd given me up. Maybe that would help make putting down roots easier. Finally, having the stability I'd longed for.

It was monumentally stupid, but there was no going back now. It was done.

I sat against my headboard, banging my head against the wall.

Jules' shadow moved across her bedroom window. The shades were always drawn, but her silhouette was backlit like the perfect torture device. Her arm whipped around almost like she was spinning in a circle, but was cut off by the edge of the window. I could almost see her dancing in her room, folding laundry, a dryer sheet tucked inside so it always smelled freshly washed, or pacing back and forth with flash-cards to study. She was definitely that kind of person.

My night was restless.

My bed felt empty, missing the warmth of someone else in the room. Not just anyone—Jules.

My mind wandered to the curly-haired brunette across the street.

I flipped on my side and pulled the shade open, even though the morning sun would blind me and despite the fact that it made me feel like a stalker.

Jules had her shade down. Did it feel weird for her to be sleeping in a bed alone after the two nights beside me? Was she tossing and turning or sleeping soundly with one of her legs thrown over a pillow, wishing it was me just as much as I did? *Get a grip, man.*

And this was why I never stayed over with anyone I slept with. These tender feelings shot to the surface way too quickly in general, and especially with someone like Jules. And she'd made her stance on what exactly we were abundantly clear. I was a great stand-in. Someone fun to hang with, but not anyone she was interested in for more than that.

Our class together was in two days; forty-three hours until the season opener, and with the pressure in my life mounting, the disappointments stacking up one after another, I kept staring out my window at the window I'd seen a thousand times before. Now I wanted to see into and be on the other side of it. Yeah, no psycho stalkers here.

Suddenly, being friends with Jules didn't feel like enough.

"Night, Jules." The semester would start and I'd be more than busy enough to keep thoughts of Jules from invading my mind. Piece of cake. That made me think of the double fudge four layer cake with the whipped cream cheese frosting she'd made.

I squeezed my eyes shut and covered my face with my pillow. I was crushing hard and I didn't want to make things weird for her. Tomorrow was a new day.

———

WITH MY CLASS SCHEDULE IN HAND, I WANDERED THE AISLES OF the bookstore wishing I'd kept some of that agent money to pay for books. At this point, I could've bought a new car with how much I'd spent on textbooks for the past four years.

My football scholarship covered tuition, room and board, but books? I was on my own.

I signed someone's Fulton U jersey with the tag still on it from downstairs where the clothes section was.

They held it out for Keyton to sign.

"If only we could pay for all this stuff with autographs." He handed it back to the guy who turned around holding up the jersey like his new prized possession.

"Do they take a kidney as a deposit for these things?" I pulled another book off the shelf. Everyone was back on campus now, which meant the level of recognition shot through the roof, especially with the season starting in a day.

Keyton switched his blue plastic basket from one hand to the other. "Not enough. They'd probably want both." He grabbed a sketching pad off the shelf of the aisle we wandered down.

I peered inside his basket. There were packs of different types of pencils in there along with some colored pencils. "You draw?"

He tugged a book from the shelf and dropped it on top of his supplies. "Sometimes."

"Will you draw me like one of your French girls?" I batted my eyelashes at him and was rewarded with a knuckle-driving punch to the shoulder.

"Jesus Christ, dude. You trying to knock me into next week?"

"Shit, sorry. I'm so sorry. I wasn't thinking."

I rubbed my arm. "Don't worry about it. One hell of a punch."

"Is that Jules?" He changed the subject so quickly my head snapped up. Also because of the name in question.

"Where?" I looked around for her horn-rimmed sweetness.

"Right, there. Hiding behind the shelves at the end of the row."

I ducked down and spotted her trying to look inconspicuous and at a vantage point where she absolutely had to have seen us.

"We can see you, Frenchie."

She shot straight up, banged her head on the shelf, and

her basket tumbled to the ground. Down on all fours, she scrambled to pick up all her stuff and rubbed her head.

I bridged the space between us and bent down, grabbing some of the books that had spilled out all over the floor.

"Berk, what are you doing here?" She said it like a kid caught with their hand in the cookie jar.

"Waterskiing. How's your head?" I curled my fingers at my side to resist the urge to rub her sore spot.

She blew a strand of hair out of her face and rubbed the side of her head. "Damn shelves, jumping out of nowhere." Shifting the basket, she swung it back up into her arms.

"They've been known to do that. Hit and runs left and right in this place."

Her wince turned into a smile and she stuck her tongue out at me. And I shoved my book-laden basket in front of me as thoughts of what her tongue would feel and taste like on mine filled my head.

Keyton leaned against the bookcase with one arm against the top shelf.

"We're wondering if the cashier would take an organ as a down payment for these books."

"I don't think that would cover it."

She laughed at Keyton. Was he more of a guy she felt like was on her level? Someone who she'd want something long term with? An irrational jolt of jealousy zinged through me. I tackled it to the ground. *She's not a freaking bone and I'm not a rabid dog. She can laugh at whatever she wants. I love the sound of her laugh.*

Inching closer, I bumped into her basket. "What are you doing today?"

"Avery from B&B wanted me to come in at noon to start my internship. I might stop by Elle's and pester her, but she's crazy busy with all the big events happening right now."

"Nix sounded like he was ready to deck someone last time I talked to him. Somebody was giving her a hard time." I dragged my finger over the spine of the books on the shelf like I was checking them out, but I wasn't. I was checking her out.

"Yeah, this PR and events big wig guy." She ducked to the bottom shelf and grabbed a book, slipping it into her basket.

"Are you going to their place to watch the game?" Maybe I could give her a ride over.

Keyton stood beside me observing like this was National Geographic. I shot him a *get lost* glare.

"Probably. We'll see. All you guys are going and there's not loads of room in their apartment." She laughed and checked the books on the other side of the aisle.

"There's always room for you, Jules. Of course we all want you there."

Her smile brightened.

With pointed eye directions from me, Keyton finally took the damn hint.

"Oh, right. I'm going to go look at the art supplies. I'll catch up to you two later."

Jules and I made it to the section marked for our class. I handed her the course packet and took one for mine, wincing at the price.

"Did you—"

"Can I—"

We both started at the same time. She smirked. "Go ahead."

"No, you go."

"Berk Vaughn!" an excited voice shouted over the bookstore din like a glass smashing in the center of a crowded restaurant. "Oh my god. We saw Keyton and he said you were over here."

Thanks a lot, man.

The girl's face had that familiar, excited look. Oh shit. There was more than one girl here.

I barely had time to get my basket out of my hands before the more aggressive girl took a running leap and hit me.

This shit never happened to Nix or Reece.

"Sorry for being in the way." Jules took another step back.

Someone pulled out their phone and started taking pictures as she smashed her cheek against mine, knocking Jules over.

"Hey, watch where the hell you're going," I ground out to the girl holding up her iPad to take a picture or record a whole documentary, while trying to move out of the vise grip on my arms.

The fans dragged Keyton over from wherever he was hiding and forced him into picture time.

I kept trying to get Jules' attention and untangle myself from the fan octopus without stiff arming anyone. Maybe Jules would bail me out. Drag me away from the growing circus as more people showed up with Fulton U swag for signing and chattered about the draft and Reece's first game right around the corner.

And then she was gone. The gentle swing of her ponytail and delicious sway of her hips disappeared down the escalator. She'd left me, and I tried to pretend that didn't hurt, but it did. Not to say the circus didn't get old real fast, but it would've been a hell of a lot better with her at my side instead of the thirty snapping wolves.

I might just need to make a pit stop at a certain bakery later today. And it was somewhere she couldn't run away from me.

CHAPTER 16
JULES

After peeking out my blinds for a solid twenty minutes, I'd made a mad dash for my escape from my house. Berk had already caught me once trying to avoid him; twice in a row would make it even more painful. Why'd he have to be so cute? And gorgeous? And the center of attention?

Not that I'd be able to avoid him for long. The smells from anything I baked wafted across the street like a cartoon, straight into his nostrils. It would only be a matter of time before he was back at my house, but I needed a little more time to get myself together before the Berk Bombardment began again. More time to shore up the sandbags in my stomach to stop those butterflies in their tracks.

"Where you going, Jules?"

I yelped and jumped. "Could you not do that?"

Zoe sat on the couch with her computer on one side of her. "Do what?"

"Sneak up on me."

"I've been sitting here this whole time."

"I'm not used to other people being here. I'm going out." I

turned and ran smack into a bare chest. Peeling myself off Mr. Hardbody, I stared up at him.

He was in a towel again. One of mine. "Do you own pants?"

"Yeah." He shrugged and smiled, walking past me with two bottles of water.

"Plan on wearing them anytime soon?"

"Eventually." He flopped onto the couch and lifted his foot, propping his leg up.

The front door slammed behind me. I think that was the fastest I'd ever moved in my life. Watching a full penis promenade wasn't on my list of things to do today.

I showed up at the B&B with my apron, not really sure if I'd need it. We hadn't gone over everything during the tour, which had mainly been Max shoving more food into her face.

Using the code Avery had given me, I tugged the back door open and flood-light levels of brightness slammed into me.

Shielding my eyes, I stood in the doorway waiting for the aliens to beam me up.

"Yay, you're here." Avery's voice sliced through my preparations for probing.

I walked inside, trying to blink away the blindness.

She bounded up to me in her cap-sleeved B&B top and jeans with her hair piled up on top of her head.

"What's going on?"

"There's been a slight change in plans." She pulled me into her office and laid it all out.

"They're doing a reality show about the bakery?"

"Not a reality show like they follow us around all the time, but they're going to do episodes where I make my most popular menu items and then post them up every week or a couple times a week. I have no idea." She dragged her hands through her hair.

I knew that feeling all too well. Taking her hand I gave it a squeeze.

"You've got this, Avery. It'll be amazing."

"Standing in front of a sea of lights and cameras isn't really my thing."

"I don't think it's something most people like, but you'll do an awesome job."

"Sorry that this is your first day. I'd have called you earlier, but I knew you were away for the weekend and I didn't realize they'd be here as early as I was to get everything set up. Holy crap there are a lot of lights."

"My face was 2.5 seconds away from melting off."

"But you're here now and I won't be alone. Thank god." She clung onto my arm. "Everyone else is actually getting work done and I figured since you're new and I'm walking through the recipes anyway, it would be a good way for you to learn."

My stare went on for way too long as I cycled through all the reasons I shouldn't be in front of the camera. Especially a camera that would be broadcasting my image to who knew how many people.

The little voice of Dr. Schuller came ringing back. I'd already run away once and I couldn't leave Avery hanging.

"I'll be right there at your side."

She let out a sharp breath and her shoulders relaxed a millimeter. "Thank you." She threw her arms around me and squeezed me so tight my arms started to go numb. Max strolled into the office. "She got you to do it, huh? Did the big pouty eyes and squeezed your hand?"

"If you're talking about the video thing then yes. What about you?" I rubbed my chin. "With a mouth as big as yours, it seems like you'd have been a perfect fit."

Max's eyes got wide and she braced her hands on the chair, staring at me with her mouth wide open. And looked between me and Avery before letting out a belly laugh that vibrated the air in the room. The three of us laughed and I wiped at my forehead, happy I hadn't misjudged the room with that one.

"Oh, shit, Ave. You pick them well." Max wiped at the tears forming in the corners of her eyes. She was the kind of bad-girl beautiful that made guys fall all over themselves to get their shot at cracking through her rock hard shell—and probably ended up cradling their bruised balls instead.

"I curse way too much to be considered a Bread & Butter brand ambassador. Avery would shit a brick if I burned myself and let out a string of four-letter words."

"Instead she's stuck with me." I'd meant that to come off a lot more lighthearted than it did. It fell to the floor between us all like a lobbed dummy grenade.

"Gah, I'm so sick of you pretty girls playing the I'm-so-plain card." Max clutched her hands to her chest and batted her eyelashes. "Oh no, no one will like me with my cute glasses and giant boobs. Whatever will they think?" She unclasped her hands and dropped the sugar sweet voice. "You're perfect for this, I can already tell."

"How?" I lifted an eyebrow.

"First off, I've tasted your stuff and it's amazing, so you know your way around the kitchen. Second, you've got that young, bubbly personality with a hint of snark, and you look so damn cute you're about to send me into a diabetic coma. It's a total I'll-bake-you-muffins-and-whip-up-some-chicken-noodle-soup-if-you're-sick look."

"Thank you?" Compliments somehow dripped off her tongue like insults and I wasn't sure how to react.

"Don't worry, you'll get used to it. I've got sort of a prickly personality. You're still taking the job, right?"

"I think Avery's getting my uniform now."

Avery grimaced. "Crap, I almost forgot. When I say uniform what I mean is shirt. It gets super hot in here once we start baking, so you'd freaking burn up in that long sleeve, what the hell is that? A thermal?"

My eyes widened and I tried to play it off like I wasn't in practically a sweater when September had just rolled in.

"If you can survive even five minutes with Max and not go running for the hills, you can handle anything." Avery rummaged around in a box of t-shirts and I prayed for once that she wouldn't have anything in my size. Just what I needed—to be standing in front of cameras with my bingo wings flapping in the wind.

Sorry, Dr. Schuller. I meant my strong arms that allow me to lift my way through life and carry the weight of my burdens.

"Yes, found one. This should fit you."

She held up a pastel pink top with short sleeves—very, very short sleeves—and the B&B logo printed in black on the front.

Don't panic, Jules. Don't panic. Just don't think about the last time your arms saw sunlight and hope you don't burn under those big camera lights out there.

"You can change in my bathroom." Avery pointed to the small door I hadn't even noticed before. "I'll wait. I don't want to go back out there alone."

"Great." That sounded as enthusiastic as a fish walking into a sushi bar. With a thumbs up, I ducked in the bathroom and changed. Folding my shirt up, I pushed aside the fact I was going to be on camera in a t-shirt. I'd made it through the engagement party gauntlet in a freaking flapper dress. This was a slam freaking dunk.

I was feeling more naked than I had in a long time as Avery and I walked back out into the bakery. Nearly tripping over a bunch of cables laid in front of the office door, I righted myself and followed Avery to the camera crew getting everything ready. Tripods, cables, even more lights.

"Look who I found." Max hopped up on one of the counters and took a bite out of a brownie.

Avery and I followed Max's outstretched hand and my butterflies burst out of hiding.

"Berk, what are you doing here?"

I tugged at the edges of my sleeves. That whole bathroom pep talk went poof in an instant and I didn't have any liquid courage as back up.

He'd never seen my arms before.

"You said you'd be here today and I needed to pick a few things up for the guys, so I thought I'd swing by. Figured, maybe you could give me the employee discount."

"I'll give you something, all right." Max wasn't even trying to hide her gratuitous ogling of Berk's ass. And what a fine one it was.

"You didn't have to come." My voice was all breathy like a screen siren from the 40s.

"That's so sweet." Avery bumped my shoulder. "They're still getting set up. I'll let you know when we're ready."

Berk was confusing me. I'd made it clear I wasn't expecting anything from him, but here he was.

"I didn't want to miss your first day, plus Marisa attempted cooking at the house and I want to avoid the salmonella blast zone before my game on Saturday."

"I totally forgot."

He frowned. "You don't plan on coming?"

"No tickets." I shrugged. "It's probably sold out."

"There might be a way I could get you one." He looked over his shoulder.

The stampede in my chest was on the horizon. His strong jaw and lips that had whispered so close to mine were there again.

"If you can score me some of those donuts with extra sprinkles." He pointed to the baker's rack stacked high with deliciousness.

My smile was un-hold-back-able. "I'll see what I can do."

"You two are making my teeth hurt," Max chimed in from her perch on the counter.

"Where the hell did you get popcorn from?"

She threw a handful into her mouth. "I have my ways." She waved her hands like a magician in front of us and wandered off to pester Avery.

"Let me check with them about the donuts and I'll be right back." I backed away, headed for the two bickering friends under the skin-blistering lights.

"Take your time." He shoved his hands into his pants and a peek of that muscular v winked at me from under his shirt. This level of sweetness and hotness, even in a bakery, was too much.

"Who's the hottie?" Max rested her elbows on the counter and shoveled more popcorn into her mouth. Where the hell did that even come from? I glanced around the room. Not a kernel in sight.

"He's my friend."

"Not from the way he's checking out your ass, he isn't." She lifted an eyebrow with a wide smile.

That's not possible. My brain's auto-responder to deny any interest any guy might have in me kicked in. It had saved my butt more than once. That hot guy waving to me at the bar? Yeah, no, that wave was for the delicate brunette in six inch heels behind me. That cocky smile from the guy in the car passing by? He's looking at his reflection in the store window behind me.

"It's true." But maybe...

I looked over my shoulder at her little, knowing mhmm.

Were my signals getting crossed?

Was he here to talk to me about professing his love for my sister before the wedding—no, but it was damn hard to get my hopes up.

Right about now I wished I could write him a letter. *Do you like me?* With a checkbox for yes or no. And what the hell happened when he found out I was TLG? How would he feel knowing I'd ditched him and run away and hidden, just like I wanted to do now? He'd probably hate me and never want to speak to me again.

Writing him those letters had set a part of me free that I'd never been able to give voice to before. With a big bottle of wine and some intense blushing, I'd written out everything I wanted to do to him and everything I wanted him to do to me. It was freeing to be that open about a part of myself I kept wrapped up tight and buried under three layers of clothes.

After the first few letters, I hadn't needed the wine to write the words. His letters—the fact that he'd actually replied—had been all the fuel I'd needed.

And I missed sharing bits of myself outside of the bedroom daydreaming. Telling him about the music I loved dancing to, or a new place I'd explored in the city.

But then the whole thing with Alexis and the cake happened and I knew I had to end it, because daydreaming was all it was, all it could be. It was getting my hopes up that someone was into me and that was never the way it turned out. And, yes, he showed up at my house at all hours, but that didn't mean anything more than that he liked chowing down on whatever I pulled out of the oven and keeping me company now that Elle had moved out. We were friends. It was sweet that he didn't want me bumping around the house all by myself.

And no matter how much batter I'd spilled watching him grab something out of the cabinets with his biceps bunching, or stretching and showing off a happy trail I'd be more than happy to follow, I had to keep all that on lockdown and pent up inside.

He hadn't stopped whatever casual on-and-off again thing he had going on with Alexis, so how was real-life me going to compete with the on-paper vixen persona I'd crafted?

He had groupies—ones who would run me over with

their car to have a piece of him. Women flinging themselves at him all the time. Beautiful, skinny women, and that was just the ones in the area. He'd go pro and there'd be women all over the country vying for his attention. Almost-kiss or not, it was no competition. Hands down, I'd lose. So, no matter what, I wasn't going to write another letter and poke that slowly-healing bruise.

"Avery, we're ready to start filming when you are," one of the crew guys called out.

"Are we ready?" Avery leaned over the counter, giving me a reassuring smile.

"Screw you guys, I'm out of here." Max jumped up like someone had zapped her with a cattle prod, and rushed off to the sidelines.

"One second. Berk wanted to know if he could have some donuts. I'll pay for them."

Avery laughed. "Give him as many as he wants. Eye candy gets paid in treats around here."

The back door opened. "Jesus Christ, is this the new security system? 'Cause it's working." A big guy filled the doorway, shielding his eyes, squinting at the floodlit brightness. I'd seen his face before, on billboards around the city. He made a beeline straight for Avery.

I jumped out of the way and grabbed a box for Berk's donuts.

"*That's* her husband?" Berk stared at the two of them, slack jawed.

"From the way he kissed her and is talking to her baby bump, I'm going with yes. You know him? He looks familiar."

"Hell, yeah. That's Emmett Cunning. The hockey player. He's the reason the team won the cup last season."

The lightbulbs fired, zipping my mind back to the pictures in Avery's office.

I stuck a bunch of donuts in the box and handed it over to

Berk, who slipped one out and took a bite before I'd even released the box.

"Jules, we're ready."

"Wish me luck." My smile was as weak as ten-second tea.

"Don't worry." Berk reached out and captured my hand. "They're going to love you." He ran his thumb along the back of my hand.

My cheeks reddened and I nodded, ducking my head. But I wasn't able to completely avoid eye contact as Max crouched down against the wall catching my gaze. Hers darted from me to where Berk held my hand.

I laughed and shook my head and trudged back to my inevitable death by embarrassment in front of a camera crew and my new boss.

We ran through everything we'd need for the recipe, with Avery showing me where everything was. Everyone else hustled around keeping the shop running, which had more than a few new customers now that news of the video crew had spread.

Berk looked happy as hell leaning against the wall and talking to Emmett. And I wanted him here. I hadn't even known I needed him here, but I did. Having him look at me with his smiles and mouthed words of encouragement kept me distracted enough that they were nearly finished filming before I'd had time to crank my freak out up to eleven.

A little flushed and with trembling hands, I helped Avery through the video as Max shouted out comments that were rolling in online.

"This is live." I nearly dropped the entire bowl of melted chocolate.

"Who's that beside Avery? She's adorable," Max threw out.

And now my face was probably glowing red like a stop-light in a snowstorm.

"They're right." That comment came from much closer.

"Now the comments are asking who the deep-voiced hottie is."

Berk waved off his chance to appear on screen.

My ears were on fire. My arms were out. A bead of sweat rolled down my back, but the world was still spinning. I was conquering my fears, and so far, so good. I looked up from the dough Avery was rolling out and caught Berk's eye.

His thumbs up melted my heart. What other fear might I be strong enough to face head on? One that looked and smelled and tasted like Berkley Vaughn?

CHAPTER 17
BERK

J ules looked up at me while they finished up their video. Everyone on the sidelines had their phones out following along with the live feed.

Everyone loved her, and why shouldn't they? She was awesome. Under the lights, her skin was glowing and she had that extra pinkness in her cheeks she always got when she was embarrassed. It only made me want to tease her even more to see how much deeper that shade could go.

"People are losing their shit over there." Emmett "Badass on the Ice" Cunning stood beside me like it was no big deal. I wasn't huge into hockey, but when your local team wins a national championship, you take notice—especially when their city-wide parade passed right by campus.

"Women baking something mouth-watering has a certain appeal to it."

"Tell me about it." He had a dreamy look in his eye as he watched his wife put whatever it was they were making into the oven.

"What's it like once you go pro? You know, having a girl and a family and stuff?"

Emmett peeled his eyes away from Avery and blinked at

me like he was coming out of a trance only she could put him in. "It's got its ups and downs, but if you're solid, there's nothing to worry about. Are you and Jules solid?"

I shoved my hands into my pockets. "We're not together."

"But you'd like to be." His knowing look told me I wasn't exactly stealthy about my feelings, which made it even harder that Jules ran every chance she got.

I nodded. All the things I'd tried to lock down when it came to Jules rushed forward. Standing on the sidelines watching her and being able to go over and lay a kiss on her in front of everyone. Seeing her looking up at me with a smile that was just for me. Feeling her nestled up against me with my arm around her waist so everyone would know that she was my woman and I was her man.

"It's harder for them than it is for us." He lifted his chin toward them as the overhead lights shut off.

"How?"

"They're the ones left behind while we're traveling all over the place. And they're always going to be the wives of professional athletes. That comes with a lot of catty bullshit we'd never even think of. The guy fans will shout at you on the street about a shitty play or come up and drunkenly hug you. The female fans get the claws out when it comes to them. Lie about you to try and break you up as though you'd hop into bed with them if you were single. You've got to protect them from that as much as you can, but they've also got to be able to ignore what they can and withstand the rest. It's not easy." He walked off with open arms and pulled Avery into a big bear hug.

That gave me pause. I'd cut my arm off before I'd do anything to hurt Jules. She was one of the most genuinely sweet, kindest people I'd ever met. And I didn't want anyone saying or doing anything to hurt her.

"How'd I do?" She was glowing with a nervous, bound-less energy and bouncing on her toes.

"The views that rolled in were insane. You two were an awesome team."

"But don't get any crazy ideas. She's my best friend." Max leaned over, butting into the conversation.

She was a little off the wall, but I could tell her heart was in a good place.

"I wouldn't think of it for a second. I'd never come between besties."

Max made a grumbling sound like a grizzled sailor before pulling Jules into a hug. "You did good. Killer stuff, and I'm so glad I won't have to do it now. If you'd totally blown it, I was on deck."

"Thanks for the vote of confidence."

"You're welcome." Max stomped off and accosted Avery and Emmett.

"I actually did it." Jules beamed with pride and radiated happiness.

The camera crew left a bunch of stuff up, and Jules and Avery worked out their schedule for the rest of the month. She was still on cloud nine as we drove back to our street.

Once parked in front of her house, I turned off the engine.

"Thanks for the ride. I'm pretty sure I would've fallen asleep on the bus after my adrenaline high wore off, and I'd have crisscrossed the city until morning."

"Any time."

"Did you start on the work Buchanan assigned? You'd think he could at least hold off on his curmudgeon attitude until classes actually start." She was talking a mile a minute and only chancing split-second long looks in my direction.

"Jules." I dropped my hand onto her leg.

She stopped mid-word, her muscles tightened under my hand. "Yes." She looked a second from ditching out of the car and rolling up onto her lawn like a stuntman making a quick getaway.

"I know what you said before, but—"

A sharp knock broke the building tension in the car. "Berk!"

I dropped my head against my head rest, letting out a growl of frustration. Was I going to have to paddle a boat out into the center of the Schuylkill River to get a second alone with her? Universe—this joke isn't anywhere near funny.

"You're needed. I've got to get through all that work. Let me know if you need any help or anything."

And then she was gone.

The car door closed and the door to her house wasn't far behind it.

"Berk!" Another knock on my window.

I threw open my door. "What?! What could possibly be so important that you couldn't wait for me to get out of my damn car?"

The guy wearing a Fulton U jersey with my number eleven on it backed up a step. "Sorry. I didn't want you to miss practice or be late to class. You've got a flat tire." He pointed at my back driver's side tire, slowly leaking air with a nice piece of metal sticking out of it. *Shit.*

"Thanks, man. Sorry for snapping at you."

"No problem. Tension's high with your game coming up. Do you want me to help?" He looked ready to sprint off and grab his toolbox.

"Sure, that would be great."

I only hoped the donut spare in my trunk would hold up for the next few months and wasn't flat already.

———

MY PHONE WOKE ME AT ONE IN THE MORNING.

I'd only been asleep for two hours, after reading over the email from Buchanan that came with a metric ton of homework we needed to have ready for the first day of class.

He couldn't have sent that out earlier? Maybe given

everyone a bit more time to complete it all? But I didn't want to show up to the first day of class empty-handed.

I hadn't expected a distress call from Alexis as soon as it felt like my eyes were closed. She was stranded down at the shore, so I'd picked her up and made the two hour drive back to campus just in time for practice.

The same song and dance we always did.

"You need to be more responsible."

"I'm having fun."

"You can't keep doing this."

"You didn't have to come. I could've figured it out on my own."

"Then why did you call me?"

"Fine, next time I won't."

Which then led to me telling her that of course she could always count on me and not to try to get out of a situation she couldn't handle on her own. I'd always be there for her.

I walked like a zombie to my cabinet and didn't even try to hide it.

LJ looked up from his notebooks and textbooks at the kitchen table. "You look like shit."

Rooting around back there, I grabbed one of my Twizzlers and shoved it into my mouth, trying to keep my eyes open.

"Are you finished with classes for the day?"

"One more." I lifted the coffee pot with the barest hint of coffee left and poured it into my mouth, grimacing at the cold, bitter taste and the grittiness.

"Are you going to make it?" He cracked his back.

"Have to. I've got Buchanan." I inhaled the strawberry licorice.

LJ grimaced and closed his books. "Good luck with that. Why'd you take that class? There are much easier ways to get your diploma."

"Who needs a diploma when we're going pro?" I willed my eyes open and pushed off the kitchen counter.

"You, maybe. With Coach killing me in practices you'd at least think I'd get more game time."

"It's better than it was before with none."

"He keeps going on and on about this being for my own good. All I see is him pissed that Marisa's staying here."

"You didn't see that coming?"

He shrugged. "She could've died, man. Showing up to her building on fucking fire, I don't think I've ever been that scared in my life. The stuff with my dad when he got sick, that was slow. Long days in the hospital. You could brace for it. But with her, she could've been gone in a blink."

Just like my mom, but she was still out there somewhere.

"Now we're trying to keep her from killing us all with food poisoning."

"Whenever she used to come over to my house, she walked into the kitchen like there was a ticking time bomb in there. Her house was always take-out. She can speed dial for Chinese, pizza, and cheese steaks with the best of them."

"Maybe you should show her how."

"Then I wouldn't get to cook for her anymore." He ducked his head and let out a huff. "I've got to go. I'm going to drag myself to Marisa's presentation thing."

"Such a good *friend*."

His glare made the dig worth it.

"I'm going to grab a quick nap on the couch."

"Make sure you set an alarm so you don't oversleep."

I nodded, too tired for words and walked out of the kitchen, dragging my bag along the floor. Thank god Keyton had brought this new couch. It was so much more comfortable than our old torture device masquerading as a couch. I lay down and the mid-afternoon light washed over my face.

Taking out my phone, I set the timer for forty-five minutes. That would give me enough time to get my ass up and back across campus before class started. Plenty of time.

My eyes shot open and I jumped up from the couch,

staring out the window. The afternoon sun was no longer beaming me in the face. I snatched up my phone off the floor, still vibrating with its silent alarm that had been going off for *thirty minutes*.

I snatched my backpack up off the floor and leapt off the porch, missing every step on the way down. I made a beeline straight to my car and raced to campus. I should've just found somewhere to crash on campus. So stupid.

Feet slipping on the tile floors, I rushed around the corner of the liberal arts building. I slung my backpack up onto my shoulder and slowly turned the knob to the door. Buchanan's back was to the class and he was writing on the board.

Jules sat toward the middle of the room with her notebooks neatly in front of her and another on the desk beside her with her bag on the chair. Her pointed gaze shot from the seat to me and back to the seat.

She'd saved a seat. For me.

Trying to be quiet, I squeezed between two of the desks to get there. Lifting my backpack, I made the tight squeeze and picked up the bag Jules had put on the seat.

"Mr. Vaughn, I made it very clear in my email to the whole class that lateness would not be tolerated." Professor Buchanan didn't even turn around from the whiteboard.

"I'm sorry I'm late. It was unavoidable."

"It wasn't. You'll lose five percent off your final grade and you can leave now. Get the notes from one of the other students who made it a priority to be here on time." He crossed his arms over his chest, holding his whiteboard marker like a sword.

My shoulders dropped. Already down five percent and I hadn't gotten to show him the true depth of my stupidity yet. Could a guy catch a damn break?

Jules shot up from her desk. "He was buying me tampons!"

CHAPTER 18
JULES

"He was buying me tampons." The words were out of my mouth before I could think of something better to come up with. Like he was getting my medicine or rescuing my dog from a burning tree—not that I had one, but the professor didn't need to know that. No, I went straight for the vagina problems: A professor's kryptonite.

Someone's desk chair combo squeaked across the floor. Probably as they were craning their neck to see which psycho had shouted out 'tampons!' in the middle of a full college ethics class.

"Excuse me." The professor's wide-eyed gaze swung to me.

A few people snickered behind me and my stomach knotted. Well, I was in it now, might as well pull out all the stops.

Leaning forward like I was telling him a secret and not broadcasting it to the entire class, I laid it on as thick as I could. "Professor Buchanan, I have an extremely heavy flow and I wasn't sure I could make it to the student center without bleeding through my clothes, so I asked Berk to buy some for me. He was in the classroom before you even got here with me, but then he left to go get the tampons."

"Wha—" The professor stared at me.

I side-eyed Berk, telling him to open the bag.

He moved his hands like if he touched the zipper he'd die of radiation burns.

With another nod from me, he gingerly unzipped my bag sitting on his desk.

I leaned over and shoved my hand inside and grabbed a handful of my emergency stash from my purse. The cotton-packed missiles were wrapped in bright paper wrappers. I raised them in the air, waving them like a pirate ship flag on the high seas of my period cruise. "See, super heavy duty."

Berk stared at me, slack jawed. Hell, half the class did—scratch that—the entire class stared at me like I was under-going a werewolf transformation in front of their eyes. My neck and cheeks were on fucking fire, but I had to save Berk from being unfairly punished.

I waved them at the professor. "Heavy flow." I repeated the words, slowly enunciating every syllable.

Buchanan mumbled and sputtered. "Please put those away. I'll allow it this time, but in the future, please take care of your personal needs before class."

"Thank you, Professor. And I will do. You know how those periods are sometimes. They jump out of nowhere and hit you like bam."

"Do you need to…" The professor eyed the door, clearly afraid that one false move from me and we'd have a re-enact-ment from The Shining going on.

"Right. Yes, I'll go take care of that."

I did a ginger duck-walk out of the classroom with my wad of tampons in my hand, and walked to the bathroom. I splashed some water on my face to look appropriately femi-ninely distressed and waited for what felt like an appropriate amount of time to deal with a period snafu of such epic proportions that you'd blurt it out in front of the whole classroom.

When I went back inside, the professor didn't even bat an eye as I slid into my seat. Berk mouthed 'thank you' and I tamped down that little giddy thrill that fluttered in my stomach.

The rest of the class went along without a hitch, except for the looks people kept shooting toward my ass like I was going to shoot up off my seat like a geyser at any second.

"Acting has shot to the top of your list of talents." Berk walked backward in front of me as we crossed the main quad after class.

"What acting?"

"In there with Buchanan and the..." His Adam's apple bobbed up and down. "Tampons," he whispered and looked over his shoulder.

"Oh, you mean the heavy-duty, super-absorbent tampons? Sure, you can have one." I raised my voice.

His eyes widened and he stopped mid-backward walk.

I burst out laughing, skirting around him. "You saved me during my sister's engagement weekend and at B&B, I figured I should return the favor."

"It means a lot, Jules." He switched from in front of me to walking beside me, bumping into me with his backpack that felt like he was transporting boulders.

"What do you have in here?" I reached for it.

He swung it to his other shoulder. "Just some crap. Nothing to worry about. Back to more important things. If I got screwed this early on, it might mess with my eligibility to play this season, and I can't let the team down like that."

"It's important to you that you not let them down."

"It's the best thing going in my life. Got me through some tough stuff."

"When you were a kid."

He stopped. "Yeah, how'd you know?" He looked at me

and my stomach dropped like an ice block had crashed into me. That was something he'd told me in his letters. In person, Berk talked like there'd never been a cloud in the sky, let alone bringing up something hard from his past.

"We're only seniors. I figure you had to have played before in high school and stuff."

He started walking again. "True. It got me outside and doing something physical. A way to burn off all that energy and pent-up emotions."

"I'm glad you've found something so important to you."

"And the paychecks won't hurt, which is why I need to kill it this season to get a good draft pick."

"How can they deny your skill on the field?"

"Know a lot about football?" He cast me a sidelong glance that required an underwear change.

"Even someone as uncultured as me can see how well you guys were doing in the last game."

"Half of us, anyway." He dragged his hands over his face. "Do you want a ride back to your place?"

I felt like the nerdy girl getting offered a ride home by the star football player. I guess that was appropriate, because that was exactly what was happening.

"I'll repay you in peanut butter cup double chocolate cupcakes."

"I'd give you a ride for free, Frenchie, but that doesn't mean I won't take you up on the offer."

MY PHONE BUZZED AS WE PULLED UP TO THE FRONT OF MY house. I stopped with my foot resting on the curb. Laura's name flashed on the screen.

"It's my sister."

"Tell her I said hi." Berk leaned over the hood of his car

looking like he was starring in the next Marvel movie; all he was missing was the leather jacket and the motorcycle.

For a split second, I thought about saying the call had been dropped just to squeeze in a little more Berk time now that I wasn't avoiding him. Then guilt pitted in my stomach. What kind of sister did that make me?

"Hey, Laura, what's up?"

"Can I come over to your place?"

For a stunned minute, I lifted the phone from my ear and stared at it.

"Hello?" Her small, tinny voice escaped the phone.

"I'm here. Sure you can come over." I motioned to my house and Berk nodded, waving and taking off to his side of the street.

"I'll be there in five."

Was something wrong with Mom? Laura never came over —well, except for that one time before the engagement party. I hadn't even known she knew where I lived.

I barely had time to put my bag down before she knocked on the door. Had she been waiting around the corner? I opened it and she barged in, wringing her hands and looking disheveled. Disheveled for her, which would be supremely polished by anyone else's standards.

"Laura, what the hell is going on? You're freaking me out." Was she going to call off the wedding? Suddenly had the crashing realization that she'd been a jackass to me my entire life? Just wanted to go out to lunch?

"Chet wants roses in the wedding." She paced like he'd said he wanted to club baby seals during the reception.

"And that's a problem?" I kicked the door closed and crossed my arms over my chest.

She threw her hands up. "Of course, it's a problem. We're supposed to be having peonies. Shades of pink peonies. But roses will ruin everything. They're trite and expected. This is supposed to be a trendsetting wedding. We need peonies."

And here I'd thought it was something serious. "They won't ruin everything. I'm sure the florist Mom has working it will make sure everything is perfect."

"He squeezes his toothpaste from the middle. And he leaves the milk out on the counter every time he uses it."

"Like a monster."

She stopped and faced me. "Thank you! I tried to tell Kaitlin, Gretchen, and Beth about it and they blew it off."

"That was a joke. It seems like you're freaking out over nothing. Or stuff you should talk to him about."

"There's two months until the wedding." She looked down at the couch before perching on the edge like she was afraid she'd catch something from it. Honestly, I didn't blame her. If I lifted the fitted cover I'd bought for it, she'd probably have an out of body experience.

"I thought you were getting married in the spring."

"Mom moved it. Discussed it with Chet and changed the date. The mayor's daughter is getting married in the spring and Mom doesn't want to compete for attention."

"Of course she doesn't." My eye roll was barely contained. "But it's your wedding. Why don't you tell her no?"

She tilted her head and stared at me with a look that only people who'd been in the trenches of childhood together could share.

In the grand scheme of things this wasn't a big problem— it was barely a problem—but when had Laura ever had to deal with anything real? When hadn't Mom and even Dad been there, brushing aside even the most minor inconveniences to make her happy? So I could see how in her head this was like flunking out of a semester or having someone smash into your brand new car.

"Right." I nodded. "It's not something I can help with. I'm surprised she sent me an invitation at all."

"You're used to her being mad at you all the time. How do

you talk to her?" She looked to me as though I had any answers when it came to Mom.

"I don't, not unless she forces me. You're the favorite. You should be able to tell her what you want."

Her humorless laugh summed that up. "Her favorite as long as I do everything she wants. For my senior prom I told her I preferred a different dress over the one she picked. She didn't talk to me for two months and cancelled all my credit cards."

"What? No way." That was my sophomore year. By that time I'd decided steering clear of both Mom and Laura was best for me.

"Yes way. You were too busy hiding out at school and going straight to your room, so you never noticed."

I sat on the couch beside her. "Why didn't you tell me?"

Her cheeks pinked up. "I—I guess I didn't want you to know." She clasped her hands on her lap. "It was always me and Mom, and you and Dad. And then once Dad died, it was only Mom, so I felt like I had to keep her happy."

"There is no happy when it comes to her. At least not that I've ever found."

She made a small sound. "You just have to know what she wants."

"Everyone and everything to be and do exactly what she wants. I can't do that anymore. And you shouldn't either."

"I don't have a choice." She wrung her hands in her lap and looked around my place. It wasn't much, but hell, I was in college. But compared to the cushy place Mom had put her up in during college, this was probably a half step above a homeless shelter in her mind.

"Of course you do."

"You've always been fine on your own. I'd like to actually have my mom like me," she snapped. Then her eyes widened and she shot up. "I didn't mean that, Julia—Jules, I'm sorry. I'm just really stressed out right now."

I'd never had the wind knocked out of me, but I'd imagine this was what it felt like. A burning in my chest. Hard to catch my breath. And a pain radiating out through my body.

"I shouldn't have come." She picked up her bag off the couch.

And just like that, our sisterly bonding disintegrated into a pile of ash, like that tray of cookies I'd baked during finals last year. I'd had to throw the whole cookie sheet away. But I couldn't do that with my family. They were all I had left. My only connection left to my dad.

CHAPTER 19
BERK

Rubbing my towel over my head, I stepped out of the shower. I wiped the steam off the mirror and wrapped a towel around my waist. Weight training sessions sucked ass. It was all the physical exhaustion of being on the field without the benefits of hitting anyone. I wrapped the towel around my waist and opened the bathroom door.

"Berk, hurry up. The game's starting in twenty minutes," Keyton called up the stairs.

"I'll be down in five." I checked my phone for any texts and threw on a t-shirt and some sweats. Damn, I wanted a beer, but during the season we kept that to a minimum, and only on weekends. This season was the most important one of my life and I wasn't going to throw it away over partying. Next year, all this would be worth it. Everything in my past would be a distant memory once I finally got the security that came with a seven-figure paycheck. But I still had to get through the season.

At least some of us were already living our dream. I jogged down the steps.

"Should I grill some burgers and hot dogs?" LJ stood at the bottom of the steps.

"A little late now. Reece's game is starting in less than five minutes." Fans stood in the stadium waving their team banners. One of us could be playing in that stadium once we were drafted.

"Damn, Nix was always the one cracking the whip on this shit and getting us organized."

I knew the feeling. I missed the guys too. Marisa and Keyton were our roommates, but Nix and Reece had been like brothers.

The front door burst open. "Did it start already?" Nix came barreling in with his arms loaded with food.

Keyton, LJ, and Marisa cheered.

"You saved us. Marisa was offering to cook."

Everyone shuddered. Her cooking was more likely to send everyone straight to the ER than have us full for the game.

"Good thing we're here, so you don't have to." Elle walked through the door balancing a plate of cookies.

I hopped to the bottom of the steps. "Are those Jules's?" I peered past her through the open door to the house across the street.

"They are." She smiled.

"Is she planning on coming?" I dragged my fingers through my hair.

"I'm not sure. Why don't you ask her?" Elle nudged me out of the way with her elbow.

"Since you're her friend and all, maybe you should invite her." I followed Elle.

"Not my house," she called out over her shoulder.

I'd been trying to play it cool with Jules. Flirty texts were one thing, but I didn't want to be the clingy stalker guy who couldn't stop thinking about her, and invited her to everything after one almost-kiss.

THE STADIUM REECE PLAYED IN DWARFED OUR OWN, BUT THAT didn't mean we would give any less heart. Our first game of the season was against St. Francis University—STFU to their student body no matter how much their administration tried to make it SFU.

At the line of scrimmage, my fingers sank into the short, perfectly manicured grass. Johannsen stared back at me through his face mask.

"Had a nice summer, Vaughn?" He sounded like he was grinding glass with his teeth.

"Serenaded any other girls since last semester?"

He'd been stalking our street last semester and we swore he was going to try to torch our house or some other insanity fitting him, so imagine that jaw-dropping shock when we woke up one morning and he was out on the small patch of lawn a couple houses down, singing his damn heart out to a girl.

"Met with any agents lately?"

My head shot up, breaking my stance just as the call for the snap came. For a split second, I lost my contact with the ground as Johannsen shouldered past me in a way too familiar way and nearly broke through the line.

Regaining my focus, I shifted my weight and banged into him. I wrapped my arms around his chest and pushed him to the side, narrowly missing Austin as the ball sailed over our heads.

Johannsen hit the ground and was up on his feet in a split second. He got in my face, banging his helmet into mine.

"Enjoy your season, Vaughn." His sneer could've peeled paint off a car.

Even with my solid block the rest of the game turned into a clusterfuck. The defense might as well have not been on the field with the times STFU strolled into the end zone. LJ managed an interception in the final quarter when Coach finally let him off the bench, but it wasn't enough. With the pressure on, Austin couldn't compensate like Nix would have been able to.

Our first game of the season ended with a morale-crushing 12-43 loss. Somewhere in the stands Jules had watched that bloodbath. Not exactly how I wanted to kick things off.

We all stood up to shake hands at the end of the game. There was silence from our lineup. I took the front right behind Austin. "You did your part."

"It wasn't enough." His head dropped.

"We'll pull it out. Everyone loves a comeback, right?" Keyton piped up from behind me.

"At least you guys got more than eight minutes on the field." LJ leaned out of the line.

"You made your time count," I called back to him. We needed him out there on defense. Whatever Coach had against him was seriously fucking with the team mojo. Everyone was uneasy about the possibility of getting on Coach's bad side for some unknown reason and being dumped on the sidelines. Coach pushed LJ harder than anyone in practice, he was one of our best players and he was riding the bench more than any senior with his talent should.

We walked past the other team, shaking hands and good gaming it. Familiar dull green eyes glared and loomed over everyone else.

"Have a good summer, Vaughn?" Johannsen shouted, still three guys from me.

"Yeah, it was fine." What the hell was his deal? He played every game like it was life and death. That it wasn't just our futures on the line, but the ability to keep breathing.

"I'm coming for you next game, Austin."

"Like you weren't coming for me this time." Austin shook his hand and didn't grimace as Johannsen squeezed.

I shoved at Johannsen's shoulder, breaking his grip. "Back the fuck off him. Maybe you've had your bell rung one too many times, but you need to chill."

"He protects you on and off the field? How precious." Then he turned his sneer to me and his whole face shifted like his own personal rain cloud now included thunder. "But who protects you?"

I hadn't thought there was anything more frightening than Johannsen's sneer; I was wrong. His smile was straight up nightmare fuel.

"Don't let him get in your head. You've got this." I clapped Austin on his shoulder. The plastic meets flesh sound ricocheted off the cement ceiling of the tunnel and cut through the trudging noise of everyone heading into the locker room.

There were no massive celebrations, Gatorade pours and yelling. There was only the slow march toward the chewing out we were all getting once the locker room door closed.

But at the end of the tunnel like a damn lighthouse in turbulent seas, Jules stood beside a couple of security guards, clutching a box to her chest.

I left Austin behind and made a beeline straight to her. The navy coat and white scarf were topped off with a cute hat with a little fluffy ball on top. She looked like something out of a still life painting of winter. All she needed was a mug of hot chocolate, or maybe a pair of ice skates.

"Sorry about your game." She nudged her glasses up, even though they hadn't fallen. It was a little quirk of hers she did whenever she was nervous.

"It's okay." I sounded like Coach had just made me run ten laps. My heart rate was kicked back into higher gear than when confronting Johannsen. "Did you bring me something?" I nodded toward the box in her hands.

I waved her through security and stepped down one of the hallways off the tunnel, keeping an ear out for the Coach shouting my name for not being inside the locker room for my reaming with along with everyone else.

She cringed. "I might've jumped the gun with these."

I lifted the box lid with one finger. With a letter on each cupcake, the word "Congrats" was spelled out. Swiping my finger across the top of one, I scooped up a dollop of the rich chocolate frosting and stuck it in my mouth. Heaven on earth. The only thing that could possibly taste better than this frosting would be Jules' lips.

Dropping the lid, I stared back at her. "It was you. You jinxed us."

"What?" Her eyes widened and her lips parted as she shook her head. "No, I didn't mean to."

I couldn't even string out the teasing with how miserable she sounded.

"It was a joke, Frenchie." A ripple of hesitation between us. I pulled a bit of lint off her coat. The perfect cover for letting my fingers skim across her neck. "Thanks for thinking we'd pull out the win." I took the box from her hand, not letting her use it as a buffer between us. My day was shitty, but there was one balm to make me forget I'd even played today.

"Next time I'll write a more generic message." She kept her eyes trained on the number eleven on the front of my jersey. "Like, 'Interesting Game' or 'Great Uniform'."

"You plan on coming to my next game." There were light freckles across the bridge of her nose. The ones I'd first seen in the greenhouse and kept discovering new ones. Tiny little footprints across the tops of her cheeks. I wanted to know everything else about her I hadn't seen yet. What else was there to discover about Jules? I wanted to write the encyclopedia.

"If a certain player can get my ticket again, I'd love to." She tilted her head and her gaze bounced up and away again.

I didn't want that. I wanted her gaze on me. Her thoughts on me. Her body screaming out for me as much as mine yearned for hers.

"That can be arranged, especially if you keep promising me after-game treats. Consolation or celebration, I'm up for them anytime."

Her laugh came out as a tight stutter. "That could be interpreted as a little dirty."

I'd hire a damn skywriter if that's what it took.

"If it still needs interpretation, maybe I should be a bit clearer." I ran my finger under her chin.

Her gaze lifted away from the box to meet mine. "Clearer?"

"Much." I set the box on the floor—for once food was the last thing I was thinking about, but that didn't mean I didn't appreciate all her time and effort. I'd watched her in the kitchen enough times to know how much attention each cookie or cupcake got before they made it into anyone's hands.

My adrenaline pumped in my veins, a thumping throbbing that wasn't going away now that we were off the field. I wasn't going to play the game we were playing anymore, not without going for the win.

I dropped my pads and wrapped my arm around her back, sinking one hand into her hair, letting my fingers wind around her silky, inky curls.

A small gasp shot from her lips and I couldn't hold back my smile. I was filled with the feeling that made you forget everything else and want to bottle up that single moment of pure, unrelenting and unparalleled joy.

"Much." And I wasn't taking any chances this time. Voices rang out against the concrete around us. Players, coaches, and everyone else in this gridiron circus flowed past us, past our little island in the middle of madness. But I couldn't hold it back any longer; like a dam in a torrential rain storm, I was overwhelmed by her.

And kissed the shit out of her.

The electric fire of desire coursed through my veins and the only antidote was her touch.

CHAPTER 20
JULES

His lips were soft and unyielding all at once. Fireworks erupted in my head. A colorful, sparking display with a new road lit up with each press of his lips and swipe of his tongue, which was nearing the grand finale.

I sank into him like I'd lost all motor functions.

He cupped the back of my neck and controlled the kiss. Delving deeper and deeper into my mouth and stealing away every breath like it would be his last. His tongue danced with mine like we had out on the dance floor, only his tongue wasn't nearly as polite. A raging heat burned in my stomach and that traveled lower, creating a throbbing ache between my legs.

I squeezed my thighs together and moaned. The sound escaped the seal of our lips. If anything, it spurred him on.

His hand tightened against the small of my back, pressing me against him.

I was sandwiched between him and the cool concrete.

"Your lips make me forget about everything else. They make me forget about losing, about the hundred people in the hallway beside us, about anything not centered on this mouth. How'd you get so fucking sweet, Jules?"

I didn't get a chance to respond. Not that I wanted one.

He was sweaty. He smelled like intensity and determination all rolled up into one, and I wanted to climb him like a tree. The whole stadium could've collapsed around us and I wouldn't have wanted to stop. His lips were enough of a balm to heal anything.

This was unlike any kiss I'd experienced before. It was all-consuming, heated and hungry. Like he was hungry for me and couldn't get enough of me, not like he was going through the motions or giving me a perfunctory peck to pave the way to the main event. He was kissing me like this was the main event and I was the center of his world.

Another kiss accompanied by a full body flush and tingling toes. My head swam and I clenched his jersey even tighter in my fists, pulling him even closer, if that were possible.

A sharp and throaty cough broke through our protective bubble. Followed up by another.

We broke apart, panting, staring at each other shell shocked, and turned our heads toward the end of the hallway at the same time.

"Coach is ready to rip us all a new asshole. You won't want to miss it." Keyton stood at the end of the hallway.

"Coming." Berk picked up the box of cupcakes and put it in my hands. "Take these, I'll want to have some after Coach is finished with Ass Reaming 2020. Wait out here and I'll be back as soon as I can. Can you wait? Maybe twenty minutes?"

"Of course."

His smile could've lit up the stadium for the rest of the season. With one more quick peck, he bolted after Keyton and left me standing there with my box of cupcakes, trying to figure out what I'd just gotten myself into.

Berk had kissed me.

Berkley Vaughn kissed me, Julia Kelland.

I was glad his after-game meeting took half an hour. It took me that long to process that I wasn't hallucinating, that he had actually been there and the lingering taste on my lips wasn't the early warning sign of a stroke.

He burst out of the locker room, and the smile on his face while everyone else looked like they'd had their fingernails pulled out wiped away the last bit of doubt swirling in my head.

Get out of there, Jules. That's no place for you to live.

"I'm starving for another taste of cupcake." His mouth said cupcake, but his eyes said me. And I was here for it in the biggest way possible.

I opened the lid to the box and he snagged a cupcake, barely unwrapping it before inhaling the whole thing.

"You're going to be running that bakery before the semester's over or those people are insane. If you're not selling these then the whole world is missing out."

My cheeks flushed in a different way this time. The compliments were always so much harder to bear for me. Criticism, I could stand there and take. It had taken years of training, but I was generally good at not letting whoever it was see me flinch.

But compliments made me want to run away or dodge them like bullets in the Matrix. Maybe it was a fear that one day all those good things anyone said about me would be gone in a snap.

"You're going straight home, right?" LJ jumped onto Berk's back, hands pressing down on his shoulders. "First game of the season tradition."

"Are you sure you want to do this?" Berk shook him off.

"The first game was already cursed. We need to make sure the rest of the season doesn't have the same issues."

"Is Keyton in?"

"I've been told, and I'm in." Keyton threw his duffle over his shoulder.

"Marisa is getting everything ready as we speak."

"Hopefully not any food." Keyton shuddered and held his arm over his stomach. "After her grilled cheeses, my ab workout took me a week to recover from."

"What did we tell you about eating anything she made?" Berk laughed.

Keyton pushed open the door at the end of the hall leading out to the parking lot. "It's cheese and bread! How in the hell can you screw that up?"

Most of the cars were gone. Although most people didn't need a reason to party, everyone had been pretty deflated in the stands after staying on their feet for the whole last quarter, hoping the Trojans would pull out the win.

"Marisa finds a way." LJ clapped him on the shoulder. "Can I catch a ride with you?"

Keyton nodded. "We'll see you at the house."

Those two took off.

Berk looked over at me.

The autumn chill in the air sent a shiver down my spine— or it could be the close proximity to Berk? I stared down at our joined hands. The same ones we'd been holding the whole time the guys had been there, while everyone was leaving the locker rooms and could see us. I'd braced myself for the cartoonish double takes. Questions about me being a little old to be a Make A Wish kid or even just a "why the fuck are you holding her hand?" from his other teammates, but so far nothing. Maybe I was just that good at fading into the background.

"What are you doing for the rest of tonight?"

Confusion had set in for sure.

"What did you have in mind?" I didn't think it was what I wanted, because I definitely wasn't inviting Keyton, LJ, and Marisa along.

"A little friendly competition." That was not what I was expecting in the slightest after he'd kissed me so well I'd forgotten seventh grade algebra.

"Sure?"

"Was that a question or are you in? This is a serious game we play. Tradition."

I nodded as he threaded his fingers through mine. A few heads turned our way, probably trying to figure out what exactly he was doing with me. I ducked my head and let him pull me along.

The engine of his car roared to life and I relaxed a bit, now safely inside and away from all the eyes at the stadium.

He drummed the fingers of one hand along the steering wheel, and the other—well, the other was on my leg. Fingers wrapped around my thigh, giving me a squeeze every couple of minutes like a reassurance that he was there. Like he was saying, 'yes, I am touching your leg, and I plan on touching a whole lot more of you in the future.' My whole speech about keeping things casual had fallen on deaf ears and I'd never been happier to be ignored in my life.

All this time I'd been trying to keep that wall between us solid and immovable, but I should've known Berk would be the one to knock it down, just like he did on the field.

Inside the house, we were loaded up with Nerf dart ammo like the Nerf zombie apocalypse was on its way.

"How are there this many different types?"

Berk stood in front of his closet door, which had them all arranged against the wall like a true arsenal. There were baskets for the clips neatly arranged under the wall of weapons.

"You take this seriously, huh?"

"I always take my fun very seriously." He smiled while tightening the ammo loop over my shoulder and across my chest.

Somewhere in the house, someone blew a whistle and it was on.

"It's every man for himself, since we have odd numbers, but I'll go easy on you." He winked at me.

"We'll see." We both took off out of the room.

Battle plans were drawn up—literally. We used shot glasses and the landing by the stairs to lay out the plan of attack. There was no messing around when it came to Nerf in this house.

With a battle cry from Marisa, we were off and the Styrofoam darts were flying.

Down in the basement, we regrouped for our second round, sweaty and a little out of breath. I wasn't the only one drenched in sweat, and that made me feel better. We hid out behind the washing machine with our backs against the cold metal. I wouldn't be caught dead crawling around in my basement—well, maybe I would be caught dead there. Some kind of monster or overdeveloped mold would probably grab me by the legs and murder me. Which was why I always high-stepped it up the stairs once I had put in a load of laundry and turned off the lights. But we were here with our Nerf guns locked and loaded, ready for the fight.

We were playing every man or woman for themselves, although Keyton was teamed up with Marisa. The mini-fit LJ had thrown when they both shot him in the forehead was kind of adorable. We had them on the run and regathered our ammo.

The distinctive clatter of an ammo cartridge hitting the ground was my opening. I popped up, leapt over the washing machine, rolled on top of the pool table to my feet and got them both from above.

They both cursed and groused. I turned my head at the slow clap from the stairs.

"You were like a gazelle. Damn, Jules. You leapt over the washing machine and then did a spin move in the air."

Everyone stopped and stared at me.

My shoulders came up a bit, and if I were a turtle I'd have climbed inside my shell.

"Well-deserved win, then." Keyton helped Marisa up off the floor.

LJ scowled. "There's leftovers from Nix's." He turned and went right back upstairs.

"You kicked ass." Berk's words licked their way up the back of my neck. His breath ruffled the damp hairs at the base of my neck and sent a full-body shockwave through me.

"Not quite yet." I grabbed onto the support pole beside me and swung around, letting one more dart hit him square in his chest.

He stared back at me, slack jawed, watching the orange and blue tipped Styrofoam fall to the ground. "You shot me."

"You said it was every man for himself." I held up my hands like I was helpless in going against the rules.

"Cutthroat to the end." He shook his head.

"I have my moments." I shrugged, twirling my gun on my pointer finger.

"What was the spin move you did right there? Looks like you've spent a little time on the pole." He said it jokingly, the way they all teased each other, but I wanted to tell him, to share another part of myself with him.

He bent down to pick up some of the darts off the floor.

"I do have experience."

He cocked his head to the side.

"You know. With the pole."

His eyes widened.

My tongue felt like it was in knots and I was flustered. "With pole dancing. Not with actual stripping or anything. I have a pole in my bedroom; it's skinnier than this one, but that was what happened with the leap and then with the swing I did right there." I gestured to the support pole.

Berk stayed in his crouch like he'd been frozen solid and then he moved in a blur.

He grabbed my hand and tugged me up the stairs, the darts long-forgotten and dropped to the floor.

"We're leaving. Eat without us," he shouted to everyone standing in the kitchen, portioning out food onto their plates.

His legs were a hell of a lot longer than mine, and unlike our jog at Kelland Estate, I could barely keep up.

"Berk, where the hell are we going?"

CHAPTER 21
BERK

I didn't even bother to close the door.

Charging across the street, I was seconds from throwing Jules over my shoulder. My hard on made it hard to run, but we came to a not-so-gentlemanly agreement to suffer through the sprint for the reward at the end of the tunnel—Jules.

I was so pissed we'd gotten that pole removed from my bedroom when we moved into The Brothel last year. Catching random people doing their own strip shows in my room wasn't exactly the best way to get any studying done—and it also gave the wrong impression about me.

Damn, that would've been a sight to see—Jules in my bedroom showing off her skills. But this was better. This was so much better. Her house was empty. No one to interrupt. No one to see everything she was going to show me.

All those times I'd seen her in her room through the shades and I'd thought it was just her dancing. She was dancing, alright. On a freaking pole. And I wasn't going to miss this next performance for the world.

"Ah, Berk, what are we doing?" She stumbled to keep up, her sneakers slapping on the pavement.

I turned to look at her over my shoulder. "You can't drop the pole dancing bomb after that move you pulled back there and think I'm not going to want to see."

She tugged against my hold on her hand as we hit the top step of her porch. "You want to see me dance?"

"Why the hell do you think I'm seconds away from throwing you over my shoulder?"

"I don't know." She pushed her glasses up the bridge of her nose in that adorable, I'm-stalling-for-time-way. "Cause you thought it was super out-of-bounds for me to mention it and didn't want anyone else to hear what I'd said?" She looked down at her shoes and shrugged.

"Jules, if you don't show me all your moves, I might have to use my imagination, and I don't know if you want me doing that."

She peered up and the corner of her mouth lifted. "Maybe I do."

We rushed inside and didn't take the standard pit stop of the kitchen. She led the way, keeping my hand in hers as she climbed the steps. Like I was going anywhere. At this point, she'd have to call the cops to get me to leave.

Walking up the stairs was crossing a barrier that we'd erected between us. It was crossing an invisible line drawn across all our interactions, and doing it now I couldn't believe I hadn't blown through that thing ages ago. Her steps were quiet even on the creaky stairs.

We stood in front of her door. She glanced at me over her shoulder and bit her bottom lip. "I've only ever danced for one other person."

A blaze of irrational jealousy ripped through me thinking about her dancing for some asshat.

"Elle isn't exactly going to tell me if I suck, though."

The tightness in my shoulders relaxed. Not an asshat. Elle, her best friend. I could deal with that. But the anticipation of seeing Jules dance made it hard to stand still and keep all the blood from shooting straight to my dick.

She let go of my hand and opened her door.

The floor-to-ceiling golden pole gleamed in the light from the hallway.

"I'll find some music."

"I'll find the light switch." I'd never been in her room before. Scanning the space, I spotted the lamp beside her bed. It would cast less light than the ceiling light and hopefully not put on a full display for anyone out on the street. Maybe I'd let her know I could see her dance from my room. Or maybe I'd keep those private shows to myself.

Her head shot up. "We can do this without the light."

"No, Jules, we really can't. I didn't come all this way to not see you." I reached under the lampshade and turned the knob. The double click was the only sound in the room.

She jumped when the soft light flipped on. "Music." Dragging her hand through her hair, she scrolled through her phone and the Bluetooth speaker dinged, announcing it was connected.

My skin prickled with the anticipation of watching her. Of her watching me watch her. And letting her know there was nowhere else I'd rather be than here.

Holding onto the pole up high above her head, she spun around, keeping her body straight and out at an angle from the pole. Damn impressive upper body strength. A fun summer song came on and she lifted her leg into a split against the pole.

Flexibility con-fucking-firmed.

"Once, my leg slipped off and I banged my forehead on the pole. It looked like I'd gotten into a fight with a vacuum cleaner." She laughed, peeking over at me.

"I'm sure no one noticed."

"The spot was as big as a half dollar, but at least I hadn't banged my nose."

She did a few more solid moves, but kept her gaze as far away from me as it could get.

"I feel like you're holding out on me, Frenchie." I tried to keep my voice light, keep the weight of desire out of my voice, so I didn't scare the shit out of her.

Like she was making a decision, she stood in front of the pole and squeezed her fists at her sides. "I can only show you what I can really do if I take my clothes off."

A wheeze shot out of my mouth. I held onto the edge of the bed, so I didn't tackle her to the floor and peel every piece of clothing off her with my teeth.

Damn, I needed to touch her.

I needed to touch her more than I needed my next breath.

I needed to touch her to make sure this wasn't all a dream and the beautiful sight in front of me didn't disappear before I could.

She was so gorgeous it hurt not to touch her.

"Not naked, but there's no point in changing into my pole gear when I'm already in boy shorts and a sports bra." She kept her back to me and slowly unbuttoned her jeans. The pop of the button and slide of the zipper had my dick straining against the metal zipper of my jeans.

Like she'd change her mind if she thought about it too long, she whipped her top off. I'd been to a couple strip clubs with some guys before, but this was a striptease that blew all the others out of the water.

The song switched and she took her hair down. It fell over half her face, obscuring her eyes.

"You got this, Jules," she said under her breath.

She sure as hell did. Most girls would start with the porn star hair flips and flash as much skin as possible; that was their prerogative.

But Jules freaked out about a dress showing some cleavage.

Jules let a curse fly here and there and glanced around like the swear police would come lock her up.

Jules baked congrats cupcakes for my game.

Jules was here with me when she could be anywhere else.

Jules was a secret sexy goddess who had a pole in her bedroom.

I couldn't hold back my smile. How had I ever not seen how brave she was? How indescribably beautiful?

Grabbing the pole, she raked her fingers through her hair and spun around more freely than she had before. She dipped and swayed to the music. As she came around the pole again she looked up at me, nervous, like I'd be anything but ready to come out of my skin with the need for her.

Whatever she saw in my face made her smile and she didn't look away. With the pole against her back, she sank down, balancing herself with one hand.

"I'll do some tricks now. You might want to sit back, some of these moves can get a little wild."

Following instructions, I leaned back and braced my hands on the bed, a little worried about the growing erection I wouldn't be able to hide.

Gaining speed, Jules leaned into the pole, and using her arms and legs ended up in a full split, doing a slow motion spin around like some insanely sexy cake topper. The routine continued, each move sending tingles through my fingertips.

She maintained eye contact with each move, always making sure I was watching. How could I not? A boldness developed and then she wasn't just doing the moves, she was dancing. Dancing for me.

Flipping her hair back, she danced toward me. Her skin glistened and shined. I was sure she was even sweeter than she'd been before. I'd tasted her lips, now I wanted to taste all of her.

"What did you think?" She stood between my open legs. Her chest rose and fell. The tips of her nipples pebbled even through the fabric of her bra.

"I think you've been holding out on me and I'm going to need you to make that up to me."

Her smile faltered for a second.

"How about this?" She spun around and tucked her hair over her shoulder, peering back at me as she sank lower. Excruciatingly slowly, until her ass rubbed against the front of my jeans. Damn, did I wish I was wearing breakaway pants right now.

She ground her hips to the rhythm of the music.

I couldn't hold back anymore. My fingers sank into her soft flesh and I gripped her hips, pulling her back.

"I thought you weren't allowed to touch the dancers."

"Good thing we're not at a strip club. Do you want me to stop?"

Her fingers tightened on my thighs.

I bit back a groan.

"No, I want you to keep going."

I skimmed one hand along her stomach and up over her bra. "How far?"

She stilled for a second and grabbed onto my hand on her hip. Slowly, like she didn't want to spook me, she pushed my hand lower, down to the front of her boy shorts. Using my fingers, she massaged the front of her pussy, using me as her own personal sex toy and I was a second away from coming in my boxers like it was my first time.

"I'm not going to be able to control myself, if you keep doing that."

She let out a shuddering breath as I took over the massage, circling my fingers and touching her through the fabric, finding her clit.

"Who said I wanted you to?" She moaned.

Stopping all exploration of her body, I shoved my hand into my pocket, tugged out my wallet and fished out a condom quicker than I'd ever done anything in my life. I flung off my pants and with one hand I rolled on the condom.

With the other, I tugged down her shorts, the fabric fraying a little and threads ripping.

"Careful." She laughed.

Pulling her down onto me, I guided my throbbing cock inside her. "We're way past careful, Frenchie." Her velvety heat tightened around me as she sank down onto my lap.

I pumped into her with hard, ruthless strokes, barely able to contain myself. I wanted her facing me, I wanted her under me, wrapped around me.

She hissed and I wrapped my arms around her waist, tugging her back against my chest. "You good?"

"Don't you fucking stop." Her head dropped back to my shoulder.

"There she is." I nipped at the smooth expanse of her neck.

"Who?" Her hips swiveled and she ground down on me.

"Fuck!" I dropped my hand between her thighs. Her wetness coated my fingers as I parted her folds and found her clit.

She shuddered against me, dropping her hips faster and I met each thrust driving up and into her. The thunderclap of my come was rolling just over the horizon, but I wasn't getting there first. Hell no.

"Who?" Her smile turned into a moan as she repeated her question.

"The real Jules." I circled her clit and her muscles seized and she tightened around me so hard black spots danced in front of my vision. She shouted my name loud enough for the university president and half of campus to hear. I squeezed her tighter, wrapping my arms across her chest and spilling into the latex between us.

With numb fingers and toes, I panted against the back of her shoulder. The salty, sweet taste of her skin lingered on my lips.

"What the hell was that?"

CHAPTER 22
JULES

He chuckled and kissed my back. "I was going to ask you the same thing."

My head buzzed and my body tingled as aftershocks of my orgasm ripped through my body. "It's not always like that with you?" I braced my hands on his thighs and lifted.

His arm tightened around my waist, not letting go.

I looked at him over my shoulder.

A strange, borderline angry look passed over his face. "No. Is it like that with other guys?"

My gaze shot to the floor. "No." What the hell had that look been?

His hold loosened and he ran his hands up and down my sides. The flutter-light touch made me break out in goosebumps. "It's never been like that, Jules." The words caressed the back of my neck, still glistening with sweat.

I nodded and leaned back against him, savoring his heated skin against mine. The self-consciousness about sitting fully on his lap and not trying to brace my weight on my hands or legs wasn't there. Berk's entire body enveloped me and for the first time, I really felt dwarfed by him. After giving myself another five seconds to imprint this moment in my mind, I braced my hands on his knees and lifted off his lap. I groaned and attempted to walk. I was like a newborn baby deer.

He steadied me. "Careful."

The gentle concern in his voice sent a thrill through me that had nothing to do with the ache between my thighs.

Now there was the awkward indecision. Did I grab my clothes and put them on? Get under the covers?

"How long have you been dancing?" Berk didn't seem at all fazed by our nakedness. Well, he still had his jeans mostly on.

"Since freshman year. I dragged Elle along to the studio and I loved it." I spotted my robe hanging off my closet door. SpongeBob wasn't exactly sexy, but I didn't have a pastel, silky robe to slip on.

"I can tell." His hand circled my wrist as I tried to walk toward my robe. "Teach me something."

A laugh burst free from my lips. "You want to learn?"

He shrugged. "Why not? It's always good to learn new things."

"Okay, let me just grab some shorts." I started to walk away, but he kept his hold on me.

"No, like this." His hungry gaze traveled up and down my body.

"It's going to be hard to do with this getting in the way." I wrapped my fingers around his growing erection.

He sucked in a sharp breath through his clenched teeth. "You let me worry about him."

I ducked my head and laughed. "If you say so."

The pole dancing lesson turned out to be one long string of excuses for Berk to rub his body against mine, not that I was complaining. Although, I was doubled over at the serious look on his face as he did a slow turn around the pole, keeping his arms straight and walking through the air. His upper body strength was insane.

"How'd I do?" He smiled at me, stepping toward me until my back banged against the pole.

"Not bad for your first time."

"We can schedule my next lesson soon, but I'm more than a little distracted." In a second, his gaze switched from playful to hungry.

"You are." My chest heaved and my words came out breathy.

"And it's all your fault."

He dipped and slid his hands behind my knees and around my shoulder, scooping me up before I could scream 'no, you'll break your back!'

Crossing the space between the pole and my bed in less than two steps, he set me down on the bed.

His erection was at head height and standing tall—and thick. Had that seriously been inside me? The ache between my legs deepened.

My mouth watered. I reached for the waistband, slipped my hand inside.

A groan broke free from his lips as my fingers curled around his rapidly-growing cock.

In here, I was bold Jules, pole dancer extraordinaire. And Berk didn't seem to mind one bit.

"You're killing me, Frenchie." He closed his hand around my wrist, helping me keep time with a rhythm he liked. I wanted more of that. I wanted to know what a flick of my wrist would do as I hit the end of my stroke and was rewarded with a groan. I licked my lips to taste him.

"I was going to say the same thing."

But every time I went for it, he blocked me.

He trailed his thumb over my bottom lip. "If you put your mouth on me, I'm done for, and I want this to keep going."

I was sweaty and felt like I'd run a marathon, and I'd

never felt more beautiful than when he looked into my eyes like he wanted to eat me up.

He grabbed a condom, rolling it on and pressed into me slow and steady, stretching me and settling his hips between my thighs like he never wanted to leave.

With a slow cant of his hips and a grind against my clit, I flew apart in a matter of minutes.

Resting my head on his chest, I trailed my fingers up and down his abs. A freaking six-pack, but I couldn't feel self-conscious in the afterglow of my multiple orgasms.

I'd have never thought Berk was a cuddler—not with the way he'd taken up a permanent spot on the floor at Laura's engagement party. But I wasn't going to say no to his strong arms wrapped around me.

"We should do this again sometime." I peered up at him, pressing my lips against his chest, hoping he wouldn't shatter my fragile hope that he'd want this again too.

A slow rumble rolled through his chest. "Oh we're going to be doing this more than just sometime, Frenchie. I'm setting up a permanent appointment in your calendar. It'll be sandwiched in right after class and before baking, that way I can watch you bake in nothing but an apron."

After everything we'd just done, my cheeks went red at the dirty picture he'd painted in my mind.

CHAPTER 23
BERK

I watched her for way longer than I should've. Probably longer than a non-stalker would, but I couldn't stop myself. The perfect curve of her eyelashes. The small indents on either side of her nose from her glasses. The way her full lips parted as she breathed. I wound a strand of her hair around my finger.

She was soft and warm nestled against me. I loved the way my fingers sank into her hips. How I never worried my grip would be too hard or rough. The sheet slid down more over the curve of her breasts with each breath. A hint of her deep pink nipple peeked out, teasing me like her salted caramel chocolate chunk cookies with the hint of espresso.

Blood rushed to my cock and I was seconds away from taking myself in my hand. It would be a miracle if I didn't get a hard on every time I smelled vanilla from here on out. It was like it was embedded in her skin, sweet and heady, just like her. I wasn't going to pounce on her while she was sleeping.

Her eyelids fluttered and I rested my head against the pillow, trying to pretend I hadn't been committing every line of her face to memory.

A date with Jules. An actual date. That would maybe end with another slow dance under the moonlight. I could only hope an act of god didn't interrupt this time.

We were doing things backward, but I was determined to do this right with her. Show her this wasn't some bang and run thing. She'd told me before she wanted casual, but I wasn't a casual guy, no matter what people thought about me. The assumption that football player equaled manwhore wasn't lost on me. And I didn't exactly scream responsible guy most of the time, but I wasn't scared to show her that side of me—okay, maybe I was a little bit.

Hell, I hadn't been with anyone since I started trading letters with TLG, but I couldn't feel guilty about being with Jules. Last night had been blow-the-back-of-my-head-off amazing. She was an indescribable kind of perfect for me. The kind that made my heart ache that I'd only just found her and was ready to get down on my knees so I didn't have to wait another day without knowing her beauty.

"Are you going to watch me sleep all morning?" She grumbled with a smile and her eyes still closed.

"I was just amazed a person could have such crusty eyes after only four hours of sleep."

Her eyes snapped open and she wiped at them with the heels of her hands.

I grabbed her wrists to stop her from scraping ninety percent of the skin off her face. "I was joking, Jules. You're perfect. Not an eye booger in sight."

She glared and poked at my chest. "Jerkface."

"How can you be so cruel?" I wrapped my arms around her, tickled her and blew raspberries on her neck.

She finally relented, laughing until tears were in her eyes. "Fine, you're not a jerkface." The words came out in pants.

"What am I then?" I didn't let her out of the circle of my arms.

"My new favorite audience member." She stared into my

eyes with so much openness and joy it made me want to keep her in bed and show her every single way she was mine.

I could stay here for the rest of my life. And I wanted this moment to stretch on for eons to come. The warm, early-morning sun streaked through her slatted blinds, lighting up her hair and making the deep chestnut brown glow. The gentle swell of her curves was pressed against my body.

Everything about her made me want to never let her go. She was the kind of woman I'd dreamed of one day being at my side. Beautiful. So warm and caring, and with a hint of a potty mouth.

I could imagine coming back from practices or away games to a house filled with smells that made my mouth water—and Jules standing in the kitchen with a body that did the same.

"Let's go out," I blurted out so fast Jules jumped in my arms.

"We've been out plenty of times."

"Yeah, I know but there's somewhere I want to show you."

"Where?"

"A special place."

"I'm at B&B this afternoon."

"No problem, I can pick you up from there or meet you at T-Sweets."

"We're going to T-Sweets? I love that place."

"No, we're going somewhere even better, but it's nearby." Everyone on campus flocked to T-Sweets. It had taken the old real estate advice of location, location, location to heart and found itself a prominent spot right on one of the main streets off campus, but that didn't mean it had the perfect ice cream. That was reserved for Fire and Ice, a place I'd found a few blocks away, and I wanted to take Jules there. Keep the intrigue high and show her the special spot. Where else could you order an ice cream sundae and s'mores at your table? It was new, and once winter set in people would be all over the place, but for now, it would be a special place just for us.

"Sounds like a date." She laid on her side with her head propped up on her arm. Her hair was all over the place and her eyes looked even bigger without her glasses on. Eyelashes framed those beautiful chocolate eyes currently raking their way up and down my body.

"It sure does." I kissed the tip of her nose.

This was a perfect moment, the kind they make slow motion in a movie so you get every excruciating detail of the action. Her beauty was heart-stopping. The kind where you know someone inside and out, and everything about them only takes what you already liked to the next level. She was the kind of girl you didn't come back from. The kind who'd always have a place in your heart to keep you warm on those nights alone long after she'd kicked you to the curb because she deserved better than you.

But I was here now, and I'd keep the fires going as long as I could.

CHAPTER 24

BERK

Jules kicked me out at ten saying she had homework to do, which was about right because I had some papers that weren't going to write themselves, no matter how long I tried to type using only my mind. We had the day off practice to recover. A chance to rest up before Coach brought down the hammer for even more drills once we were back on the field.

After closing my notebooks, I jogged downstairs. The house was quiet, which meant LJ and Marisa weren't here.

Two days away from Jules would be torture. Maybe I could sweet talk her into a care package filled with her newly baked treats. She didn't have to know what I'd be doing while I ate those cookies. Damn, I was becoming a baked goods perv. And it was all her fault.

Keyton looked up from his sketchpad, pencil stilling against the textured paper. "What's with your grin? Has TLG finally returned?"

"No, I've got no idea." I should probably take the letter out of the mailbox or write her an updated one. I'd swapped out the letter a couple times since the first unanswered one, but I needed to write a new one after last night. "I haven't checked today."

"Look at you. There was a time you'd plow over anyone to yank open that mailbox."

I shrugged. "Things change."

"Was that you coming back this morning after an early run or did you stay out all night?" He went back to sketching.

"When you moved in, did that start up a curfew I didn't know about?"

"Nope, just wondering how long we'll need to wait before we can give you crap about charging across the street with Jules last night, and maybe score some extra cookies. Those peanut butter chocolate chunk cookies were so damn good I had an out-of-body experience. You two have been doing this little dance for a long time. Plus, I won the bet." He grinned, pumping one arm over his head triumphantly.

"You made a bet on whether or not I'd hook up with Jules?"

"LJ swore you'd crack at the end of last semester. Marisa said it would be the first week of classes." He looked up from his drawing. "I said you'd hold back as long as possible. Seeing you blazing out of here dragging Jules behind you like you were a second from banging her on the living room floor, I'm surprised you lasted as long as you did."

"It's official, you all freaking suck."

"We know. But that's what roommates are for, right?"

I grumbled and glared.

"You working out today?"

I cracked my neck. "Do I have to?"

"Only if you want to play tomorrow."

"Shit." Coach's edict about getting in even a light twenty before game day was coming back to haunt me. "Do you still need to go? I need to get in a session this afternoon. I've got a date tonight."

"I already went this morning." He closed his sketchpad. "But I can spot you."

"Meet back down here in five."

Keyton and I headed over to the gym with the guitar he didn't play.

"Do you actually play, and you're just super embarrassed or something?"

He set it down against the wall in the locker room.

"No, I need to take it somewhere after this."

"We'll be expecting you to pull a Johannsen and serenade us all by the end of the year."

"Not on your life. Do you want to work out or not?"

We blazed through the workout along with a few other guys. Even more poured in as we were leaving. After we finished the workout, I grabbed a shower and Keyton slunk off with the guitar he didn't actually play.

Back home, I rushed through all my assignments to get ready for my date with Jules. Shaking out one of the button-downs hanging up in my closet, I wondered if Jules would like it.

I opened the front door and my phone vibrated. Smiling, I pulled it out and my smile dropped. A message flashed on my screen.

ALEXIS: I might be in a little bit of trouble...

Shit. Maybe I could make this quick. I headed back inside.

"Forgot your wallet?" Keyton looked up from the books spread out all over the kitchen table.

"No, my backpack."

"I thought you were walking to get ice cream."

I rushed upstairs to grab my backpack without another word. The last thing I needed was to go over yet again, why I couldn't just abandon Alexis.

ME: Where are you?

This couldn't keep happening, but I didn't know how to fix it. How to get Alexis to see she didn't need to keep going out with these loser guys. She was worth so much more than that. But she couldn't see it, no matter how much love and attention her mom and dad showed her. If anything, it made her pull back even more.

And I felt that, deep in my bones, I knew what it was like to not believe anything good was real. Hell, look at Jules. I could practically feel the countdown timer ticking above my head, but that didn't mean I'd go out of my way to fuck things up. For Alexis, she was like a damn magnet for shady shit she had no business going near.

My phone vibrated in my cupholder. A name flashed up on the screen. Mason. And the message rolled in. My heart pounded. I tore my eyes off the glowing screen and back onto the road. Just my luck, I'd crash when I finally had an answer about my mom. I pulled over into the emergency lane on the highway, my leg bouncing up and down. I needed to find Alexis, but if he had information for me, I needed that now.

MASON: I have a new lead. I've got a last known address in Pittsburgh fourteen years ago in March.

That was less than a year after she left me. I'd been shifted to so many homes by then. Emergency placements where I'd barely had time to learn the names of the other kids in the houses and the amount of stuff I owned dwindled as each placement meant another thing stolen, lost, or left behind. I rubbed my knuckles along the center of my chest, like I could massage away the thudding pain like a muscle cramp from lifting too much.

MASON: I might need more money.

ME: There's no more money. I don't have anything left.

MASON: Then I'll have to improvise. It might take me some extra time. I'll get back to you with the outcome soon.

I squeezed my phone, seething, and slammed my hand against the dashboard.

I'd already put my future in jeopardy by giving him the money I had. Waiting another year when Mom could be out there wasn't an option. I needed to know now, before I was drafted, before I was a professional football player, if she loved me. If she'd ever loved me at all before dropping me off on my dad's doorstep like a Dear John letter gone wrong. Dropping me off on my birthday with the last wrapped present I'd ever received. I'd been booted from my foster family with Alexis after two months. Two weeks before Christmas. No, I needed to know now.

When you achieved anything big, hit any level of fame and fortune, people from your past came crawling out of the woodwork. I needed to know now, before I had anything for someone to want to take a piece of, that Mom cared. Now, before there was any kind of agenda based on what she could get from me... If she found me because she saw me on TV, it wouldn't be the same.

Otherwise, I'd always wonder.

And that was my night going from spectacular to bad to even worse.

With a shaky breath, I switched to a different message, trying to cool my rising anger.

ME: Running a little late. I'll be there as soon as I can.

JULES: Okay, just let me know if you need to reschedule.

ME: No, I've got an errand to do and then I'll be there.

I'd make it up to Jules and then it would all be okay. I just needed to clean a few things up, namely my sister, who couldn't keep herself out of trouble.

———

I CLIMBED THE THREE SETS OF STAIRS AND BURST INTO THE apartment. A guy's head whipped up and I charged at him, tackling him around the waist and taking him to the ground. The anger clouded out the panic at what Alexis might have gotten herself into this time.

Grabbing onto the front of his shirt, I slammed him back

to the floor. He wrapped his hands around my wrists, trying to throw me off.

"Where the fuck is she?" I growled.

His eyes widened and he shook beneath me. "Who?"

"Don't screw with me. Alexis. She said you wouldn't let her leave. Where is she?"

"The redhead?"

Was this asshole that dumb? "Yes, the redhead. Where is she?"

He let go of my wrist and pointed a shaky finger down a darkened hallway to the right. "I got home from work after a twelve-hour shift and there's some random chick in my apartment. I asked her who the hell she was and she ran into the bathroom."

I shoved him back down again and got up.

"She's been in there for hours. My roommate brought her home. He left, won't be home until the morning, and I don't know what the hell is going on, but I've got to piss," he called out from the floor.

Not paying attention to his bullshit, I knocked on the one closed door in the hallway.

"Go away. I called my brother; he'll be here any minute."

"Alexis, it's me."

The bathroom door cracked open and she stared at me through the crack. "You're here!" She threw the door open and hugged me with her hands away from my body. "You came."

"You told me you needed my help. Of course I came."

The distinct, acrid smell of nail polish wafted from the bathroom.

"Let me get my stuff." She bounced back inside like I was picking her up from a day at school, not from nearly beating the shit out of a guy who she'd said wouldn't let her leave the bathroom.

She screwed the cap on her nail polish bottle, careful of her fingers.

"You were painting your nails?"

"What else was I supposed to do while I was stuck in here?" She stood in front of me with her bag looped over her shoulder.

"I don't know. Maybe leave?" I wrapped my finger around her arm and pulled her toward the front door.

The guy who I'd nearly knocked out stood across the living room. "Sorry about that, man."

"Always the redheads," he muttered under his breath before bolting back down the hallway we'd cleared. The bathroom door slammed before we got out the front door.

The walk to my car was in dead silence. It was already late and Jules had to be wondering where the hell I was.

"Alexis, I could've killed that guy in there."

"Unlikely. Maybe a black eye or something."

I tightened my grip on the steering wheel. "And you think that would be okay? Some dude comes home from work after a long day and we fuck that long day up even more."

"You're overreacting. Thank you for coming to get me." She blew on her nails.

"Are you serious right now?"

She jumped at the boom of my words. "I'm sorry, okay. I didn't know who the guy was. I figured maybe he broke in or something, so I freaked and ran into the bathroom."

"For hours."

"Then he was pissed so I thought the best thing to do was wait for reinforcements to arrive."

I dragged my fingers through my hair and grabbed my phone.

"Who are you calling?"

"I'm late for a date right now and am late because I was rushing to you. I can't keep doing this, Alexis. I can't."

She gently took my phone from me and tucked it under

her leg. "No texting and driving; it's not safe. I won't do it again. I promise." She turned in her seat and pressed her palms together, the hostility draining from her words. "I overreacted. I get that and I'm sorry."

"Me coming to your rescue isn't helping. And I won't always be there to do it. You've got to start making better choices for yourself."

"You just don't want to help me anymore." Her voice was mouse squeak small.

"I want you to not need help anymore. One day you're going to get yourself into a situation even I can't help you out of. Stop trying to force yourself down a bad path."

"And what path should I be on?" She folded her arms across her chest, nails out, wouldn't want to smudge.

"Any path. Go to school. Get a job. Something."

She tilted her head to the side. "Will you help me?"

"Help you?"

"We can look up some college programs. Applications should be available for next year right now. We can sit down and hash it all out."

"You're being serious?" If she figured out her life, or at least got off this self-destructive path, it would keep me from worrying so much when I did get drafted. What if I ended up on the other side of the country? Even if I didn't, I'd be crisscrossing the coasts. If she was serious, I couldn't let this chance go.

"Super serious. School could be good for me." She crossed her heart and held up her hand palm out. "If you help me, I'll do it."

"Okay, but if we do this, you have to follow through."

"One hundred percent." She pulled out my phone and started googling. "My phone's dead." She looked at me with sincerity in her eyes. "I can get there with your help, big bro."

And she knew once she pulled that card out I'd do anything for her. Getting her set up on a path would take one more worry off my plate. It would keep me from needing to make hours-long trips to random neighborhoods to rescue Alexis.

And maybe she'd finally be safe and let herself have a future.

CHAPTER 25
JULES

"Aww, that apron's adorable." Avery pushed a baker's rack filled with ten trays of donuts to proof toward the oven.

The apron was made from a vintage fabric with a cherry pattern on it and had a red frill around the edges. "I bought it at a farmers market over the summer."

"It's perfect. What are you making today?"

"Black Forest cupcakes. After we film today, I wanted to give that a shot before I head out."

Max strolled in. "These videos are freaking gold."

"Don't you have clients or something? You're always here." Avery latched the oven door.

Max leaned back against the counter and picked up one of the molded chocolate pumpkins from a baking tray. "'Appointment only' means I set my own schedule and only have to deal with people when it's absolutely necessary." Her bright blue tank showed off her full sleeve of tattoos on one arm, the colors of the ink matching her hair.

"Aren't you freezing?" The short sleeves we wore at B&B were bad enough. I'd die showing that much skin.

"The ovens in my cramped back-of-house are like a

furnace. Plus, all my crazy creations burn a lot of brain power." She tapped the side of her head.

"Your poor clients." Avery blew her hair out of her face, fixing her ponytail.

"Rich people love eccentricity. It's my number-one selling point. They feel like a rebel when they walk into my shop. They get a cake with a look and taste like no one else has ever gotten before. Plus, I serve shots at my tastings." She winked, pulled a flask out of her boot, and took a swig.

"You provide the full-service experience." I dipped a spoon into my batter and tasted it. *Salmonella eat your heart out!*

"Hell yeah, I do. And if after a few shots they decide to throw an extra tier onto the cake, we'll that's better for everyone, don't you think?" Her grin was contagious. She was nothing but trouble, in the very best of ways.

"We're going to film two today and be sneaky. We'll pretend the one for later is live, since the weather is supposed to be terrible next week. Then you can work on your recipe." Avery slid some baking trays onto the counter as I measured out the ingredients we'd need for today.

"And trying out a few things off-screen means we won't have to go through the soufflé debacle again."

Our attempt at a chocolate soufflé had made some pretty delicious chocolate syrup.

"The viewers were entertained."

"They were? At us failing?"

Max hopped up on the counter, kicking her feet. Her hair was rainbow-colored now and matched the piercing just below her nostrils. "Loved every second of it and want you guys to try it again. You haven't been checking out the social media profiles?"

I shook my head so fast my neck hurt. "All you said I needed to do was show up in the videos. Nothing about checking on the profiles after the content was uploaded."

That was the only way I could keep myself from spiraling into a panic attack at the thought of hundreds of people watching me, even though I'm sure most of them were watching Avery.

"Everyone's super supportive and blown away by you two."

"It's totally cheating calling you a home cook, but what's a little deception between friends." Max snapped her gum and winked at me.

"Can you get off my counters please? Who knows where your ass has been."

"I can tell you exactly where it's been, Mrs. Cunning." Max hopped down and grabbed a donut covered in chocolate and rainbow sprinkles off the rack of newly frosted ones. I was sensing a theme.

"No man candy to watch you today?"

"No, but I did boot him out of bed early this morning." I kept my head down, mixing the batter we were prepping for the after shots later.

Max dropped her donut on the counter and nearly knocked me off my feet with her shove to my shoulder. "Shut the front door! I was ready to take bets you were going to fight that until the day you died. Hell, yes, I knew you had it in you!" She grabbed her donut and smiled at me.

"Is that why you're walking funny?" Avery laughed and bumped me with her hip.

"You two are the worst."

"Tell us all about that tasty dick you got." Max hopped back up on the counter.

My jaw cracked through the floor and was headed straight for the basement.

"Not in front of the baby, Max," Avery laugh-hissed and shoved her off the counter.

The camera crew interrupted their quest for more details

—not that Max would've been deterred, but Avery sent her back to her own shop to meet clients she had coming.

"She's a handful."

"Whoever snags her heart is going to have their work cut out for them."

"More like their balls cut off for them." Avery exhaled sharply and shook her head. "Maybe one day she'll let it happen."

The lights flicked on like a solar flare burning our retinas, and we were off.

————

I wasn't going to check the time again. Looking at the clock on my phone didn't somehow magically make it speed up. Berk had said he'd be a little late. I crossed my arms over my chest and rocked back and forth from my heels to my toes, craning my neck to look past the people walking up to T-Sweets. Was I supposed to meet him somewhere else? Inside? We hadn't finalized the location, so I thought this was where I should be. Maybe I'd gotten my wires crossed.

My half-smiles with people I made eye contact with made me more self-conscious with each passing minute. Had I gotten the time wrong? I checked my messages. Still nothing. But I couldn't help but catch the time at the top of the screen.

Twenty-eight minutes. It was twenty-eight minutes after we were supposed to meet. I could call Elle and ask her to have Nix find out from one of the guys if something had happened to Berk, but that ventured into overly-attached girl-friend territory—not that I was his girlfriend. Besides, it was only twenty-eight minutes.

The tiny pinpricks of insecurity clawed at the door in my mind labeled Insecure as Fuck. We'd slept together last night. I'd danced for him and we'd banged so hard the walk over to

B&B and T-Sweets had been with ginger, gentle steps. And now he hadn't responded to my calls and texts.

Were they all over at the Brothel, waiting to laugh at me when I finally got home? Were they taking bets as to what time I'd show up, how long I'd wait before realizing it was all a joke?

I squeezed my eyes shut and held my fist up to my forehead. *Don't do it, Jules. Don't go there. He's not blowing you off. He didn't sleep with you only to walk away laughing this morning. That's not what's happening. Just stop.*

Taking a deep breath, I opened my eyes and looked around at everyone getting in the very last scoops of ice cream before T-Sweets shut down for the winter. They were laughing and smiling, eating delicious ice cream. A few people were making out. I'd wanted that to be me. Maybe not the making out part—I didn't need to be around ice cream with Berk, making out and having everyone staring at us and wondering what the hell he was doing there with me. Six-pack abs meets Pillsbury dough girl.

This isn't helping, Jules.

I sent him another message.

ME: Hey, I'm here at T-Sweets. But it's a while after we were supposed to meet. I'm heading home. I hope you're okay.

After ten minutes of no response, I left and went home, kicking rocks like Charlie Brown the whole way. What did I do when there were too many feelings? I pulled out my trusty recipe cards and got to work. *Maybe he'd been mangled in a car wreck. Maybe he was knee deep in co-eds. Maybe he'd been abducted by aliens. Maybe I was a freaking idiot.*

At nearly one am my phone vibrated on the counter. My head snapped up from the kitchen table and I peeled a cupcake wrapper off the side of my face. Taking a deep breath, I got up and checked the message.

BERK: I'm so fucking sorry. I had to do a thing and it

went way later than I expected and I didn't have a charger.
I'll make it up to you for sure.

 BERK: Some next-level making it up to you.

 BERK: Shit, you're probably asleep. Sorry if I woke you.

 BERK: Talk tomorrow.

 BERK: I miss you.

I smiled at the small glowing screen and climbed back into bed with my phone tucked under my pillow. Good thing I hadn't let my imagination run wild. I hadn't gone into a panic spiral. Well, staring at my bedroom ceiling at one am wasn't exactly cool as a cucumber. But I drifted off to sleep, cuddled up against my pillow that still smelled like him.

———

I SMOOTHED OUT MY SKIRT AS THE FALL AIR NIPPED AT MY uncovered legs. The cinnamon sugar smell wafted up from my arms. I balanced the plastic container with the lid securely snapped on in my hands as I climbed the steps to The Brothel.

Freshly baked muffins for breakfast, that was totally normal. It wasn't a desperate attempt to make sure he was okay. Besides, I wanted to see him, and I wasn't going to wait around for him to show up. I needed to take charge, right? Be proactive. Stop letting life happen to me.

Be confident for a change.

I knocked, but it was so freaking early, I didn't want to wake everyone else. Slipping the key out of the spot behind the porch light, I checked over my shoulder making sure their new hiding spot wouldn't be discovered. Who was I kidding? The only person out this early on campus was the mail man. Opening the door, I said 'hello'.

I walked into his place like he always walked into mine. Climbing the stairs, I tugged at the hem of my skirt. An honest-to-god skirt. While it was only walking across the street, it was the first time I'd worn a skirt with my legs out, other than the engagement party, since I was probably ten years old. I wanted him to see me in it, and if he was promising next-level making it up to me, why not make it easier on both of us?

They weren't salted caramel cookies, but I knew he'd like these. I couldn't wait to see his face when he took a bite. I loved the sounds he made when he ate whatever I made. Who didn't love some freshly baked coffee cake muffins first thing in the morning? And if I was lucky, maybe we'd get in some early morning cuddles. He'd pull me into his bed and we could doze and play all morning until he had to leave for the team bus for his game. With a quick knock, I opened the door, smiling wide.

"Morning, sunshine, I thought I'd—"

Only it wasn't Berk in his bed. It was a girl. A petite redhead with freckles, a serious case of bedhead, and no pants on. And she was wearing Berk's t-shirt. The faded FU one that was fraying around the bottom of the sleeve.

"Who are you?" I asked even though I didn't want to know the answer. I didn't want to know the name of the girl who'd just punched a hole right through the little fantasy I'd been dreaming up in my head.

"I'm Alexis. Are you lost?"

The tunnel vision started, like I'd been punted down the deepest well on campus. 'Alexis' came out slowed down, like someone was playing the entire world at half speed. This was Alexis. This was the girl I'd baked a cake for. The girl all the guys said was bad news, but Berk kept talking to. All through our letters, after the engagement party and after two nights ago he was still not only talking to Alexis—but apparently banging her too.

He'd stood me up last night to bang his ex—or current —girlfriend.

I couldn't breathe. Air stalled in my lungs like my head was being held underwater and I was clawing for the surface.

The burn was sharp and slamming at my ribs. A small wheeze made it past my lips.

She slipped out of bed with her arms crossed over her chest. She was small. Skinny with long legs that made her appear statuesque even at her height. And she looked totally pissed off that I was there. "Who are you?"

My chest was so tight every attempt to breathe created a new crack. If I moved too quickly I was going to shatter.

I needed to get out of there before my humiliation was complete.

"I'm no one." I spun around and rushed back down the hallway. The bathroom door opened as my foot hit the top step. I wouldn't break down. Not here. I'd save that for once I was on the other side of the front door. A complete collapse of the brave Jules I'd tried to be. She was gone.

"Jules?"

My fingers wrapped around the banister and I was frozen like someone had laid down an entire tube of Crazy Glue.

It was Berk's voice. And everything froze.

CHAPTER 26
JULES

"Jules, what are you doing here so early?" He didn't sound angry or defensive. More like pleasantly surprised. His arms wrapped around me and he kissed the back of my neck. This didn't make any sense. Shouldn't he be trying to rush me away, or coming up with excuses?

"I baked you some coffee cake muffins." I lifted the container, still not turning around.

"You're the best, you know that?" He reached over my shoulder and took the container from my hand and laced his fingers through mine. "Since you're here, there's someone I want you to meet."

He tugged on my hand, freeing me from my self-imposed staircase prison.

On numb legs, I let him lead me back toward his room.

He pushed on his bedroom door and I half expected what I'd seen inside to be a figment of my imagination. Maybe I'd made it all up because I was incapable of letting myself be happy. Maybe there wasn't a half-naked girl in his bed. The door opened fully and there she was looking pissed with her phone in her hand.

Berk grinned. "Alexis, this is Jules."

Her gaze flicked to us standing in the doorway like we were an inconvenience to her already shitty morning.

"Jules, this is Alexis." He held out his hand, pointing at the girl on her phone. "My sister."

The words went into my head, but somehow they got scrambled and didn't make a bit of sense.

"Your sister?"

He nodded and flashed a sleepy smile, rubbing his eye.

"Alexis is your sister?" I pointed at her.

The depth of her frown increased and she glared at me.

"Yeah, she got stranded last night and I had to go pick her up."

"Alexis is your sister."

He turned and looked at me with his eyebrows scrunched together.

"I know we don't look alike." His sigh was a long-suffering one, like he'd had to have this same conversation more than once, the same as me with Laura. "But she's my sister."

"On a good day," Alexis grumbled from the bed.

"That's not something you need to throw in every time I say it, Alexis." He said her name pointedly, like he'd had to tell her a million times to stop touching his stuff or stay on her side of the car. "And will you put some pants on? What if the guys wake up and see you?" Berk rummaged through his drawers.

"I don't know, a couple of them are pretty hot. Especially the new one. What's his name again?"

"You're not dating any of my roommates." He flung a pair of sweatpants at her, hitting her in the face.

"Who said anything about dating?" She grinned.

"Not cool. Don't even go there. Pants."

"Not like I'd do anything with any of your goody-two-shoes friends, Berkley." She rolled her eyes and shoved her legs into the sweatpants.

"At least none of my friends would strand me a hundred miles from anywhere."

"But that's what keeps life exciting. Plus, I have you to bail me out." She threw on a devil-may-care smile. "That's what big *brothers* are for, right?" She stressed the word brother like it was a concession she was giving, calling him that.

"What about next year? What about if I get traded to Seattle or LA or I'm at an away game and I'm hundreds or thousands of miles away? Then what?"

She shrugged.

They fought just like I'd imagined a normal brother and sister would, like in TV shows. God knows I wasn't a good person to evaluate normal sibling relationships. But... he hadn't stood me up to bang someone else.

I wasn't the other woman.

Alexis was his *sister!*

Finally snapping out of the temporary paralysis that had me stuck in the doorway, I crossed the room and held out my hand to Alexis, Berk's sister. His little sister. A giddy laugh bubbled up and escaped my lips.

"I'm Jules. It's so nice to finally meet you. Berk said you liked my cake."

She looked at me like I was a complete psycho, but put down her phone and shook my hand.

"Ah, you're the cake girl. I wondered which one of his fuck buddies he'd gotten to do that for him."

Wow, she was certainly... rude.

"Dude, Alexis, don't be an ass. And she's not a fuck buddy." He cut me a sly grin. "And I paid for that cake." The baked good smell filled the room when he lifted the lid off the container and wolfed one down. "I'll make some coffee. These deserve coffee." He held up another one triumphantly.

A moment of panic shot through me at being left alone

with his sister, who was fascinated by anything in the room that wasn't me. "I'll come help you."

I walked down the steps still trying to catch my breath. In the span of ten minutes, almost a year's worth of pain and doubt had been erased. Berk didn't have some bad news chick he banged every so often that everyone hated. He had a little sister who got into trouble who he had to rescue, and all the guys hated....

Her being a little sister probably had something to do with it, as well as her sunshine and gumdrops personality, but she wasn't sleeping with Berk, so that was a huge plus in my book.

I opened the cabinets to get a couple mugs. I was jolted out of the running calculus in my brain by the rough pads of Berk's fingertips skimming along the backs of my legs.

"Don't think I didn't notice that you wore a skirt," he breathed against the back of my neck, nipping at my shoulder. His hands were joined by the hard press of his erection through his sweatpants. "Did you wear that for me?"

I clutched the mugs to my chest and nodded.

"Ready for some next-level apologizing?" He dropped a kiss to the crook of my neck. The soft but insistent pressure of his lips made my stomach flip.

A cascade of pleasure danced along my spine. The weight of his body pinned me against the counter. He inched his hands higher, giving himself a little space between our bodies to cup and squeeze my ass.

I held onto the edge of the sink, trying to keep myself upright. "I'm always ready for you." The words were shaky and hungry for his touch. I craved it like my next sugar high.

"Berk, please don't bang your girlfriend in the kitchen." An annoyed voice broke the trance we were in.

He jerked back and I whipped around, smoothing my skirt down to make sure I wasn't flashing Alexis. Berk's sister.

His red-haired, looked-nothing-like-him sister. My gaze jumped between Berk and Alexis.

With mugs of coffee poured for everyone, Berk gave the run down on what had happened last night.

Alexis's gaze was laser focused on the side of my face. Every time I caught her out of the corner of my eye, her unflinching gaze was on me. It was a little unnerving. Did she not like me? Was she overprotective? Had she disliked Berk's other girl-friends? Was I his girlfriend? Had he had other girlfriends? He hadn't corrected her when she'd called me his girlfriend!

The questions raced through my head, whipping even faster around like a roller derby championship.

Doors opened and closed upstairs and footsteps hammered on the floor above our heads as the rest of the house woke up.

"You live across the street?" Alexis picked up the coffee cake muffin and poked at it like she was inspecting it for poison.

"That crap shack across the street is what I call home."

"It's way less crappy than it used to be," Berk butted in. "I've helped her fix a few things."

Alexis scrunched her shoulders up and shot me a squinty-eyed half smile. "How adorable." She took a bite and there was a flash as the brown sugar and cinnamon crunch hit her tongue. Her eyes widened and even though she fought warming up to me, she couldn't beat the sugar siren.

That was the look I lived for.

A thud hit the stairs like someone had been thrown down each step.

"Do I smell a Jules special delivery?" Keyton rounded the base of the stairs and tossed his duffle beside the front door.

"Coffee cake muffins."

Keyton grabbed me and pulled me in for a hug, kissing the side of my face. "You're our savior. Stale bus bagels with those tiny little pods of cream cheese weren't going to cut it today."

"Could you not paw my girl?" Berk brushed him aside and tucked me in under his arm.

"Your girl?" Alexis and I said it at the same time.

I stared up at him.

He broke his glare at Keyton and looked down at me. "Of course. I mean, if you want." The uncertainty in his gaze made him even more adorable.

"I do." I rested my hand against his chest, the muscles bunching under my fingertips.

Sneaking a glance to the side, I could see Alexis trying to light my hair on fire with her eyes.

He leaned down and pressed his mouth against my ear. His breath whispered against my skin and sent shivers down my spine. "When I get back, we're going to make this official, Frenchie." He palmed my ass, giving it a squeeze. "But, I've got to go pack."

"I can help."

"Stay here and enjoy your muffins. You can keep Alexis out of trouble." He let me go and raced back upstairs.

Turning like I was in a horror movie, I slid back into a chair.

"You're Berk's new girlfriend." She drummed her fingers against her mug.

"Seems that way. Are you in school too?"

"No." She took a sip, completely content not to speak another word to me.

"Taking a gap year?" I added more sugar to my coffee. And cream. Okay, so it was sugar and creamer with a splash of coffee at this point.

"No."

Alrighty then. "What do you think your chances are, Keyton?"

He spun around and sloshed hot coffee on his hand. "Sonofa—"

I hopped up and grabbed a kitchen towel and helped him dry it off. "Sorry."

"It's my fault for being a dumbass; I zoned out."

"Thinking about the game?"

He evaded my gaze. "Something like that. What did you ask?"

"How's the season going? Do you think you'll make it to the championship again?"

"Our chances are good. We're solid, and after last game, Coach has the defense ready to push the other team into the parking lot once the ref blows the whistle."

Berk came downstairs and walked me out the front door with his backpack slung over his shoulder. The rest of the guys flowed around us and into Berk's car.

"If she steals anything…" LJ glared at Berk.

"She won't. Will you, Alexis?"

Alexis stood with her arms crossed at the top of the steps. She rolled her eyes and inspected her nails. "No, I won't."

He turned back to me and cupped my shoulders with his hands, rubbing his thumbs in circles that made me feel like I was in my own romance movie—not the one where I was the plucky sidekick doling out advice, but the one where I got the guy. The insanely hot, adorable guy who looked at me like Berk did.

A horn blast broke the moment and Berk *thumped* the roof of his car.

"You'll watch the game?"

"Every second."

"Good. I'll miss you." He took my chin between his thumb and finger and laid a kiss on me. This was a gasping-for-breath, forget-your-name kind of kiss that only reminded me of his promise and exactly what we'd done two nights before. "And I'm counting down the days until I'm back here. Will you wear a skirt for me again?"

"I only have the one."

"I don't care if it's made out of toilet paper. I want to see those legs."

I laughed against his lips.

With one more planted kiss, he let me go and jogged around to the front of his car.

"Bye, Jules."

"Bye, Jules," LJ and Keyton chorused through their open windows.

Waving to the car as they pulled away, I crossed my arms over my chest. Now my bare legs felt a lot more naked without Berk there. Maybe Alexis and I could hang out.

I turned and the door slammed before I could even take a step in that direction, so I headed home.

Sitting at my desk, I grabbed some stationery I hadn't touched in months. Careful not to pull the color I'd used with Berk, I wrote out a message to Alexis.

Dear Alexis,

I'm so glad we were finally able to meet. Sorry for waking you up this morning! I know how much I hate it when a random person just barges into the room where I'm sleeping with a box of coffee cake muffins and stares. That was my attempt at a joke, sorry again.

If you're going to be around for a while, I'd love to meet up sometime. Or I could make you a cupcake version of the cake I made for your birthday. I was so happy to hear you liked it. I'll stop now, but here's my phone number if you ever want to hang out. I'd like to do something special for Berk this semester with all the craziness going on with football, so if you have any ideas, let me know!

JULES

Sealing it up, I darted back across the street, hoping she'd answer the door.

Alexis opened the door and immediately crossed her arms.

"I wanted to give this to you." I held out the note to her and kept my smile as relaxed as I could.

She stared at it with an eyebrow raised. "Is it an invitation to your eighth birthday party or something? Who writes letters anymore?"

I swallowed, my throat tight like I was standing in front of a judge. I wanted Alexis to like me. She mattered to Berk and was obviously an important person in his life.

"There are a few things I wanted to say and I thought it would be easier this way."

She plucked the envelope from my fingers and closed the door before I could say another word.

Well, that could've gone better.

CHAPTER 27
BERK

The temperature had dropped so quickly, the rain felt like needles shooting straight through the face mask of my helmet. Our breath hung in clouds in front of our faces at the final line of scrimmage.

Austin shouted out the call and back went the snap. The play was over in seconds. We were already up by ten, but now it was officially over.

We raced down the tunnel, sweat, grass, and mud caked onto us.

"Who invited the freaking hurricane to the game?" Austin shook out his hair like a dog, splattering me.

"Keep that up and next game, I open a pocket for the defense to take your ass out."

He held up his hands in surrender.

"How's your arm?"

He rotated it and held onto his shoulder pad. "Feels good. Perfect. I could finally open up out there because someone gave me the breathing room I needed."

Guilt still blindsided me that I'd never noticed how much Nix's arm was killing him. It had been painful enough that he'd made the choice not to go pro. I'd seen him take a few hits and get drilled into the ground more than once, usually when I was hit by three guys gunning for me, but he always got up.

"Hell, yeah!" LJ rushed up and jumped on me, nearly knocking me to the ground, his uniform just as muddy and wet as everyone else's.

"Nice touchdown."

"At least I've got something coaches can look at for this season." His grin barely fit on his face. "Marisa was probably freaking out at home." He got a far off look in his eye.

"And then she'd bust your balls about not doing it sooner."

LJ nodded. "True, she would. But that's our thing."

"We've noticed," Keyton popped in to add that right along with me.

Everyone showered up after Coach's post-game talk that was less fire-and-brimstone and more fiery poker.

In my room, I lay in bed staring up at the ceiling and thinking of only one thing. Jules. She'd worn a skirt. I wanted another taste of her. I wanted those soft and supple legs wrapped around my waist.

How running my hands along her skin made my heart race like I was going for the world record in the hundred-yard dash.

How she looked at me and saw so much of me I never let anyone else see.

How with my arms wrapped around her, I felt safe, and the closest I'd ever come to having a home.

She was the most beautiful thing in the world to me and it scared me more than losing the next game or not making the draft. Because I'd never had anything as beautiful as her in my life. And that made it so much harder. It would end; it always did. She'd see something in me that showed her I was a fucked-up kid who didn't know how to do this adult thing, and she'd find a guy who did and said all the right things all the time and could give her exactly what she needed.

The engagement party had been fun, but I'd never felt completely comfortable, always worried I'd do something to embarrass her. It wasn't something Jules liked now, but what about later, once she was over her college rebellious phase?

Would I be the odd man out without their private school upbringings and trust funds to fall back on? Where we'd come from was so different. She was first class and I was steerage all the way—hell, I was the guy shoveling coal into the furnace with barely a possession to my name. What would happen when she finally realized that?

My phone buzzed beside me.

JULES: Great game. Sorry if you're already asleep or out partying or something.

Her sweetness distilled into a single text. I called her back before I finished reading the message.

"Are you out partying?" she asked.

"Only if you consider a batch of caramel crunch cookies and my textbooks a party."

"With you, that's definitely a party."

"Studying hard?"

"Not as hard as I should. I'm going to work out a little bit to get the knots out of my shoulders."

"We can work out together when I get back. I'm sure you're a much better gym buddy than Keyton." Jules being all hot and sweaty before we got hot and sweaty made my roomy sweatpants feel like a damn speedo.

"I don't usually go to the gym. It's strictly the pole."

"Why would you say that to me when I'm a couple hundred miles away? Now all I'm thinking of is you in those boy shorts with your thighs wrapped around that pole, spinning around."

"I never should've told you."

"No, you should've told me earlier. All this time you were keeping secrets from me. Promise me there aren't any more."

Her side of the line went so quiet, I checked to make sure the call hadn't dropped.

"No more."

"Good. If you'd told me you were also moonlighting as a go-go dancer, I'd be in a taxi back home right now."

She half-laughed and half-yawned.

"Long day?"

"B&B was crazy. People love watching other people bake. And now I'm the new recipe writer. Apparently, people also like watching me write out the ingredients lists and they turn that into a graphic that flashes up on the screen, so that's been added to my list of duties."

"I'm sure you've got perfect swirly girl penmanship."

"It's nothing special." The words came out stilted. Of course she wouldn't think it was anything special. It was probably the most perfect handwriting known to man. Like TLG. Her handwriting had always been so neat. Never a crooked line or crossed-out misspelling.

"We're recording again tomorrow at three."

"The bus is back on campus at two. I can meet you there."

"You don't have to do that." She powered through another yawn. "It's a long bus ride back."

"Once again, Frenchie, I don't do anything I don't want to do. And I want to see you."

"Okay. I want to see you too." The sleepy droop to her words made me want to pull the covers up and over her, running my fingers through her hair as she slept.

"I won't keep you up. Rest up and I'll see you tomorrow."

"Tomorrow."

———

I PEELED OUT OF THE STADIUM PARKING LOT, BARELY GIVING LJ and Keyton enough time to close their doors.

"Have you placed bets against our team or something this season? You trying to take me out?" Keyton clicked his seatbelt in.

"I'm in a hurry."

"Why? Did Alexis do something to the house? Is Marisa okay?" LJ leaned forward, grabbing onto the headrest of my seat.

I turned, glaring at him. "Jules is filming another one of her videos at B&B and I want to be there to support her."

"Oh." LJ sat back.

I barely came to a complete stop before I ejected both of them.

With seconds to spare, I jumped out at B&B and popped back to where they were filming.

Jules' face lit up. Every light in the place was trained on her, and her eyes glittered with a happiness that made me want to drag her across the table, swipe the baking supplies to the side, and kiss her like she deserved to be kissed.

"Everyone in the comments wants to know why Jules looks like Santa just showed up with a huge sack full of presents." Max manned her station at her laptop behind the scenes. "And now they want to see the hottie."

"How'd they know he's hot?" Jules called out.

"I might've been a bit overly descriptive in my appreciation of his male form." An incoming kitchen towel shower rained down over her.

"Max!"

"We're going for more views, right?" She shrugged and licked the icing off her fingers.

"You might as well go up there before they beat down the door."

"Seriously?" I stared at the lights and cameras. Without my uniform and helmet it wasn't my normal comfort zone.

"Come on up, Berk. You can do some heavy whipping for us and get those view spikes." Avery waved me over.

Jules lifted her chin and smiled and I took the invitation.

"And we've got one of the Fulton U Trojans here." Avery held out her hands in her best showcase model pose.

"Off a big win." Jules grinned up at me and I couldn't help myself. Keeping things as PG as possible, I stole a kiss like a robber in the night, even though I really wanted to throw her over my shoulder and carry her into the closest dark room to sample everything I'd missed over the past two days.

"They're definitely loving you, Big Man." Max rubbed it in from her safe spot behind the camera.

Jules covered my hand with hers.

There was a tightness in my chest. One that wasn't from pain or hurt, but from how hard it was to contain all the feelings she brought out in me. There was the hungry side of me that couldn't wait to get her alone, the proud side of me that wanted nothing more than for her to be in front of these cameras and under the spotlights just like she deserved, and another part of me that couldn't believe she was mine. Even if this didn't last, even if she kicked me to the curb tomorrow, at least I had today. And I wanted to live in this perfect, vanilla-scented moment forever.

"Earth to you two." Avery snapped in front of our grinning faces, breaking the cheek-achingly sweet moment we'd been stuck in. "Let's get baking."

I was tasked with jar opening and heavy mixing. Apparently, there was something going on in the comments section about my gray sweatpants and arm veins. Max chimed in from time to time with the comments coming in until she stopped all together. It seemed my appearance hadn't been the ratings boost she'd been banking on. She closed the laptop and stuck it on the shelf under the counter.

We wrapped everything up and I got to take my girl home with some warm, old-fashioned sour cream donuts. I didn't know they could get any more delicious, but I'd been wrong. Dead freaking wrong.

"You're seriously not going to eat one?"

Jules had the box balanced on her lap.

My mouth watered for two different reasons.

She shook her head. "I'm good. I'll split one with you."

"Split one? Are you insane? I could inhale that entire box on my own."

She rubbed her chin and tapped a finger against her lips. "I made a few of them with extra large holes in the center. How would you feel about a donut blow job?"

I swerved into the other lane.

Jules' arm whipped out and grabbed onto my arm to pull us back.

A horn blared and I held up my hand in a wave of apology. "Are you trying to kill us both?"

She laughed and shook her head. "I didn't think you'd nearly run us off the road."

"I didn't think I'd ever hear the words donut blow job. Looks like Frenchie is full of secrets."

"Nope. Totally boring." She toyed with the edge of the cardboard box.

"Says the pole dancing baker throwing out sex acts involving baked goods."

Cresting on the edge of the speed limit, I got us back to our street in record time.

"That was fast." She brushed her hair out of her face after my Formula One parking job.

"Not nearly fast enough. Out Frenchie. Out right now." I flung open her door and pulled her out of her seat and up the stairs to her place in seconds flat.

We barged into her house like we were on a raid and skidded to a stop when I spotted the half-naked dude walking from the kitchen to the living room. Jules banged into my back.

I glared at him. "Who the fuck are you?"

"Jesus, Nick would you put some freaking pants on. Berk, this is Nick. Nick, this is Berk."

Jules grabbed my hand and dragged me toward the stairs.

"That's Zoe's boyfriend. He's apparently forgotten what pants are."

"Since when do you have a roommate?"

"I've always had a roommate. She was our roommate when Elle lived here, but she never showed up. She's here now with a plus one. Don't worry about him. There's a donut in this box with your name on it."

Her fingers tightened on my t-shirt, pulling me away from the murderous looks I was shooting toward Towel Guy and refocusing my energy toward this little experiment Jules was determined to undertake. Who was I to get in the way of sexual exploration?

CHAPTER 28
JULES

'd never look at a donut the same way again. Before now, I hadn't known blow jobs could be so funny, but Berk sitting on my bed propped up on his hands, watching me with tears of laughter in his eyes, I finally called it.

I burst out laughing and wiped at the tears on my face. My sides hurt and I doubled over, clutching my sides. "Cosmo lied."

Or maybe cake donuts weren't the right type to try this with, or maybe Berk was just too damn big for any further attempts at a donut blow job. "There was an attempt."

"There were three attempts." He motioned to the broken donut pieces sitting in the box, taking a bite of one of the non-dicked dunked donuts.

"I want to give it one more try."

"Jules, seriously? I think we've proven it's not going to work."

"Let me have my fun." I parted my lips, sucking his thick mushroom tip into my mouth.

"Holy shit." He threaded his fingers in my hair, tugging at the roots as I licked him from base to tip. The sweet sugar combined with his own musk created a heady combination I wished I could bottle up.

Every hiss and groan ripped from his throat sent another thrill through me and I squeezed my thighs together as I was kneeling on the floor.

Using my hand to work his velvety erection, I looked up at him.

Our gazes collided and his thigh muscles bunched under my hand.

He jerked his hips back, pulling himself free from my mouth and squeezed the head of his cock. "Fuck, Frenchie your mouth is too damn good. I was a second away from coming."

"Why didn't you?" Who pouted about a guy not coming in her mouth? Me apparently, when it was Berk.

"Because I need to get inside you and I need to wash all this residual sugar off my dick first." A mischievous glint in his eye, he took my hand, helping me up from the floor.

"What do you have in mind?"

What he had in mind was the soapiest, sexiest shower I'd ever had in my life.

I braced one hand against the wall and another on his shoulder.

His fingers sank into the top of my thigh, anchoring my leg over his shoulder as he sucked my clit into his mouth. Each tug on the most sensitive part of me demanded more pleasure, louder moans, and even more gasps.

My knees shook and his arm wrapped around my waist was the only thing keeping me up. I dropped my head back, squeezing my eyes shut at the avalanche of sensations pulsing through my body. My orgasm raced toward me in the rearview mirror, only a split second away from catching me.

And he stopped.

My head snapped down and I stared at him wide-eyed. "What the hell?"

He stood up, teasing my pussy with his fingers.

"Now that we're all clean, it's time to get dirty." He grabbed a towel off the counter and dried me off, taking his time like we had all night. I was ready to come out of my skin, jump on him and nail our bedroom door shut.

Barely wrapping a towel around me, I tugged him into my room without even checking on whether or not the coast was clear.

He laughed, holding his towel around his waist. "In a rush."

I glared and he kicked the door closed.

"It seems someone's eager." He spun me around and pushed me up against the door. Capturing both my hands, he put them over my head and stared into my eyes.

"It's my turn to make it up to you, Frenchie." He kissed and licked along the curve of my neck.

I squeezed my thighs together, ready to explode if he didn't move his attentions a bit lower. My breath came out shuddering and shallow.

"You can make it up to me by getting inside me right now."

"I think you'll like this better." He didn't let go of my hands until I let out every expletive known to man.

With a strength I didn't think anyone had, he lifted me and carried me over to the bed. My sexual torture was only just beginning and I was here for it.

My toes curled and my back arched off the bed. I'd never known sex could be like this—well, I had from the last time Berk drove his cock into me as I clung to him trying to catch my breath, but this was even better.

The noises coming from my mouth were halfway between wounded animal and a bliss so hot it felt like the two of us would be welded together.

Berk's hips pounded against my thighs and his fingers

sank into my flesh, grabbing my ass like I was his only life raft in a raging sea.

Panting, I held onto him as he held onto me.

He collapsed on top of me, ruffling my hair with each breath. His body weight settled over me, not crushing me, completely wrapped up with me. Blanketing me with his warmth. I dropped a kiss on the top of his shoulder.

"You nearly killed me, Frenchie." He lifted his head and brushed the sweaty hair back from my forehead, kissing me. His tender smile sent flutters of happiness through my chest. The light brought out the caramel streaks in his mossy eyes and I was suddenly very happy he'd wanted to have the lights on. I wanted to bask in every moment and not miss a thing.

"Aren't you supposed to be the athlete?" I ran my fingers along his side, tickling him.

He laughed and jerked away, tugging himself free from my body.

We both groaned. My heated flesh ached and throbbed in the very best of ways. In a way that made me want to grab him and pull him right back on top of me.

He got up and ducked out of the room to get rid of the condom.

I rolled onto my side, not reaching for the blanket like I normally would've. He'd already seen all of me and there was nothing about our session that made me think he had a problem with it. He walked back in—I swear, dick first, with a cloth in his hand. "I'm an athlete, but you're a next-level girl, Jules. I've got to step up my game."

"What's that for?"

"Taking my game to the next level." He grabbed my ankle and pulled me down to the edge of the bed.

"I don't follow."

"You will." He ran the warm, wet cloth along the insides of my thighs.

Goosebumps broke out all over my body. I let out a hiss as the cloth rubbed against my clit. "Is this the next level?" The words were choppy and shuddery as the pretense of cleaning me up was punted out the window.

"No, this is." He dropped to his knees and slid his hands under my thighs, anchoring me in place.

And in a flash, his tongue was on me. In me. Everywhere all at once. My hips bucked, but I didn't get far. Damn he was strong. I wasn't exactly a waif. "I thought this was foreplay. We already had sex."

"You think I'd only want to go down on you before sex? Frenchie, I'm ready to eat you any freaking time and any place." And then his tongue did a magical thing that made me forget my name, how to breathe, and what my body felt like when it wasn't attached to a live wire of pleasure.

"Fuck!" I screamed and grabbed onto his hair, holding on for dear life through the sexual tsunami that was Berkley Vaughn.

———

"If you could have one thing in the world right now, what would it be?" Berk brushed my hair back from my face.

He smacked my hand when I snaked it down his stomach through the covers. "Not that. So freaking naughty, Frenchie."

"If I can't have that…" I tapped my finger to my lips and a pang of sadness nudged at my heart. "Books my dad used to read me."

"The Peter Rabbit ones?" He rubbed a messy curl between his fingers.

"You remember that?"

He nuzzled the top of my head. "There's nothing I forget when it comes to you."

"Those ones." Pushing aside the sadness, I focused on right here, right now. "What's the next game I can come to?" I traced my fingers across his chest and my body buzzed and tingled, basking in the afterglow of sex beyond anything we'd done before.

I'd run out of the bathroom practically naked. We'd had wild, crazy, loud sex in a house with other people. And I didn't even care. He was a sexual distraction magician.

"We have a home game in a couple weeks, right before Halloween." His quick squeeze of my ass made me not hate the size of it. It made me sink deeper into his clutches, enjoying the way he didn't seem to want to let go and the way he growled against my neck, making my stomach flip.

"Can I come dressed up?" Lifting my head, I stared up at him, breathless and ready for another round. He had the uncanny ability to make me feel like nothing bad could touch me when I was in his arms.

He skimmed his fingers down my spine.

Goosebumps broke out all over my body and I bit back a moan.

"I have a few things I'd like you to come dressed up as."

"Getting arrested trying to get into an FU game isn't on my list of top tens."

"How do you know what I wanted you to dress up as? Maybe I was going to say a nun." He chuckled. His chest rumbled under my ear.

"Damn, and I wanted to dress up as a stripper. But I think your idea will be a better fit."

"Hold on a second." He wiggled his fingers into my side.

I shoved at him and rolled away laughing. "No take-backsies."

Hopping off the bed, I searched the room and grabbed my robe. Outside of the bed, the floorboards were like ice cubes and a shiver shuddered through me.

"Nun, it is." Triumphantly, I tied the fluffy sash of my robe.

"How about you dress up as a nun for my game and we

can have a private costume party back here?" He propped his head up with his arms, every muscle and vein prominent and tasty.

There wasn't an ounce of fat on him. Tanned. Solid. Athletic. He could've been a sculpture brought to life, and he was here with me.

Behind these curtains and in these walls, everything else faded away and the voices in my head—the ones that had been there for so long I wasn't sure if they were my own words or not—weren't nearly as loud.

"That might be something we could arrange." I swung the sash in a loop.

His phone buzzed on my nightstand. He scooped it up and his forehead creased.

"What's wrong? Did Alexis steal something again?" I meant it to come out as a joke, but after what the guys had said and how Berk always came to her rescue, I wondered if she hadn't gotten into some kind of trouble again.

"No, why would you say that?" He set the phone down again.

"That was a really bad attempt at a joke. I'm sorry. Is there something wrong?"

The frown lines and creases disappeared and he relaxed back against the headboard.

"Everything's fine, except for one thing. Why are you out of bed? It's getting cold without you." He pushed back the blankets, showing me a few more muscles I hadn't explored.

"I was going to make us some French toast. Maybe some bacon and eggs."

"I have a better idea." He pushed back the blankets and swung his feet around to the floor. "Why don't I cook and you can ogle me for once?"

My head bobbed up and down. "Yes, please." My grin at how homey that felt was uncontrollable.

He grabbed his jeans and slipped them on.

I looked out the window behind him and ran to it, staring out wide-eyed. "It's snowing."

"In October?" He turned and looked out the window beside me. "They said we'd be getting some weather, but freaking snow?" The snowflakes didn't dance to the ground blanketing it in a gentle blanket. It was coming down like this was the day before Christmas. There wasn't anywhere we needed to be. The fridge was stocked. What better way to spend a snow day than with Berk?

I grinned at him and rushed to my closet. "Come on. Let's go out there."

CHAPTER 29

BERK

'd always hated snow. For a long time I'd hoped to get drafted to a team somewhere warm where it never hit. Growing up, snow meant walking through it with soggy socks, frozen toes, and plastic bags wrapped around my feet.

No one was buying me boots or snow pants to go out and play or have snowball fights in it. It meant freezing temperatures in my bunk and dreading the morning when I'd have to slide my already frozen feet into ice-cold shoes. No, snow was public enemy number one, right behind rain.

But watching Jules run around in an adorable blue and purple knit hat with a white pompom on top made me want to move to a winter wonderland. Her cheeks were bright red. The dark wisps of her hair stuck out from the bottom of her hat as she ran around with her arms out at her sides, getting covered with flakes like the most beautiful statue ever sculpted.

"Do you think we'll get enough to make a snow man?" She opened her mouth, catching flakes on her tongue and laughed. The snow whipped at us from all angles. The flakes clung to her eyelashes under her glasses, and the sight left me breathless. Another piece of my heart mailed to her in that second in a signed, sealed, and delivered envelope. I could imagine her doing the same thing with two little kids at her side, a boy and a girl that both looked just like her.

And that vision was so vivid, so real, that I had to take a step back. The dreams of a kid who'd never had a family jumping way ahead of where we were now. There was so much uncertainty and there always would be. That restlessness never went away. I was always waiting for the other shoe to drop.

It started coming down even harder, sleet mixed with snow.

Shielding her eyes with water-splattered glasses, she looked over at me. "We should probably go in, huh?"

"We can stay out here as long as you want."

"You don't even have gloves." She stared at my bare hands in my pockets. "Come on, let's go in." Holding out her mitten-covered hand, she pulled me in close against her body, cradling my hand in hers.

Inside, she took off her hat and shook out her hair, stomping her boots by the door.

I toed off my sneakers and hung up my coat beside hers.

She blew into her hands and took mine, cupping them and blowing her warm breath on them.

"I may have gotten a little carried away out there. Whenever the first snow hit, my dad would take me outside and we'd run around and play for hours and make a snowman, even if it was only three inches tall. So I always love the first snow. It reminds me of him and being a kid, back when everything was easy."

She looked up at me, still trying to warm my hands.

Things had never been easy for me as a kid. Now I was bigger and stronger, and I didn't have anyone telling me I'd be shuttled off from one place to another. I couldn't steal the joy of this moment and her connection to her dad from her.

"I've always loved the snow too." I tucked some of her hair behind her ear. "You ready for some breakfast?"

She nuzzled her cold cheeks against my newly-warmed hands. "I'm ready to ogle." With a smack to my ass, she pulled me into the kitchen.

My cooking skills weren't on par with Jules's, but I tried my best.

"These eggs are phenomenal." She scooped up another hearty forkful and I wasn't sure if she was humoring me or not. "And I love the pancake shapes. Is this a mouse?"

It was supposed to be a heart. "Yeah, it's a mouse."

"The best mouse pancake I've ever had. The bacon is also delicious."

"It's hard to go wrong with bacon. Although, you haven't seen Marisa cook."

"I've heard the stories. How did she make you all sick from pasta with canned sauce?"

My stomach clenched at the memory. "I don't know and none of us want to find out. I don't know how she's survived this long. She's built up an immunity or something. A bionic stomach that could withstand even nuclear testing."

"Poor LJ."

Our lazy morning watching the snow and drinking hot chocolate with mini marshmallows was ended with a text— from Alexis.

"What's wrong?" Jules raised her head, looking over at my phone.

"It's Alexis. She went out last night with a friend and now she's trapped in the snow and needs me to come get her. I've got to go." I braced for Jules to be annoyed at the intrusion on our time—a common thing that had come up in past relationships when Alexis needed me.

"Why don't I come with you? I've got some extra warm clothes we could bring her."

"You'd do that?"

She stared at me with a puzzled look on her face. "Of course I would. She's your sister. Let me help."

Driving over to Alexis didn't feel half as bad as it normally did, with Jules manning the radio in the seat beside me. I ran my hand up and down her thigh even though the heat was cranked up. We slid on the ice a couple times, but the spare tire I still had on the car managed to get us to her.

I sent her a text and she came running out in a pair of heels and skirt barely covering her ass.

"That's a pretty dress."

"Not in a blizzard." She'd have frostbite on her kneecaps by the time she got to the car.

I got out and opened the back door.

"Berk, you're here." She hugged me. "Why are you opening the back?"

"Because Jules is sitting in the front."

Alexis smile dropped and she peered inside. "You brought her?"

"She offered to come along, and she's got some weather appropriate clothes for you."

With a grim look, she slid into the backseat of the car and I closed the door.

We were back on the road and the wipers could barely keep up with the snowfall, which had turned from winter wonderland to a white out snowman massacre in the hour-long car ride here.

The spot my car had been parked in earlier was already snowed in. Throwing on the hazards, I got out to get a shovel.

"You two go inside, I'll park and meet you in a few." At least most people weren't stupid enough to go out, so the spot was still there, just a bit more snow-covered than when I'd left.

"I can get a shovel and help." Jules leaned over the center console.

"Get Alexis inside and I'll handle the heavy lifting." I

winked at her and closed the door.

The two of them got out, Alexis wearing the extra coat Jules had brought with her hands hidden in the sleeves, looking like she was twelve again.

They disappeared and Jules came back out a few minutes later.

My sweat froze on my exposed skin and my coat felt heavier by the minute as the snow kept falling.

"What are you doing out here?"

"I was going to run home and get some provisions. Hot chocolate. Some stuff from the freezer. I figured it would make the snow day more fun."

I let go of the shovel with one hand and wrapped my arm around her, tugging her close against me. "That's a killer idea. Save a mug for me." Our lips were icy hot and steam rose between us.

"Of course." Her words were breathless, just the way I liked.

With her arms out like she was on a balance beam, Jules skidded across the street. Her front door opened and closed behind her. Three-quarters of a cleared parking space later, she came back out with her arms loaded up with containers stacked on top of containers.

Sweating my ass off and freezing at the same time, I barely cleared the space in time to help her up the steps.

"That was fast." Her winter-chapped reddened cheeks glowed. This was what she loved to do. Feed other people and make them comfortable and happy. She sure as hell made me happy.

Inside the house, you'd have thought she'd shown up with water to a group wandering through the desert.

"Jules, you're the best."

"If I'm ever snowed in anywhere, I want to be snowed in with you."

"These are so good, I hope we never have to leave this

house."

They laid it on thick, trying to keep the chocolate, vanilla, and sugar goodies coming.

"Alexis, go upstairs." I'd noticed her sulking in the corner, having removed Jules' warm jacket. "There's some sweatpants and a thermal up there. You know where they are."

Her frown deepened. I shrugged. "Fine, freeze your ass off if you'd like, but don't expect me to bring you any chicken noodle soup when you've got the flu."

"I'd hate to take that dress off, too, if I were you. It's really pretty," Jules chimed in.

I tucked her under my arm.

Alexis's gaze bounced from me to Jules and she stormed across the room. "Fine, I'll put on your clothes. Thanks, Berk."

She disappeared upstairs and Jules turned to me, nibbling her bottom lip.

"I don't think she likes me very much."

I rubbed her nose with mine, the deep freeze from outside finally thawing. "She has a hard time with new people sometimes. How could anyone not like you? And you brought cookies. That's a guaranteed friend-maker. Don't worry. She'll warm up to you."

Her smile told me she wasn't really buying it. I'd have to talk to Alexis about how I felt about Jules and make sure Alexis didn't give her a hard time. It wouldn't be the first time she'd gone all protective on me with a girl I was interested in.

Jules wasn't some football groupie or someone trying to hitch a ride on my pro career. My going pro was probably the only way I'd even be good enough for Jules. She was used to living life a certain way, and without that draft pay check, I wasn't going to cut it with only a business degree. Not that she ever made me feel like I was a kid from the wrong side of the tracks, which made me want to give her the moon and stars. She deserved them. Every single one.

CHAPTER 30
JULES

Berk, LJ, and Keyton were in the basement, checking all the water valves after a message from their landlord. My landlord would most likely send me an inflatable raft if I told him there was a leak in the basement.

Marisa was on drink duty. And I was in the living room with Alexis.

She'd trudged down the steps wearing rolled-up sweatpants and a thermal, choosing those over what Marisa and I had offered to her. With her feet tucked up under her, she'd been engrossed in her phone since the guys left.

Taking a deep breath, I grabbed some cookies and made my way over to Alexis, who hadn't even acknowledged the letter I'd written her or me for that matter. So, she hated me. I wished that was something new I was dealing with. But this time I didn't want to let things lie. She was important to Berk and I wanted to find out more about her, maybe even be at least friendly if friends was pushing it too far for her.

"Did you want to try one of my salted caramel cookies?" I held out the container in front of me and stood in front of her.

"No." She didn't look up from her phone, swiping her finger over the colorful candy on her screen.

"If you're not a fan of those, I brought a few other kinds over."

Looking up like I'd just offered her a roach sandwich, she crossed her arms over her chest.

"I don't want any of your baking."

Being Brave Jules, I set down the container and sat on the coffee table across from her. "You don't seem to like me, and I'd like to find out what I did."

Her lips twisted and she continued to stare.

"Did you read my note? I'd really like for us to be friends."

"Why?"

"Because I care about your brother and he cares about me too."

Alexis's head snapped back like she hadn't thought I'd call her out or hadn't noticed the eye-daggers she'd been shooting my way since she'd slipped into the back of the car. She stood up, appearing a lot taller than her five-one stature. "I have all the friends I need. And I don't need another fake friend who only tolerates me because she's trying to bone Berk."

"I'm not. I mean—" My cheeks heated and I'm sure my neck was a nice deep crimson.

"That's not why I'd like us to be friends."

"Really?" She tilted her head to the side. "If Berk weren't in the picture, you'd still want to be friends with me?"

"If our paths crossed, sure, why not?" I shrugged.

"I liked the letter chick better. At least I didn't have to pretend to like her."

"The letter chick. Was she his ex?" I wasn't above a fishing expedition.

"The one he's head over heels for. The one he talked my ear off about for months solid before you showed up. I'm pretty sure he's still hung up on her. She was everything he wanted in a woman, according to him." She said that last bit like she was chewing on broken glass.

My heart did a little flip. And then the guilt hit came. I needed to tell him. If he cared that much and thought she'd abandoned him, that had to hurt. He deserved to know.

"Excuse me for not thinking this thing you've got going on with him is going to last. It never does."

And that was what I was afraid of most. How would he react when he found out I'd been lying? Which was worse, me lying as TLG or me lying as me?

"I get that you want to be a good sister and protect him and we'll last however long we do, but I'd still like to get along with you. I don't want you to think I'm trying to push you out."

She sneered. "He'd never let that happen."

"Exactly, so you shouldn't feel threatened."

"I don't," she snapped.

"Then there's no reason for us not to get along."

"Maybe I just don't like you. Why do we have to get along? Are you one of those people who has to be liked by everyone? Is that why you show up with the big smile and the tractor trailer of baked goods? Because you can't stand the idea of someone not liking you so you bribe them into it?"

I took a step back.

Hostility radiated off her and she was hitting that nail head on. Who could dislike someone who showed up with cupcakes and cookies? I'd been using that since middle school to get people to like me—or give me a chance. Or at least get people to not let their friends be shitty to me in case they didn't get whatever I decided to bake and bring into school that day. Not that I'd had a chance to do much of it with my mom around watching everything I put into my mouth like a hawk.

And I'd carried that over into college. New student orientation, here's some no-bake peanut butter balls for everyone. Once I'd gotten a kitchen, there was no stopping me.

"I don't want any hostility between us to affect either of our relationships with Berk."

She smirked. "Oh, it won't. He's always been there when I need him and there's no one out there who can stop him."

"I'd never want to."

"You'd be the first." She eyed me suspiciously. Who had Berk dated before me to make her so wary of anyone new in his life? What kind of women had he been with that made Alexis so distrustful?

"I'm willing to prove it to you."

"Maybe you can. In your letter you talked about doing something special for him this semester." She rubbed her chin. "His birthday is coming up soon."

I leaned in. "His birthday? He didn't mention it."

"He doesn't like to make a big deal out of it, but maybe you'd like to do something for him." She looked at me out of the corner of her eye. "A surprise party?"

"That's a great idea. I'd love to do something for him. Would you be up for helping?"

The corner of her mouth lifted. "Totally. That would be a good chance for us to get to know each other better. What did you have in mind?" She leaned in close and I went through a few things off the top of my head.

Direct Jules for the win! I'd been upfront with Alexis. Talked to her and look at us now, practically best friends planning a surprise for Berk's birthday. Well, maybe not best friends, but at least she wasn't staring at me like she was auditioning for a Mean Girls remake.

CHAPTER 31
BERK

"We can store the booze out on the deck to keep it cold." LJ took the lead up the steps.

"We've got a game in two days; this is not the time to get blitzed."

He turned at the top of the steps and spread his arms out wide. "Not like I'll be in for more than a play. What does it matter?"

"If you don't ask Marisa to talk to her dad, you're never going to get enough time on the field."

"I'm not going to put that on her. She's been at my side through some screwed up shit. I can do the same for her."

"At the expense of your future?"

"What's at the expense of your future?" Marisa walked out of the kitchen with a pitcher filled with brightly-colored booze.

Keyton shook his head. "Is no one else going to say it? Really? Fine, LJ's been sidelined by your dad for ninety percent of our games… because of you." Keyton threw it out there and it landed on the floor like an undetonated grenade.

"I told you to shut the hell up." LJ lunged at Keyton. I

grabbed him, my arm coming up around his neck as he went for Keyton's.

"Because of me." Marisa's gaze ricocheted between Keyton and LJ.

LJ stopped his struggle and spun around. "It's not because of you. It's because he's being an unreasonable asshole."

"Because of me." She stared at him with hurt brimming in her eyes. "Because I'm making you come to his dinners."

He stepped forward reaching for her arm. "It's not a big deal."

"It's a big deal if it's keeping you from playing." She jerked back, crossing her arms over her chest.

"And you've done way more than that for me." He let his hand drop, but moved closer.

"This is your future we're talking about. This is all you've ever talked about. What you've wanted since we were ten years old." Flinging her arms out to her side, she shook her head like none of this made sense. I'd learned that a hell of a long time ago.

"And it'll happen."

"Not if you're not playing most of the games. You said it was because you'd slacked off in the pre-season, but he's stopping you from starting this season because I've dragged you to his house every week."

"So what? The time I'm on the field, I make it count. It's my turn to be there for you. After everything you've done for me and for my family, of course I'd do that for you."

"How many times have I told you, you don't owe me anything? There's nothing left for you to repay. There's no ledger with your debts tallied up."

"I don't give a shit. My dad wouldn't be alive if it weren't for you. I'll freaking follow you wherever you want me to go."

His dad wouldn't be alive? We all knew their relationship

went beyond friends, but it looked like there were way more serious things they'd been keeping quiet.

"I'm not... I don't want you following me around doing whatever I want because you feel indebted to me. We're supposed to be friends—I don't want you feeling like I'm lording something over you that I'd have done no matter what to help Charlie."

She shoved the pitcher at me, the contents sloshing over the side and pouring down my chest.

Her footsteps shook the house as she charged upstairs and slammed her door.

"What the fuck?" LJ stared at the empty steps. "What did I say wrong?"

We all stared at each other in stunned silence, and at him with questions.

He sunk his fingers into his hair and yanked at the roots. "She was a bone marrow donor to my dad. Our senior year of high school. He had cancer and a rare bone marrow type. My family was tested and none of us were a match. Marisa helped me put together a big drive and she got tested. She was a match. Missed walking at graduation to do it. He literally wouldn't be alive without her."

"Maybe she's afraid that's the only reason you're still hanging around. Or like she's an insurance policy in case your dad gets sick again." I held onto his shoulder.

"Girls don't like feeling like you're not with them for them," Jules threw out from the living room. She was sitting next to Alexis and they looked like they were getting along. Maybe Jules could butter her up on the college angle some more. Them getting along would be a bow on all the madness going on right now, even if Alexis made me want to strangle her sometimes. She was slow to trust, but if anyone could win her over, it was Jules. Who couldn't love every sweet thing about her?

"We're not even dating." LJ banged his head against the wall.

"Never? It's really never crossed your mind?" Keyton lobbed that out there. He was on a roll today.

The awkward silence crept in and he scrubbed his hands down his face. "We did try. For, like, a split second senior year and then everything hit the fan once my dad got sick and it was easier being friends. If I'd lost her then... I don't think I'd have made it, bone marrow or not."

"Maybe you need to show her that you're not just keeping her around or indebted to her because of what happened with your dad. Maybe show her you'd like things to change between you, if that's what you want."

I headed upstairs and peeled my shirt off in my room. The sticky mixed-drink concoction had soaked through to my skin.

Jules slipped into the room. "It smells like a sorority house in here."

"There must have been half a bottle of grenadine in whatever Marisa was mixing."

"It did have the added benefit of me getting to see you with your shirt off." She pushed off from the door and walked over to me. Extending one finger, she ran it down my stomach and sucked it into her mouth.

Her lips wrapped around it and I wrapped my arm around her waist, tugging her tight against me. She was the sexiest woman in the world, and she was all freaking mine.

"I'm about to start a snow dance to get a few more inches to fall and keep classes cancelled."

She walked her fingers along my chest. "Alexis said your birthday was coming up."

My sexy feelings shrank. I fucking hated my birthday. I didn't even think the guys knew when my birthday was. It was the worst day of my life. The day my mom had dumped me at my dad's. The day I'd stood in the doorway watching her fade away in the back seat of a taxi. She'd left me with a birthday present, a carry-on suitcase and more crushing pain than a kid should ever know.

"It's not a big deal." I shrugged, trying to play it cool.

Growing up as a foster kid in the placements I'd gotten hadn't meant homemade cakes and well-wrapped presents. It meant the teacher announced it in class and everyone bombarded me with questions about what I'd be getting and why I wasn't having a party. Even now, there was always a prickling claw of terror in my gut whenever the day rolled around.

"We should do something."

Long after-class parties where moms brought in cupcakes or invited everyone to a kids' play place with invitations stuffed in our lockers—I hated my birthday for all those bad memories that resurfaced as the day got closer and the new ones had been piled on top.

"No, we don't have to. I'd rather just spend the day with you. We can go grab a movie or I can have Marisa make another pitcher of these drinks and you can have your way with me."

Jules peered up at me, the hungry desire naked in her eyes. My sweatpants were a second away from becoming a camping tent. "Who said I need a pitcher of drinks for that?"

"That's a one-way ticket to me not letting you out of this room for the next twenty-four hours."

"Your sister's here!" She pushed at my chest laughing. I loved that she called Alexis my sister. There was never a question in her voice or one of the strange looks everyone always gave us, and that made me love Jules even more.

That slammed into me hard and I tightened my hold around her waist. I loved her. And it would only be a matter of time before I lost her.

CHAPTER 32
JULES

"I'm about to run into work, but I love the idea of making it like a kid's party."

"Berk never got to have those parties when we were growing up, so the sillier the better." Alexis had warmed up even more after our snow day, even insisting on calling instead of texting to talk about Berk's party.

"You're thinking streamers, balloons, party hats?"

"The works. He'll love it." She actually sounded happy; maybe we'd gotten off on the wrong foot and things were slowly turning around.

"I hope I don't accidentally let anything slip. I'm terrible at keeping secrets."

"You've been pretty good at it so far." There was a weird tone to her voice, almost accusatory.

"I'm here at work, so I've got to go. Thanks again, Alexis."

"Don't worry about it, Jules." She ended the call and I slipped my phone into my pocket.

We were filming and I didn't feel like I needed a trashcan on hand to puke, so today was a win. The last few shows had gone well and people were loving everything we made. Standing beside Avery, I'd thought people would keep putting in requests for me to step out of frame, but Max kept saying that everyone loved the way we interacted.

It wasn't so scary to get up in front of everyone once those nerves wore off. Why had I thought this would be such a nightmare? It was actually kind of fun.

"Are we ready?" I walked into B&B without a single knot in my stomach. The butterflies were firmly in place, but usually melted away after the first few minutes.

Max slammed a laptop closed and shoved it behind her. Avery stood beside her and the camera lights were all off.

"What?" The not-there knots turned into a pit. "What happened?"

They both let out deep sighs in unison. "Let's go sit down in the office." Avery wrapped her arm around my shoulder.

I waited for some snark from Max about stealing her best friend, but nothing came. That made it even worse. Max scooped up the laptop and followed us.

"Did I get the date and time wrong?"

"No, you're right on time." Avery sat on the edge of her desk. Her bump was growing every day. She had a massive hockey baby in there, so it was only a matter of time before she was rocking the basketball look.

"You're freaking me out. Whatever it is, please just tell me what I did. Did I forget to turn off the oven or something?"

Avery covered my hand with hers. "You did nothing wrong. I need you to know that. Know it, Jules." She squeezed my hand.

I nodded. "Okay, so why are you two looking like you've seen a ghost?"

"Did you—" Max stopped and rubbed her hand along the back of her neck.

"Someone just tell me." It came out like a screech, the panic finally boiling over.

"You were going to find out, no matter what. After Berk popped into the last video the views spiked a lot. Things were great and then they weren't. The comments changed. We figured it would die down and we'd just delete them all, but then something new was added to the mix and it added fuel to the fire." Max's grim look turned the pit in my stomach to a yawning cavern.

"What—" I licked my sandpaper-dry lips. "What were they saying?"

She shook her head and opened the laptop. "If there was a way to hide it, trust me I'd have taken it out back, rolled it up in a carpet, and buried it out in the Pine Barrens. But it's not stopping. These are asshole trolls, but you can't be walking around blind out there."

She turned the glowing screen toward me.

My smile stalled on my lips and I scanned the screen. In bite-sized comments, dripping with venom and humiliation, I scrolled through my life being shredded. Bile raced up my throat.

Dough Ho gets her sticky hands on a six-pack hottie.

Dough Ho.

I scrolled down the page and let out a sound from the deepest recesses of my fears and insecurities as one of my letters to Berk appeared on the screen.

They knew I was The Letter Girl.

'She must give next-level head to get a guy like that.'

'What's a hottie like that doing with the Pillsbury Dough Girl?'

'Her vag probably tastes like cinnamon rolls. That's why he's with her.'

And those were the kind ones. I clapped my hands over my mouth, trying to keep those noises from being wrenched from inside my chest. Someone took a screenshot from one of the videos and circled every roll and pucker on my body. Those problem areas I'd hated but had somehow convinced myself no one else really noticed. Oh they'd noticed all right. And they'd gone into detailed analysis of every way that I sucked and wasn't good enough for perfect Berk.

Avery closed the laptop and wrapped her arms around me.

My shoulders shook and I tried to breathe through the burn in my chest and tears pooling in my eyes.

Max enclosed us both in a hug, and that was what broke me.

Ragged sobs wrenched free from my mouth and I buried my face in their shoulders. This was what I got. I was Icarus and Berk was the sun. I'd tried to be so careful. Not let my guard down too much or fall too hard too fast because I knew what it would mean for me. He had women lined up around the stadium for a chance to give him a lap dance and here I was the Dough Ho who didn't make any sense standing next to him. It was like it was against the laws of nature and people couldn't help but point it out.

Max and Avery rocked me until my sobs turned to tears and tears faded to hiccups and sniffles. I lifted my head and wiped at my eyes with my hands.

Avery grabbed a box of tissues off her desk and gave me one.

"Thanks." It came out small and ragged, just like I felt right now.

"Is that note from you?" Max leaned in, keeping her hand on my shoulder.

I kept my gaze trained on the floor and nodded. Then I spilled the whole sordid story of the letters.

"And you never told Berk?" Avery held onto my hand.

I shook my head. "I—we weren't supposed to happen. He wasn't supposed to be this great guy who was interested in me. Once he was, I didn't know how to tell him I'd been lying to him all this time." The words caught in my throat, which squeezed even tighter.

"He'll understand."

I wiped at my face with the back of my hand. "I don't know if I want him to." What if once he saw these comments the lightbulb would go off? He'd turn and look at me and go, oh yeah, why the hell *am* I with you? The violent churning in my stomach got worse and I scanned the room for a trashcan.

As if conjured by my thoughts, my phone buzzed in my pocket. I looked at the screen.

BERK: *Where are you? Are you guys not filming today? I was looking forward to watching you ;-)*

Panic shot through my chest. I shut it off and shoved it way down deep in my bag. That was too much right now. Everything was slamming into me rapid-fire like a machine gun of pent up repercussions I'd somehow been awesome at dodging up until this very moment. Now they were all converging and hitting the bullseye with every single round.

Avery and Max assured me that all social media would be scrubbed, and told me to take as much time as I needed. I took a taxi back to my house. All I wanted to do was crawl under my sheets and not come out until the school year was over. Everyone would know. Everyone would judge. Everyone would be watching me.

I flung the taxi door open and froze a half-step out.

Berk sat on my front steps. Once he saw me, he stood up.

He knew.

Why else would he be here waiting? His gaze was trained on me like he was seeing me with new eyes.

I couldn't face him right now.

"Can we talk later?" Like the scaredy cat I was, I scurried up the steps, bypassing him, and shoved my key into the door lock.

"Did you write the letters?"

"Berk, can we talk about this later?" My heart attempted a speedy exit from my throat. I opened the door.

"No, we need to talk about this now." He wrapped his fingers around my arm, holding me in place. "LJ showed me some post saying you were The Letter Girl."

Which meant he'd most likely seen everything else everyone had said.

"Yes, it was me." Turning slowly like I was walking toward my executioner, I faced him, only meeting his gaze for a split second.

"Why didn't you tell me? Why'd you lie to me?" He raised his voice.

"Because I couldn't open myself up to all this." People stopped along the street to watch the show.

He looked behind him and stepped forward, shielding me and corralling me into the house. The door closed behind us and I was trapped inside with him.

"Jules, look at me."

I couldn't. The tears were back. They prickled at the backs of my eyes and I blinked to try to keep from dissolving into a puddle. "I think we should back off for a bit."

"Because I found out you're The Letter Girl?"

"You know that's not why." I took a deep breath, breathing through my nose even though it burned.

"Tell me what's going on."

I licked my lips. "Things are moving really fast and I think it would be best to chill out for a while."

"You're breaking up with me." Hurt radiated from his voice.

"I'm barely to a place where I can look at myself in the mirror and not want to wear a snowsuit. I've hated myself for so long, and I've hated the way I look for so long, and I'm finally coming to a point where I'm okay with being me— most of the time. But what happened today…"

I shook my head and squeezed my eyes shut. "What's happening right now, with people talking about the letters and me and you together as though I'm a circus freak? I'm working hard on loving myself. I know I can get there. But I can't do it under the searing spotlight at your side. I can't do it when I know people are constantly looking at you and back at me and wondering why the hell you're with me."

"Because you're beautiful and sexy and kind and bake a killer cookie." He ducked his head to catch my gaze.

Squeezing my fingers, I stared at the floor between us. "I want to be strong enough for this, Berk. I do. But I'm not and I can't force you to spend the rest of however long this lasts reassuring me every three seconds that everyone we pass isn't thinking the same thing."

"I don't care what other people think."

"I know you don't, but I'm not there yet."

"If you're worried about other people around here, maybe go home for a few days. Lay low there and hang out with your mom and sister. Things will blow over."

A hysterical laugh bubbled up from my stomach. "From the frying pan into the fire. Who do you think drummed these things into my head for the past twenty-two years? Do you know what it was like for me growing up?"

He stared at me like he couldn't fathom anything other than a picture-perfect childhood shattered by the death of my father.

"But your mom was nice enough."

"To you. She was so nice to you, but every word from her was trying to cut me down. Like seeing me happy for even a second offended her."

"I'm sure it's not—"

"I don't even know if my own mother loves me." My voice cracked and my nose was a split second from running. Another ugly cry was rushing to the surface and I didn't need him here to experience it. "How about that? How's that for some honesty? She's the one person who's supposed to love me unconditionally and I'm fifty-fifty on whether she'd even care if I disappeared off the face of the earth. Those are issues I'm still dealing with, and I can't add being on your arm to that—not now."

"We don't have to end things because some asshat put things up on the internet. I don't even know how they figured it out when I couldn't."

"It doesn't matter. You deserved to know the truth and I'm sorry I lied."

"That doesn't matter now." He reached for me and I stepped back.

"Do you know what she said at Laura's engagement party?"

"No." The word was small and quiet, like he didn't want to scare me away.

"She said 'It's a wonder he sees anything in you at all.' She threatened to cut me out of the wedding pictures if I didn't lose weight. I've been getting that from her for as long as I can remember."

"Watching everything I put into my mouth like we're rationing. Criticizing me during every shopping trip because I can't fit into the same clothes as Laura."

"I don't care what other people are saying. And I don't care that you're The Letter Girl. I'm fine with it—more than fine with it."

Tears trailed down my cheeks. "But I'm not. This is a tightrope I'm walking and I'm three minutes from flying into the kitchen and eating half the stuff I baked over the past week, but I won't. I can be strong right now, but every day, knowing that's what's going on? I'm not that strong, Berk. I'm just not. This is my breaking point."

I put my hand on the center of his chest and pushed him toward the porch.

"There's no way I can make it out unscathed."

He covered my hand on his chest with his own. "Who said you had to? Who said any of us do?"

I looked up at him. "I do." I pushed a little harder and he cleared the door. Closing it behind him, I locked it and sank to the floor, burying my face in my knees.

"Jules." Berk banged on the door. "Jules, don't run away from me. Don't push me away." The 'again' hung in his words. I was doing this again.

I muffled my tears and rushed upstairs, burying my head under my pillow.

I was a fucking coward and I'd lost the best thing that had ever happened to me. Better that than have him realize over time just how much better he could do as the prying eyes and judgement wore me down to nothing.

CHAPTER 33
BERK

Jules was The Letter Girl. She was the woman I'd fallen in love with through her words and the one I'd slowly discovered my feelings for right across the street.

The whole time I fought my feelings for her, it was because I'd been afraid of betraying—well, her. She'd kept that from me. The letters I'd read and re-read hundreds of times. The woman I'd finally said goodbye to in my last letter, she was Jules all this time.

I wasn't sure how long I'd stood on her porch, knocking and calling her name. Any longer and someone would probably call the cops on me for harassment. The pain in her eyes made me want to tear the place apart and find out who exactly had hurt her—other than her own family.

I walked back across the street in a daze. A swell of emotions so tangled and mixed up, I could barely hold onto one for longer than a second. Crushing sadness, confusion, anger that she'd kept this from me, relief that I'd finally found TLG and then devastation at losing her again.

And she was pushing me away, acting like we were so mismatched when we weren't. No one would think that—she was amazing. That's what they'd see. No one who knew Jules could hate her... but she'd said her mom and sister were awful to her?

None of it made sense. She seemed more stressed about strangers' opinions. What was that about?

"Did you get any treats from Jules after you busted her?" LJ came down the steps.

"She broke up with me." Stunned, I stood in the living room, trying to remember how to breathe.

"She broke up with you." LJ held onto my shoulders. "Why?"

"She said something about not being able to live under my spotlight."

"I don't blame her after the shit people have been spewing online. I've reported as much of it as I could. Give her some time."

"What stuff? Show me." Once they'd told me about Jules being TLG, I'd jumped off the porch and rushed to her house. Anything else didn't matter in that moment, except finding her and getting some answers. Now that need for answers was killed by the ache in my chest. What had I missed? What could anyone say to make her break down like that and push me away?

Marisa fired up her laptop and pulled up a whole bunch of sites and the comments sections. Ones I wished she hadn't. The Dough Ho. That's what they called Jules. And a whole shit load of other screwed up things. Their comments made me want to knock on every one of their doors and punch them in the face.

I sat on Marisa's bed and buried my head in my hands. "Why are they picking on her? She's fucking gorgeous. She's everything anyone could ever want in a girlfriend. Why do they even care?"

"It's juicy gossip. Her letter wasn't exactly PG, more like XXX. How'd they even get it?"

"No idea." I raked my fingers through my hair. "For a

while I was carrying them with me everywhere. One of them could've fallen out of my bag."

"But how'd they figure out it was Jules?" LJ leaned against Marisa's desk.

"No idea. Maybe when classes started up, they figured out her handwriting or something? We've got a freaking CSI team out there doing handwriting samples. These assholes don't have anything better to do?"

I scrambled up the steps to my backpack. The one I always had with me, and ripped it open. The bundle with the present in it was tucked to the side like it always was. Shoving my hand down deep toward the bottom, I hit the stack of letters that I'd stashed there. I pulled them out and snapped off the rubber band.

Marisa and LJ stood in the doorway.

The thick stack bounced on my bed, falling over. I fanned out the letters. "There's a few missing." I'd written dates on the top corners of them.

"You take that backpack with you all the time." LJ picked up one of the envelopes. I snatched it out of his hand.

It was bad enough when I'd thought these letters were from The Letter Girl, but now that I knew these were from Jules, no one else was getting their hands on them.

"I know I do." I raked my fingers through my hair, tugging on the roots. "I should've left them here. I shouldn't have taken them with me. Someone must have gotten into my backpack and taken them."

"Who would do that, Berk? Why would they take a couple letters and not any of the other stuff in your bag?" She sat on the edge of my bed.

"I don't know. Maybe someone wanting to be an asshole or embarrassing me or something. Get at me through Jules." I clenched my fists at my sides. Whoever had done this deserved to get their ass kicked. My heart ached for Jules. I wanted to storm back across the street, bust down her door and be the big spoon until she felt better.

Her tears were like razor blades to my heart. All I wanted to do was protect her from all this. What Emmett had said to me made so much more sense now. They couldn't attack me, so they went for the soft target, trying to tear Jules down.

And the stuff about her mom. That hurt, knowing I'd been there and she'd been in pain—that her own damn mom had made her feel like she was anything less than the beautiful, kickass Jules she was. I'd thought my mom walking out was bad, but now I didn't know what was worse: being abandoned or having to look at the person every day and never feeling like they loved you, or waiting for another emotional blow from them.

"This is all my fault." I banged my head against the wall. "If I hadn't been carrying these things around with me everywhere, they'd have never gotten them."

Marisa and LJ exchanged looks. "Why would some random person do that? And why would they want to drag Jules into this? To embarrass her? Why?"

"Because people are assholes."

"Who's had access to your bag?"

"Everyone. Like you said, I take it with me almost everywhere."

"Come on, man. Some random person isn't going to rummage through your backpack to take a letter they don't even know is in there."

This line of questioning wasn't going anywhere I wanted it to go. "Then who did it?" I pushed off the wall, going toe-to-toe with LJ.

"Dude, chill out." He pushed his hands against my chest.

"Fine, I'll say it. You can come and glower at me. It was probably Alexis." Marisa wedged herself between me and LJ.

My head snapped down and I stared at her. "Why in the hell would she do that? You're out of your minds."

LJ always went straight to Alexis whenever anything went wrong. If it was me being late somewhere or something going missing, his knee-jerk conclusion was always Alexis, but that wasn't the case—well, maybe fifty percent of the time.

"You didn't see the way she was looking at Jules the two times I've seen them meet?"

"She has a hard time meeting new people and trusting them."

"She also looked like if she had a voodoo doll of Jules, Jules would definitely have been in trouble."

"Alexis would never do something like that to me. She'd never hurt me like that. Look at you and LJ. You jumped in here in a split second trying to chest bump me away. Would you hurt him like that? You're best friends. Me and Alexis are family."

"Then how'd they find out the letter was Jules's?"

Something Jules had mentioned about the recipes...

"They put up her handwriting on each one of the web shows. And if a letter fell out of my backpack, maybe someone matched it up that way. It doesn't have to be Alexis's fault every time anything goes wrong. She's my sister and she wouldn't do that to me. Besides, she's never even seen Jules' writing. She wouldn't hurt me like this." I had to believe she wouldn't. Because doing that to Jules, exposing her private thoughts to me, knowing who it was? That was beyond anything Alexis had ever pulled before. That bordered on unforgivable. I didn't have many people in the world I could call family, and losing one of them would kill me.

LJ and Marisa looked at each other again like they were speaking some kind of telepathic twin speak and shook their heads. "I hope you're right, man." LJ squeezed my shoulder and the two of them left the room, looking back at me like a dude who'd just lost a leg saying he could walk it off.

No matter how these letters were released, they were out

in the world and I'd deal with the consequences. TLG was Jules. All those conflicted feelings I'd had about liking Jules when TLG and I were still writing, keeping her at arm's length not only because of Nix, but because I didn't want to betray TLG—I should've been pissed off. I should've wanted to yell at her for lying to me, but now that I went back over everything in my mind, I couldn't keep the smile off my face.

I'd found TLG. She hadn't just dropped me and walked away. She'd been right across the street baking for me every day, smiling at me from behind those glasses from her favorite spot with her head on my chest. She'd been in my bed. She'd been too shy to tell me it was her. She was real and in the flesh—and had just broken up with me.

But I wasn't going to go down easy.

The crap Jules was telling herself about all this, the insecurities she'd been good at hiding and slowly overcoming—that was something hard to come up against. I had twenty-two years of that myself, but I wasn't going down that easy. I wasn't going to let her push me away because she was scared.

I was scared too, but I was scared that she'd shut me out and walk away from what we had. A plan formed in my head and I got to work, going to my desk and throwing open the bottom drawer. This was exactly what I needed. The perfect thing to show her she'd always been on my mind and that a little viral sensation wasn't enough to scare me away. She was so much stronger than she thought, but now it came down to whether or not she thought I was worth the risk.

CHAPTER 34
JULES

"Remember what you said to me when I was lying in bed after my break up with Nix?"

I rolled my head to the side and stared at Elle. My hoodie, the one I used to wear every day, that I'd had to search through piles of clothes to find, now covered me like a blanket. It had been weeks since I'd worn it, but I needed the safety of its soft gray cocoon. "You're completely right to wallow and I'll bring you more chocolate chunk cookies."

The corner of her mouth lifted. "Not quite."

"A pep talk isn't what I need right now."

"But it's what you're going to get."

I lay in my bed, staring up at the ceiling. "I can't. I really can't. Not right now." I breathed through the burn in my nostrils like I was seconds away from breaking down again.

"How about I lie with you then?"

I nodded and the bed dipped as she swung her legs up and settled down beside me.

"You have nothing to be embarrassed about." She tilted her head toward me.

"When people look at you and Nix, they get it. You make sense. Despite knowing you'd been seconds away from removing his balls with an ice cream scoop and the whole getting-him-arrested thing, I never, ever batted an eye at you two dating."

I sucked in a shuddering breath.

"But with me and Berk. We don't make sense to people. They can't figure it out. Like why in the hell is *he* with *her?* Is it pity? Is it a dare or a bet? A fetish? And it's only a matter of time before he starts to wonder the same thing."

"You know him and you know that's not the type of guy he is."

"But can I take that chance? He would destroy me. Not even on purpose—this is bad enough, but once I'm in even deeper than I already am? How could I come back from that? How do you recover from having a piece of your soul shredded? It's so early and I already feel like I was halfway there." The tears pooled in my eyes.

I didn't even know how long Elle stayed with me before leaving for an event they were scrambling to get back on track after the snow. She took the liberty of hiding all my electronics to keep me from tying myself to a whipping post of scrolling social media. And my mother's messages had been particularly helpful.

Julia, do you have any idea how embarrassing this is for our family?

Julia, we're going to have to rethink your participation in your sister's wedding. We don't want to cause a scandal.

You'd think we were Kennedys or members of the royal family with how important keeping up appearances was to my mother. But for once, her words weren't the most hateful things I'd had said about me. People behind their keyboards had certainly had a field day with my outing.

Their words floated in my brain, looking for a nice soft place to burrow and infest my thoughts. Classmates from high school had backed up the big reveal with notes I'd scribbled in their yearbooks and everyone was a handwriting expert now.

The internet pitchfork mob had ruined everything. I wouldn't get to lay in Berk's arms at night. Watch his face when he walked into the house for the party Alexis and I had planned.

She'd given me her phone number, thawing the ice between us to frigid water. My plans for Berk's birthday were in play. Anytime I texted her with an idea she'd replied immediately with a 'Call me!' Maybe my letter had gotten her to see I wasn't just a user. I could only imagine the women falling over Berk all the time. When we talked last she'd suggested I recreate a kid's birthday of sorts. Kind of like the ones you'd have back in the classroom that everyone loved so much because it meant cupcakes instead of whatever math worksheet the teacher had planned.

Now I'd have to let Alexis know the party was cancelled. I curled up even tighter. Maybe she could still throw it without me. My heart felt like someone had taken a hammer to it—the claw end. A birthday party would help take Berk's mind off how I'd slammed the door in his face as he asked me not to.

A figure loomed in my doorway and I screamed.

"Jesus Christ!" Nick jumped and stepped into the light, clutching his chest. His bare chest. With a towel wrapped around his waist. "Are you ever dressed?!"

He tightened his grip on the towel. "Sure, for classes and stuff. And it looks like you're having a moment, so I wasn't sure how to bug you."

"Bug me for what?"

"That pomegranate body wash you bought is all gone. Do you maybe have some more?"

My laugh was pure disbelief. I shoved up off the bed and stalked to my closet, grabbing my spare bottle and shoving it at him.

"You're the best, Jules."

"I've been told."

My stomach rumbled.

"Might want to take care of that. Also, you've been locked up in your room for days. It's getting a little rank in here." He fanned his face. "Maybe air it out a little." He walked farther into my room toward the windows.

"Touch them and die." I glared at Mr. Towel.

He raised his hands in surrender, backing into the hallway. "Sorry, just trying to be helpful."

I trudged downstairs. There had to be some sliced turkey and cheese in there. Maybe some chips. Not that I needed chips. I stared down at my body. The body I'd worked so hard to love and accept, but sometimes—sometimes it was so hard.

The doorbell rang after the first bite of my sandwich. Divine intervention?

Opening it, there was no one there but the inky darkness of night. When the hell had the sun set? I stepped back to close it and spotted the bundle of notes, with the same paper Berk always used, with a daisy on top of it.

I looked out over the porch, but the street was silent. Taking it inside, I closed the door and opened the bundle. The notes had dates written across the top. I headed back to the kitchen to open them.

TLG where are you? It's been over a week since your last letter. I didn't think you were serious about ending this. That's it? If you don't want to meet, we don't have to, but don't just end what we have like this.

I slammed my lips together, trying to hold back the swelling emotion.

Please don't end things this way. I can't tell you how much your words mean to me. Can you walk away like this didn't mean anything?

The words swam on the page as tears welled in my eyes.

Just let me know you're okay. Did I do something wrong? I'm sorry if I was too pushy.

I squeezed the letter to my chest, breathing through the ache in my heart. His sadness radiated from these letters. He'd never let me know, actual me. When he came over and talked about finding TLG the depth of his pain over the letters stopping never came through, but I had hurt him. I dropped my chin to my chest and my tears fell onto the neatly printed words.

Please.

A quiet sob shook my shoulders. *Berk, I'm sorry.* I squeezed my lips together and flipped to the next one.

I'm not even sure why I'm writing these letters anymore. I guess sometimes you felt like the only person I could really talk to. But I thought I should tell you, I've met someone. I think you'd like her. I don't know why, but I think you would. I hope you're okay.

My throat tightened and I flipped to the next one. This one was dated over a week ago, before the Dough Ho blow up.

This will be my last letter. Remember that girl I told you about before? I'm crazy about her. She's kind and beautiful and makes me want to tell her things that would scare her away in a heartbeat. Things that I told you that made you stop wanting to talk to me. I don't know how, but I'm going to show her how much she means to me without sending her running for the hills.

And I hope wherever you are, you're happy.

I wiped at my tears and clutched the notes to my chest. Once again, I'd pushed him away. Once as TLG and now as me. I'd hurt him twice trying to protect myself.

Another knock on the door stopped me in my tracks.

I rushed to the front door and threw it open, looking at the floor and instead of another note, there were a pair of legs, attached to Berk.

"Berk."

He stared back at me with red ringed eyes and I hated myself a little more. And that was why I was in this mess in the first place. I hated that I couldn't be the perfect daughter my mother wanted. I hated that I couldn't keep the family together as my dad would've wanted. And I hated myself so much that I'd shoved Berk straight out the door when all he'd ever been was amazing to me. He'd made me feel like I mattered from our first handshake with a wide smile that made my heart gallop in my chest.

The uncertainty in his eyes and the way he shifted from foot to foot made the tears I'd just wiped away rush back in.

"Hey, Frenchie. Can I come in?" He shoved his hands into his pockets.

I nodded, swallowing against the vise grip around my throat as I stepped back to let him in.

"I—" we both started at the same time.

An awkward huff shot from my lips. How did I even begin to say I was sorry?

"Jules, I'm crazy about you." His Adam's apple bobbed. "I needed you to know that. And… I know I promised I wasn't going to say anything to send you screaming from the room, but I want to be completely honest with you. I love you."

I gasped and his letters fell from my fingertips, dancing their way to the ground through the thick air laced with hope and possibilities between us.

"And I needed to say that. If you're going to walk away from me, I don't want there to be any more secrets between us. I'm head over heels in love with you. Hell, I even felt like I was cheating on The Letter Girl with how much I liked you even from the beginning. And I see you, Jules.

"I know there's so much shit out there about women and their bodies and I don't want you to think I don't see you. I love your curves. I love your thighs and how strong they are when you wrap them around my waist."

He wrapped an arm around me, tugging me close. "I love your arms. I love how you can use them to swing around that pole upstairs." Dropping his arm, he threaded his fingers through mine. His gaze lifted. "And how you wrap them around my neck." He pulled my arms up around his neck, my fingers brushing against his thick hair.

"But you're not someone who's been in the spotlight. I don't even know what catty bullshit and terrible things you've listened to for who knows how long. And I don't want to see you get hurt." His words were whispers across my lips.

"If you need me to go and you don't want to be with me, then I'll respect that. I can't force you to put up with everything that comes with being with me or force you to love me back." His voice cracked and tears glittered in his eyes. "But I hoped you might." Those last words were whisper quiet against my lips.

My tears couldn't be held back. Words stalled in my throat and I tried not to ugly cry all over him. I'd never had someone so nakedly ask me to love them. Wasn't that always me? Wasn't I always the one searching for approval? Searching for love?

"I do, Berk." I ran my fingers along the back of his neck. "I love you so much and it scared me that one day, after people kept saying the things they were saying online about me, that maybe one day..." I slammed my lips together. They quivered and I sucked in a deep breath. "That maybe one day you'd start believing them."

He crushed me against his chest, his heart thundering in time with mine. Burying my face in his neck, I hugged his head to me. "I don't give a shit what anyone says. I learned that lesson a long time ago. They can say whatever they want, but it's me and you, okay?"

Taking my face in his hands, he brushed at my tears with his thumbs. "It's us. Tell me when you're upset, but don't run. Because now that I know you love me, I'll never stop the chase. Can you promise me that?"

I nodded, staring into the eyes that had seen deep into my soul. The ones with the golden flecks that always looked at me with a tenderness I'd never expected.

He squeezed his eyes shut and rested his forehead against mine. "Thank you, Frenchie."

His lips were on mine in a flash. And his hands were under my shirt and mine were under his. Backing me into the kitchen, he tugged down my pants and palmed my ass, squeezing it and carrying me to the table.

Knocking my notebooks and baking sheets to the floor, he was on me and I whipped his shirt over his head.

We were hungry and frantic. Stripping our clothes off, he barely had time to roll on a condom before he sank into me. Sticking one hand between us, he strummed my clit like an instrument he'd practiced for years. His thick head opened and stretched me until I screamed out his name. The orgasm cascaded over me in only a couple of minutes. Panting and sweaty, we looked at each other and laughed before getting off the table. I'd never bake in here again without blushing.

Boneless and satisfied by the intensity of the whole day, he led me upstairs.

He peeled back the blankets and we climbed into bed. I closed my eyes, dozing beside Berk.

He brushed his fingers through my hair.

And I relaxed against him, snuggled up close with my arm draped across his waist. He flicked off my bedside light and we were bathed in darkness.

Pressing a kiss to my temple, he whispered against my skin, "Just warn me before you find someone better, okay?" His arms tightened against me and I squeezed my closed eyes shut even harder against the hurt I'd caused him.

I'd done that to him and made him feel like I might cut out on him at any moment, but I wouldn't do it again. I'd never make him feel like he didn't stack up or deserve my love. That word hit on a spot in my heart and I knew it was true. I loved him. That was the only reason I'd have run screaming for the hills like I had. I loved him, and I'd make sure he knew it.

CHAPTER 35
BERK

My Hail Mary pass had landed safely in the end zone. Jules' gentle breaths now breezed across my arm, the weight of her nestled against my side. All was right with the world again. But not quite. My mom was still out there somewhere. So many things hung in the balance, but the rising tide of that turmoil wasn't as high and heavy with Jules by my side. And my football season teetered on the brink of disaster.

And there was the undercurrent of fear that someone would expose what I'd done. That at the worst possible moment, my need for resolution and closure—for answers, was going to kick my damn teeth in.

Someone had connected Jules' handwriting to the letters they'd taken from my bag. Why was someone going through my stuff? Why had they exposed Jules' letters to me like that? To hurt me? To hurt Jules? The puzzle of who'd found Jules' letters to me and published them hung over my head and the breadcrumbs of what that meant for my future was an unshakable prickle of fear. What else were they digging into, and why? Did they want money? I didn't have any. Or were they waiting to use it as something later once I had money? A threat I couldn't face down made me uneasy. LJ and Marisa's little super-sleuth suggestion had shoved a new terrible thought into my head, so wrong I didn't even want to entertain it. Alexis was family. She'd love Jules as much as I did.

There was still so much wrong, but this was the rightest thing I'd felt in a long time. A contentment and a happiness that made everything else pale in comparison.

"Good morning." Jules stretched like a cat, pressing her breasts against me.

Morning wood had nothing on what I had right now. She might not see it, but Jules was the sexiest woman I'd ever met. She made it so easy to fall into the dream land of breakfast at the kitchen table laughing and smiling, and late nights making her scream my name. It wasn't only the amazing sex —I saw a *home* with her in our future. The complete picture. There wasn't anyone more perfect for me than her. And I'd spend as long as I needed to make her believe it was true. But there was still a bit of unfinished business left hanging.

"There was a lot going on last night."

She dropped her gaze and nodded, taking her position against my chest.

"And we didn't talk about everything." I kissed her temple.

Lifting her head, she stared up at me. "What else is there? I'm an open book."

I pushed her hair back behind her ear. "I want to know when I get to experience everything The Letter Girl promised me." Jules doing half the things TLG described sent me from damn-I-need-that to I'll-kill-someone-if-I-can't-touch-her-now territory.

Her eyes widened and her breath caught. "Everything."

"Everything." I tapped her on her nose. "You've been holding out on me big time, Frenchie."

The sides of her neck and up to her cheeks were bright

red. "I wouldn't say that." She toyed with the edge of the blanket covering us.

"Why not? Those letters were holy shit levels of hot. I'm talking disappear-into-my-room-for-an-hour and can-only-cool-off-with-a-cold-shower hot."

"Really?" Her voice pitched up and the flush of her cheeks set in deeper.

I took her chin between my fingers and tilted her head up. "How many times do I have to tell you, Jules. I'm into you. Whether it's in letter form, cookie form, pole dancing form, sitting in your sweats on the couch watching TV form, or any other way you want to show me what you're all about, I'm here for it. I'm here for you."

———

WITH EVERYTHING THAT HAD HAPPENED, IT WOULD HAVE BEEN easy to stay at home, but Jules wanted to go out.

I wanted to protect Jules within the safety of our walls, but she made the decision and I wasn't going to give up the chance to show everyone how crazy I was about Jules, leaving no doubt in the mind of whoever was trying to screw with my season that they'd failed—hard.

"We don't have to." I squeezed her hand.

Jules stood beside me with her purple-and-pink hat tugged way down on her head and her jacket zipped up, so only her glasses and the wisps of her hair pushed down by the hat were exposed.

"No." She straightened her shoulders. "I need to do this."

My brave, beautiful woman. We walked to campus, her mittened hand in mine, and I dared anyone to say a word. For them to utter a syllable of what people had been spouting online.

Once at Uncommon Grounds, she tugged her hat off and slipped into the booth across from me. Every few seconds, with every flicker of movement or time the door opened, she shot a quick glance over her shoulder.

I ordered our drinks and came back to her, sliding into the seat beside her. Dropping my hand to her thigh, I squeezed it and whispered against her neck, "No one is going to say a word to you."

"Probably because you're glaring at anyone looking in our direction."

"I do that anyway. I wouldn't want anyone to get any ideas about trying to steal you away."

She snorted. "I don't think that'll be a problem."

"One of these days you'll see yourself like I do."

She turned to me and held my gaze. Her uncertainty and vulnerability simmered just under the shield of her gaze. The one she dropped for me. She swallowed and covered her hand with mine. "I hope one day I can."

We left Uncommon Grounds and no one said a word. With every new customer into the shop Jules had relaxed the slightest bit. Everyone was really brave behind a keyboard, but they'd never have the guts to spew half the shit they did online to her face.

She banished me back to The Brothel from the bottom step of her porch with a kiss to tide me over until our self-imposed study sessions were over. Coach would also be expecting us to get in our workout even if there was two feet of snow on the ground.

I made it halfway across the street when a sight I wouldn't wish on my worst enemy rocked up on my side of the street.

Johannsen leaned against his car with his hands shoved in his pockets like he was enjoying the freezing air. The grungy, dirty snow piled around his feet matched his personality to a tee.

"What the hell are you doing here? Come for another serenade?"

Like he couldn't help himself, his gaze flicked to the house a few down from The Brothel where he'd stood out in their postage stamp front yard and sung right along with his guitar.

But she'd moved out. We'd helped Brick move Willa out at the end of last school year. She'd transferred to another school halfway across the country.

"No, I'm here for you." His smile teetered on friendly, which made it even worse.

"Sorry if you expected an invitation inside. We've got a game on Friday, that'll be more than enough of seeing you for this season."

I stepped onto the first step of the porch.

"Except, maybe you won't be playing, since you're not eligible and all." His heavy Northeast accent from way above the tristate area was like nails on a chalkboard.

"What the hell are you talking about?" I swung around and stared at him.

He shrugged, his smile widening. "How are things with Felix? I hear he's a very generous agent."

Ice cold prickles that had nothing to do with the snow on the ground ran down my spine.

"I'm sure it was a very lucrative arrangement you came to."

"You're talking out of your ass." Never let them see you sweat and never admit to anything—unless you were covering for something even bigger. I'd learned those lessons well, growing up.

"It's always nice to have some money for things like taking your girl out." He nodded his head in the direction of Jules' house.

I snorted. "Have you seen my car? You think if I had a pile of cash from some agent I wouldn't have a much better ride?"

"Nah, you're not that stupid. But there are other things money can be spent on. And Felix looked real damn excited to be talking to you at Kelland this summer."

"I go a lot of places and I meet a lot of people. I don't know what the hell you're talking about. You spying on me or something?"

"Don't flatter yourself. Unlike you, I work for what I have and I'm not about cutting corners or breaking rules to get what I want. My summer job has given me a lot of insight into what makes these rich people talk; a few glasses of champagne and they can't keep their lips closed. So he was real chatty about how he works his client. And you're now a client."

So Johannsen was the waiter who'd knocked me sideways and vanished at the engagement party. "Why would I throw my entire future in jeopardy? Why would I break the rules when I'm so close to the draft?"

He shrugged. "Cause you're greedy just like everyone else."

"Like you. What about you? You think you know this thing about me because of some rich guy talking at a party, but I know something about you. How about family being off limits? Especially the family of opposing players? You act like this whole street didn't see you stalking Willa Goodwin's place and busting out your guitar."

"That has nothing to do with this." His nostrils flared and he pushed off the car.

"Maybe this is your guilty conscience talking when it comes to breaking rules, but you stay the hell away from me and quit talking about things you know nothing about." I walked away, still keeping him in my sights. That's the last thing I needed, a freaking sucker punch.

"We play a game next week."

"And?"

He crossed his arms. "And my team needs that win."

"Why should I give a shit?"

"Anonymous tips can come in all forms. I'm pretty sure you have to let the officials look at things like your bank records if they ask for them. Refusing is an admission of guilt. Your bullshit 'family is off limits' rule doesn't come close to the thick-ass book of them they have for college football. Think about that one, Vaughn." He flung the door to his car open and revved the engine before kicking up salt and snow as he charged up the street.

And there it was. I stood staring after the shadowy threat that had been looming over me since I'd taken the money. Only it wasn't in the shadows anymore. I'd lulled myself into thinking this was a threat far off and possibly without any actual merit, but here I was, and this had the power to destroy everything I'd worked for in a blink. The life I'd been trying to build and the future I'd dreamed of would implode. He had the power to destroy me, and I'd given him everything he needed to get the dirty job done.

CHAPTER 36
JULES

Berk had his arm draped over my shoulder, running his thumb up and down my arm.

My feet were tucked up under me and I burrowed my face in his side.

"How are you scared by this?" He held out his hand toward the TV with the evil alien creature pointing his glowing finger toward the kids hiding him.

"He's a walking, talking testicle. Is it almost over?" I held onto his shirt, using it to cover my eyes.

"It's ET! He's a childhood classic."

"His stretchy neck and freaky fingers weird me out. I used to have nightmares about him."

"About him what? Breaking into your garden and making the flowers grow?"

"No, I had bunk beds growing up, thinking I'd have sleep-overs and stuff, and I always thought I'd wake up to his big bulging eyes staring at me while I slept."

He didn't even try to muffle his laugh. "Why not sleep on the bottom bunk, then?"

"So he could touch me with his glowing penis fingers?"

He bent over, nearly knocking me off the couch, gasping

for breath through his laughter. "Penis fingers? I don't even want to know what kinds of guys you were dating before me, if you think those fingers look like penises." He wiped the tears from his eyes and pushed himself up off the floor.

I grabbed a pillow and whacked him with it. "Shut up. How long do we have until you have to be at the team bus?" I stretched and laughed at how his gaze laser focused to the gap where my shirt rode up. Normally, I'd be shoving it down, beet red with embarrassment, but I prolonged the stretch a little longer. Maybe we'd sneak in a little fun before he had to leave.

"About an hour and a half." He bit his bottom lip.

An insistent buzz broke the little eye contact tug-of-war we had going on. He scooped his phone up and tapped the screen.

"Shit, it's Alexis, I've got to go." Scanning the room, he spotted his keys.

"What about the game?"

He cursed under his breath and dragged his fingers through his hair. "She's stranded."

"I can go." Jumping up from the couch, I looked for my coat. It would give me a chance to talk to her about putting the final touches on his birthday party. "I'll go get her. You don't have time to get there and back." I grabbed his arm as he was already halfway out the door.

"I can make it."

"Berk, you don't even know what she needs."

"She needs *me*," he snapped. "I'm not going to ignore her."

I jumped at the sharpness in his tone.

"I never said I wanted you to not help her." My fingers bit into his bicep. "Let me come with you. Then, if she needs something I can stay, or once you know she's okay you can leave and I can get her back here or to her place—"

He stopped, and turned back to me. "Sorry."

A flicker of hope.

"She asked me to come alone. And I need to extract her from whatever mess she's stumbled into again." He slipped his hand around the back of my neck, running his callused pads against my nape. "Thank you for offering and being so concerned, but I've got this. And it's better if I go alone. I can handle it." He leaned in and pressed his lips to mine in a feather-light kiss. His small smile of reassurance did anything but.

———

THE BEAD-ENCRUSTED, LONG-SLEEVED DRESS WAS EXACTLY THE kind of thing I'd hoped Laura would choose for her brides-maids. It had a high scoop neck that highlighted my collar-bones. The flowing skirt was forgiving on the hips and thighs —and I couldn't help but think that Berk would hate it. I could see him now, ruffling the skirt of it, looking for a slit or threatening to make it a backless dress.

I ran my fingers along the gentle pleating and gathering, letting the smooth fabric glide across my skin. I was fairly exposed, for me, but it felt okay. And I didn't feel like I wanted to grab the nearest hoodie and jeans. When had I started feeling like a parka wasn't the only appropriate form of clothing for me? Maybe when a certain football player made it loud and clear that he appreciated every bit of skin he got to touch.

"Julia." The harsh snap of my name from my mom was even more biting than usual.

I shook my head. "Sorry, what were you saying?"

She looked at me through my reflection in the mirror.

"Will we have to let this dress out before the wedding or are you going to hold yourself together until then?"

The barbs didn't sink as deeply as they used to. "I've been the exact same weight for the past two years, Mom."

"Part of the problem. But if you're around temptation in that bakery every day…"

"Mom, please, can you not." Laura touched Mom's arm. "It looks very nice, Jules."

That was the first time she'd ever called me Jules. And stuck up for me in front of Mom.

Mom sniffed. "All I'm trying to do is make sure your day is memorable. That everyone will be talking about it for months to come."

"I know. Thank you. It will all be just like you planned." A flicker of an emotion that wasn't anywhere near that of a gleeful bride crossed Laura's face. "Perfect."

"It will be." Mom looked at Laura like she'd never looked at me. Like she wanted nothing but the best for Laura—like she loved her. I looked away from the mother-daughter display and stepped away from the mirrors.

Mom stood. "I'll try on my gown and then we can go get lunch."

"I've got to go to my internship."

"The invitation wasn't an open one. You should be watching your weight, anyway." And with that little nugget of preciousness, Mom swanned out of the room.

"Jules…" Laura trailed off and raised her hands in a futile attempt to smooth things over. "Are you okay after the internet stuff? With the bakery and Berk?" She pulled me down to sit beside her on the champagne-colored couches opposite the wall of mirrors.

I was surprised she'd even heard about that. "I am now. Thanks for asking."

"Why didn't you tell me you were working at B&B? I love that place. I watched some of your videos." She looked at me out of the corner of her eye like we were passing notes behind the teacher's back. "You two are so fun together. And everything you bake makes me want to eat my phone screen."

"Really?" I leaned closer, still not sure I'd heard what

she'd said. Was she being sarcastic? She actually liked what I was doing? In all the years I'd baked, she'd never even tried anything I'd made, as far as I could tell. But she'd watched my videos. Emotions welled up inside of me, a longing for the kind of closeness I'd always wanted with her. But the cautious side of me reined them in. I'd had my hopes kicked like a puppy by her once already, but she looked so sincere.

"It's easy to see how much you love it. And it reminds me so much of Dad. I'd come back from shopping with Mom and the place would feel so warm and smell so good. You two always loved spending time in the kitchen together." There was a hint of sadness there.

"You could come by to watch us film sometime."

"That would be okay with Avery?"

"Of course, but you'd have to put up with Max. Some of her snark might burn a bit, but you get used to it. Don't let the tattoos fool you—she's secretly nice."

"Max Hale?"

"Pretty sure that's her last name."

"Holy crap." She looked over her shoulder. "I tried to get an appointment with her for my cake." She leaned in like this was a state secret. "Mom vetoed it, of course, and it didn't matter anyway because her waiting list is, like, eighteen months long, but, damn, her stuff is amazing. There was one at a charity event I went to a couple weeks ago. Everyone couldn't stop talking about it—usually those things look beautiful but taste terrible, but it was amazing." Her eyes widened. "Nothing like what you've made, but it was so good."

"No offense taken. I'll send her your compliments. And I'll let you know the next time we're filming something. We've taken a little bit of a hiatus."

"Since the incident?"

I nodded.

Mom came back in with her just off-white enough to pass as a not-white gown.

That's when I spotted it. An eye roll almost imperceptible to the naked eye, but Laura did it. She caught my gaze and every muscle in her body tensed. I did my own much more exaggerated eye roll and she buried her face in her shoulder.

"Something entertaining happening?" Mom stared at me in the mirror.

Covering my laugh with a cough, I lifted my hand to my mouth. "Nothing, Mom, just something funny a friend did."

"Hopefully it's nothing you're involved in that might cause us even more embarrassment."

"Nope, just a video of me pole dancing." And with that, I excused myself to change.

There would never be anything I could do to change her. It was time I accepted that and stopped looking to my mom to be anything more than she'd ever been to me. I didn't need to keep putting myself through the torture that came with trying to please her.

My worst nightmare had happened. I'd been exposed up on the internet in front of everyone. I'd had intimate details of my inner thoughts flung up online—and I was still here. Breathing, laughing, and living.

Since my dad's death, I'd always hidden and tried to fade into the background. Better to have someone glance right past me than see me and decide they didn't like what they saw. Well, I'd had that anonymity ripped away from me like the world's stickiest Band-Aid. Damn, had it hurt, and I'd been red and raw for a while, but now that it was done I had one word for anyone who had a problem with me—fuck you. Well, that was two words, but you get my drift.

Did I want to lose weight and be able to squeeze into clothes I could buy in any store, even those places Laura and Mom visited regularly? Sure.

Would I ever be one of those girls? Who the hell knew?

But I deserved to be happy just as I was, regardless of size, and I deserved the love of someone like Berk. And I wasn't going to let my doubts about my self-worth get in the way of that anymore.

I came out of the changing room and waved bye to Mom and Laura, who mouthed 'sorry' to me. Maybe we could salvage something of our relationship if we were out from under the watchful eye of our mother.

———

THE SMELLS FROM B&B WAFTED DOWN THE STREET OVER A BLOCK away. My stomach rumbled. I rummaged around in my bag for my power bar. I'd learned the hard lesson about filling up on cream-filled donuts and cupcakes at the shop. Hello, stomach ache. You'd think I'd have learned my lesson baking at home, but something about having someone else craft these delicious treats was like a sugar-coated drug.

I pushed the backdoor open. "Hey, Avery."

"Hey." There was a gentle slope to the way she said the word. It held all the questions without needing to say more. Glad you're here. Are you okay? Is there anything I can do for you?

"I'm here and ready to work."

"We're not going to record anything today, but I figured the three of us could work on some stuff. How's that sound?"

"Perfect."

"Why don't you go grab Max and we can get started?" Avery wrapped the apron around her waist, her bump meaning she couldn't wrap it around and tie it in the front like she usually did.

With all the time I'd been at B&B I'd never been in Max's store. I'd passed by the outside, but she was always at Avery's and I was usually trying to keep myself from hyperventilating ninety percent of the time, so tours weren't on my to-do list.

The door that connected the shops was in the front, right beside the front-of-house tables where customers sat and the cases housing everything that Avery and the rest of her team made.

On the other side, it was like I'd been transported into a trendy industrial loft. Exposed brick covered one wall and the duct work ran along the ceiling. A spray-painted intricate woven flower design covered one whole wall. The bright colors matched Max's tattoos and hair color perfectly.

"Max," I called out.

There were sofas and a small table along one side of the room.

Black and gray slate serving platters were lined up alongside the massive bar, all lit up with bottles of booze and bubbly. That was one way to get people to shell out a shit-ton on cakes. Get them drunk. Maybe I could get her to make something small for Laura since she'd talked about how much she loved Max's work.

I peeked into the back room.

Max had headphones in. The long white cables disappeared into her pocket.

Massive mixers and ovens were crammed into the small space. The heat had to be crazy when it was all going.

She sat on a steel stool with her foot bouncing around on the bottom rung and her hair held back from her face.

It was freezing despite her previous assertions that it was hot in the back, but her steady hand spackled an intricate design using a mini version of what someone laying plaster might use.

"It's beautiful." I dropped my hand onto her shoulder.

A yelp erupted from her mouth, and she jumped off the stool and spun around, whipping the ear buds out of her ears.

"Jesus, Jules! You scared the shit out of me." She clutched the front of her shirt and set down her icing trowel.

"Sorry." I held up my hands in surrender, still laughing.

"Yeah, I can tell from your face you're real sorry. Next time you'll meet the business end of my spatula."

Draped across her workbench was a black suit jacket and tie.

"Looks like someone's been getting some business ends taken care of back here." I lifted the jacket, holding it out with my finger. The label inside the jacket was hand stitched in. And the designer…

"Max, whose jacket is this?" My gaze swung to hers.

She grabbed it off my finger. "No one's." She shoved it and the tie into a filing cabinet and slammed the metal drawer shut.

"You can't scrunch and shove a jacket like that. It's worth, like, all the money." I reached for the handle.

With a quick smack to my hand, she bumped me out of the way. "And I'm sure it's long forgotten. Avery said we were waiting on you to get the recipes for the next round of videos just right." She stopped and turned. "How are you doing?"

I turned my hands palm up and shrugged. "Still breathing."

"Sometimes that's all we hang onto." A flicker of sadness flashed across her eyes. "Let's get to work."

We worked together on the recipes, with Max swiping more than her fair share from the trays ready to go out front.

"It's a wonder you manage to get any to the customers with her around."

"Tell me about it. I think I've had to increase my overall production by twelve percent to take the Max Factor into account."

"I'm right here, you know." Max's words were muffled through the funnel cake donut she was inhaling.

One of the girls from the front poked her head through the swinging doors. "Someone's here for you."

"For me?" Avery wiped her hands on her apron.

"No, for Max."

"For me?" she choked out from behind the sugar-coated pastry.

"Tall guy. Looks like he should be riding a white stallion through Fairmount Park."

Max jumped down off the counter and walked to the door, peering out the small window. "Shit. Not him." She stood with her back to the door, mumbling to herself before lifting her head and catching our open-mouthed, wide-eyed gazes.

"There's a dude here to see you?" Avery rushed around the counter.

Max stopped her with two hands to the chest. "Oh, no, you don't. Let me get rid of him and I'll be right back." She pushed backward through the swinging door.

Avery and I rushed to the door and looked out the window.

"Damn, he's tall."

"He's the jacket guy." I could spot that tailored style anywhere. I relayed my earlier discovery of a bespoke blazer that could pay the rent for a city block for a week, and Avery stared even harder, like she'd be able to hear through the door if her eyesight were a little better.

"I guess it wasn't long forgotten after all."

Max threw her hands up and grabbed him by his impeccably tailored sleeve and dragged him outside.

Instead of closing the door after him, she went out with him and they both disappeared around the corner.

"I can't wait to wring this story out of her." Avery crossed her arms over her chest with a wide grin.

CHAPTER 37
BERK

The semester and our season marched forward until they ground to a halt at the one spot in my life that made me feel like a seven-year-old kid again. I read his text over ten times sitting outside of the location he'd dropped a pin on.

Hey, Kid, I didn't want to say anything until I knew for sure, but here's the last address I have for Elizabeth Vaughn. Sorry I couldn't deliver this to you sooner and sorry it's not better news.

Leaving Jules that morning with a kiss on the forehead while she slept, I'd driven for two hours. Through my windshield, I stared up at the wrought-iron fence with the block letters welded in place.

Dayton Memorial Cemetery.

I don't know how long I sat in my car staring up at the gray sky hoping this was a mistake, that he'd screwed me over and made this all up. I got out of the car and freezing rain pelted my skin, stinging and numbing at the same time. The vise grip in my chest blotted out everything else. Rain soaked into my thermal, weighed my jeans down, and sent rivulets of water into my sneakers.

The dude behind the small desk in the little shack by the entrance jumped when I tugged the door open.

He wiped a napkin over his face and stood as I got closer to his desk. "Did you need some help?"

Water dripped off the ends of my hair and poured down my face. My body was rocked by shivers, my lips trembling with the cold and emotions I tried to hold tight, but the edges were fraying and I was teetering at the precipice.

"I'm looking for someone." My voice was harsh and gravelly. I slid the damp piece of paper with her name on it across the desk to him. The ink had run, making my handwriting barely legible.

His eyes widened and he stared down at it. His gaze narrowed and he looked from me to the paper.

"I need to know if she's here."

Peeling the paper off the desk, he lifted it and went to his computer. Each press of the keys made it harder for me to see. The warmth of the tears pooling in my eyes was sharp against my frozen skin.

He took a bite of his sandwich like what he said didn't have the ability to shred my world. "We have an Elizabeth Anne Vaughn."

"Her middle name was Caroline." A zing of hope rushed through me. Maybe Mason hadn't been as good as I thought. Maybe he'd fucked this up and gotten it wrong.

"Hmm." He scrolled a little more, the sharp noise of his mouse setting my teeth on edge.

"Elizabeth Caroline Vaughn. Born on August twenty-eighth." I sent up a prayer to no one in particular. *Please let this be wrong.*

With a click of his mouse, he glanced from his screen back to me.

"Looks like we have your Elizabeth over on plot 837."

"Are you sure?" I braced my hands on the desk.

He tilted his screen so I could see. Her full name. Her birthday. All right there in black and white.

"Hang on, kid."

The rest of his words were drowned out by the roar in my ears and the hammering of the rain. The door slammed behind me and I flew back outside and into my car. I didn't want his pity.

My breath collected in front of my face in a puff of steam. Each mini cloud dissipated and clung to the windshield, fogging it up from the inside.

A primal scream ripped from my throat, raw and unstoppable.

My phone buzzed and pinged in the cup holder.

Dragging my gaze from the nothingness in front of me, I picked it up. The last message rolled in. The angry sliver of red at the end of the battery icon mocked my stupidity for not keeping it charged and not having a cable with me.

KEYTON: The game is in an hour. Coach is looking for you.

The screen went dead.

Reanimating like new life had been breathed into me, I threw my car into drive.

With my fists white knuckled on the steering wheel, I flew down the roads, trying to remember my route here without my phone's map to guide me.

The lights from my headlights bounced off the patches of wetness in the road. I was speeding into I'm-definitely-getting-pulled-over-by-a-cop-if-they-catch-me territory.

One second, my biggest worry was a ticket, and the next everything went sideways. The road and my tires were no longer on speaking terms. Black ice. I skidded on the patch and flew across all three lanes. Whipping the wheel around, I corrected for the slide and my car lurched to a stop less than a foot from the guardrail.

I dropped my head to the steering wheel. Opening and

closing my hands around it, I let out a breath and tried to get my heart rate under control.

Shaking it off, I checked my mirrors and pulled out into the slow lane, but my car wasn't moving like it should. I climbed out, and the other cars whipping by with their headlights on high showed me exactly what the problem was.

My donut, the one I'd been riding on for months, the one I wasn't even smart enough to get a replacement for with the money from my agent, had decided that this was the perfect time to add another cherry on top of my shit sundae of a day. Tattered pieces of shredded rubber sat where the tire had once been.

Standing on the side of the road, I screamed into the frosty, freezing air. I slammed my hands into the roof of my car, denting the shit out of it. I kicked the side panels and raged against the piece of metal that hadn't done a thing to deserve my ire. Here I was, sitting on the side of the road, all alone.

———

THE PARKING LOT WAS FULL BUT SILENT, EVERY CAR EMPTY, THE tailgaters long gone inside.

Inside, the crowd roared and my blood pounded in my veins, kicking down the door to my heart. The game had started forty-five minutes ago.

And I was fucked.

Racing past stadium security at the team entrance, I darted into the locker room and changed. One of the special teams' coaches walked in as I laced up my shoes and shook his head. Not a word, but the look said 'way to throw your future away, kid'.

The biting cold was no better inside the stadium. The giant heat cannons on the sidelines provided momentary reprieve, but once I stepped out of their line of fire, it was back to icicles.

Everyone on the sidelines stared at me as I walked toward Coach.

"Don't do this." Keyton jumped up from the bench.

The first half ended and the offensive line came off the field. Everyone headed back toward the tunnel and into the locker rooms for the half time motivational speech.

Coach jogged straight past me, looking through me like I wasn't even there. His clipboard in his hand and headset still on, he moved alongside the team.

"Coach, I need to talk to you. I'm sorry I'm late." I spun to catch up.

"I don't have time for you, Vaughn." He kept his eyes straight ahead. "I only have time for people who care enough about this team to show up for their damn games." He ground out those words and blew straight past.

Standing outside the locker room, I banged my head against the cinderblock walls.

"You thought not showing up was enough to save your ass." Johannsen's labored breathing to my right pushed away the pain and provided a laser focus for the building storm inside my head.

"This has nothing to do with you. I wasn't here and my team is still kicking your ass. They didn't even need me."

"How's it going to end up once they realize you've fucked them for the whole season?" He stood in the hallway. His bright red jersey like waving a flag in front of a bull.

I charged at him, not taking a second to think, and met his face with a fist I'd held back for too long.

Every nerve ending was firing like I was out on the field bracing for another hit. My skin tingled, sparking like a misfired firework ready to destroy anything in its way.

For the angry kid standing on a doorstep to a house that would never be home.

For the scared kid thrown from place to place always feeling unwanted.

And for me, the guy who thought he might find that happiness that would never be there again.

I rammed my shoulder into his stomach.

His back slammed into the floor and his fist connected with the side of my head.

My ears rang.

Shouts echoed all around me as security charged toward us.

"Stop them!" A screech broke through the security pile up we had going on.

"Ezra, stop it!" a woman screamed.

Johannsen's eyes widened. His bloody lips parted and his head whipped around, searching over his shoulder as he let go of my jersey.

Willa Goodwin stood on the outskirts of the madness with tears in her eyes. And in that moment, I was glad Jules wasn't here. I'd rather face down anything other than her fear and disappointment—almost anything.

Moments later, I sat in the Coach's office, Johannsen's blood still on my knuckles. The water from my uniform dripped into a puddle on the floor around me.

The clock on coach's desk ticked with each passing second.

"Can we get this over with so I can go home?" Every cell in my body teetered on the edge of complete collapse and an explosion that would take out anyone around me. My legs bounced up and down. I tightened my grip on my knees. Hot and cold flashed through my body; I was on a spiraling roller coaster and there was no ride attendant to let me off.

I squeezed my fists together in my lap and stared down at them. My fingers were still numb. My whole body was numb and my brain was foggy like I was underwater.

"You're about to go home for good. What in the hell happened out there? First, you show up late, taking a spot off the roster from someone who showed up on time, then you lose it out there with a fight that could've cost us the game on a technical."

"I'm sorry."

"That's the best you've got for me." He slammed his hand down on the desk.

He'd always been a fair coach—LJ situation aside. He wasn't one to yell and scream and get in your face. He did the whole quiet disappointment when you screwed up and managed to chew you out without screaming at the top of his lungs, but right now I was beyond caring about anything.

"Maybe Johannsen will want to tell me what your scuffle was about? That have anything to do with you being late?" His eyes bored into mine, drilling down deep to the center of my soul. Any other day I'd spill my guts to him, but not today.

My nostrils flared. It was too much, and the only way to keep it together was to shut down.

It was like I'd been kicked down to the bottom of a pit and all I could do was react. There was no thinking, no higher brain function. It had all been bashed out of my head by one text and a visit to a cemetery. The one thing I'd hoped for, for so long—that I'd finally get answers—was gone. She was gone. Forever.

And I couldn't say it out loud yet.

At some point the words, 'Get out,' left Coach's mouth, and I did. On autopilot, I went through the motions.

The locker room was empty. Everyone had gone home. Even without me, they'd won. I didn't want to face them. I didn't want to see the accusation in their eyes that I'd screwed up and hurt the team. Or worse, that they'd figured out they could do it all without me from here on out.

Jules stood waiting for me inside the tunnel. It seemed they'd kept the news of my fight quiet. She was all brightness and light, but even now my smile was brittle, forced. All I wanted to do was lay down beside her and hold her. I wanted to feel her arms wrapped around me and bury my head in her neck and wake up tomorrow when this nightmare was over.

"What happened?" She covered my hands with hers and she brushed over the small cut on my eyebrow.

I winced as she ran her finger over it.

"I was in the stands right before kick-off and got a message from Keyton saying you weren't here. Where were you? Did you play? I kept looking for your number, but I wasn't sure if I'd missed you out there."

"I didn't play. It's been a long day, Frenchie."

"Were you hurt? Are you okay now?" She fussed, searching my face and my body like she'd be able to diagnose whatever was wrong with me, if she could just see it with her eyes. "Was it Alexis again?"

Why was that where she immediately jumped? My defenses were up for my sister who was trying to do better. She was. It wasn't a crazy party or random person's house. She'd been at the library and her phone had died just after she called me. She knew it wouldn't have lasted long enough to order a taxi, but she was also embarrassed about needing my help just to fill out the applications and didn't want Jules to see her struggle. I got that. Deep down, I understood not wanting other people to see your cracks.

"Can we go home now?"

"Of course, where's your car?"

I tilted my head to the side. "Remember that part about it being a long day? My car broke down. My phone was dead. I was stranded."

She ordered a taxi, and for once something today went right and we only had to stand in the looming shadow of the stadium for a few minutes before it showed up. Rummaging in her purse, she pulled out a power charger and plugged my phone in.

"You can keep that one. Think of it as a birthday present."

The muscles in my back tightened. My birthday. Today.

After everything that had happened, I'd mercifully forgotten to look at the date. With that reminder, it all came rushing back, making me want to find a wide open place to scream until my voice was gone.

She fidgeted beside me. "If it *was* something going on with Alexis, maybe I could help."

"Why does this keep coming back to Alexis? Can you drop it? It's got nothing to do with her."

She snapped straight forward and stared out the front of the car.

What was I doing? I dragged my hands down over my face. Her probing questions for what went down anytime I was in a bad mood kept drifting back to what had Alexis done. What had Alexis screwed up now? And that reminded me, like a sore spot you had forgotten about, but hit all over again. How many women had I dated who had a problem with Alexis? Who had tried to get between us and push her out of my life? There was no way for Jules to help what was wrong with me, and the mentions of Alexis in that tiptoe way of hers ratcheted up my walls.

Jules turned to me and took my hand. "I don't want you to think I'm blaming Alexis, but I don't like seeing you upset. And sometimes you clam up when things go wrong, and I want to help." She traced her fingers along my knuckles. "I don't want you to feel like you're alone."

"Thank you, Jules." I rested my head against hers for the rest of the trip to the house.

Alexis was the only thing close to family I had left. What would happen next year when I was gone? Would she be safe? Or would she pull one last stunt with the wrong guy that went too far and end up in a spot just like my mom? A clawing dread pounded in my stomach.

At this point, was I even going to get a chance at the draft? Coach had dismissed me, telling me he'd figure out my punishment later.

I opened the door to the house and someone flicked on the lights, blinding me. An attack? I stepped in front of Jules.

"Surprise," a chorus of voices shouted. A small painted banner hung in the doorway to the kitchen. 'Happy Birthday, Berk.'

Jules radiated a giddiness that pushed down the rising bile in my throat.

Today was the day I'd lost my mother twice, threw away my football career, and now had to stand in front of fifty people and pretend my world wasn't disintegrating in front of me.

CHAPTER 38
JULES

I couldn't hold back my giddiness and flung my arms around his neck. This would help pick him up. He'd had a shitty day, but the team had won and now there was cake.

His hands came up slowly, hesitantly, and the small prickles of doubt flickered.

"Is this okay?" I leaned back, catching his gaze.

He looked over my shoulder at everyone else. "Now is not a good time. I told you I didn't want to do anything for my birthday." He kept the words low. Not quite clenched teeth, but teetering on the edge.

A knot formed in my stomach.

"I know, but I thought it would be a nice surprise. A way to celebrate a win and your birthday and the game."

Alexis came in and looked around the room. Finally, a little back up. She'd be able to show him how much fun this could be. The party itself and half of the details had been her idea, and I appreciated all the little tips she'd given me along the way.

"A birthday party?" Her eyebrows dipped low like this was some alien ritual she'd been dropped in the middle of.

She hugged Berk and I swear she sniffed him, going up on her tiptoes.

"I wanted to come by because I know how hard today is for you and how much you hate anyone even mentioning your birthday." Her pointed glare turned the knot in my stomach into one looped around the top of an anchor sinking to the bottom of the ocean.

She'd mentioned it to me.

She'd given me the idea to have a party, knowing Berk would hate it. She'd set a trap and I'd fallen for it. I'd been so eager for a little bit of positive female bonding that I'd let her manipulate me. Anger warred with hurt, and anger was winning.

"You hate your birthday?" I turned to Berk, meeting his fiery gaze.

"Remember when those kids teased you in sixth grade when you didn't have cupcakes for the whole class and you took on all five of them? They suspended you for, what?" She tapped her bottom lip. "Two weeks. Didn't I mention that, Jules?"

My mom had almost always been upfront with her disdain for me, but Alexis... a rage unlike any I'd ever known flooded every fiber of my being. She'd not only done this sneaky sabotage to screw me over, but she'd done it knowing it would hurt Berk in the process.

And it was like a switched flipped in my head and I saw everything she'd been doing. Everything the guys had told me about her, everything she'd done to Berk up until this point.

Everyone around us deflated a bit at the not-happy-to-see-them reception from Berk. People talked in the background, grabbed drinks, and steered clear of our little trio.

"His birthdays are always reminders of bad shit."

I glared at Alexis. "I must have missed that part."

Her self-satisfied grin made me want to scream. It was one

thing to take things out on me or hate me because I was with Berk, but to hurt her own brother? But that wasn't what she called him unless prompted or in an attempt to push me out of a conversation.

And the way she'd hugged him when she walked in. That wasn't the hug of someone who thought about someone as a sibling.

Was there a giant flashing 'moron' light above my head? Because there should be. This wasn't about me not being good enough for her brother or her fearing I was using him. This was about her not wanting anyone else as *competition.*

"Dude, what happened today? Coach was losing his mind in the locker room when you didn't show." One of the Fulton U football players passed, dropping off that nugget already three sheets to the wind.

"You didn't show." My head whipped around to Berk.

"I had something to do."

Berk's gaze darted to Alexis.

Did it have something to do with Alexis again? She was trying to sabotage his future. Standing in his way.

"What the hell is that doing out here?" Berk pushed his way through three people and grabbed the old wrapped present that sat beside his cake. "Where did you get this?" He shook it at me.

My mouth opened and closed. Alexis had given it to me. She'd said it was an old present she'd gotten him when they were growing up that he'd been waiting for the perfect time to open. Teasing and joking with her about maybe never opening it in some older-brother torture. And maybe doing it in front of everyone at a party would finally get him to rip that paper off.

Another lie. Another trap. I hated her. I don't know that I'd ever truly hated someone before, but I hated her for what she'd done.

He charged past everyone and headed for the stairs with the gift cradled in his arms.

"Berk! I'm sorry. I didn't know."

"Why can't you leave things alone, Jules?" He walked away from me like this was too much and his head was seconds from exploding. Without another word, he spun around and took the stairs three at a time.

I followed him into his room, trying to figure out how I could fix this. "This was a mistake."

"How do you mistakenly throw someone a birthday party?"

My mouth opened and closed. "Alexis…" My shoulders dipped and I lifted my arm, letting it fall limply to my side. "Alexis mentioned your birthday and that a party would be a good idea." That sounded like such a weak excuse and the look in his eyes told me everything I needed to know.

His head snapped back. "She would never. This is not the day… Especially not today." His voice was tight, like every breath was a chore, requiring every ounce of his strength. He opened his closet and put the present on the shelf. His fingers shook as he set it down and closed the doors.

"Tell me why not today. Let me in, Berk. Tell me what's going on. What happened today? You were late to the game? Do you have any idea what you're putting at risk?"

"I know exactly what's at risk."

"Then talk to me. Tell me what happened and maybe I can help. Maybe we can work on it together."

"There's nothing to be worked on, Jules. There's nothing to be fixed. It's unfixable. Not everything can be solved with cupcakes and cookies. Some of us are dealing with real-world shit that can't be fixed with a smile and a pound of sugar. You don't understand. You couldn't understand. With your country estates that ran in your family, and beautiful three-day engagement parties and your sister's wedding that'll probably cost as much as I make next year in the pros."

"*If* you make it. You didn't play because you were late! There are scouts and coaches watching every move you guys make. What could be so important you'd risk that?"

"You wouldn't understand."

"Was it Alexis? You can't be her white knight for the rest of her life. Did Alexis need help?"

"If this was about Alexis, of course I'd help. Who else does she have but me?"

"She has herself. Her parents. She can't keep hoping you'll swoop in and rescue her. It's not your job. As long as you keep jumping in, she'll never learn how to take care of her own problems."

"You have no idea what it's like to have no one. To have nothing. Absolutely nothing."

"I've lost things." My vision blurred with unshed tears. "I've lost people I care about."

"To death. They didn't choose to throw you away like garbage." He spat the words like an accusation. "Practically chuck you out a moving fucking car with one thing to remember them by and not even a backward glance."

The tears welled and my nostrils flared. I was so sad and beyond angry for that little kid being shown the cruelty of the world no one should have to face alone.

"To have to carry around the few clothes you have in garbage bags under the glare of the foster family you're leaving because they want to make sure you don't steal anything. Have you ever had to leave a house without shoes? Or drank as much water as you could from the bathroom tap because you knew you weren't eating for the next two days?"

"No," I whispered, wrapping my arms around my waist.

"Do you want to know what's in this bag?" He stormed over to the backpack beside his doorway. The one he'd brought to the engagement party, to class, and almost everywhere else. Lifting it off the floor, he tugged on the zipper and pushed it forward.

I peered into the wide-open compartment in the bag. Neat rolls of clothes. Jeans and t-shirts rolled up. Deodorant. Toothpaste and a toothbrush. Another pair of shoes shoved along the side.

"I never knew if I'd have more than five minutes to pack. It's an old habit. Keep essentials in an old backpack, so you can snatch it and run if you need to."

Tears crested down my cheeks at the pain in his eyes. I zipped the pack closed.

"You're not that kid anymore." My voice wobbled. My heart was chipped and bruised for that little boy who didn't know anyone cared. "You've done so many amazing things so far. You're graduating. Entering the draft."

"But I'm still that kid. I'll always be that kid. You don't know what it's like when you've gone through a life like that with someone else. Someone you care about when the rest of the world is telling you you're trash.

"How you'd take the fall for that person, even if they're not blood, because you've ended up in the same three homes together over two years. And she's an ally in a place where you don't even know what the enemies look like."

"You said she ended up in a good home."

He scrubbed his hands down his face. "She did. We both did. But you don't get how hard it is to trust a good thing when you grow up like we did. They were a great family. Treated us well. Treated us like their own kids, like we mattered. But you're always waiting for the other shoe to drop. In the back of your mind, you're like a zoo animal pacing and waiting for whatever comes next, and whatever comes next is never good. You're always looking for the cracks." He leaned against the wall and slid down to the floor, dropping his head. "And sometimes you make them yourself."

"What happened?" I slid down beside him and crossed my legs, setting my hand up on my knee, palm up.

He glanced over, staring at it like he wasn't sure he'd take it. Like he didn't want to take it. A part of me curled up inside and I drew it back. His hand shot out and he caught it, threading his fingers through mine.

"She got into trouble. They were great people, but they had a couple rules. No drinking and no drugs. It was to keep us safe, but…" He shook his head. "Alexis has always wanted to push buttons. She's always teetering on the edge. And she started hanging out with the wrong crowd. I warned her. Told her not to mess that place up. We were lucky to be in such a great home." He talked more to himself than me, but he kept his hand in mine. "She was only in middle school. I was in high school. I couldn't keep her out of trouble and one day, they found a stash of drugs she'd been hiding for another kid. Someone had figured she was young, so she wouldn't get in trouble."

"And she begged you to cover for her." It's what she always did; expected him to bail her out.

"No." He snatched his hand away from mine. "I did it without her even asking. Do you know what happens to girls in bad homes? Thirteen-year-old girls who are looking for affection and love in places they never should? She didn't have to ask. I did it. I told them it was mine and I'd asked her to hold it for me. I was older. Bigger. I could defend myself. So I took the fall and went to the group home. She was the only one to visit me there."

"Because it was her fault. It's called guilt. Did she get kicked out?"

"No, that's why I did it. To protect her." Shaking his head, he looked at me like I didn't understand anything, but I did.

I understood how every text I sent Alexis trying to organize party details was replied to with the 'Call Me!' Her responses were the perfect cover. Nothing she'd said had been in writing. I couldn't actually prove she'd helped plan the party or tried to sabotage Berk and me. She had plausible deniability.

I'd been so starved for any kind of sisterly affection I'd let her nail down the stakes to my own trap. And she'd used my eagerness to break what Berk and I had been building. She's used her closeness to him as a weapon against someone else who might love him.

It was selfishness on top of more selfishness. Her whole life had been one long episode of Berk cleaning up after her, and her robbing him of happiness he damn well deserved.

"She was a messed up kid."

No shit. And she was going to destroy his life.

He jumped up.

"And what's her excuse now?" I stood up too, pushing off the wall. "She went through a lot of what you did, but got to stay with the great family because of you, and unlike everything you've accomplished, she's not trying to do better. She's trying to drag you down. Everything you told me only makes it worse. She screwed you over and didn't even appreciate what she had. Look at you. Look at how far you've come. And the amazing future you have—she's trying to destroy that. She's not good for you." I swallowed past the boulder lodged in my throat.

"You keep telling me not to put up with the toxic people in my life, but you need to look at the people in your life too. You need to do this for you." I lifted my hands to his face, but he caught my wrists.

"And for you, right?" He pushed my hands away. "If I want to be with you, I've got to cut her off." He practically snarled. "Not see her anymore."

CHAPTER 39
BERK

She shook her head. "No, I'd never give you an ultimatum like that. I'd never force you to make that choice. I know you love her. And I love you." Her voice cracked. "Coming third isn't the issue. But I can't stand by and watch someone hurt you. Football comes first. I know that. And I'm okay with that." She let out a shaky breath, pushing her hands out palms-down like that was an issue long ago settled in her mind.

"You are so fierce and unstoppable out on the field. But *I* need to put *me* first. And I can't stand beside you and watch her toxic behavior tear you down. I can't do it and I won't."

I blinked, staring at her through the sawing pain eviscerating my heart. "Then where does that leave us?"

"You tell me." She wiped at her nose with the back of her hand, her eyes red-rimmed and boring into my soul.

My phone vibrated on the desk. Alexis's name flashed across the screen. The insistent buzz against the wood was a ticking time bomb in Jules's and my fledgling relationship.

ALEXIS: How are you doing? I can bring you up some cake. I tried to talk her out of it.

Why wouldn't Alexis warn me, if she'd known Jules was planning this? Especially if she'd tried to talk her out of it?

A heads-up would've been nice, Alexis.

"I can't just walk away from her. I won't. She's my sister." Why couldn't Jules see that? But Alexis couldn't see that either... There was nothing Alexis could do to get me to stop caring about her. Especially not now. She was the closest thing I had left to family. The only person who not only knew the ugly truth of my childhood, but had been there by my side for a lot of it.

From that first time she'd asked me to read a story from a tattered *Highlights Magazine* she'd found shoved in the back of a toy box, she was someone I'd never let down. I wanted to be that person for Alexis and I'd wanted to be that person for Jules. Why couldn't Jules understand that?

"I can't watch you ruin your future over someone who'd never sacrifice half the things you've sacrificed for her. Who'd knowingly do something to hurt you. You deserve better than that."

"What you're saying is I deserve you? You come in here telling me you're not going to make me choose between you and my sister and that's exactly what you're doing by making her sound awful. You think you're so much better than her? Than me?"

The door pushed open behind Jules. Alexis stood there with a party hat on and a plate with two slices of cake on it.

Jules shook her head and rushed forward to me. I stepped back. "No, we're done. I'm done with this game of pretend you were so good at playing."

She stopped trying to touch me and backed up. Her gaze darted over her shoulder and her entire body went rigid. "Alexis, let's clear this up."

"Clear what up?" Alexis stepped farther into the room with her eyebrows furrowed, looking at Jules like she had no idea what she was talking about.

"What does Alexis have to do with this? Stop trying to drag her into everything."

Jules whipped around. "Is that what you think I'm doing?"

"What else am I supposed to think?"

"Then here's something for you to think about when it comes to the always-innocent Alexis. If she hadn't been helping me—" Jules took a deep breath and swallowed. "Then how'd I know about the present? The one that apparently means so much to you, but you've never shown me. I don't know why Alexis would want to set me up, but that's exactly what she did."

Doubt jabbed at the back of my mind.

Alexis edged closer to me. "Berk, remember what happened with Gretchen?"

Gretchen was a girl I'd dated for a little bit senior year of high school, who'd never liked Alexis. Started making wild accusations about Alexis until I'd had to end things. It had hurt. A deep down kind of hurt that I hadn't wanted to revisit again.

"Why would Alexis lie?"

Jules clutched her hands in front of her face. "Why would I?" Her gaze swung to Alexis, but her words were trained on me, like daggers straight to my heart. "I hope you don't lose everything you've worked for, for someone who doesn't treat you the way they should. People who want the best for us don't try to cut us off from other people who love us."

With tears in her eyes, she gave me one last look. "Bye, Berk." She fled the room and down the steps. The patter of her feet left bruises on my heart with each step. An anchor was wrapped around my ankle and there was no escape. Anytime I finally got my head above a wave someone added another ten pounds, dragging me back under, and I was choking on the inky blackness of the waves, my chest burning for relief.

"Hey, Jules," Keyton called out from downstairs. "Where's Berk?"

And then the door slammed. Silence. Ringing so loudly in my ears I couldn't think straight. Her smile. The way she rested her head on my back and trailed her fingers down my sides. The way I held her in my arms and rested my cheek against hers. The nervous way she pushed up her glasses right before I took a bite of something new she'd made. All gone. Wiped away.

I tried to blink back the tears. Tears I hadn't let fall since I was eight. But I couldn't hold them back. An overwhelming tide crashed into my chest and wrenched away the threadbare hold I had on myself.

Throwing my arm out, my hand connected with the wall again. I braced my hands against the dented wall and hung my head. My phone buzzed again on my desk. I picked it up and flung it as hard as I could. It hit my headboard, the screen splintered into a spider web of glass, but it just kept buzzing. It bounced off the bed and onto the floor.

"Berk." Alexis's footsteps creaked on the floor.

"Not now," I bit out and squeezed my eyes shut. "Just go, please." Bracing my arm against the wall, I breathed, panting like I'd been forced to run laps for an hour.

"I'll leave the cake here for you." She slid it onto my makeshift nightstand.

As she pulled back, I wrapped my fingers around her wrist. "She said you didn't tell her about how I felt about my birthday."

"Of course I did. More than once." She stepped back with her eyes wide. Party sounds drifted from downstairs, the low rumble of music vibrating through the floor. People laughed and shouted, going on like nothing had even happened. Like fiery rubble hadn't been toppled over on top of me, crushing every inch of me like a raw nerve.

"How'd she know it was my birthday in the first place?"

"Maybe she saw it on your social media or something."

"Why throw a party? She said you knew? Why didn't you stop her?"

"She was adamant about doing it. She kept trying to rope me into it. Every time she'd text me with some big new idea, I'd tell her to call me, so I could talk her out of it."

That explained part of it. But... "So, you let me walk into an ambush?"

Her mouth opened and closed. "I... I thought after the last time I talked to her, she'd realize what a bad idea it was." Alexis licked her lips and her gaze darted away.

Another mystery. "Why are you here today? You never just show up."

She licked her lips. "I was in the neighborhood and wanted to stop by."

"Even if you're five blocks away, you always call me to pick you up." The pit in my stomach soured and I got that watery mouth feeling that proceeded the inevitable. I swallowed back against the rising bile.

"Maybe I'm turning over a new leaf. Making more of an effort." She shrugged and tried to pull off a nonchalant smile. But she wouldn't look me in the eye.

And the picture clicked like the last piece of a thousand-piece puzzle sliding into place. Every time she'd ever lied to me. Every time she'd stretched the truth or told me she'd been to the movies with friends. Or told me she didn't know what the stash was that the guy she'd liked had asked her to hold for him. And the raw ugly truth of it came barreling toward me.

"You wanted to be here when it blew up. When I walked in on a fucking sixth grade birthday party time warp."

"No. I was hanging out with some friends around the corner." She backed up a couple steps.

"Pretty convenient timing. How'd Jules know about the present?" I pushed myself up off the floor.

She shrugged and crossed her arms over her chest. "Maybe she's been poking around your room when you're in the bathroom or something." Defensiveness radiated off her like a shield, one she'd never put up around me before.

"What did you do, Alexis? How did Jules know about my mom's present?"

"Why would I do something with your present? I know how much it means to you."

"Because you knew it would freak me the hell out. It would fuck with my head. Do you know why I missed half my game today?" My words were low, like a warning growl.

She stood there mutinously silent, like I was her jailer and anything she said could be used against her in a court of law.

"I found my mom today."

Her head snapped up. "You did?"

"At the Dayton Memorial Cemetery."

"Berk—" She slapped her hand over her mouth.

"After the day I've had, Alexis, I need you to tell me the truth." My voice cracked and I pleaded with my eyes. I needed the truth. "Did you give her the present? Did you tell her about my birthday and make her think planning this was a good idea?"

Her fingers tightened on her arms. "Don't you understand what everyone else who's come after you has tried to do? What they want?"

"Did you give her the present?" The blood pounded in my veins, throbbing in my neck.

"All they want to do is use you." She rushed forward, so close she stepped on the toe of my shoe. "They don't understand where we're coming from."

"Don't make me repeat it."

"She buddied up to me, wrote me a note digging for the inside scoop on you. Trying to find ways to insinuate herself into our life."

"Into *my* life." I jammed my finger into the center of my

chest. "Or maybe to do something nice. Become friends with someone she knew I cared about. That's what people do when they love you." My words shot through the gap between us like bullets.

Alexis stumbled back like I'd shoved her. "She doesn't love you! No one really loves us except for *us*."

"I can't believe you'd do this." I spun around, unable to look at her. I stared out the window across the street. All the lights were off. Jules was over there thinking that everything else came before her when all I wanted was to be with her. My loyalty to my family over her had been misplaced, a mistake I regretted now. "You got her to throw this party knowing how much it would rip me apart inside."

"I didn't—"

"You fucking did." I jabbed an accusatory finger at her.

"I'm sorry, Berkie." She ducked her head and peered up at me.

"You can't pull that shit with this. I'm not falling for that anymore." And then it hit me, an even uglier truth I'd pushed aside. "The Letter Girl. That was you. You're the one who posted the whole thing. That sacrificed her to the damn wolves."

"She was hanging all over you in that video. And she was lying. She dated you, lying the whole time about who she really was."

"Because she was afraid to tell me. She was afraid I'd be disappointed. But you made all her fears come true. How did you even know Jules was TLG?"

"Because of that fake 'let's be friends' letter she wrote me the day we met. Who even writes letters anymore? It was so extra and fake, such a try-hard move. I recognized the hand-writing."

"Jules isn't fake like that! Were you happy when she broke up with me? Are you happy now?" My words came out like growls, teetering on the edge of feral.

"No." Tears shone in her eyes, but I wasn't swayed by them this time.

"You need to leave."

"Berk, please." She grabbed onto my arm.

I shook her off. "No, Alexis. I've put up with a lot over the years. I've helped you dodge a shit-ton more than I should have…" I raked my fingers through my hair. "But you're not the sister I thought I had. If you could do this to me… If you could do this to someone I love." I squeezed out that last word, it was barely a whisper between us. "You're not the person I thought you were." And holy fuck, did I ever owe Jules an apology.

Everything was silent. The only sound in the room, my labored breathing as my mind tried to piece together the betrayal ripping through me. All the music and talking downstairs had stopped. The same kind of pin-drop silence that had accompanied the cop showing up to drag Nix away last year.

A knock shattered that silence. Keyton opened the door. "Coach is here. He said you need to come with him right now." The grim look on his face didn't come near the weighted rock around my neck.

"I've got to go," I said over my shoulder.

"I knew it. It was only a matter of time before you abandoned me like everyone else." Alexis turned the knife a little harder from behind me.

All I wanted to do was race across the street and tell Jules she was never third in my heart, football didn't even come close to second to how I felt about her. But even though Alexis thought I'd abandoned her, I knew I'd forgive her. My eyes were opened to her problems being a hell of a lot bigger than I imagined, but she'd always be my sister.

How could I go to Jules knowing Alexis would be a part of my life? I couldn't ask her to forgive what Alexis had done.

Was it even fair to push another toxic family member onto Jules after everything she'd already been through?

In twenty-four hours my life had been turned upside down, imploded by my own stupidity. The team's season, my future, and what was left hung in the balance. I'd done too much to screw all that up already.

Every eye in the house was on me as I descended the stairs. Coach stood in the open doorway, his gaze locked on Marisa, who stood beside LJ, using him as a buffer between them.

Coach's grim gaze locked with mine. "We're going to sort this out once and for all."

———

"Rumors are flying about agents and under-the-table money. Let's have it out." Coach glared at me and I resisted the urge to shield my forehead from the incoming scorch mark.

After a talk out on the porch, I was told to report to Coach's office at six am. As I was standing outside his door, Johannsen and his coach, Mikelson, stormed down the hallway. We were all waiting for our audience with the judge and jury in my career execution. Drained: that's what I was. A bottomless pit of nothingness. What was left? Football would be gone in just a few minutes. The dream of finding my mom had come to its own cruel conclusion. Alexis… I didn't even know where to start with her. But the one piece of my life that made the cavernous void feel like the airless expanse of space was Jules.

I'd lost Jules—no, not lost—pushed her away. I'd shoved her love right back in her face and let her walk away from me. The burning ache in my chest made it hard to feel anything else. I was empty without her and what I'd lost didn't compare to that pain.

"Fighting in the opposing team's tunnel." The STFU coach, Mikelson, glared at Johannsen like he was ready to peel the flesh from his bones.

We sat beside each other in chairs that fit us like they'd been brought in from a local elementary school.

"Who wants to go first?" Coach sat on the edge of his desk with his arms crossed over his chest.

Mikelson went with the caged tiger approach, pacing in front of us like we were steaks they'd tossed into his cage after a few skipped meals.

Johannsen and I tilted our heads, barely acknowledging each other's existence, neither one of us wanting to go first.

"Nothing! That's what you two have for us?" Mikelson spit out. "How about this? How about the two of you are suspended through the rest of the season? All those draft dreams poof…" He wiggled his fingers in the air in front of our faces. "Up in smoke."

I kept my lips welded shut, expecting it all to come pouring out of Johannsen.

But he kept his lips tight. His leg bounced up and down.

"We had a disagreement." Each word was tendon tight. Johannsen kept his gaze trained straight ahead.

"Don't leave us hanging, boys. Because that's what you both are right now, like preschoolers getting hauled into the principal's office. Only you're not skipping out of here to clap the erasers after class."

The grinding from Johannsen's jaw warred with the bass drum rumbling in my chest. My fingers tingled and my mouth was full-box-of-saltines dry. I licked my lips.

"Over what?" Coach leaned down trying to catch my eye.

My gaze darted over to Johannsen. I'd have thought he'd be jumping out of his chair to give every hint of a detail he had, but he didn't seem to want to be here any more than I did.

Mikelson got in his face. "You start something and now you don't want to say a word?" Spittle flew off his lips.

"Bill, calm down." Coach grabbed Mikelson and pulled him back. "Why don't you take a walk and I'll figure this out?"

Mikelson opened his mouth, but Coach gave him the look. The one that broke down cocky freshman who thought they'd be playing first string since they were hot shit back in high school. The look that had former players of his, now NFL gods, falling all over themselves to escape the blast zone.

And without another word, he was gone and we were left alone with Coach. I'd have almost preferred Mikelson.

"Who's going to talk first?" His voice was calm and even like it always was.

"Coach." I licked my dry, cracked lips.

"It was over a girl." Johannsen shot forward in his seat. "He was pissed about a girl I was going for and this was payback." His gaze cut sideways, skating across mine.

"A girl." Even though it was a statement, the question hung heavy with each syllable.

"Brick's sister," I offered, ducking my head.

"You two were scrapping out in the hallway and you are throwing out accusations about taking money that could have my entire team's whole season stricken from the record books over the sister of a player, Jason Stringer, who graduated last year? That's what you're both telling me? That this was some team code to not mess with another player's sister gone awry?"

The seconds ticked by. Each strike of the second hand seeming to rattle the floor under the laser focus of Coach's gaze.

"Your pro careers are on the line here. Get your testosterone under control." He tapped a thick stack of papers against his leg as he leaned against the desk.

Time slipped away in front of his gaze. Hours? Was he waiting us out for hours?

"If that's what you're sticking to, then at least now you've got your stories straight. You're not getting out of here unscathed. There will be repercussions and you two had better pray we make it to the national championship or you can kiss your pro careers goodbye. Now get out of here. I'll let you know once the final punishment has been decided."

"Thank you, Coach," we said in unison and got up from our chairs.

Mikelson was ready to lay into us but Coach intercepted him, dragging him back into the office.

The tense energy pulsed in the hallway, repelling us from each other like moving truck-sized magnets.

Every scenario I'd run, I ended up off the team, my pro career ended before it began. Why wasn't it? What Johannsen did didn't make sense. He had me. He could've spilled every bit of intel he had, and Coach, being the stand-up guy he was, would've reported me. I'd be suspended. Everything I'd worked for demolished.

But he hadn't.

Without even a look my way, he took off in the opposite direction.

"Thanks, man," I offered, not even sure if he'd heard me.

He froze, his shoulders shooting up with his hands shoved in his pockets. "I didn't do it for you." Whipping his hands out, he spun around. "I'm always the fucking bad guy, right? Not the cheaters? Not the assholes who do whatever the hell they want. Living it up with all those rich assholes who look down their noses at people like us." He charged back at me. "Sure hope you like your vacation or new car or whatever other bullshit you spent it on." He spat the words out like barbs.

And I got right in his face. "You think you're the only one dealing with shit?" My voice dropped to a growling whisper.

I didn't need to broadcast my misdeeds all over the stadium. "I took the money. I didn't spend it on any of that. I spent it on a PI to track down my mom. The one who dropped me off on my ex-con, soon-to-be-lifer dad's porch when I was seven." A rolling, grinding anger that I couldn't hold back shot forward.

His head snapped back and he stared back at me. The muscles in his neck worked overtime. "Did you find her?" The sincere interest threw me, but I'd learned about letting my guard down around him.

"Yeah, I found her." I lifted my chin. "At the Dayton Memorial Cemetery." The shot at my raw wound deflated my anger and that let the pain right back in.

"Fuck."

I tipped my head back. "That's been my last few days, so before you go shouting about people doing stupid shit just because they can, think about why someone like me would do something so monumentally stupid. It was wrong. I shouldn't have done it, but I had to know."

His gaze was trained on the floor between us. "Are you glad you do? Even though the news was shitty?"

"It's better than not knowing."

There was a beat between us and he nodded. "I guess."

And he was gone.

With the bullet of the century dodged, now it was time to fix the other burning rubble of my life.

CHAPTER 40
JULES

My head pounded and I lay in bed staring up at the ceiling. I'd promised myself I wasn't going to cry —much. That crack in my chest had widened to the point that the Grand Canyon looked quaint, but the tears had run dry. Salty trails made the skin from the corners of my eyes to my hairline dry and itchy.

I hadn't called Elle. What was I supposed to say? She'd shown up after I'd already left, and sent a text wondering where Berk and I were. I wasn't surprised he'd bailed after I left, but I hadn't felt like any company. That was three days ago.

We were over. I'd broken up with him again, not because of my insecurity but because for once I'd been able to stand up for what I knew was right, so why did it hurt so damn much? I curled into a ball and buried my face in my pillow. The smells of fresh soap and sandalwood hit my nose, the exact scent of Berk right after a practice shower, lounging in my bed.

But he hadn't bothered reaching out to try and make things right. He'd chosen a toxic person over me, and I had to stop thinking about him.

I squeezed my eyes shut and counted to five.

One: I'm still here.

Two: I can do this.

Three: I did the right thing.

Four: I deserve to be in a loving, trusting relationship.

Five: The pain will go away—eventually…

Sitting up straight, I repeated the mantra over in my head. I grabbed my towel and hidden stash of shower gel and padded out to the bathroom.

Zoe's door swung open. Nick strode out with a towel around his waist.

"Not today!" I ducked into the bathroom and closed and locked the door.

"Come on, Jules. I've got class."

"Maybe take a shower at your own place," I called out and put my stuff down.

"But you've got kick-ass water pressure."

I let out a huff of laughter. Leave it to Nick to break through the storm clouds hovering over my head with a bout of his ridiculousness.

My reflection wasn't doing me any favors in the self-esteem department, but other than the sand bags under my eyes, aching in my chest, and inability to sleep I was right as rain. But I'd promised Avery and Max I'd come in today. Obviously, that had been before the birthday disaster from hell, but it gave me a reason to drag myself out of bed.

Showered and doing my best human-being imperson-ation, I made it to B&B, ducking under hanging ghosts, pumpkin garlands, and Christmas lights. Some people just couldn't hold off.

"There she is," Avery called out the second I walked in. "What's wrong?" She put down her rolling pin and walked over to me, holding onto my shoulder.

I wouldn't burst into tears. I would *not*. I refused.

The brave face I'd clung onto on the way over was shattered in a second as I grabbed onto her and buried my face in her chest.

Everything came pouring out once the door to her office clicked shut.

"His sister sounds like a heinous bitch."

"You're not even half wrong. I thought she was just a bit of a mess at first, but what she did was next-level awful. Not just to me, but to Berk."

"Let me tell you from experience, family members like that..." She ran her hand over her ever-expanding bump. "They can poison things between you so easily if you're not on the same page. And it sounds like he's still got some things to learn when it comes to her."

"It feels like someone's sawn me in half."

"Time. That's the only cure and even then, sometimes the ache is still there, but you did the right thing." My eyes filled with tears again at her reassuring arm squeeze. "Sometimes you have to think about yourself and put yourself first. I learned that lesson the hard way. You can't be everything to everyone all the time and give and give until there's nothing left of you. And she'd have undermined everything you did, planting seeds of doubt in his head if he wasn't ready to see what she was doing. You can show people all you want, but that doesn't mean you can make them see."

My shoulders sagged, the power of her quiet reassurance reverberating through me.

Max burst into the office with a cake knife in her hand. "I thought I heard crying. Who do I need to take out?"

Avery and I looked at each other before bursting out laughing.

"I've never had many friends, but I like to think I've got you." I looked to Avery and Max.

Max's head jerked back when my gaze landed on her. "Me, too?" She pointed the tip of the cake knife at her chest.

"You did burst in here threatening to disembowel whoever made me cry with that, so I'd consider us friends."

"It's not like I need a reason." She spun the handle of the knife over the backs of her fingers, looking more badass than anyone should while covered in icing and wearing a tie-dyed bandana over their hair. With a look at me, she squinted and lifted her chin. "Yeah, I guess we're friends."

"Don't hurt yourself, Miss Emotional." I turned away from her and crossed my arms over my chest.

The darting blur of her body was the only warning I got before she slammed into my back and wrapped her arms around me, squeezing me tight and rocking me back and forth.

"You got the squeeze and rock." Avery whistled. "That means you'll never be rid of her. She's like a wart you can't freeze off now."

Max let go of me and glared at Avery, barely keeping her smile in check. "Maybe someone's worried about being replaced," she challenged.

"I'd be happily dethroned, if it meant Emmett and I didn't have you literally watching us bang."

"How was I supposed to know that's what you two were doing under that desk?"

The laughing fest only grew from there, but in the background the ache was still there. *I'm still here. I'm still breathing.* I went through my mantra again.

We got to work and Max came back to steal food after one of her clients left the shop.

The cashier poked her head through the door. "You've got a visitor."

"Not again." Max threw down her donut.

Avery and I looked at each other. Max had been a steel trap, locked up like Fort Knox about who her tall, dark, and handsome visitor had been. Every question was met with a glare or a growl.

"Not you, Max. It's for Jules."

I wiped my hands on my apron. My heart thundered in my chest. As hard as it would be to face him, I'd wondered if Berk would show up. Pushing through the door, I scanned the space beyond the door cases and my eyes widened.

"Laura? What are you doing here?"

She had her hands clasped in front of her. "You usually recorded on a Tuesday, so I took a chance that you'd be here. I've been meaning to come by for a while."

"What do you want to try?"

"You can pick. I'm sure you know better than me."

I recoiled at the dig.

She dropped her hand onto my arm. "Because you're working here and helping make all this amazing stuff." With a small squeeze, she let go.

Grabbing a couple plates, I kept peeking over at her, trying to figure out why she was here. Why today? Her hair was up in a simple ponytail, but it didn't look like it had been shellacked to within an inch of its life. She wasn't even wearing heels with her jeans.

"Here's a blueberry cake donut and pumpkin spice sugar cookie."

"Thanks." She slid one of the plates closer to her.

We sat together in silence, her crunching bites of the pumpkin-shaped sugar cookie the only sound at our table. The rest of the place was empty. Even the cashier had left, probably trying to escape our awkwardness.

"The wedding is on Saturday."

"I know. I'll be there." For a second, there was a claw of fear down my back that Mom had sent her here to disinvite me. It was like a reflex, but sitting across from her, I wished she would. My guilt would be absolved and I wouldn't have to sit through a ceremony and reception with people faker than the bags sold on South Street.

"Of course you will be. What do you think Dad would

think?" She peered up from her plate with the corner of her mouth quirked up.

"He'd probably freak out at the price tag. And hate the fact you're not having it at Kelland."

"What do you think he'd think of Chet?" Her head ducked again and she picked at the bright crystalized sugar on her cookie.

"If you're happy, I'm sure he'd be happy."

"And if I'm not?" Her gaze locked with mine.

"He'd probably tell you not to do it." I covered her hand with mine. "You don't have to marry Chet if you don't want to."

She snatched her hand back. "You're jealous. Of course you'd say that." Her face was the perfect reflection of Mom's dismissal.

My chair screeched across the floor as I shot back like she'd smacked me.

Jumping up from her seat, she grabbed my hand and squeezed it tight, switching chairs to the one beside me. "I'm so sorry, Jules. I didn't mean that. It was a knee-jerk reaction." She petted my hand, keeping her vise grip on me, so I couldn't get away. "In reality, I've always been jealous of *you*."

Well, now I was glad she was holding onto me because I'd have fallen out of my chair if she weren't holding on.

"You were jealous of *me*? Since when?"

Laura barely stopped her eye roll. "Since you got to go to Kelland most weekends with Dad, and Mom had me playing pretty, pretty princess. He never cared about you getting dirty or staying up late and eating ice cream. It was like they were divorced while they were still married, and I got the short end of the parenting stick."

"Mom's still here." I squeezed her hands in mine.

Peering over at me out of the corner of her eye, her lip trembled. "Do you ever wonder what things would have been like if it were reversed? If we'd lost her instead of him?" She pinched her lips together and blinked, quickly, dropping her gaze.

"Sometimes, but I can't power up my time machine, so I try not to dwell on it too much and remember the fun we did have. And I look for that in my life now, trying to find people who make me that happy."

"I don't think I've ever had a happier day than when Mom was sick and I got to go with you two to that carnival."

"You puked, like, three times." I laughed, grabbing onto that happy memory and wanting to keep it close to my head.

"The funnel cake, caramel apples, and popcorn were so worth it." She wiped at the corners of her eyes. "You let me ride with him as much as I wanted that day." Her lips twisted and she took a shuddering breath.

"You didn't have a chance to hang out with us often. I figured you deserved to."

"You're a great sister." Her voice cracked. "If I've never told you that before."

Fanning her face, she checked the time on my phone. "And I've got to go. Time to be fake happy for fake people I fake like." She slung her bag onto her shoulder and pushed back from her chair. With a real hug that made my ribs ache, she turned to the door.

"If you're looking for permission to not go through with it?"

She stopped, but didn't turn around.

"You don't need it from me. You don't need it from anyone. You can make that choice. You've got to decide what kind of life you want to live and not let anyone else's expectations kill that dream of a happy life. We only have one."

With a glance over her shoulder and a tight-lipped smile, she pushed out the door and left me in the empty bakery.

Still breathing.

CHAPTER 41
BERK

My palms were sweating and I'd already been through a hundred conversations with myself on the way over before I knocked on the door and took a step back.

It swung open and her eyes widened.

"Berk, what are you doing here?" Alexis hung on to the door like it was the only thing holding her up.

"We need to talk."

She nodded and let me in.

The awkwardness in the room was like sitting in a doctor's office waiting for a terminal prognosis.

Alexis's sweater sleeves were tugged down, almost covering her hands that were sandwiched between her legs, which bounced up and down, her heels tapping against the ground with each fall.

"Is this where you make it official?" She brushed her hair back behind her ear, keeping her gaze trained on her knees.

"Make what official?"

"Where you tell me you're done with me? That after all you've done for me, you're finally over it?" She crossed her arms over her chest and ducked her head.

"Alexis, you're my sister. I'm not going anywhere. No matter how many times I say it and show it, it hurts that you don't believe me."

"I want to." She wiped her eyes. "But it's hard."

"And no one can blame you for that, but what you did was wrong. Fucking wrong." My throat tightened. "Why would you do that to me? Hell, forget me, to Jules? And I don't even want to think of who else you've done something like this to in the past. This jealousy or whatever it is, it can't keep going on."

"I'm sorry."

"You can't spend the rest of your life waiting for it to all come crashing down or trying to bring it on by doing crazy things. Stop trying to make people prove they love you. You have a chance. A chance a lot of kids who grew up like us don't get. I love you and I'll always love you, but I can't keep letting you sabotage yourself, and I won't let you stop me from having the future I've worked for and deserve."

Her micro-nods were followed by watery eyes that she wiped at so hard, there was a red band across her face. "You've always been good to me, and I'm sorry. Mom and Dad have been trying to get me to see a therapist for a long time, and I finally took them up on that offer. I want to do better. I need to do better."

I dropped my hand onto her knee. "That's a great start. Don't keep pushing away the people who care about you."

"I'll try." Her pinched smile would've been enough to get me to believe before, but not now. I'd wait for her to follow through, but let her know I'd be cheering her on from the sidelines. "And I'm going to tell Mom and Dad about the drugs."

I shook my head before she finished the sentence. "Don't. It's in the past. You don't have to throw away what you have with them for something I'm never going to get."

"They need to know. They should know the truth about

you—and me." Her sadness was so palpable I could taste its acrid sting in the air.

"You're their daughter. That's all they need to know. I don't need you to do that to prove anything to me." I scrubbed my hands down my face. "It's been a long day. I'm heading home." Getting up from the couch, a small piece of broken fragments of my life slipped back into place. Slowly, I'd rebuild this.

"Thank you for coming, and tell Jules I said thanks, too."

"I'm here because you're my family. Jules doesn't know I'm here. We're still broken up. I haven't seen her since the party."

She rushed forward. "What? Why? You know I lied." Her voice was so sharp it made me recoil. "Why didn't you go to her?"

"I screwed up big time with her, and maybe it's better that I don't bring even more chaos into her life."

"But—"

"Drop it. Focus on you and don't worry about this."

I opened the door and a new plan formulated in my head. Outside, I tugged my zipper up against the cold rushing through the city streets. Taking out my phone, I scrolled through my contacts searching for a name I'd never thought I'd message.

Hey, it's Berk. Jules' Berk. I could use your help.

CHAPTER 42
JULES

stood in the doorway to the church, sneaking in a call to Elle to take the edge off the wonderful day's festivities. I especially liked the highlights so far. My mom 'forgetting' to book me in for the hair appointment and failing to give me the correct times for the 'getting ready' photography session.

It was only a matter of time before she requested I be sent off for another errand when the pictures were taken after the ceremony.

"Why didn't you tell me you were going alone? I'd have come with you." Elle chastised me on our call.

"I needed to do this myself. Plus, I didn't need you threatening to disembowel Chet again."

"The look on his face, though. Think of the wedding pictures."

"Oh I know." I ran my hands down over the sheer lilac layers of the dress. "Make it through the day, that's my mantra."

"This is a terrible time, but do you want to talk about him?"

The 'him' needed no naming and I'd made Elle promise

not to tell Nix. That was the last thing I wanted to happen. To create a rift between him and Berk. He needed people in his life who cared about him and weren't doing everything in their power to hold him back.

I ended my call with Elle. The long sleeves helped with the frigid nip in the air that was way too cold for an October afternoon, and they almost made me feel comfortable. But that didn't mean I was prepared for who I saw sitting on the stone bench near the stairs to the church.

The gray skies mirrored my mood. My heels clicked on the stone steps and crunched on the gravel.

"What are you doing here?" Just when I'd thought my day couldn't get any worse.

Alexis stubbed out her cigarette on the stone and stood as I approached.

"Hey, Jules." She had bags under her eyes and looked wrung out.

I crossed my arms over my chest, the beading and sequins scratching my skin. "What are you doing here?"

"This looked like as nice a place for a stroll." Her half-hearted chuckle was met with my dead-eyed stare.

I squeezed my own arms, hugging them tighter to my chest.

"I came to apologize." Her lips tightened and she dropped her gaze. "I was a possessive, psycho bitch and I used my history and relationship with Berk to undermine your relationship and try to turn him against you."

My eyes widened, and I dropped my arms to my sides. Did I need to jam my finger in my ear to make sure I'd heard that correctly? My lips parted, but words failed me. I'd figured she was a pro at gaslighting and that would be her tactic, but brutal honesty? Color me freaking surprised.

"Whenever he's had a girlfriend in the past, or anyone even approaching that level, they've always hated me.

They've always said I wasn't his real sister and he needed to just walk away."

I tilted my head.

"Okay. Okay." She waved her hands in front of her. "Maybe I was part of the problem in some of those situations?"

"Maybe?"

"Fine, I was a huge bitch. Some of them were honestly awful. Princesses in front of him and vipers behind his back, gloating about the things they'd buy once he was drafted and how he'd forget about me, but others..." Her shoulders dropped. "I caused trouble and did everything I could so Berk would come to my rescue. But—" The words stalled in her throat. "Have you ever known someone who cared about you and you couldn't figure out why? Like it didn't make any sense and you never knew when they'd just stop." She stared past me.

"Yeah, your brother—at first."

Her gaze cut to mine. "I guess we're more alike than I thought. I've known Berk since I was seven." She ran her fingers through her hair, her scarlet strands catching in the almost-winter wind.

"Maybe I put myself into shitty situations hoping he'd swoop in to save me. He's my brother, even when I've denied it." Her gaze darted to mine. "It would only be a matter of time before he'd stop thinking of me as his little sister, realize what a fuck-up I was, and kick me to the curb."

"You know Berk would do anything for you. He doesn't need you throwing yourself into insane situations just to see him." My throat tightened and I clenched my hands at my sides, not wanting to ask the question, but needing to know the answer. I relaxed my fingers and ran them along the tulle of my dress. "Do you love him? Like, *love* him, love him?"

Her head shot up. She stared at me wide-eyed, already shaking her head. Her mouth opened.

"Don't lie." I shot her a glare. "You owe me the truth at the very least."

She clamped her lips shut and rubbed her arm. "Maybe for a while I thought I did. A way to keep him closer. Or make sure he'd never—"

"You should know better than anyone that sleeping with a guy doesn't mean he won't leave."

She snorted. "True. But no, I don't. Sometimes I think it would've been easier if I did and he did and then it would run its course and I wouldn't have to live with the fear of him walking out of my life forever. He'd already be gone."

She sliced her hands through the air in front of her. "Not that it would ever have happened. He's always had one hundred percent clarity when it came to our relationship, which is why you were so damn scary, Jules."

"Me?"

"Of course, you. He's so in love with you." Tears glittered in her eyes.

I opened my mouth to stop her.

"No, I've known him longer, remember?" She smiled at me with a wry look. "He's head-over-heels for you. I've never seen him like this with anyone else, except for The Letter Girl, but she wasn't a threat because she was only pen and paper. Except she was you. And you're real. You're the real thing, and sometimes it feels like he's the only person I can count on, and I went a little crazy because I felt threatened. If you two were together, he'd eventually stop needing me to need him, because he'd have you.

"And that's why after you wrote the letter to me, I went up to Berk's room and found one of your old letters and saw it was the same handwriting." She dropped her head. "It was me. I'm the one who put all that out there connecting the two of you. I hoped if he saw you weren't perfect—that you'd lied to him—that maybe he'd break up with you."

A confirmation of a tiny whisper that had been at the back of my mind. "Does Berk know it was you?"

She nodded. "Now he does. I don't think I'm coming back from this. When he found out what I did and how much it hurt you—" The word caught in her throat. "I can't tell you how sorry I am." She lifted her gaze and there was a heart-squeezing sadness in her eyes. "There's nothing I can do to make up for it. Those were private notes between you and him, and I exposed that. He... I... What I deserve is for neither one of you to talk to me again. I deserve him not wanting to be my brother anymore."

"He'd never do that, Alexis."

Her humorless laugh escaped in puffs of breath. "I know that—now. But just because someone's your family, that doesn't mean you can keep hurting them over and over again and get away with it. He has every right to cut me out of his life. It's what I deserve."

I wanted there to be anger. I wanted to rage at her and take all that anger and sadness I'd felt once those letters came out and blast her with it. But another part of me wanted to thank her for that trial by fire where I'd come out the other side more sure of myself and less afraid of what the world thought about me. "I would never tell him not to be your brother, Alexis. And he's never going to stop loving you and being your big brother."

"Do you have any idea how hard it is for me to trust that?" She squeezed her eyes shut. That ache in my chest got a bit deeper, not just for those two scared kids who'd clung to each other when their worlds were being torn apart, but for the adults they'd become, trying to navigate the scariness of the world and the uncertainty that never really left.

She sniffled. "Do you know how hard it is for me to trust anything or anyone?"

"But using that against Berk to try to keep him small when he's made for much bigger things isn't okay."

She sucked in a shaky breath. "I know. That's why I'm here. I want to win you back for him—because you're both good for each other and deserve real love."

"I'll admit I don't know much about being a good sibling, but he's not going to walk out of your life. He's not going to leave you behind, even when you think he should. All his talk about walking away from toxic people…"

Alexis winced.

"But you're his sister. Be the kind of sister he deserves."

"Julia, could you please get in here?" My mother's hiss split the freezing air and added a whole new level of frost. "In the natural light, I can see how that dress is fitting you. Would it have killed you to switch to salads only after the fitting? We'll have to change to all-indoor photography now."

My mom stormed back into the church.

"*That's* your mom?"

We both stared after her disappearing form, trailing a just-off-white-enough train through the open church doors.

"That's my mom." I'd promised myself I wouldn't roll my eyes on Laura's wedding day.

"What a massive bitch." Alexis's spot on my shit list shifted a bit. "She's the one getting married?"

"Nope. My sister is getting married to my ex-kind-of-boyfriend."

Alexis's eyes widened. "Seriously? At least it's not your mom, I guess."

"Silver lining." I huffed, the corner of my mouth lifting.

"The mom who isn't getting married—she's in a white dress."

"Technically, it's champagne."

Alexis squinted. "It looked pretty white to me."

I chuckled. "Me too."

"Damn."

"I'm glad you both had each other. I can't imagine what it was like for you two growing up the way you did, but you don't have to keep being the scared kid. Look at what Berk's done. You can do the same."

"I don't think I'd look nearly as good as he does in the uniform." Her small, sad smile didn't reach her eyes.

"No one could."

"Julia," Mom's exasperated call split the peaceful air outside.

"Give me five minutes." My tone brooked no argument.

Mom jolted, stuttering, before going back inside.

"Want me to sleep with the groom? Give your sister a taste of her own medicine? Add some extra fun to the festive occasion?" Alexis swung her gaze around to me. "Really shake things up?"

The seconds ticked by, and I'd like to say my immediate response was no, but damn if I didn't think about it for a full five seconds. "Nah, I wouldn't wish him on you."

"Fair enough." She dropped her head.

"Has he contacted you?" She ran her nails along the back of her hand.

Razor blade to the heart.

"No, but I want him to be happy. And so should you."

"You make him happy."

My smile was filled with a sadness that dredged the wells of my resolve. *Just keep standing upright.* "Not happy enough."

"Don't let the shit with me screw this up. I've screwed up enough things in his life; I can't add you to it too."

"And I have to think about what I need. He's... it's complicated, even more complicated than I want to admit, but I think it's best that we not see each other right now." It was the mature thing to do. The one that made the most sense. I needed to come first with someone, even if that someone was me.

"Jules..." Laura walked up behind us looking like she'd seen a ghost. Her pale face looked even more stark under the sun-kissed makeup the artist had applied this morning.

"Did mom give you one of her pep talks?" I'd been cornered by her for more than one and always felt like I was walking out of the rubble of a bombed-out building afterward.

She stared down the path leading to the street. "Not mom."

"You're scaring me." I stepped in front of her and held onto both her shoulders. "What happened?"

"I thought I'd sneak in a kiss from Chet before all the madness really settled in. I went to the little room they said he'd be in before the ceremony started." She broke off from her thousand-yard stare and looked at me. "And he was getting a blow job from one of my college roommates. I invited her to the wedding, even gave her a plus one."

I wrapped my arms around her.

"Seems like my offer came a little too late," Alexis said.

Laura broke our hug. "What offer?"

"Don't worry about it." I waved her off. "What do you want to do?"

"Do?"

"You just caught Chet getting a blow job seconds before your wedding. What do *you* want to do, Laura?"

"I—I don't know." She shook her head like she was in slow motion.

"He's cheated on you and you're not even married yet. Is that the kind of life you want to live?"

The distant crunch of leaves under tires, murmur of voices inside the church and my heart hammering in my ears were the only sounds. She stared over my shoulder at the end of the long driveway to the church.

Meeting my gaze, a streak of conviction blazed across her eyes. "No." She shook her head. "No, I don't want any of it."

I grabbed her hand. "Then let's get the hell out of here."

"How do we do that?" She looked to me with worry painted all over her face.

Alexis jumped up and down with her hand raised in the air. "I'm excellent at causing disruptions. I'll go in there and do my thing. You two grab what you need and get out of there."

Laura looked to me like I was the older sister. I squeezed her hand and walked back to the church. "Stay here, I'll be right back."

I turned to Alexis. "You sure you're up for this?"

Alexis interlocked her hands and cracked her knuckles. "It's what I do best." Climbing the steps to the church, she messed up her hair. With a thumbs up over her shoulder to us, she burst through the doors of the church. "Chet, how could you? You told me you were going to marry me. And what about our baby?"

A collective gasp so loud they probably heard it all over the tri-state area whooshed out of the doors.

I ducked into the room where we'd stored everything for the ceremony and grabbed my purse and a set of keys to the classic car Chet had borrowed for their big drive to the reception. The voices in the church got louder. People shouting and scrambling bodies drowned out the organ music even before it came to an abrupt stop.

Swinging the keys overhead, I joined Laura outside. "You ready?"

She stared up at the looming and imposing church and looked back to me. "Ready."

"Let's do this."

CHAPTER 43
BERK

J ogging across the street, I straightened the bow I'd tied around the box cradled in my arms. The lump in my throat grew with each step I took until it was hard to breathe. The steps groaned under my weight and I prayed Jules hadn't heard, probably at her spot in the kitchen in front of the oven, sliding in a cookie sheet full of treats that would taste even better than the last ones, excited to share them with whoever needed a little piece of heaven to brighten their day.

Alexis told me she'd gone to see her, completely following along with her promise of total honesty. More of my life's baggage forced onto Jules. The look in her eyes as I'd lashed out, trying to bury my own pain. It was still hard to think about.

I'd carved out a part of my heart when I pushed her away. When I didn't believe her. There wasn't anything I wouldn't give to erase that from her mind, but I could do something small that might give her a bit of the memories she'd missed out on.

Crouching, I set the box down. Part of me wanted to stay to see her face, but the protector in me didn't want to hurt her any more. The last thing she needed was me standing there waiting for my pat on the back for this. I'd done this because it was the right thing to do, not to win her back or get credit. She deserved it and she should always get all the goodness there was in the world—end of story.

I stared at the door with a longing stronger than any I'd experienced before. I wanted to find my mom and be there for Alexis, but I wanted Jules just as much. Those feelings were different, making me crazy when I wasn't near her. I needed her, but she didn't need someone like me fucking up her life and hurting her.

I'd held her in my arms, brushed away her tears and found myself in her. I'd had a home, something I'd longed for since I could remember, and I'd thrown it away.

Walking backward, I had one foot on the top step when the door swung open.

Jules came out with a plastic container tucked under her arm, fixing her glove, and froze with it halfway on, staring back at me wide-eyed.

The coward in me wanted to make a break for it. Just sprint down the block like a lunatic caught peeking in a window or checking door handles for an unlocked one.

"Berk." Her breath came out in a single puff.

"Hey, Jules."

"There you are. I've been dreaming about these all day." A male voice punched right through our little bubble of past mistakes and heartache.

"Hey, Nigel. I was on my way to you."

My stomach knotted. Who was this guy? Was she moving on already?

He had that perfectly layered t-shirt-sweater-coat combo that always made me feel like I'd stepped inside a furnace.

"Not quickly enough." He hit the steps with his gaze squarely trained on Jules. Not until he got to the second to last one did he even look at me. I'd looked at her the same damn way.

"Hey, I'm Nigel." With his hand out like he expected me to shake it, he stared at me.

Nigel had perfectly-aligned teeth that looked like they'd been brushed and flossed since his first tooth came in. And exactly the kind of guy who'd dote on Jules.

Had the air suddenly been sucked out of the atmosphere? "Berk." I squeezed his hand.

He shook his hand when I let it go. "Great grip you've got there. Now, for the reason I came." His gaze wasn't on me anymore. He walked toward her with his arms extended like he was going to wrap her up in his embrace. She'd moved on already.

"Megan's been bugging me all damn day to get over here and get these from you."

"It's no chicken soup, but I hope it helps. They're still piping hot, so she should be happy." Jules put the container in his hands.

Confusion set in.

"If someone had run them over with their car, she'd be out on the street with a spatula to scrape them up." He laughed. "Thanks, Jules, you're the best." The lean in for a kiss was so fast, I nearly snatched the back of his collar. I'd followed him all the way up from the step.

But it landed solidly on her cheek.

"Don't worry about it. It's kind of my thing." She did a little cute head tilt.

Nigel turned around. "Nice to meet you, Berk with the crazy grip. I've got to get these back to my girlfriend." He shook the cookie box and took off down the stairs.

"His girlfriend."

Jules rocked up on her toes and nodded. "His girlfriend, Megan. My partner for Buchanan's class."

My partner had made a deal to do all the work this semester if it meant he had a free pass to any Brothel parties we had for the year. Easiest trade of my life.

"Oh."

"Did you think he was here for me?" Her half-huff, half laugh and eye roll oozed disbelief.

"What's it going to take to get you to see how irresistible you are?"

She snorted and dropped her gaze and caught the box out of the corner of her eye from the speed of her double take. Sucking in a breath, she dropped, picking up the box like it held the Queen's Crown Jewels.

"Is this…" Her eyes were riveted to the box, taking in every fold and crease. She ran her fingers down the spines of the books reverently, as though touching them too hard might wash away the memory of her father's touch. "The books. How did you get them?"

This time when she looked at me with tears in her eyes, it tapped a place deep inside. One where I was sharing those happy memories with her, even though I'd never been there when she last read these.

"Your sister helped me get them."

"She did?" Jules clutched them tight against her chest, teary eyed with a look of awe on her face. "I haven't heard from her since we Thelma-and-Louise it out of her wedding. Things got a little awkward once we got back to the house. There were presents everywhere. Wedding stuff. Laura said she needed to be alone for a bit, I didn't know if she was mad at me."

"Making a big choice like that doesn't happen without some second guessing, but people can change, grow. Family dynamics are always hard and complicated, but she wanted to do this for you, she just needed a little help." Help like a window jimmied open, three locks picked, one drawer brute-forced open, and someone to vault over the back fence when their mom came home earlier than expected.

"Thank you, Berk. This… I don't have words for it. Thank you." The streetlights made her eyes sparkle. Her mossy green gaze was like a lake on a summer's day, and I never wanted to leave.

"You deserved them. I can't believe I ever thought your mom was nice."

She snorted. "You don't exactly have the best track record with character assessment." Her eyes widened and she shook her head, taking a step forward and holding out her hand. "I'm sorry. I didn't mean that. Alexis came to me to apologize. She seemed sincere, like she's learned a lot with this whole experience."

"I didn't put her up to that. I didn't want her to bother you after... you know."

"I know." A sad, glum nod to go along with the melancholy space between us that was never there before.

"There's been... Talking about my character assessment ability—" I took a breath to gather my thoughts. *Don't hold back now.* "There have been other people in the past who've tried to get between us. They'd hone in on the fact that we weren't blood related and use that as a reason she shouldn't matter to me and I shouldn't matter to her."

"That had to be hard."

"It was, but it doesn't excuse what she did. And I don't expect you to forgive her. She's—she's got a lot of work to do. How've you been?" I reached out my hand before shoving it into my pocket.

"Okay. How about you?" She lifted her gaze to mine.

"Honestly?"

"Always."

"I feel like someone's run over my heart with a tire made of cleats. I keep waking up in the middle of the night and looking out the window at your room and I want to be in there with you. I want to be holding you and rubbing that spot on your nose with the freckle cluster that kind of looks like a tiny strawberry."

She lifted her hand and rubbed it along the bridge of her nose.

"And I want to call you, or even write you letters, because I miss you, Frenchie. I miss you so much that even with all the people I've lost in my life, it's you who keeps me up at night because you're part of my heart. You're part of my soul and I swear..." I choked through the words, pushing past the tightness in my throat and the tears in my eyes.

"I promised I wouldn't do this, that I'd give you space and not make showing up here like this, but fuck it. I love you so much that my future that was once so crystal clear is a wasteland stretching on as far as I can see when I try to picture it now without you."

"You've got a great future ahead of you. You've already made it through so much."

"It doesn't mean anything if I can't get another private dance lesson, if I can't sit at our kitchen table and watch you work your magic, if I can't hold you in my arms and tell you how much I love you."

She opened her mouth, but I charged forward, needing her to hear everything.

"People fuck up and who knows what the future holds. And before you say anything, I want you to know, Alexis is family, but you're my forever. I can't promise she won't fuck up, same as I can't promise I won't fuck up. But I can promise that I'll always believe you and love you. The blinders are off when it comes to her, but she's still going to be part of my life. No more rescuing, no more trying to keep her out of trouble, but she's my sister." The muscles in my neck strained and I tried to keep my breathing under control. This could be a deal breaker, but I had to be honest with Jules.

"I never wanted to come between you."

"I know that. I know."

"These past few days..." She hugged the book box tighter to her chest. "I've missed you so much too." Her watery smile was the first ray of sunshine after a turbulent storm. A ray of hope. "And the future I'd never been able to picture for myself was clear after I walked out your door. It was bleak, lonely, and not filled with even half the love I feel for you."

I rushed forward and wrapped my arms around her. The hard edges of the box dug into my chest, but I didn't care. I'd sit on a bed of nails to be this close to her again.

She laughed, skimming her fingers along my jaw and looking into my eyes with that kind of open love that made her Jules. I'd never take it for granted again.

"And you were never the third best thing in my life, Jules. Never. I'd never play a game again, if it meant I could be here with you."

She brushed her fingers against my lips. "It was never about forcing you to choose. There's enough room in here for more than me." Her hand slid down to my chest.

"I know, but everything else falls away when I'm with you, and I don't ever want to lose that."

"Neither do I, but I have one important question for you." Her lips thinned to a line, her face transforming into finals-week seriousness. She lifted her chin, meeting my gaze. "Ready for another dance lesson?"

I laughed, rubbing my nose against hers. "Always."

CHAPTER 44
BERK

My hand shook in hers. She covered mine with both of her mitten-covered ones. Letting go with one hand, she picked up the present from her seat. The one she'd held on to the whole way here.

The afternoon air was sharp and crisp. There wasn't a cloud in the sky; even though our breath hung in clouds in front of our faces, the sun shone.

A tremor rolled through my body. Her fingers tightened around mine, running along the back of my hand. She reached up and put her other hand around my arm, molding herself to my side like she was prepared to jump out and protect me if I needed it. And I did.

We walked into the caretaker's office. This time I wasn't teetering on the edge and soaked completely through.

My Adam's apple bobbed. I cleared my throat, trying to form the words. "Can you please let me know where Elizabeth Vaughn is?"

The caretaker looked up from his desk and his eyes widened. "You're back." He leaned over and opened a drawer. "You left so quickly last time, I wasn't sure if you'd be back."

I nodded, every muscle in my body tense almost like I was poised to outrun the pain of what was to come. Jules tightened her hold on me.

"I'm here. You're not alone." Her whispered words soothed the edges of the ache burning deep in my heart. She was here and she'd always be here for me.

"She's over by the old oak tree. Here's a map." He circled a gravestone amongst others lined up neatly in rows. "If you need me to, I can walk you out there."

I stared at the white paper with the simple pattern running along the border. The light blue circle on the page was scarier than anything I'd faced before. It was a kind of finality I hadn't wanted to face.

Jules took the paper, sliding it across his desk. "We'll be okay. If we need your help, we can come back." She held onto my arm, anchoring me to what was happening—to my new reality, not based on childhood dreams, but the here and now.

"I understand." The caretaker's tight nod said this wasn't the first person he'd had paralyzed in his office. "Oh, and this is for you." He held out a plain white envelope, well, it had once been white. Now the edges were yellowed. Who'd written that? When? I still didn't even know how long my mom had been buried here.

Jules took the envelope from his hand with two fingers, keeping the present firmly in her grip and gently nudged me toward the door.

I walked without feeling anything. Each step was numb and deadened. Slowly, with a measured gait that stretched our trip into what felt like weeks, we made it to the spot near the oak tree.

"This is it." Jules stopped, standing at the end of the row. "She's the fourth one in. Do you want me to go with you?" She stared up at me with a shine to her eyes. Her tears were for me and all I'd lost, but she was still trying so damn hard to be strong. Holding out the envelope, she looked up at me.

Shaking my head, I took the envelope and present from her.

She shook her hands out of her mittens and ran warm fingers over the backs of mine.

Her eyes glittered with unshed tears and she was fighting to be strong for me. Had there ever been anyone luckier than me? Had anyone been as loved? She nodded and took a step back, not needing to say the words I already knew. She was there if I needed her.

With my gaze trained on the long row ahead, I walked toward the inevitable. The loss of Jules's warmth made me want to turn around and rush back to her, gather her up in my arms and bury my face in her neck, and smell her lemon-and-sugar scent until we were transported away from this place.

But I had to see it with my own eyes.

I walked past headstones surrounded by well-manicured grass. My fingers were shaking around the wrapped present. Some had flowers laid on top, and others were solitary sentries all on their own. The words on the small plaque nestled into the grass were her name. Tears swam in my eyes.

Elizabeth Caroline Vaughn. I set the present on top of the low-profile cut granite.

And the date of her death. June twenty-seventh.

And the year.

I sucked in a shuddering breath. It was five months after I'd ended up in my first foster home. Eight months after my birthday, when she'd dropped me off on my dad's doorstep.

I fell to my knees. The snow crunched under my body, wetness seeping into my jeans. Tears streamed down my face. I'd been looking for her for over a decade and she'd been here all along. Waiting patiently for me to find her.

Soft, smooth hands ran along the back of my neck. Jules was beside me, with her arms around me cradling my head. I buried my face in her stomach and wrapped my arms around her waist, holding onto her as tightly as I could. I knew I needed to loosen it up, but she didn't complain.

We were frozen like that for so long the muscles in my arms ached and my legs went numb. But she didn't say a word about moving. The slow and steady drag of her fingers through my hair helped to even out my breathing and made me feel like I was no longer completely alone.

Jules was here, and that made even the worst moment of my life bearable.

"I didn't read the note." Each word felt dragged from my throat, raw and creaky.

"Do you want me to read it?" Her voice was a soothing caress on a blustery day.

I nodded, keeping my head against her.

The paper fluttered in her hand and she took a long breath.

"My beautiful boy,

I love you with all my heart and I'm so sorry I had to leave you. You deserve so much more than I have to give you, and now that I know I'm sick it's only a matter of time before I can no longer take care of you. You're the only person I have left in the world, and I don't want to let you go, but I hope your father will be able to take care of you now that I can't."

Jules' voice cracked and I held on tighter to her. The cold, scratchy wool of her coat and the steady rise of her stomach with each breath reminded me that I was still alive. I was still here—with her.

The way I'd had to take over cooking at home and how my mom had stopped going to her jobs filtered back through years of memories. How she'd gotten skinnier and the fullness of her cheeks had faded away. How much more slowly she'd walked, and the way she'd clutched her side as she'd walked away from me.

"This isn't fair, none of it is, but I hope someday you can forgive

me and that you'll have the life you deserve. The life I never could have given you.

I love you with all my heart,

Mommy

"That's the whole thing." Jules wrapped her hands around my head, holding me close.

She untangled my arms from around her waist and knelt in front of me. Holding my face in her hands with the letter still clenched between her fingers, she dropped a kiss on my forehead.

"You're loved Berk. More than you could ever know. Your mom loved you. The guys love you. Alexis loves you. I love you." Tears brimmed in her eyes. "And that will never change. Losing your mom—" Her voice gave out and she wiped at her eyes with the back of her hand. "That'll be something that you always carry with you. But you have a family that loves you and will always be there for you."

I nodded. I could barely breathe, let alone make a sound right now.

Dropping to the ground, I pulled her into my lap. With my arms tight around her, I lifted the wrapped present off the headstone.

My hand shook and Jules cupped it, holding the present with her fingers wrapped around mine.

This was the last present Mom was ever going to give me. The last time I'd ever get anything from her. The tight creases of the paper, now worn away over the years, had been made by her.

"There's no rush. You don't have to do this today." Jules turned in my lap, nuzzling against the side of my face.

"I want to do it now. Will you help me?" I looked to her and she squeezed her lips together and nodded.

We worked slowly, deliberately, peeling away the worn tape, careful of each crease and edge.

Inside, the green knitted bundle was tucked neatly in a roll. My fingers rubbed against the cardboard sides as I reached inside. Unfurling it with care, I squeezed my eyes shut. Green and white with the number 11 on the front. It was so small. Had I ever really been that little? It was hard to picture.

Tears welled in my eyes. "Some of the kids at school had gotten jerseys when the new football season started. I begged my mom for one. I was such a pain in the ass. We were eating beans and rice on a good day and I wanted a stupid football jersey, when there was no way we could afford it."

"You were a kid." She cupped my cheek with her gloved hand. "They aren't known for being reasonable." Her gentle smile for that stupid kid was almost too much. Swallowing past the tightness in my throat, I pushed on.

"I don't even know when she made this. She was always working—always." My voice cracked. "But a few months before she left, we'd found a huge bag of yarn in the dumpster near a craft store. She made me gloves, a hat and a scarf—practical stuff. But I still bitched about that damn jersey." I ran my fingers over the white 11 and turned it over. My name was knitted in big block letters on the back. My favorite number. My number now. "A kid who had no idea what real life was like and how bad things could get. I never got to tell her how much I love this." My nostrils flared, and the frigid air bit at my skin against the falling tears.

"She knew." Jules covered my hand with hers, tracing the letters along the top.

We walked back to the car hand-in-hand, and I couldn't take my eyes off it. She had to have stayed up all night even when she was dead tired, working on it whenever she had a spare moment.

Back at Jules' house, I sat in the kitchen and laid the jersey out on the table. I squeezed Jules' hand.

"Do you want to get it framed?" She ran her fingers over the number 11 and smiled.

"Maybe later." I held the edge between my fingers. "I want to hold on to it for a bit." A vision of a little girl in glasses with eyes just like her mother was so vivid I could almost reach out and touch her. She'd run across a huge back yard in fall wearing this. I ran my fingers over the soft yarn. Something her grandmother had made. I had a piece of my mom, and I'd be able to share that with her.

The little girl with her mom's eyes and loving spirit would sit on my lap on the back steps and I'd read her one of her favorite books, *The Tale of The Flopsy Bunnies*.

"Of course." Jules got up and walked behind me, draping her arms around my neck and pressing herself against my back.

Wrapped up tightly in her arms, I took a breath and imagined what it would've been like to have my mom see my face when I opened it. To have her see me walk out onto the field as a professional football player.

"She knew. All the things you think she's missing out on. She knew you loved her and she knew you'd find your happiness." Jules kissed the back of my neck and grabbed some of my favorite cookies.

The front door opened and it sounded like a parade was charging into her house.

"We're in here," she called out.

And the doorframe of the kitchen nearly burst away from the wall as everyone piled inside.

I set down the jersey. Nix had his arm wrapped around Elle. Reece and Seph poked their heads out from behind them.

"What are you doing here?" I turned to Reece. "Didn't you have a game last night?"

He grabbed me and pulled me into a hug. "It's the craziest thing about planes—they're in the air all the time. Jules called us up and said we should all come over for something new she'd baked up. How could we turn down that invitation?"

He patted me on the back. "Plus, she said you needed us. All you ever have to do is ask and we'll be here."

"We thought you knew that by now." LJ came up and gave me a hug.

"I do, but everyone needs a reminder sometimes."

"Monumentally stupid move with that agent, man." Nix punched me in the arm. "But I get why you did it. If I knew my mom was out there somewhere, nothing would've stopped me. Do we all need to go pay Johannsen a visit?"

I shook my head. "No, we've come to an understanding. He's cool."

"Not too sure about that."

"Fine, not cool, but he's backed off."

"Probably that six-inch bruise covering half his face."

"Maybe."

I looked over at everyone crammed into the kitchen. Elle helping Nix raid Jules' stash of goodies. Marisa and LJ keeping the table between them like they were magnets repelling one another as far as possible. Seph and Reece laughing at Nix attempting to steal an entire sleeve of mini chocolate peppermint cookies.

"Is Coach going to let you play?" Keyton stood beside me with his hands in the cookie mystery box where everything you pulled out was a prize.

"I have to sit out the rest of the season until the playoffs. Johannsen choked up like he was facing down the mob. One second, he was practically skipping, ready to fuck me over, and then he said nothing."

"Maybe he grew a conscience," Keyton offered.

"Nah," everyone replied in unison and went back to talking and laughing, pulling up chairs.

Marisa broke out the blender to make some drinks, even though it was freezing outside.

Jules came up behind me and wrapped her arms around my waist. "What's up?"

I ran my arms over hers, letting her squeeze me tight. The weight of her embrace blanketed me in a love I'd never thought I'd find. I pulled her around to my front and clasped my hands at the small of her back.

"Nothing's up. Just taking it all in."

She turned her head to the side, looking at our ragtag group of friends. "It's a good day, isn't it?"

Even with everything I'd been through today and the emotional nosedive I'd taken visiting my mom's grave, she was right. I hugged her tighter to me and kissed her temple with a heart so full, I couldn't hold back my smile. "It is. The best day, and I can't wait to make a lifetime of memories like these with you."

EPILOGUE – SPRING FLING

"You don't have to prove anything to anyone." Elle tugged at the neckline of my shirt like a doting mother.

"Weren't you the one telling me to let these girls loose?" I tugged the bottom of the shirt, pushing the neckline back where it was.

"This is a stupid tradition."

"You always wanted me to go to more parties." I laughed at her narrowed gaze. "I'm in a T-shirt and jeans. You're acting like I'm walking outside in a pole dancing outfit with tassels on my nipples."

"Does Berk know you're going out in this?"

"He's not my keeper, Elle. And yes, he fully supports whatever I want to do or wear." Although it had taken a few baked-good-bracketed bedroom sessions for him to agree not to growl at anyone who looked at me sideways.

I checked myself out in the mirror. The special-order T-shirt had arrived just in time for the campus Halloween do-over with much better weather. Philly in late October wasn't known for its amazing weather, so decades ago, the campus planned their own version for the Friday before spring break.

Better weather, and a long stretch off after to recover from the debauchery.

Elle stood beside me in a Princess Leia outfit complete with cinnamon roll hair buns. Instead of taking one look at her and grabbing my sweatshirt and hiding, we finished up getting ready and I was excited to go to the party. Not that we were traveling far, but a party at The Brothel would have been beyond my imagination only a year ago. So would the fact that I'd slept in Berk's bed just as many nights as he slept in mine, and that he looked at me like I'd walked off a Paris Fashion Week runway every time I stepped into the room.

My costume wasn't even a costume—although I did have a headband with a cupcake on it and a giant wooden mixing spoon I could use like a staff—but my shirt was the cherry on top.

In big bold letters across the front, it spelled out DOUGH HO.

"We're going to a party at The Brothel, it's hardly like I'll be strutting around City Hall in this. I can laugh at it now. And you know what? I can't say I haven't dipped my fingers in a hell of a lot of dough, so..." I shrugged. "We're going to have fun." Loading our arms up with containers of cookies, we set off on our short journey like two Little Reds in search of our Big Bad Wolves.

The music from The Brothel and half the houses on the block filled the air with a pulsing, rumbling beat.

"Remember when I called the cops on them for these parties?" Elle linked her arm through mine.

"You're saying that like it was a one-time thing. Was the tally ten by the time you and Nix started bumping uglies?"

She swatted at my arm. "Ew. But let's say that maybe I was a little over the top." Holding her fingers up almost touching, she looked at me through the gap.

We stopped at the bottom of the stairs to their porch and burst out laughing.

She opened the door and all heads swung our way. I straightened my back, not shrinking away like old Jules might have.

"Hell, yes!" someone called out from the crowd of people in the living room. "Jules is here!"

"My queen, may I relieve you of your parcels of deliciousness?" Keyton crossed the room and knelt in front of us, crossing an arm over his chest in his Roman soldier uniform, complete with shield and sword. Touching each shoulder with my spoon sceptre, I knighted him and handed over the goods. Within seconds, he was mobbed and people grabbed handfuls of the cookies.

"I think that means they like them," Elle stage-whispered to me.

"Keyton gets first dibs on the cookies? Not cool." Berk walked out of the kitchen with two red plastic cups in his hands. They didn't exactly go with his toga and the gold leaf crown wrapped around his head, but the butterflies in my stomach didn't care. Their wings had gotten bigger, and every time he looked at me I felt like the luckiest woman in the room—hell, the world.

Taking one of the cups, I took a sip. "It's not my fault he beat you to the punch."

"No, I was getting you punch."

"Touché."

"You didn't save any for me?" Nix walked in looking like Elle had told him Santa wasn't real. Dejected, he held onto both cups, clutching them to his chest.

I couldn't stop my laugh at his crestfallen expression, especially since he had a giant green alien inflatable attached to his back with fake arms around his waist so it looked like he was being carried away.

She cupped his cheek. "Don't worry. There's a whole box for us back at the house."

He wrapped his arms around her, crushing her to him and almost spilling the drinks on her.

"What about me? I'm the one who made them."

Berk wrapped his arms tighter around me and whispered against the back of my neck. "You saved some for me, didn't you?"

I shuddered, trying to keep my knees under control at the gentle caress of his lips against my skin.

"There's an even bigger surprise waiting for you." I turned, our mouths less than an inch apart.

"If it's a kiss, I'll be a happy man." A whisper-soft brush of his lips against mine.

I ran my hands up and down his arms around his shoulders. "You're too easy to please."

"Only when it comes to you." He planted a kiss on me. A deep, sweet kiss that made everything lighter and brighter around us.

"We're here!" The door banged open. A flurry of hula hoops with Styrofoam balls stuck to them surrounded Seph. Reece helped her through the doorway, laughing the whole way.

The volume increased now that we had an actual professional player here. With an exchange of fist bumps and bro hugs, Reece got Seph situated with her costume complete with a bright yellow sun helmet.

"It's not spatially accurate, but I took some artistic license for this special occasion."

"Everyone forgives you, Seph."

"I've never gotten to dress up for Halloween before, let alone make my own costume. The glue gun was treacherous, but I persevered." She held up a triumphant fist.

Berk came back in with a tray of jello shots, which disappeared before he got to me.

"Don't look so sad. I saved one for you." He pulled a small plastic cup with red gelatin inside from under his toga.

"Do I want to know where you were hiding this?" I laughed and threw it back.

"You do not."

"Thanks for thinking of me."

He slipped his arms around my waist. "Always."

———

"THERE'S A SMALL POT OF THE SALTED CARAMEL SAUCE AT MY place with your name on it." She smiled at me with that mischievous look in her eyes. The one that meant she'd learned a new pole dancing move, ordered a new outfit just for me, or had something delicious for me to taste.

Every day with her was an adventure in what it felt like to be so loved it was like living in a dream. She was my dream girl, and no matter what, we'd have our dream life filled with all the love we'd been searching for all our lives and could finally share with one another.

Wearing her Dough Ho costume, she looked good enough to eat. The reminder of the phrase that had contributed to breaking us up wouldn't have been my number one choice, but the way Jules worked the room in jeans that hugged her curves pushed aside any worries I'd had. She was so much stronger than she knew, and I'd be by her side every step of the way from here on out.

"Is Alexis coming?" She locked her fingers around the back of my neck.

"No, she's home studying for the pre-college program that starts in May."

"More studying? After her two-month SAT cram session, I'm surprised she can see straight." We rocked back and forth to a song with a much faster tempo, but I didn't care. With Jules, every song deserved to be a slow dance.

"And the applications, but the real work starts now that

she's in. I much prefer getting phone calls about helping with Scantron sheets and financial aid applications."

She fixed my crown, trailing her fingers along my scalp. "You're a great big brother."

Stitched, healed and smoothed, my heart belonged to her. Without a word from me, she knew that deep down thing I longed to hear. She took what I longed to hear and put it out into the world to show the truth of everything I'd always doubted.

"And I love you." Her lips pressed against mine, sweet, soft, and eager all at once. She was made for me, and I'd spend the rest of my life giving her every beautiful thing she deserved—starting with my love.

Slipping my hand along the back of her neck, I deepened the kiss.

Keyton burst into the room waving and clicking the metal tongs together. "LJ's supposed to be helping me with the grill. People are hungry."

Chuckling against her lips, I pecked Jules. "I'll get him." I took the stairs three at a time. We had promised people some chargrilled burgers, and we had to deliver.

"LJ, Keyton says you're on grill duty." I flung LJ's bedroom door open.

If we'd been in a movie, this was the moment when I'd have been holding a bowl of marbles or beads for no reason, and they would dramatically fall to the floor. The two of them broke apart, staring back at me like I'd caught them trying to hide a body. Marisa released the grip she had on the back of LJ's hair and he extracted his hand from under her bra and shirt.

Slowly, like measured movement would mean I hadn't seen this, she climbed off his lap.

Jerking her shirt down, Marisa turned her back to me with fire-engine-red cheeks. LJ's belt jingled as he tugged up his zipper and fastened his button.

"We'll be down in a second." He moved toward me, breaking me out of the deep freeze I'd been in standing in the doorway.

His face was grim, flushed and sweaty. "Give us a second." The door closed in my grinning face.

Jules jogged up the stairs. "Did you find them?"

"Yeah." I braced my arms across the doorway. "But they're gonna need a sec."

"Why are you smiling like that?" Her eyebrows scrunched, her gaze darting from me to the door.

"No reason." I took her hand leading her downstairs. "Let's say things are about to get a whole lot more interesting around here."

THE LETTERS

1. …Just the thought of those big hands all over my body makes me wet. I use a toy on myself, pretending it's your fingers inside me. I've never come so hard in my life as when I'm panting your name and pushing myself to the next orgasm….

2. Who is this? If this is one of the STFU guys playing a joke or something? It's not funny.

3. No joke, Berk. I slide my hand under the waistband of my boy shorts and sink them inside myself, pumping three fingers at a time with my back arching off the bed, wanting it to be your touch.

4. If you're real, tell me who you are. These letters are seriously hot.

5. I had a dream about you last night. You had me pinned against the wall, your cock slamming into me, and I wrapped my legs tightly around your waist, taking every inch of you. I came twice and lay in bed sweaty and still unsatisfied because you weren't there with me.

6. If you want it to be my touch, then let's stop with

these letters. I'm going to burn a hole in my palm at this point re-reading these.

7. Some things are left better to the imagination.

8. Not this. You've got to be feeling just like I am. Your hands or your toys aren't making half the fire we will. I can't get you out of my head.

9. I licked my hand clean, after my middle of the night dreams, pretending it was your cum. I bet you taste good.

10. ...When can we meet? I've read your letter ten times already and wrapped my fingers around my cock thinking about you. Give me a name I can call out when I'm ready to come...

11. ...No name. You've already got one for me. The Letter Girl...

12. ...That's not good enough. You've got me at a disadvantage. You know who I am, you know my name. Hair color? Eye color? Anything—help me picture the woman who turns me inside out with her words. Did you touch yourself thinking about me today?

13. I touch myself thinking about you every day. How your cock will feel stretching me, filling me up so I can feel you everywhere. I dream of tasting you, running my tongue along the head of your cock and trying to take all of you. I have brown hair, but that's all you're getting...

14. Now you'll have my head swimming thinking about every brunette woman I pass. Give me more. What's your favorite movie? Song? I'll play it and think of you.

15. I've always been a John Hughes fan.

16. Me too. Who doesn't want all their problems wrapped up neatly at the end of a 90 minute

movie? Give me something else about you. Do you go to my school? Are you in any of my classes?

17. We might've had a class together, or maybe I've seen you on campus or on the field.

18. So you're writing to me because I'm a football player.

19. Not really, although I do love the way your ass looks in those pants.

20. I think I'm blushing. There's nothing sexier than the taste of your pussy on my lips. Sucking on your clit will be my appetizer, but sinking into your pussy will be the whole damn meal. When can I have you for dinner, Letter Girl?

21. None of my other letters made you blush?

22. No, those letters only made me want to rip this campus apart to find you and do everything to you that you've written about over the past couple months.

23. I can't say I would mind you Hulking out in a mad dash around campus, but I think you're more of a Thor type of guy.

24. No way! Cap all the way, although I'm not nearly as clean cut.

25. But you do have America's ass. ;-) All that gym time pays off, and not just on the field.

26. I approve of your objectification.

27. Sunny side up all the way. Maybe fried.

28. I threw up in my mouth. Scrambled FTW! Add some cheese on it and I'm set.

29. I'm not kidding. I didn't even realize there were curses in half those movies until I got to college.

30. Sometimes I feel like I can tell you anything.

31. You can.

32. We can't meet. This was never supposed to be more

than our letters. Real life… Real life ruins everything.

33. This will be my last letter. This was the most fun I've had in a long time, so thank you. Yours, The Letter Girl

———

Thank you so incredibly much for spending some time with Berk and Jules and the rest of the FU gang! Many of my stories reflect feelings I've felt at one point in my life, but Jules was especially close.

Her struggles with accepting herself are ones I've wrestled with and continue to wrestle with and I hope someday to be as kickass about it all as she is.

I can't believe we're already on the third book of the Fulton U series! Time flies and there's still so much story to tell.

———

If you'd like another day with Berk and Jules, head over to https://BookHip.com/MAFLFW to grab a little more time with them.

EXCERPT FROM THE PERFECT FIRST

She was looking for a first. She just became my only.

THE PERFECT FIRST

MAYA HUGHES

Seph - Project De-virginization

The jingle sounded again as the door to the coffee shop swung open. My head snapped up and my bouncing leg froze. The sun shone through the doorway and a figure stood there. He was tall, taller than anyone who'd come in before. His muscles were obvious even under his coat. He paused at the entrance, his head moving from side to side like he knew people would be looking back, like he was giving everyone a chance to soak in his presence. His jet black hair was tousled just right, like he'd been running his fingers through it on the walk over from wherever he'd come from. The jacket fit him perfectly, like it had been tailored just for his body.

I glanced around; I wasn't the only one who'd noticed him walk in. He seemed familiar, but I couldn't place him. He bent forward, and I thought he was going to tie his shoes, but instead he wiped a wet leaf off his pristine white sneaker. Heads turned as he crossed the floor toward me. Squeezing my fingers tighter around the notecards, I reminded myself to breathe.

He glanced around again and spotted me. The green in his eyes was clear even from across the coffee shop. Dark hair with eyes like that wasn't a usual combo. He froze and his lips squeezed together. With his hands shoved into his pockets, he stalked toward me with a *Let's get this over with* look. That didn't bode well. He stood beside the seat on the other side of the booth, staring at me expectantly.

My gaze ran over his face. Square jaw. Hint of stubble on his cheeks and chin. My skin flushed. He had beautiful lips. What would his feel like on my mouth? I ran my finger over my bottom lip. What would they feel like on other parts of me? My body responded and I thanked God I had on a bra, shirt, and blazer or I'd have been flashing him some serious high beams. This was a good sign.

He cleared his throat.

Jumping, I dropped my hand, and the heat in my cheeks turned into a flamethrower on my neck. "Sorry, have a seat." I half stood from my spot in the booth and extended my hand toward the other side across from me. The table dug into my thighs and I fell back into the soft seat.

Sliding in opposite me, he unzipped his coat and put his arm over the back of the shiny booth.

"Hi, very nice to meet you. I'm Seph." I shot my hand out across the table between us. The cuff of my blazer tightened as it rode up my arm.

His eyebrows scrunched together. "Seth?" He leaned in, his forearms resting on the edge of the table. He was nothing like the guys from the math department. They were quiet, sometimes obnoxious, and none of them made my stomach ricochet around inside me like it was trying to win a gold medal in gymnastics at the Olympics.

I tamped down a giggle. I did *not* giggle. The sound came out like a sharp snort, and I resisted the urge to slam my eyes shut and crawl under the table. *Be cool, Seph. Be cool.* "No—Seph. It's short for Persephone."

He lifted one eyebrow.

"Greek goddess of spring. Daughter of Demeter and Zeus. You know what, never mind. I'm glad you agreed to meet with me today."

"Not like I had much choice." He leaned back and ran his knuckles along the table top, rapping out a haphazard rhythm.

I licked my lips and parted them. Not like he had much choice? Had someone put him up to this? Had something in my post made him feel obligated to come? I hadn't been able to bring myself to go back and look at it after posting it. Shaking my head, I stuck my hand out again. "Nice to meet you…"

He looked down at my hand and back up at me, letting out a bored breath. "Reece. Reece Michaels."

"Very nice to meet you, Reece. I'm Persephone Alexander.

I have a few questions we can get started with, if you don't mind."

"The quicker we get started, the quicker we can finish." He looked around like he would have rather been anywhere but there.

Those giddy bubbles soured in my stomach. A server came by with the bottled waters I'd ordered. I arranged them in a neat pyramid at the end of the table.

"Would you like a water?" I held one out to him.

He eyed me like I was offering him an illicit substance, but then reached out. His fingers brushed against the backs of mine and shooting sparks of excitement rushed through me. Pulling the bottle out of my grasp, he cracked it open and took a gulp.

My cheeks heated and I glanced down at my cards, flipping the ones at the front to the back.

"I have a notecard with some information for you to fill out."

Sliding it across the table, I held out a pen for him. He took it from me, careful that our fingers didn't touch this time. I'd have been lying if I'd said I didn't want another touch, just to test whether or not that first one had been something more than static electricity. He filled out the biographical data on the card and handed it back to me.

I scanned it. He was twenty-one. Had a birthday coming up just after the New Year. Good height-to-weight ratio. Grabbing my pen, I scanned over the questions I'd prepared for my meetings.

"Let's get started." *Just rip the Band-Aid off.* Clearing my throat, I tapped the cards on the table. A few heads turned in our direction at the sharp, rapping sound. "When were you last tested for sexually transmitted diseases?"

Setting the bottle down on the table, he stared at me like I was an equation he was suddenly interested in figuring out. And then it was gone. "At the beginning of the season. Clean bill of health." He looked over his shoulder, the boredom back, leaking from every pore. *Wow.* I'd thought guys were all over this whole sex thing, but he looked like he was sitting in the waiting room of a dentist's office.

"When did you last have sexual intercourse?"

His head snapped back to me, eyes bugged out. "What?" I had his full attention now.

"Sex? When did you last have sex?" I tapped my pen against the notecard.

He sputtered and stared back at me. His eyes narrowed and he rested his elbows on the table.

I scooted my neatly lain out cards back toward me, away from him.

"No comment."

"Given the circumstances, it's an appropriate question."

The muscles in his neck tightened and his lips crumpled together. "Fine, at the beginning of the season."

"What season?" I looked up from my pen. That was an odd way to put it. "Like, the beginning of fall?"

"Like football season."

The pieces fit together—the body, the looks from other people around the coffee house. "You play football." That made sense, and he seemed like the perfect all-American person for the job.

"Yes, I play football."

"When did the season start?"

He shook his head like he was trying to clear away a fog and stared back at me like I'd started speaking a different language. "September."

"And…" I ran my hand along the back of my neck. "How long would you say it lasted?"

His eyebrows dipped. "It didn't last. It was a one-night thing. I don't do relationships."

Of course not. He was playing the field. Sowing his oats.

Banging his way through as many co-eds as possible. Experienced. Excellent.

I cleared my throat. "No, I didn't mean how long did you date the woman. I meant, how long was the sex?"

The steady drumming on the table stopped. "Are you serious?"

I licked my Sahara-dry lips. "It's a reasonable question. How long did it last?"

"I didn't exactly set a timer, but let's just say we both got our reward."

"Interesting." I made another note on the card.

"These are the types of questions I'm going to be asked for the draft?" He took the lid off the bottled water.

The draft? Pushing ahead, I went to the next line one my card and cringed a bit. "Okay, this might seem a little invasive." I cleared my throat again. "But how big is your penis? Length is fine. I don't need to know the circumference, you know—the girth."

A fine spray of water from his mouth washed over me. "What the hell kind of question is that? I know you're trying to throw me off my game, but holy shit, lady."

———

Persephone Alexander. Math genius. Lover of blazers. The only girl I know who can make Heidi braids look sexy as hell. And she's on a mission. Lose her virginity by the end of the semester.

I walked in on her interview session for potential candidates (who even does that?) and saw straight through her brave front. She's got a list of Firsts to accomplish like she's only got months to live. I've decided to be her guide for all her firsts except one. Someone's got to keep her out of trouble. I have one rule, no sex. We even shook on it.

I'll help her find the right guy for the job. Someone like

her doesn't need someone like me and my massive...baggage for her first time.

Drinking at a bar. Check.

Partying all night. Double check.

Skinny dipping. Triple check.

She's unlike anyone I've ever met. The walls I'd put up around my heart are slowly crumbling with each touch that sets fire to my soul.

I'm the first to bend the rules. One electrifying kiss changes everything and suddenly I don't want to be her first, I want to be her only. But her plan was written before I came onto the scene and now I'm determined to get her to re-write her future with me.

Grab your copy of The Perfect First or read it for FREE in Kindle Unlimited at https://amzn.to/2ZqEMzl

HONESTY TIME

Thank you for reading The Third Best Thing! It was an emotional rollercoaster navigating Jules and Berk's journey. Jules...I'm not sure any other way to say it, other than—I want to be her when I grow up.

She's so much bolder and more fearless than I've ever felt I could be. I learned a lot from her throughout the book. There was more than one lesson I needed to learn myself.

And sweet, sweet Berk. Not hardened by his past and so full of love and acceptance for the people around him, flaws and all. I love him so hard and a lot of those gentle touches and words bursting with love are inspired by how Mr. Maya has been my rock since day 1.

I hope their story brought you joy and you're looking forward to what comes next. The questions have come by email, DM and posts in my group. Yes, that side character you loved, they're getting a story! When or what will be something I'll tell you about later. ;-)

ACKNOWLEDGMENTS

Jules and Berk was one of my most emotional stories to date. So many of Jules's insecurities and pressure are ones I've faced. Her feelings hit so close to home as well as that need to accept and love herself.

I hope you enjoyed her journey and fell in love with Berk just like I, ahem, I mean she did! ;-)

Thank you to my editing team, Tamara Mayata, Tex, and the Sarahs Squared! Karen is the master of wrangling me and keeping the Maya train on track. Thank you a million times!

I loved all the messages from so many readers, bloggers, bookstagrammers as they waited for these two. The eager anticipation always keeps me smiling and so ready to serve them up to you!

If you haven't read any of my other books, turn the page for more wonderful stories featuring baked good, found families and hot guys!

Maya xx

ALSO BY MAYA HUGHES

Fulton U

The Perfect First - First Time/Friends to Lovers Romance

The Third Best Thing

The Fourth Time Charm

The Fulton U Trilogy

The Art of Falling for You

The Sin of Kissing You

The Hate of Loving You

Kings of Rittenhouse

Kings of Rittenhouse - FREE

Shameless King - Enemies to Lovers

Reckless King - Off Limits Lover

Ruthless King - Second Chance Romance

Fearless King - Brother's Best Friend Romance

Heartless King - Accidental Pregnancy

CONNECT WITH MAYA

Sign up for my newsletter to get exclusive bonus content, ARC opportunities, sneak peeks, new release alerts and to find out just what I'm books are coming up next.

Join my reader group for teasers, giveaways and more!

Follow my Amazon author page for new release alerts!

Follow me on Instagram, where I try and fail to take pretty pictures!

Follow me on Twitter, just because :)

I'd love to hear from you! Drop me a line anytime :)
https://www.mayahughes.com/
maya@mayahughes.com

Made in United States
North Haven, CT
15 August 2022